Epico Bayou

For Linda,

Enjoy this mystery!

Charlie Russell

Also by Charlsie Russell

The Devil's Bastard

Wolf Dawson

Epico Bayou

A Novel

Charlsie Russell

Loblolly Writer's House
Gulfport, Mississippi

Loblolly Writer's House
P.O. Box 7438
Gulfport, MS 39506-7438
Visit our website at www.loblollywritershouse.com

First Edition: July 2009

This book is a work of fiction. Names, characters, and incidents are products of the author's imagination. Any resemblance to actual events or persons is coincidental. Any scenes depicting actual historical persons are fictitious.

Library of Congress Catalogue Number: 2008910962
Russell, Charlsie.
    Epico bayou: a novel

    ISBN 978-0-9769824-2-5
    1. Mystery – Fiction

Book design by Lucretia Gibson
Copy editor, Nancy McDowell

Printed and bound in the United States of America.

For Ryleigh Anna Slagel
then, now, and always my very first grandbaby

Historical Note

In the fall of 1779 Spain, ally of Britain's rebellious American colonies, moved forces north from New Orleans into British West Florida, capturing first Baton Rouge, then Natchez. Mobile fell to Spain in 1780, and the British provincial capital at Pensacola succumbed in the spring of 1781, ending British hegemony in the Gulf Coast region.

The area south of the Natchez District to the Gulf of Mexico and from the Mississippi River east to the Perdido River, Spain named Feliciance County, and before the ink dried on the Treaty of Paris ending the American Revolution (1783), Spain began seducing Protestant Anglo-Saxons into the territory. Spain correctly perceived that the young United States, no longer restrained by London's carefully manipulated approach to foreign policy, would prove a dangerous enemy. Spanish strategy was to create a buffer of disgruntled expatriots between the United States and Spain's lucrative holdings in the southwest and Mexico.

Americans, many seeking opportunity, others disillusioned with the revolution and separation from the motherland, were on the move. Spain's offers of fertile land, clemency for honest debtors, exemption from taxes and military service, and free access to trade in New Orleans brought them to the area in droves. It was during this period that English and Scots-Irish pioneers settled the Buena Vista community (now Handsboro, Mississippi) on Bayou Bernard, the latter named for a free-Negro blacksmith and sheepherder, who lived on the north shore of the bayou.

In 1800, Spain returned to Napoleonic France New Orleans and the land west of the Mississippi, which France had ceded to

vii

Spain in 1762 as French prospects in the French and Indian War dimmed. Twenty days later, Napoleon sold the territory to the United States, and the capitol of Spanish West Florida moved from New Orleans to Pensacola. The United States claimed the rest of West Florida, from the Pearl River east to the Perdido River, to be part of that "ancient" territory of Louisiana and was, therefore, included in the sale. Madrid countered that France had not ceded that land to Spain in 1762, but Spain won the territory through military conquest during the American Revolution. Spain continued to maintain strong military forces in Baton Rouge, Mobile, and Pensacola.

During the first decade of the nineteenth century, cotton planting, sugar processing, and the timber industry, along with black market trade, piracy, and trafficking in stolen slaves, flourished in Spain's Feliciance County. At home, the Napoleonic Wars impaired Madrid's ability to control West Florida. Misfits, malcontents, seditionists, traitors, pirates, and thieves came and went at will in what are now Mississippi's six southernmost counties. Lawlessness spilled into the Mississippi Territory, thus the United States, where self-proclaimed patriots sought refuge after wreaking havoc inside Spanish territory. Madrid discouraged further settlement of the Mississippi Territory to the north by placing unpopular duties on American trade with Mobile. Within Feliciance County, Spain had set the stage for revolt.

In the fall of 1810, rebels overthrew Spanish authority. For seventy-four days prior to its annexation by the United States, the Republic of West Florida reigned over what are now the southeastern-most parishes of Louisiana and Mississippi's six southern counties as well as the southern parts of Lamar, Forrest, Perry, and Wayne counties. In April of 1812, Congress created the State of Louisiana, which included the area west of the Pearl River to New Orleans. It designated the area east of the Pearl to the Perdido River part of the Mississippi Territory—an action Spain protested. Spanish claims to the territory ended in 1814 with Spain's withdrawal from Mobile following the British defeat at the Battle of New Orleans. Mississippi became a state in 1817.

At that time, Hancock County extended from the Pearl River to Biloxi Bay and north to the 31st parallel.

In 1837, the Mississippi legislature issued a charter to James McLauren for the express purpose of laying out a port city to be named Mississippi City. The city was incorporated that same year—the first on the Coast. Biloxi and Pass Christian, also in Hancock County, and Pascagoula in Jackson County followed in 1838. McLauren and two other Scots-Irish entrepreneurs, John J. McCaughan and Colin J. McRae, received a charter for a railroad line to extend from Jackson to the Gulf. The railroad right-of-way was drawn and partially cleared, but a nationwide financial crisis shortly after stifled the sale of 46 lots comprising Mississippi City and compelled the legislature to cancel plans for the railroad.

McLauren, McCaughan, and McRae took the setbacks in stride. By 1841, conflicts of interests between the political center of power in western Hancock County's Pearl River communities and the growing towns east of the Bay of St. Louis, compelled the state legislature to grant a peoples' petition for separation. Harrison County, named in honor of William Henry Harrison, ninth president of the United States, was established February 5, 1841. The new county appropriated eastern Hancock County from a north-south line running through the middle of the Bay of St. Louis and east to Biloxi Bay. The communities of Wolftown (Delisle), Pass Christian, Buena Vista (Handsboro), Mississippi City, and Biloxi became part of Harrison County.

Those Scots-Irish visionaries, McLauren, McCaughan, and McRae immediately strong-armed the county's new Board of Police (County Board of Supervisors) into selecting Mississippi City as the county seat and built a courthouse at the end of Railroad Road (now Courthouse Road), along with the county jail. That particular courthouse came replete with political debates and shootouts—no doubt, one leading directly to the other. Here Jefferson Davis, only president of the Confederacy, made his last public speech in 1888: "The past is dead; let it bury its dead, its hopes and aspirations. Before you lies the future, a future full of golden promise, a future of expanding national glory, before which all the world shall stand amazed. Let me beseech you to lay aside all rancor, all bitter sectional feeling, and to take your place in the ranks of those who will bring about a consummation devoutly to be wished — a reunited country."

It would take more than Jeff Davis' words to lay aside all that rancor and bitter sectional feeling, at least in the South. It would take a war with Spain. At the time Jeff Davis made that speech, the Stars and Bars of the Confederacy still flew over the Harrison County Courthouse, on the steps of which he stood. It was not until July 4, 1898, shortly after the people of Harrison County learned of the U.S. victory at Santiago, Cuba, with Yank and Reb fighting side by side, that Old Glory once again took its place over the seat of Harrison County Justice.

Meanwhile, the Spanish-era community of Buena Vista on Bayou Bernard had grown from a lumber center to a thriving manufacturing town. In 1840, New York brothers Miles and Shelton Hand arrived and built a foundry that in a short few years was supplying the Coast's growing timber and fishing industries with the machines needed to saw logs and can oysters and shrimp. They built identical homes on either side of Lorraine Road, linked to Buena Vista and Gulf Street (Cowan Road) by ferry. The house on the east side stands today. In honor of the Hand brothers, Buena Vista changed its name in 1856 to Handsborough, now Handsboro.

For a short stretch, the Pass Christian-Biloxi Road served as Handsboro's Main Street. One mile south, along north-south Old Cowan, Tegarden, and Railroad Roads was (and is) Mississippi City and the Gulf of Mexico. The blue-collar community of Epico lay north of Mississippi City and west of Railroad Road. Today it is the middle-class neighborhood of Bayou View.

If the Stars and Bars of the Confederacy's flying over the Harrison County Courthouse for 33 years following the War Between the States hasn't already clued the reader, suffice it to say, the Mississippi Gulf Coast gave its sons to the Confederacy, and its citizens knew the deprivations of siege and Federal raids.

Union forces took Ship Island early in the War and established a prisoner of war camp there. Federal raiding parties against the mainland were common. Despite that, the mill at Red Bluff on the north shore of Bayou Bernard continued to supply gunpowder to the Confederacy until the closing days of the War.

In 1866, a group of ex-slaves received Federal grants for eight forty-acre plots along Turkey Creek west of the Epico community. The sheltered bayou enclave remained relatively isolated well into the twentieth century. Today, descendents of the original owners still occupy a number of those plots, and the community is a registered historic landmark.

Early in the 1880s, William Hardy, founder of Hattiesburg, revived that old dream of a railroad from Jackson, through the lumber towns of the Piney Woods, to a deepwater port on the Mississippi Sound. Rather than battle for old land titles and already developed land, Hardy chose a new location for the port on mostly undeveloped land, three miles west of Mississippi City. Dubbed "Cinderella City" at the time, it was officially named Gulfport. Financial depression and a squabbling legislature forced Hardy out of the plan, but the land was there, as was the charter; the missing money was later provided by Spenser S. Bullis, a New York promoter, and Joseph T. Jones, a financier from Philadelphia, Pennsylvania. It was Jones, an adopted favorite son, who brought to fruition a deepwater port for Mississippi at the newly laid out city of Gulfport, terminus of the Gulf and Ship Island Railroad (G&SI).

The visionaries who created Gulfport met with their own set of obstacles, dealing not only with construction of the railroad but with federal engineers, who insisted that dredging a deepwater port would be most easily accomplished at Biloxi. Maybe so, but dredging a channel to Biloxi defeated the purpose if the G&SI was already laid and the fresh-water timber boom was under construction in Gulfport. Jones dismissed the potential of a Biloxi port, and forsaking federal support, financed the dredging of Gulfport's channel with his own money.

Gulfport was incorporated on July 28, 1898. It has since

grown to be the second largest city in the state, swallowing up Handsboro and Mississippi City in the process.

Epico Bayou opens with Gulfport under construction and the then sovereign cities of Handsboro and Mississippi City basking in flush times with no concept that the dream that was Mississippi City's sixty years earlier would, in roughly that same period of time, annex them both. The impact of Gulfport, however, they felt much sooner, for in 1902, the voters of Harrison County chose Gulfport as their new county seat.

Brickyard Bayou, Turkey Creek, and myriad brackish, freshwater streams empty into Bayou Bernard on the Mississippi Coast. Epico Bayou is not among them. Epico Bayou is fictional, on the surface a mostly peaceful, shimmering body of water, but beneath, a dark, twisting, silt-choked stream, not unlike the mystery confronting the hero and heroine in this tale bearing its name. *Epico Bayou* is both a clear-cut murder mystery and a charade. But the mystery of the here and now disguises a darker one that began in the long-ago past and threatens not only the lives of two young lovers, reluctantly thrown together, but ultimately their hopes of a future together. More a mystery than my previous novels, *Epico Bayou* still has its share of suspense. Romance, of course, is non-negotiable. Enjoy piecing this puzzle together.

Guide to Characters

Family Members

James Lee—father to
  Matthew Lee—father to
    Darcy Clayton Lee—husband to
    Rebecca Fontaine Lee—later wife to *Lionel Augustus* and mother of
      Olivia Lee (Boudreaux)

Peter Augustus—father to
  Agatha Augustus
  Lionel Augustus—stepfather to *Olivia Lee (Boudreaux)*
  Duncan Augustus—husband to *Constance*—together parents of
    Francis Augustus
    Howard Augustus
    Julian Augustus
    Lydia Augustus (Pique)

Hugh Henry Gibson—father to
  Elaine Gibson (Boudreaux)—wife to *Edwin Boudreaux*—together parents of
    Troy Boudreaux
    Clay Boudreaux—husband by proxy to *Olivia Lee* and acknowledged son of
      Lionel Augustus

Domestic Servants

Lionel Augustus Home:

May Wilbur
Billy Wilbur
Betty Joy Wilbur
Katie Harder
Tom Buscher (deceased)
Millicent and Simon Dumont

Duncan Augustus Home:

Mabel Simpson
Sally Gordon
Floyd Hammer

Other Functionaries

Nate Phillips—Sheriff, Galveston County, Texas
Dosh Brogan—Sheriff, Harrison County, Mississippi
Maurice Tasker—Doctor and County Coroner, Harrison County, Mississippi
Benford and *Sandifer Hudgins*—Father and son, lawyers for Lionel Augustus

Chapter One

The dead were as cold as the knob in his hand, a paradox, considering how they died. He pushed, and the cabin door whined in protest. From the vicinity of the barn, a screech owl cried out to him, and the hair on the back of his neck stood on end. He hesitated at the threshold and fought the urge to seek the foreboding owl rather than go inside.

An oily film lay over him, weighing down his clothing like guilt and grief weighted his soul. Steeling himself, he stepped inside, into darkness, blacker even than this darkest of nights, and swiped a match against the rough edge of the unseen sideboard. Flame spat, and sulfur purged the sickening-sweet scent of charred human flesh from his nostrils where it had lingered for the past three hours. He reached for the cracked chimney of the lamp, and the smell of kerosene curdled what was left of his long-ago supper.

"Troy Boudreaux?"

The damaged chimney broke in his hand. In his other, the lighted match singed his fingers, and he dropped it. Darkness had scarcely engulfed him when another match flashed, and steadier hands lit the wick in the lantern.

"I'm sorry I spooked you. I've been waiting for you."

"In the dark?"

"I fell asleep."

1

Boudreaux stared at the man's face, ghoulish in the flickering yellow light, and he would have cursed this person, but his rattled brain couldn't conjure a fate dire enough to match the offense.

The intruder swallowed. "I regret the circumstances of our meeting and please accept my condolences for the loss of your brother."

"Who are you, mister, and what the hell are you doing here?"

The man glanced at the broken glass chimney in Boudreaux's hand, then extended his own. "I'm Sandifer Hudgins, Clay's—"

"Lionel Augustus's attorney." Boudreaux set the remains of the soot-covered chimney on the sideboard and took the man's hand.

"Yes, and Clay's also. Did you cut yourself?"

"No." At least he didn't think he had. Truth was, his entire body was numb. But he didn't see any blood.

"My packet arrived at eleven," Hudgins said. "By the time I made my way to your mother's boardinghouse, it was beyond saving. I understand Clay was inside. I came to tell him Lionel Augustus died three days ago."

Boudreaux stole an intact, although equally filthy chimney from a lamp sitting on the rough shelf above the sideboard. "Duncan Augustus sent Nate Phillips a telegram."

"There's more. Duncan's requested an autopsy. There's going to be an inquest."

"Why? The man's been at death's door for the past four weeks."

Sandifer Hudgins looked him in the eye. "Something's afoot. Clay was about to walk into a hornet's nest."

"A den of cottonmouths was how he referred to that mess over there."

"Ah, he discussed the situation with you?"

"I'm aware of what's going on."

"I thought perhaps you were." Hudgins shrugged, then placed a hand in the pocket of his coat. "Clay's death has wrapped things up nice and tight for Olivia. She inherits everything."

"And you came out here to tell me that, Mister Hudgins?"

"Call me Sandy, and I'll call you Troy, if I may?"

"You may."

"I came out here to tell you a tale." He pulled an envelope

2

from his coat pocket and held it up. "But before I get started, be advised that I am aware of this. I found it in a coffee tin out in the cookhouse." He hooked a thumb in the direction of a can now sitting on the dining room table. "Went out there to make myself some coffee while I waited for you. I was tired, been traveling since six Tuesday morning." Hudgins handed him the envelope along with an apologetic smile. "Forgive me for being nosey, but I couldn't resist a peek inside Olivia's distinctive stationery. Why, I asked myself, would Olivia Lee be corresponding with her new husband's brother?"

Boudreaux's palms were sweating, but he resisted the urge to remove the violated letter from its envelope. "I still don't know what you want with me."

Hudgins lifted the lamp from the sideboard and placed it in the center of the little round table Elaine Boudreaux had pilfered from her boardinghouse and given her husband years ago. "I told you I had a tale for you, son," Hudgins said. He nodded to the envelope in Boudreaux's hand. "Given the contents of that letter, I do believe you might be more amenable than ever to listening to it."

In the shadowy dimness of the small dining area, Boudreaux glanced at the letter in his hand, then pocketed it. "And what, exactly, is your story about, Sandy?"

Hudgins took a seat at the table. "A fascinating story of Elaine Gibson Boudreaux, Lionel Augustus, and one Troy Boudreaux, Elaine's first-born son."

If the story was one he hadn't already heard, fascinating was not the word to describe it. Boudreaux reached for a chair.

Hudgins turned up the wick on the lamp and asked, "Could you tell me one thing before I get started?"

"Depends on the question."

"Did you kill your brother for his bride?"

3

Chapter Two

Olivia opened the bedroom door and stopped short. The scent of chilled air on leather, spiced with sandalwood, checked her search for the man she suspected of having forced a groan from the upper-story joists. She glanced over the dim corners of the room, then stepped inside. The lingering smell of coal gas overwhelmed those more pleasant scents, grounding her in the here and now, then her heartbeat quickened at the unexpected site of Uncle Lionel's service revolver out on his dresser. She went to it and picked it up.

"Put it down," Boudreaux said.

The lovely Olivia Lee Boudreaux spun and watched him emerge from his hiding place behind the bedroom door. "Where did you..." she said, with a step his way. Then she stopped. "Do I know you?"

"No," he said, but he swore she had thought she did.

She cast a furtive glance to the open door. "What are you doing up here?"

"Searching the room."

"For money?"

"For weapons."

He watched her wrap a finger around the trigger on the gun. She hadn't done as he said and put it down.

"And you found one," she said.

He nodded at the revolver. "That's right, Missus Boudreaux, if you want something done right, best do it yourself."

4

Confusion etched her brow, and she sidestepped in the direction of the open portal. "I'll call my servants."

He pushed the door, and it shut with a clap. "You gave Millie and Simon permission to go home after the funeral, and I heard you tell May goodnight before you came up here. I know you and I are the only ones left in this house, Olivia, and your Uncle Duncan's place is nearly a mile away. Now put the gun down."

She wrapped both hands around the butt of the Colt and pulled back on the hammer. "Who are you?" she asked.

Those of them who'd left Mississippi after the War and gone to Texas had heard she favored her mama, beautiful and, obvious to him at least, suffering the ills that blessing bestowed.

"Answer me," she said, "and tell me what you're doing in my house."

He studied her, alert for weakness. The Colt was too large for her, but she was holding it pretty darn steady. "I'm your loving husband, sweetheart. Clay Boudreaux."

"*You* are Clay?"

"I am."

Again, she stepped toward him, but stopped abruptly when he bristled, and from the way she looked at him, he might as well have slapped her. Then she raised her chin and appeared to look right through him. "Clay is dead."

"Unfortunately for you, I am not."

Refocused now, she said, "And again, who are you?"

He frowned. "Since you're so darn sure I'm not Clay, would you believe I'm Troy Boudreaux?"

"Clay's brother?"

"You know of another?"

"What are you doing here?"

He took a step, and she braced. "Don't you dare come any closer. Why are you here?"

The woman who moments ago had dared to approach him had hardened. He glanced at the gun, then her. "To collect what's owed me, I reckon."

"What's owed you?"

5

He held her gaze. "For killing Clay."

"For killing...but Clay...Clay died in a house fire."

"You're not going to try and convince me you believe that fire was an accident, are you? I'd have thought you'd been pleased with that tactic. I would have been, for sure, right up till your henchman tried to kill me." He cocked his head. "My, my, Missus Boudreaux, you'd have thunk I'd grown horns the way you're staring at me."

"You killed him?"

His chest tightened. "I shot him."

"But why?"

"Because he tried to kill me."

"Clay tried—"

"Your henchman."

She opened her mouth, shut it, then whispered, "Oh, my dear God."

"I beg your pardon?"

"Clay's death wasn't an accident?"

"That fire wasn't an accident."

She was studying him, weighing what she was going to say next, and he wished he knew what was going on behind those highly touted eyes of hers. "Well?" he prodded.

"I must confess I'm somewhat bewildered. This will create a mess. More investigations, another inquest."

"A killer to pay off."

She narrowed her eyes. "Which explains the henchman, no doubt."

"Are you trying to be funny?"

"I can assure you I am anything but amused."

"Yeah, I imagine my turning up, instead of him, puts a real crimp in your plans."

"Indeed."

"You're one cold-hearted little heifer for only nineteen."

"I'm not the one who claims to have murdered my brother."

"No, you plotted the death of your husband, but I was referring to your partner in crime."

6

"I thought that was you," she snapped.

"The other one. Your henchman. The man I killed in New Orleans."

She stared at him.

"Who was he?" he asked.

"I have no earthly idea."

"Give me his name."

"You go to the devil."

He straightened. "If you don't tell me who helped you plot Clay's murder," he said, "I'll beat it out of you."

She stretched out her arms, settling the Colt in front of her like a shield. "You are not going to beat anything out of me, Mister Whoever-the-devil-you-are." She dropped the barrel of the gun six inches and pulled the trigger.

Click.

Olivia had braced for an explosion, and at the near silence, she almost fell forward. Again, she pulled back on the hammer and squeezed. The pounding of her heart might have drowned the report of the gun had there been one.

She riveted her gaze on the undaunted man who had invaded her home, and he reached into his coat pocket and pulled out a fisted hand. One by one, he dropped six bullets onto the carpet.

He raised his brow, as if he expected her to say something. What that could possibly be she had no idea, so she grasped the impotent pistol by its barrel and slung it at his head.

He ducked, giving her time to fling the bedroom door wide. Behind her, he cursed, but she was out the door and on the landing, which extended over the foyer below. Fifteen feet in front of her, the stairs descended in a graceful curve to the front entry. She tripped, righted herself, hiked her skirt, and...

Her foot snagged a petticoat, jerking her head down and curling her body into a juggernaut that ploughed headfirst into the balcony railing, its giving more wrenching to her physical being than the heat searing her head and shoulders. She grasped the spindle next to the hole her flailing body made, then fell through the bannister with the force of a condemned man falling through a gallows' trap, popping her elbow and yanking the anchoring spindle free.

Fingers bit into her right arm, cutting short both her fall and her scream, but doing nothing to still her raging heart. She looked up at the man straining to hold her. Twenty feet below them, broken rail and spindles clattered against the marble floor. She whimpered, then started to look down.

"Look at me!"

She snapped her head back up and reached for him with her free hand. He grasped her above the elbow and pulled her waist-high onto the landing, then leaning forward, wrapped an arm around her buttocks and heaved her back onto the balcony.

Olivia's palms sank into the deep carpet, and she pushed herself to her knees. Fighting yards of black satin, she crawled from the exposed edge, the locket around her neck swinging like a pendulum. She huddled against the wall, then caught the locket in her right hand and held it over her heart. Next to the broken rail, the man rose, and she held her breath until he sat at her feet.

"That was very graceful, Olivia."

"It's my size. Everything I do appears graceful." She swallowed. "Why didn't you let me fall?"

"You know, sweetheart, aiming for my leg was stupid. When you find a strange man in your house, you need to kill him."

"If you recall, I can't do my own killing. I have to hire henchmen to do it."

"Well, the mercy you intended me had nothing to do with why I pulled you up."

"Then why?" she asked.

Damn those questioning eyes, so blue they were purple. As the story went, Olivia's mother had those eyes, shuttered windows to a selfish soul. "Because I need you," he said.

"What do you mean?"

"I'm taking my inheritance." His gaze moved over her. "At least the part of it I want."

8

"Meaning me to take or leave at your pleasure? I was not part of the inheritance, you fool. I am a beneficiary, as was Clay."

"I've got news for you. You are as much a part of Clay's estate as this house and the sundry businesses Lionel Augustus managed to accumulate over the past thirty years." His gaze swept her head to foot. "Like he accumulated your mother and you. Rebecca Lee passed on, you he saved for Clay."

Her nostrils flared. "On the contrary, he gathered up Clay for me."

Yes, well, the truth of that lay in how one viewed Lionel Augustus's objectives. Boudreaux stood and offered her a hand. She looked at it.

"Take it," he said.

Her eyes moved from the extended hand to his face. "I don't want it."

He reached down, grabbed her arm—she yelped—and he yanked her to her feet, where she twisted, trying to pull free. The scent of gardenia filled his nostrils, fever his blood, and he spun her so that her back was to him. He circled his arm around her waist and pulled her against him. "You're getting it anyway."

In six long strides, he had her back in Lionel Augustus's bedroom and the door locked behind them. Key in hand, he turned and made a show of pocketing it. "To make sure you make no more mad dashes through the railing."

"No one here is going to willingly believe you're Clay."

"You'll convince them."

"Why would I? Howard Augustus sent word three days ago that Clay Boudreaux died in a fire, and that sits fine with the rest of the family."

"To include you, I'm sure."

"You're sure of nothing, Mister Boudreaux."

"You should have waited for notification from authorities in Galveston County. The sheriff over there doesn't know who he found in that house; therefore, the coroner hasn't pronounced Clay Boudreaux dead. And there's no doubt in my mind that you'll vouch for me."

9

"You're overplaying your hand, if you think you can coerce me into partaking in such a sham."

"Overplaying my hand? A favored expression of your late granduncle." Boudreaux arched an eyebrow. "Do you like to gamble, madam?"

"On a sure bet."

"Not much fun in that, but I am a sure bet."

"And I think you're bluffing."

"Ain't necessary, sweetheart. You exposed your hand when you tried to have me killed."

"In Galveston or New Orleans?"

"Both."

She drew in what appeared to be a calming breath. "And why, pray tell, do you think I would agree to such chicanery?"

"Because of the letter."

"What letter?"

"The letter you wrote propositioning"—he smiled—"Troy to kill Clay for you. Foolish, writing a letter that would implicate you in murder."

"My sentiments exactly. I never wrote any such letter."

"Well, somebody did, and whoever she was, she wrote it in your hand and signed your name to it."

"I want to see it."

"It's safe where you can't get your hands on it."

He stepped to where she stood in the middle of the room, and she wrapped her fingers around the locket hanging against her breast. "I do not believe you have anything to implicate me."

"Oh, I have the letter, Olivia. Anyone who'd plot to kill her new husband, sight unseen, was a sure bet to try to eliminate his assassin next." He straightened and noted how her body tensed with his move. He started around her. "That letter's my insurance if you ever want to try another trick like that. I left detailed information as to its location in the event of my, shall we say, untimely death. The sheriff of Galveston County will retrieve it."

He stopped, her back to him, and when she didn't move, he brought his lips to her ear. "You could end up on the gallows."

She whirled, and he laughed at her. For the first time in days, he thought of her as a sexual being.

"I will not have relations with you."

And a mind reader to boot. He raked his eyes over her petite body, grinned, and stepped around her to the bed. She stepped aside. Out of the corner of his eye, he watched her watching him. The threat of sexual coercion could prove a viable form of duress.

From the night table, he picked up a copy of *The Three Mus* —

Olivia's small hand covered the title. She took the book from him and returned it to the table.

"I beg your pardon?"

"It was Uncle Lionel's. I was reading it to him...I don't want you to lose his place."

"You expect him to finish it?"

"I might finish it."

He sat on the bed and fell back on the chintz spread. "I might read it myself. Better yet, maybe I'll let you read it to me, too, Olivia." He patted the mattress. "Right here, beside me."

"I'll forgo the pleasure, thank you."

He sat up and pulled off a boot, then started struggling with the other. "You know, it might be hard to keep up appearances, us not sleeping together. What will the servants think?"

"That you and I do not know each other very well."

He stretched out the length of the bed. Damn, his feet didn't even reach the end of the mattress, a luxury he hadn't experienced since he was seventeen. With a hum, he sank further into a feather pillow and weaved his fingers together behind his head. "That might work for a day or two," he said. "Simon's not going to be fooled much past that."

"And what concern is it of Simon's?"

"I have my reputation to think of."

"None of the servants live here, Mister Boudreaux."

"But I do. I'm lord of the manor, sweetheart, and I plan to enjoy the role."

"If you think..."

Outside, oyster shell crunched in harmony with the spin of

11

carriage wheels and the chink of harness. Olivia turned to the windows overlooking the front of the house. He rose, stepped in front of her, and pulled the velvet drapes aside. Olivia moved up beside him and craned her neck to see who was driving up. Pleased or displeased, he couldn't tell, and he dropped the drapery.

"Dear Aunt Aggie, I do believe, with her niece, the beautiful and vivacious Lydia Augustus Pique, Uncle Duncan's youngest."

"You, sir, appear to know more than you should. Are you trying to make me suspicious?"

He thrust his hand around the back of her neck and yanked her to him. For a moment he basked in the fear reflected in those now not-so-shuttered windows to a selfish soul, then he brought his face close to hers.

"I'm trying to make you see how precarious your position is, sweetheart. Now listen. I am Deputy Sheriff Clay Boudreaux, and I am your secret partner now. I'm going to find out who your accomplices are, so you better think real careful what you tell Aunt Aggie and Lydia about me. I'm aware you could be in cahoots with them and Duncan, but, tell me this, whose side do you think they'll be on when they find out I have evidence implicating you in a plot to murder Clay? Even if they could, do you think they'd help you? They'll leave you to swing alone, while they divvy up the estate, and I think you're smart enough to know it."

He eased his hold and started to pull back, then stilled when her arms snaked around his neck. She jerked him back. His gaze dropped to her lips, full and pink and moist and gently parted and, no doubt, deliciously soft. Her sweet breath filled his senses, already drunk on the scent of gardenia, and he hardened.

"And you listen to me, you bastard," she said, her warm body pressed to his. "I'm going to help you find my accomplices. And then I'm going to send him or her or them, but most especially you, to the gallows for the murder of Clay Boudreaux."

His erection melted. "I am Clay Boudreaux."

"No, you aren't." She'd already unwound those arms from around his neck and placed her hands on his shoulders. Now she pushed at him.

12

"How can you be sure?" he asked.

"Clay would never believe I betrayed him." Her glistening eyes damned him, and he watched the subtle movement of her throat when she swallowed. "And if he did," she said softly, "I would never, ever forgive him. Now take your treacherous hands off me."

He released her so fast she almost toppled backwards, but she recovered in "true" graceful fashion.

"Well, Missus Boudreaux," he said, "it seems we have reached an agreement."

Chapter Three

"I'm coming, Aunt Aggie."

Olivia stopped on the last step, and Boudreaux almost ran her over. She raised her hands to her hair and turned to him.

"What do I look like?"

"Like a woman getting to know her husband."

She tightened her lips and started around him, from where she would have climbed back up the stairs if he hadn't grabbed her arm. Knocks on the door had given way to a rude, and in his opinion, uncalled-for banging of the heavy brass knocker. "You look the way we want them to see you."

"Olivia," a disembodied voice hollered, "open this door, right now. It's cold out here."

"She's a hateful old biddy," he said.

"She is that."

"Mean as a cottonmouth and twice as ugly, I'm told."

Olivia pulled her arm free. "And who told you that? Certainly not your father. Uncle Lionel would have never spoken that way about her."

It was his calling the woman ugly that got to her, had to be. Everybody from here to Texas knew Agatha Augustus was mean. The old witch prided herself on it. "My grandfather," he said. "He didn't regard her with the same awe her brothers did."

"Fraternal respect would be a better way of putting it." She glanced around him, and he followed her gaze to where the fallen spindles and a section of broken railing lay on the floor. One story up, the damaged bannister gaped down at them, and a full story higher the foyer ceiling secured a massive, coal-gas-fueled

14

crystal chandelier, which fell more than half that distance to hang twenty feet above the shimmering entry floor.

Another sharp knock echoed through the foyer, and he took Olivia by the shoulders and turned her so she faced the door.

"I'll get the mess," he said, "you let Aunt Aggie in."

"Good heavens, girl..."

From the staircase, behind which he'd deposited the broken railing, Boudreaux watched the massive front door swing wide, followed by Agatha Augustus's entry. The oh-so-very-lovely Lydia sailed in behind her.

"...what in the good Lord's name are you doing in here?" Agatha said.

"The servants are gone, and I was—"

"I don't care where you were or what you were doing. Why is Lionel's front door locked to begin with?"

"To prevent unwelcome visitors from barging in," she said, and she said it loudly, telling him in no uncertain terms that he was the intended recipient of her response and not Aunt Aggie. Nevertheless, Lydia laughed.

"I hardly think her rudeness amusing."

"I am sorry, Aunt Aggie, but I needed something to laugh at; I've been weeping all afternoon." Still grinning ear to ear, Lydia bent and kissed Olivia's cheek. "Speaking of visitors, darling, you look as if you've been wrestling with someone. Has Julian been bothering you again?"

"I won't dignify that comment with a response," Olivia said.

"I should think not," Agatha said. "Lydia, refrain from tasteless teasing, and Olivia, come in here." With that, the family's self-anointed matriarch stepped into the front room on her left and out of his sight. Lydia leaned close to whisper in Olivia's ear before finding the hall mirror and pulling hatpins from the black menagerie of crepe, feathers, and netting that made up her head cover. She carefully removed the hat from atop an elegant coiffure of auburn hair. "Damn, I have a terrible headache."

"Lydia, talk like a lady, and Olivia, now, please."

15

Lydia unbuttoned her cloak and whirled it off her shoulders. From the way she had trussed her buxom body, Boudreaux was amazed the woman could breathe. If the effect produced by her tightly laced stays was to entice, and from what little he knew of Lydia Augustus Pique it was, she succeeded beyond compare, even in mourning dress.

Olivia hung Lydia's cloak on the coat tree, then followed the other women into the adjoining room. He removed his black dress jacket and tossed it on the floor atop the spindles, then, in stocking feet, started across the foyer, removing his tie and unbuttoning the top three buttons of his shirt as he went.

"Would you like me to take your coat," he heard Olivia say when he drew closer.

"We'll not be here long, dear," Agatha answered.

"Julian hoped you'd come back with us," Lydia said.

He could see Olivia's back now. She stood at the entrance to the front room, waiting, he imagined, his grand appearance.

"I'm very tired, but thank you. What did you wish to talk about, Aunt Aggie?"

"Your inheritance."

"What about my inheritance?"

"Well, as you know by the terms of the agreement, you were to inherit if you wed Clay Boudreaux, per Lionel's request."

"And I did."

"Yes, my dear, by proxy. Unfortunately, the marriage was..."

He walked up behind Olivia and wrapped his arm around her waist, then looked up to find one of Agatha Augustus's eyeballs locked on him. He wasn't sure where the other one focused. For good measure, he pulled Olivia against him and bent his head. "Let me lead," he whispered, and when he sensed no resistance, he kissed her ear, a public display of affection he knew both women would find inappropriate, if not downright embarrassing.

The old woman raised her pointed chin. "Who are you?"

"Your nephew, Clay Boudreaux."

Her jaw dropped. "It is my understanding, young man, that Clay Boudreaux is dead."

"I am pleased to report I am not." He hugged Olivia tighter. "Isn't that so, sweetheart."

Olivia placed a hand on the arm round her waist. "A happy report indeed," she said, and he laid his head against hers and smiled at Aunt Aggie.

"Howard Augustus sent a telegram—"

"That Clay died in a house fire. I've heard. The report was wrong."

The woman stepped closer. "Howard was at the scene. He received his information from Nate Phillips."

"Did he now? Well, the sheriff made a quick assumption. It was my house, but the remains were unidentifiable. I regret the discomfort my untimely demise caused everyone."

Agatha's uncoordinated gaze slid to Olivia, who he still held to him. "Have you heard anything else from Galveston?"

"I have indeed, from a Deputy Boudreaux confirming Clay was not killed."

That flippant remark earned Olivia a look of contempt from the old shrew, and he rewarded her with a supportive squeeze. "I don't believe the sheriff has sent out anything official regarding the assumed death of Clay Boudreaux," he said to Agatha, "nor would he until he was sure. Since I'm alive, and he knows that, don't expect to hear anything else."

Her smile was second cousin to a sneer. "I happen to know Nate Phillips, young man—"

"I know you do, and he knows you, too."

She studied him, at least one eye did, and finally she said, "Is he part of this, too?"

His heartbeat quickened, but before he could respond, Aggie continued, "Of course he is. He'd have to be for you to expect to get away with this."

"With what, Aunt Aggie?"

The old woman turned a half-pivot, blessing him with a full view of her infamous hook nose. "Well, Lydia, my one true niece"—she looked at Olivia—"this will certainly dampen your father's aspirations to make Olivia his daughter-in-law."

17

Lydia rose from her spot on the settee. "Yes," she said and smoothed the black satin mourning dress over her hips. "I'm sure daddy's spirits will plummet once he discovers Clay Boudreaux is actually alive." The lovely Lydia sauntered toward the rest of them congregated at the entrance to the front room. "I must say I'm somewhat disappointed myself." Her smile was for him alone. "I'd prefer you were someone else."

He cocked his head to the side.

"Someone other than my little cousin's spouse, I mean. I spied you skulking around at the funeral earlier, and I'd hoped to run across you again, under more pleasant circumstances."

"Who knows what might have been."

Aunt Aggie stepped sideways, blocking his view of Lydia and forcing him to look at her. "Or what yet might be," she spat out. "Have you spoken to Lionel's attorney?"

He tried to focus on the eye actually looking at him. "I have."

"And he's convinced as to who you are?"

"He is."

"Sandifer Hudgins?"

"The same."

Aunt Aggie's good eye found Olivia. "Well, I certainly hope you are not part of this game, little girl."

"I beg your pardon?"

"Inserting this impostor into your bed to deceive the rest of the family."

"And why would I do such a thing?"

Olivia's voice had held a subtle tremor when she spoke. Her body, still against his, echoed it. Again he brought his mouth to her ear. "To consummate our marriage, sweetheart."

She twisted to face first him, then Aggie. "And share my inheritance with a stranger? Not to mention my body."

"A horrifying thought," he said.

Olivia pulled his arm wide and stepped out of his hold. "I can assure you, Aunt Aggie, if fortune saw fit to make me a widow, the last thing I would do is rush out and find a husband."

"Until the marriage between Clay Boudreaux and Olivia Lee

is consummated, the union is not considered legally binding in the eyes of the courts."

He closed the gap Olivia had made between him and her. "Could be argued in court as 'not legally binding' is what she's trying to say, sweetheart. Until this moment, the loving family of Lionel Augustus intended to contest the will. Now they have no basis."

Lydia moved into their circle. "Daddy never intended to contest the will. He wants you to marry Julian."

"He won't be able to finagle that either," Boudreaux said.

Lydia reached out and touched Olivia's hand, then nodded to him. "He simply showed up here this afternoon?"

"I found him in Uncle Lionel's bedroom."

"And now he wants you to sleep with him?"

Olivia flushed. "Lydia, please."

"Darling, you do realize this man really could be an impostor?"

Olivia trilled a laugh. "Who would be fool enough to think he could get away with such a deception?"

"Someone who knows about the family," Aunt Aggie said and forced herself between him and Olivia. "Someone who knows about the estate. Someone jealous of another's good fortune."

Lord, the woman was almost as tall as he was, and she did look him in the eye, or would if her eyes looked straight in front of her. "Do you have a particular someone in mind?" he asked.

She drew a breath through that beak of hers. "Tell Sandifer I know what he's up to and he's not going to get away with it."

"Perhaps you should tell him yourself."

"Rest assured I will, as soon as I find which rock he's hiding under." Aunt Aggie turned on her heel and stepped into the foyer. "Come, Lydia. Let's leave these lovebirds to their tangled nest."

Lydia placed a manicured hand against the doorjamb and stretched her long body to pluck her cloak from the coat tree. She graced him with a smile, before looking at Olivia. "If it's not already too late, darling, I would suggest you stay out of this man's bed until we are sure who he is."

"Thank you, but I don't need the family to confirm anything for me."

Lydia shrugged, then glanced at Aunt Aggie before leaning close to Olivia. "You could still take her in, you know. Daddy would be ever so grateful."

"Not nearly as much as your mother, I'm sure, but it's clear to me now that my husband and Aunt Aggie will not get along."

Lydia looked from him to Aunt Aggie, then winked at Olivia. "Are you certain of that? In my opinion, they appear to understand each other rather well."

*B*oudreaux saw them out the front door and into the carriage. Olivia watched from the porch until he started back to the house, then she came inside. Consummate the marriage, her left hind foot. For pity's sake, they lived at the threshold of the twentieth century.

Behind her, she heard the deadbolt turn. Between her self-serving family and this interloper moving up behind her, she was boxed in. Aunt Aggie's ploy to break her stepfather's will came as no surprise, and Uncle Duncan's loosely-knit plan to marry her off to Julian was almost as old as she was. More disconcerting were Aunt Aggie's confronting the man about Sandifer Hudgins and Lydia's parting remark implying Aunt Aggie might know something about what this Boudreaux person was really doing at Epico Hollow, and, for that matter, Lydia's role in this increasingly convoluted plot.

"You locked the door earlier?" she asked and moved into the front room.

"I did," he said, following.

"Why?"

"I didn't want us to be disturbed. What did Lydia whisper to you when she first came in?"

Olivia, her hand around the brandy decanter, looked at the man watching her from the foyer entry. "Oh, that. She said, and I quote, 'She's come for your house.' Lydia was, of course, only half joking, because that is, ultimately, what Aunt Aggie wants."

"She's worn out her welcome at the Duncan Augustuses'?"

"There never was a welcome. She had no place to go. Uncle Duncan had gone along with her last bad investment, so he took her in."

"And now that Lionel's gone, Duncan wants her to move in with you?"

"Lydia was teasing," she said and took a sip of brandy. "Uncle Lionel made it clear he would never live under the same roof with Aunt Aggie again. Truth is, she doesn't want to live here with me, but she does want to live here. In her mind, Uncle Lionel owed her a house, and she felt she had a better claim to this one than he did since she was actually related by blood to Matthew Lee."

"And what did Lionel say to that?"

Olivia shrugged. "I don't know what his response was precisely, but she never got this house."

"And Lionel did, along with Darcy Lee's widow"—he started her way—"and his daughter. Agatha's demand for a house, I take it, was in return for the farm in Maryland?"

"Still trying to impress me with your knowledge of the family, Mr. Boudreaux?"

He stopped at the parlor commode containing Epico Hollow's collection of alcoholic spirits. "There's a lot about this family Clay Boudreaux knows, Olivia, most of which he overheard growing up. I'm not trying to impress you, just trying to confirm what I think I already know, but I do know the lay of the land."

"And may I assume Troy also overheard what Clay overheard?"

"You may."

She gave him a hard study, then said, "Yes, to answer your question. Aunt Aggie has apparently spent a good part of her life bitter that Uncle Lionel inherited the farm in Maryland, then sold it out from under her. But in his defense, he bought her two homes after selling that place. One in Marion County, which she sold when she followed him down here seventeen years ago. The second over in Biloxi, which she lost last year."

"Did she believe he was going to leave her the house?"

"Most assuredly not. I suspect he left her enough for a modest home and comfortable livelihood, his generosity as much for Uncle Duncan's sake as hers."

"And you don't think she'll be satisfied with that."

"I do not. She wants everything."

"As does Duncan."

It had been a statement on his part, not a question. "Uncle Duncan wants control of the business, yes."

"Which you would have given him."

"Never."

"You planned to run the business yourself?" She said nothing, and he turned to the crystal bottles on the commode. "Seems my arrival is wreaking havoc with a number of aspirations, which explains why somebody wants me dead."

"If you are presuming to include my aspirations in that number, sir, you may rest assured that my feelings towards you are shaping as we speak. I believe what you are trying to uncover is a premeditated plot. That, or you're part of it."

"You didn't have to know me to want me dead," he said.

"Nor you me."

"Has anyone tried to kill you?"

"Not yet."

He picked up the decanter from which she'd poured her brandy—"Peach, I presume"—then pulled the glass plug and sniffed. "Peach." He replaced the plug, poured three fingers of whiskey from the amber bottle next to the cordial, and saluted her, stating, "brandy's too sweet for my palate."

"And whiskey is too duplicitous for mine."

He downed the whiskey without a grimace. "Treacherous is a better word."

He was an educated man, at least. Middle to late twenties, Olivia judged, with a strong chin, slightly cleft. His wide mouth, sculpted like that of a darn Greek god, complemented a straight nose. Her eyes lingered on that mouth, and he smiled at her perusal. All the pieces of his physical being were falling back into place since his look of disdain upstairs had shattered her short-lived euphoria at espying him behind the door. Lydia's interest in the man needed no explanation; still, that did not rule out the possibility the two already knew each other.

She rubbed her arms. Outside, the sun was setting and the chilly December day threatened to become a cold night.

"They'll check your story, you know?" she said.

"I know, but I have Galveston covered. The only thing they'll find there is that you and I are man and wife."

"I'd like assurance myself."

"We'll send a telegram tomorrow."

"To convince me you have Galveston covered?"

He poured himself another shot. "I want you certain of that, sweetheart."

"We needn't bother. Aunt Aggie made it perfectly clear Nate Phillips can't be trusted."

"The question is whether she can trust him for good or for bad. The answer is, and she knows this, she can't trust him for bad. That leaves her at a disadvantage if she's up to no good, which, I suspect, she is. The same could be said for you, Missus Boudreaux."

"I only know *of* Nate Phillips, and suddenly I don't trust him for either good or bad, and there is nothing you could say about him, at this point, that would change my mind."

He shrugged, then clenched his teeth with the downing of a second shot. She watched him pour another, then started around him. "It's been a long, awful day."

"Olivia."

She halted and looked back. He was leaning against the fireplace now, his gaze fixed on her.

"Don't try to leave this house tonight. I'm a light sleeper."

"I'll have you know that my granddaddy Lee cleared this land from what was, for all intents and purposes, jungle almost sixty years ago. This house has withstood hurricanes and pirates, and I have it on good faith that five of Butler's thieving Yankees are buried in the basement. I have no intention of surrendering it to you or Aunt Aggie or anyone short of my own demise."

23

Chapter Four

Trouble. STOP. *Survivor.* STOP. *Enroute N. O.* STOP. *Will advise.* STOP. *Howard.*

First that, now this. Duncan Augustus looked up from the telegram sent two days ago by his second-born. Howard had been in Galveston when he sent it—to Agatha, no less—a worrisome detail in itself. The much-put-out woman had slammed the missive down in front of him only ten minutes ago after she and Lydia returned from their brief and disturbing visit with Olivia. Duncan passed the telegram to Francis, who stood in front of the fireplace.

"If I'm interpreting this message correctly, son, it means someone believed killed in that fire is alive and Howard's on his trail."

"At Agatha's behest," Connie Augustus said.

Duncan turned to where his wife of thirty-eight years sat in a wing chair near his desk. "Apparently."

She stared at him a moment, then punched a thread through her needlework canvas. Duncan looked at Lydia, lounging on the settee in front of him.

"Who do you think he is, sugar?"

Lydia, pulled the last of the pins from her hair and massaged her scalp. "I've no idea, but Aunt Aggie insists he's Troy."

"Did she give you a reason why she thinks that?"

"She is convinced Howard knew Clay was dead when he sent that first message. She says the only person who could pull off this deception would be someone who knew Clay extremely well. Interestingly, she implied Sandifer Hudgins was involved."

24

Duncan blinked at his daughter. Now, that was interesting.

Francis laid the telegram back on the desk. "From what Howard reported to you the night of the fire, Nate Phillips was like Meridian after Sherman. He was certain Clay was dead."

Duncan placed his hands steeple-fashion under his chin. "And Troy had disappeared."

"Days before," Francis added. "It had to be Clay in that house. Had to be."

Duncan leaned back in his swivel chair and said to Lydia, "When Agatha spoke with him, did you get the sense they might already know each other?"

"You think Aunt Aggie's up to something, Dad?" Francis said.

In the chair next to the fireplace, Julian fidgeted, and Connie said, "She's always up to something."

"What matters," Duncan said, "is what she's up to this time. Lydia, what do you say?"

"It wasn't so much their knowing each other as it was the impression I had that he was toying with her."

"If anything, Agatha's involved with Sandy."

"No, Mama," Francis said from his spot in front of the fire. "It sounds more like Hudgins left her out, and she's angry about it."

"Well, if that's the case, she would be, wouldn't she?" Connie said.

"What was he like?" Duncan asked Lydia, who responded by raising her arms above her head and stretching, before placing a fisted hand over her mouth to cover a yawn.

"Tall and lean, and very good-looking. What was Clay like?"

"Tall, lean, and good-looking from what I've been told."

"And Troy?"

"Tall, lean, and good-looking." Duncan caught Francis's eye. "They looked enough alike, apparently, to be brothers."

"Personalities?" Lydia asked.

"From what Lionel said about him, Clay was easygoing for the most part. Quick-tempered when riled, but cooled quickly. He's smart, loyal, and honest."

25

Lydia giggled. "Did you ever ask Uncle Lionel if he was sure Clay was his?"

"Quite recently, as a matter of fact."

"There's no doubt," Francis said. "Uncle Lionel took Elaine in after Edwin Boudreaux abandoned her—"

"Excuse me, dear brother, I know. I was making a foolish attempt at humor. Please say no more."

Unaffected by Lydia's plea, Connie looked at Francis. "Honey, you're wrong to blame your Uncle Lionel."

"I wasn't blam—"

"Everything that happened was Darcy's fault. He's the one who insisted Elaine couldn't manage the farm. He asked Lionel to take her in as a housekeeper, no less."

"Yes," Duncan said, "a beautiful woman, a lonely man. Their fornicating had to happen." He rested his gaze on his wife. "Truly Darcy has much to account for."

"Your sarcasm is unnecessary."

"I'm agreeing with you, my dear—about Darcy that is, not my sarcasm."

Connie sneered, then turned back to Francis. "Hugh Gibson had already left for Texas or he'd have probably killed Lionel and his daughter, and we wouldn't have this problem today."

Duncan looked at Lydia. "He probably considered it, but couldn't bring himself to do her in."

Lydia laughed, then asked, "What about Troy, Daddy?"

Duncan raised an eyebrow.

"His temperament? Do you know anything about him?"

"Not much."

Francis tossed a small limb onto the fire. "And Howard's been of little value."

"He uncovered that stuff about Clay and the Mexican girl," Julian said.

"Yes," Duncan agreed, "something for Olivia to ponder."

"Olivia didn't buy that cotton patch the first time you tried to sell it to her," Connie said. "What makes you think she will now?"

Duncan leaned back in his chair and swiveled to face his wife.

"The death of Margo Flores takes on greater weight for Olivia now that her dead husband has shown up on her doorstep."

"She married him knowing about the Flores woman. If she wed him without question, why should the incident concern her now. Unless, of course, you are suggesting Olivia knew all along that Clay would not be showing up to claim his inheritance."

"You think Olivia plotted to kill Clay?" Julian asked.

Duncan looked at his youngest son and realized the question had, unbelievably, been directed at him, not Connie. But Francis had already stepped away from the fireplace. "Julian, you say you want to marry Olivia, but how well do you really know her?"

"I've known her all my life."

Francis raised his eyes to heaven. "All *her* life, and it was a rhetorical question."

Duncan swiveled his chair to better address Julian. "What I meant, son, was the Margo Flores incident carries more weight for Olivia now that this person has shown up claiming to be Clay." He glanced at Connie. "My concern is that Olivia is not giving enough thought to Miss Flores's turning up dead at the same time this boon falls at Clay's feet."

"Yes," Francis said, "and we need to point that out to Olivia."

"We should and we will."

Connie squirmed close to the edge of her seat. "As much as I hate to admit this, Duncan, Agatha could be right about this person, and on top of that, you must consider that Olivia is working with him. Agatha is."

"Oh, I suspect he's working with someone all right, but I do not believe it's Olivia. She doesn't need a 'Clay', any Clay, dead or alive. Not anymore. Olivia met the requirements of the will when she married him, and you know as well as I that there is no way we can break Lionel's will based on non-consummation of the marriage. Their union is a legal contract, not a Dark Ages, Pope-sanctioned treaty designed for power mongering. The only way we'll get our hands on Lionel's money is by marrying her to Julian."

"Olivia could die," Connie said.

27

From his vantage point behind the desk, Duncan watched every head in the room turn to Connie, and he said, "Olivia's untimely demise would leave Agatha with the estate, Connie. Do you suggest we kill her off, too?"

"That's what I'm really after, dear, an excuse to kill Agatha."

"I'm pleased you find this situation amusing."

"I'm sorry your plans have gone awry, but it's not the first time that has happened, is it?"

And she was no sorrier now than she had been then.

"But the fire was an accident, was it not?" Lydia asked.

"A convenient one," Francis answered, and Duncan glanced at him.

Lydia pushed up from her reclining position and put her feet on the floor. "Do you think Howard set the fire, Daddy? I thought you sent him to Texas to gather unsavory information on Clay."

"Don't ask questions you don't want to know the answer to," Connie said to Lydia, before locking her gaze on Duncan. "She's no longer content leading you astray; now she's recruiting my children."

"Ah," Lydia said, "I see why everyone is doubly bothered by this unfortunate turn of events. Howard—"

"This is not an unfortunate turn of events, you twit," Francis said. "It's a disaster. And so you'll know, Howard went to Texas on his own."

Connie snorted like a horse, and Francis's gaze passed from his sister to his mother.

"On his own, Daddy?" Lydia said. "That is a rather frightening thought."

Duncan kept his face noncommittal, but, indeed, the thought was frightening. "Sugar, we have no reason to believe Howard started that fire. We thought fate had eliminated one obstacle, and now we find it hasn't. That's all. Now, did the man at Epico Hollow mention who had died?"

"He only said it wasn't him."

"No mention of having lost a brother?"

"Which you would assume he might," Connie said.

"Not if he's trying to trick us," Francis said.

"Did he appear angry?" Duncan asked.

"No, it seemed to me he wanted to convince us Clay was alive and he and Olivia were man and wife."

Francis placed his hands behind his back and caught his father's eye. "You think he could be Troy?"

"Agatha thinks so."

Julian rose. "If it is Troy who survived, Olivia's been duped, and I need to get her out of that house."

Connie looked at Julian and snapped, "No," then fixed her eyes on Duncan. "Don't let him go. I still say Olivia could be working with that man over there. Worse yet, they could both be working with Agatha."

"Could you explain why you think that?"

"You remember how Olivia was growing up. She detested the very thought of Lionel having a real son in Texas. I still can't believe she agreed to marry him. But think. You're the one who made a point of her not needing a Clay, but she got one anyway, didn't she? Forced on her by Lionel."

"Olivia only thought she disliked Clay because of Lionel. She considered Clay's dismissive attitude toward his father an affront and, for some odd reason, believed Lionel was bothered by it."

"I thought it was Uncle Lionel who refused to acknowledge him," Francis said.

"He—"

"Olivia was jealous of Clay," Connie said. "He was Lionel's true flesh and blood, which she could never be, but Lionel did do Elaine and the boy dirty."

"Is this the same poor Elaine, who minutes ago you suggested her father should have ritually executed? You know better than that." Duncan looked at Francis, watching them. "Lionel's relationship with Clay was what Elaine wanted it to be. She was married, so was he. She needed to get out of a bad situation, and she did."

Connie rolled her eyes. "That woman was in one bad situation after another."

"Consider what a fortunate woman you are."

"Meaning that you didn't share Lionel's good fortune when it came to women?"

"Uncle Lionel's women are dead," Julian said.

Francis stooped and warmed his hands in front of the fire. "I believe that was Mama's rather tasteless point."

"Oh, y'all stop being that way," Lydia said and leaned forward on the settee. "Daddy did have excellent fortune with his women. Mama, me, then—"

"Aunt Aggie." Francis sniggered.

That drew a laugh from Julian, and Lydia curled her lips at the both of them. "Not to mention three wonderful, legitimate sons to inherit his fortune, should he ever get his hands on it."

More relaxed in the wake of Lydia's words, Duncan winked at his daughter. Immediately thereafter, he glanced at his spouse. "Could you and Lydia excuse us, please?"

Connie glared at him, but she already knew too much. He wanted her out of this room.

With a faux sigh, Lydia rose to her elegant height of seventy inches. "Plotting murder and mayhem without your wonderful women, Daddy?"

"Not at all, sugar," he said with a smile as false as her much-put-upon sigh. "I simply do not wish to bore my beautiful ladies with business is all."

"If you were talking legitimate business, you'd be wise to ask me to stay. Don't do anything reckless. Remember that I now have money to burn and will happily invest whatever amount you need in Augustus Brick Works."

"We'd rather do business with a shark," Francis said.

She had started in the direction of the desk, now she stopped and turned full on Francis, still standing in front of the fireplace. "Here's your business tip of the week, brother: Gulfport is the future, and the men building Gulfport need bricks. I would love to invest in bricks."

"Did that old fart you married tell you that?"

"That darling old fart I married merely provided me the means

30

to invest," she said, rounding the desk and kissing Duncan on the cheek. "I got my tip—"

"From her Uncle Lionel," Duncan finished for her, and this time, it was she who winked at him, then she continued after her mother.

"We've got more immediate concerns than the rise of a speculative Gulfport," Francis said when the door closed behind her.

"We do, but if we don't come up with some capital, preferably interest-free, our creditors are going to gobble up our little chunk of Handsboro before we sell Gulfport the first brick."

"Lydia told me this afternoon she could double our operation in three months," Julian said. "Dealing with her could be our best option."

Francis scowled and looked at Duncan, who raised a hand. "You don't have to say anything, son. I've had high hopes for the past three days, too. I'm not ready to accept that Clay didn't die in that fire."

"And the man with Olivia?" Francis asked.

"If he's Troy, dealing with him will be easy. We will, after all, simply be protecting our little Olivia."

Julian started to the door.

"Where are you going?" Duncan asked.

"I'm getting Olivia out of there."

"Get back here."

Julian spun around. "Dad—"

"We're not rushing in there. Not yet." Chest tight, Duncan rose from his chair. "I need time to think this out."

"And Howard's on his way home," Francis said, rocking back on his heels. "He'll be able to shed some light on this mess and maybe even where Olivia fits in it all."

Chapter Five

𝔄 door squeaked outside the bedroom of the recently dead Lionel Augustus. On the bed inside, Boudreaux opened his eyes. Damp cold had penetrated the room over the course of the night, a minor discomfort which kept him semi-alert. Good thing, too, because Olivia was venturing forth.

He didn't think she'd go far, but he could not simply dismiss suspicions she was working with someone in this mess. Julian Augustus was smitten with her. Boudreaux had known that for years, but from what he'd been told, Olivia didn't return the man's feelings. That didn't mean she wouldn't be willing to use him. Hell, the whole darn clan could be part of the plot.

He watched her shadow block the light beneath his door, but he remained relaxed, his head on the pillows, and gave her time to get down the stairs.

When he heard a soft clatter—the result, no doubt, of her collision with the pile of spindles he'd shoved into the hall behind the stairs—he moved his legs over the side of the bed.

The foyer chandelier hung level with and fifteen feet beyond the gaping balcony rail. He contemplated following her downstairs in case she was meeting someone, but opted instead for her bedroom.

The dim light from the chandelier illuminated a path across her carpeted floor, and he followed his shadow to the bureau beside her bed. The scents of gardenia and woman heated his skin and hardened his manhood. He hadn't made it this far yesterday afternoon, and the chance she harbored a weapon nagged him. He lit the coal oil lamp on the chest, brightening the room enough to register the muted shades of rose and green flowers woven into the oriental carpet. Beside the lamp lay the locket she'd been wearing the afternoon before, and he opened it to find a young Darcy Lee, decked out in Confederate finery, staring back at him. His gut burned. "Her being your daughter won't stop me," he told the image and snapped the locket shut.

From the way the bed was rumpled, Olivia slept on its right side. He squeezed his fingers into the down pillow and cringed at the unpleasant sensation of wet linen. Nonetheless, he picked it up, stuffed his face into it, and breathed her perfume. The damp pillowcase kissed his cheek, cooling his ardor, and he pulled back, ready to return the pillow to its place on the mattress. But where the pillow had been, he discovered a sheet of ruled paper filled with words written in an all-too-familiar hand.

The strain of the past three days slammed into him. Weary, he sat on the bed and skimmed the letter Clay had written his bride. Not much of a damn letter in his opinion, and when he'd finished it, he picked up a tear-soaked handkerchief from the bureau and held it between his thumb and forefinger. She'd buried the man she'd loved as a father a little more than twelve hours ago. Signs of her grief should hardly be considered a surprise. Again, he glanced at the letter, then pushed it back beneath the pillow and rose.

This room, with its lavish moldings and high baseboards, was smaller than his, but still large. A rose-colored spread lay folded back at the foot of her cherry bed, and he glanced at the closest of four delicately carved bedposts. The matching three-drawer bureau by her bed, dressing table, and highboy furnished this side of the room. A huge wardrobe, not matching, stood on the wall near the door he'd entered. The highboy rose almost seven feet off the floor, and he wondered what practical use the petite Olivia derived from its upper drawers, but inside a lower one, he found a white silk nightgown. For a moment he luxuriated in the cool smoothness of it and wondered what she was wearing now.

Seven letters spanning twelve years. Clay wrote the first in 1885—he'd have been fifteen. In all, he made only two references to his older brother, neither disparaging. On July 13, 1886, he'd written that Troy had finished school and had moved out to his father's ranch to live permanently. In 1890, he made reference to Edwin Boudreaux's death and the fact Troy intended to remain on the ranch and raise cattle and hogs.

That same summer, Clay went to work for the Galveston County sheriff. Both Elaine Boudreaux's boys were making their own way and causing their mother little concern. She died two years later, and Clay inherited her boardinghouse, the one Lionel Augustus had paid the full mortgage on when her father, Hugh Henry Gibson, died years before.

The last letter, written eight months ago, said nothing Olivia didn't already know. For two years prior to its crafting, her Uncle Lionel had been trying to persuade Clay to return to Mississippi and take over his business. Here now, with a strong, decisive script, Clay again told his father he hadn't decided to leave Texas, but he would think on it. Then three months ago, Lionel, his health failing, had gone to Galveston alone and talked to his son face to face. The talks proved fruitful and landed her in the circumstances where she found herself today.

She traced the signature on the letter. She'd received her only letter from Clay less than three weeks ago. He'd written to ask how she felt about the proposal and closed by telling her he would humbly take her for his bride "if you are willing."

...if you are willing.

She wed Clay Boudreaux by proxy, in Texas, at her uncle's insistence, two days before Lionel Augustus died. She brought her finger to a halt at the end of the "y" in the word "Clay."

"I was willing," she said.

"Willing to what?"

Olivia jumped when he spoke, then jerked her head up and glared at him, standing at the threshold of the office door.

"Having second thoughts regarding your done deeds?"

"You have no idea how much so," she answered with a stuffy voice.

She was dressed not in seductive silk, but in a white flannel gown with matching robe. Trimmed with eyelet and pink ribbon, the ensemble was as feminine as it was chaste...and challenging. She had plaited her hair, but loose strands twisted and curled around her face, still pretty despite its red-rimmed eyes.

"What are you doing down here at three-thirty in the morning?" he asked.

"I might ask you the same thing."

"I followed you."

She waved her hands over a small accumulation of letters on top of the desk. "I'm reading Clay's letters to his father."

"That shouldn't take you long," he said and flopped in the wing chair in front of her.

Excessive had been the word that passed through his mind yesterday when he'd first seen this dark-paneled room. Large pieces of upholstered furniture and Boston fern-filled planters sat amidst walls of bookshelves; unadorned floor-to-ceiling windows ran along the back wall; and a huge black walnut desk and accompanying leather chair, Olivia's present throne, sat atop a rich carpet in the middle of the room. Centered above all, and casting a halo-like glow over both of them, was a gaslight. He rested his eyes on the ugly thing. "Trying to find out what I really thought about you? You should spare yourself the humiliation."

"Further proof you are not who you claim. There is nothing insulting toward me in these letters."

"My point exactly. There is nothing about you, period, in those letters."

"And you believe that would bother me?"

"Possibly."

"Well, it doesn't. But if you must know, Troy was the topic I was interested in."

Olivia folded the last letter and placed it atop the others, but when she reached for the ribbon to retie the stack, he sat forward and held out a hand, palm up.

"And did you find out anything?" he asked.

"Nothing of value."

35

He shuffled through the letters, all the while shaking his head. "You should have attempted to find out what you could about Troy before you contacted him, don't you think?"

"It would seem, sir, that he has made contact with me, and I feel somewhat at a disadvantage."

"I'm Clay."

"Even if you are, I still need to know about Troy."

"You know all you'll ever need to know. Why don't you ask about Clay?"

She sat there for a long moment, studying him, then said, "How did Clay feel about me growing up?"

"He never thought much about you at all."

"I thought about him a lot."

"How so?"

"I hated him."

She was going somewhere with this conversation, and the expectation pleased him even if her words did not. "You didn't even know him."

"It was a childish, little-girl kind of hate in deference to the man I loved, but it was very real."

"And do you still hate him?"

She pushed a wisp of silver-blond hair behind her ear. "I'm sure he, or you if you are he, would think so, but no; I'd reconciled myself to his being a petulant, self-pitying brat years ago. Then, when Uncle Lionel started to woo Clay back here, he told me my reasons for disliking Clay were unjustified, and I had no business forming opinions in the first place. He said his decision not to acknowledge Clay had nothing to do with his not wanting him, but was made in deference to Elaine Boudreaux's wishes. She wanted her marriage to work and for her and Edwin to make a good home for both her boys. He said he'd respected that. I've always suspected Uncle Lionel said what he did to curb my temper as regards Clay; nevertheless, over the past two years, I had grown quite ambivalent toward him. I gave my stepfather the benefit of the doubt because I loved him so. Now you tell me why Clay didn't like his father."

"I didn't dislike him. I didn't know him. He wasn't part of my life. I don't look like him, I don't think like him, and I don't want to be like him."

"Did Clay think of Edwin Boudreaux as his father?"

"I called him Daddy."

"Edwin knew Clay wasn't his?"

"Yes, he knew."

"Did Clay trust Troy?"

"Without question."

"Did Troy trust Clay?"

"Implicitly."

"If that's true, then why would anyone approach Troy to kill Clay?"

"Because that person is an idiot, Missus Boudreaux."

"Which rules me out, Mister Boudreaux. Now, I would like to suggest two other possibilities for your alleged letter."

He laid his head against the back of the chair. "Go ahead."

"First, someone is purposefully trying to make me look bad in your eyes."

"Make you look bad? Olivia, if you didn't write that letter in my possession, someone is trying to frame you for murder."

"Fine, we agree—"

"Only if you grant me my qualifying if. What's your second possibility?"

"You are delusional about your brother, no matter which one of you he is."

He frowned. "Are you saying I couldn't trust Troy?"

"I'm saying Clay couldn't trust Troy and Troy couldn't trust Clay."

"And why do you say that?"

"I'm simply giving you possibilities to consider."

"Based on what?"

"I have a brain, and I use it."

"Olivia, I have a brain, too, and a sometimes above average ability to deduce things. Your two alternative possibilities are based on something, and I would like for you to tell me what."

37

She laid her forearm on the desk and leaned toward him. "I know that I did not write any letter to Troy offering him money to kill Clay. How does that compare to your superior deductive reasoning?"

"Pretty basic, and, at present, unprovable. How about that mumbo-jumbo about my not being able to trust Troy and vice versa?"

She studied him a moment, raised her chin, then sat back.

"Well?" he persisted.

"Was Troy jealous of Clay?"

He hated being answered with a question. "Why would he be?"

"Because of Lionel Augustus's money."

"We've always known about Lionel Augustus's money. Troy's thought on the subject was that the price of inheriting that money would be too high, but I was under fire from Nate Phillips to do my familial duty."

"By marrying me?"

"To protect you actually."

Her mouth dropped open. "So Clay was to be my protector?"

He nodded.

"Ha! At present, I am officially a widow. The only thing standing between me and a fortune is a man blackmailing me with evidence he refuses to reveal and insisting I acknowledge him as my co-heir. Once he has established himself as Clay Boudreaux, he has everything to gain from my demise. I can't tell you how comforting I find those prospects."

"So, Lionel Augustus was correct in believing you couldn't take care of yourself."

"An example of your superior deductive reasoning, Mister Boudreaux?" She rose from the chair so fast he thought maybe he needed to get up himself, but didn't want her to think she'd cowed him into rising.

"Well, let me tell you this, sir. Lionel Augustus loved me. He wanted me to inherit his estate and help run his business. I greatly resent your suggestion that I am simply part of this estate to be protected and invested in like a darn pine tree. You implied the same thing this afternoon, and I would appreciate hearing no more of it."

"If that were true, Olivia," he said softly, "why have Clay wed you at all? Your Uncle Lionel could have left you everything. I—"

"Clay."

He frowned at her. "Very well. Clay didn't want it."

She sat down slowly. "He wanted to give something to his son."

"He wanted a male at the head of his empire, sweetheart, and he wanted Darcy Lee's progeny taken care of. Our marriage guaranteed both."

Her eyes didn't tear, and he was glad of that, but his words had wounded her. Still, he couldn't help but believe she'd realized this from the beginning, which could account for her decision to eliminate Clay and take everything.

She cocked her head toward the bank of windows. "I hear Chester."

Boudreaux hadn't heard anything; but Olivia rose, and the chair rolled away from her.

"He doesn't like the cold. I need to let him in." She stepped out from behind the desk. "Enjoy reading Clay's letters. Maybe you'll learn something."

He rose and tossed the letters on top of the desk. "I know what's in the letters. I'm going to help you find the cat, then I'm going back up to bed with you."

Olivia had to call the cat; she hadn't really heard him, but he did come. Boudreaux had stood at the kitchen door, as if he expected her to summon a person. Then he'd stayed close on her heels through the narrow back hall into the foyer and up the stairs, her heart pounding harder with each step she took.

He stopped when they passed the door to Uncle Lionel's bedroom, and when she looked over her shoulder at him, he'd asked, "Disappointed?"

"Only in that you've robbed me of an excuse to claw your eyes out."

"Kitten scratches, Olivia, not even as bad as what old Chester could do. Bites and kicks and screams. None would do you any good, should I persist with what you imply."

"Are you trying to frighten me, Mister Boudreaux?"

"I'm reminding you that I am a nice man."

"Why should you care what I think of you? After all, I'm not a nice woman."

He shrugged. "I'm doing my best not to believe a word you say."

Chapter Six

$\mathcal{B}$oudreaux paused in front of the hot air furnace hidden one floor below the main level of the house. Epico Hollow had been built in 1841 on an excavated knoll, overlooking the point where Epico Bayou flowed into Bayou Bernard. The back of the living area sat on eleven-foot-high brick pillars. What had originally been a great, covered lower level had, years later, been enclosed with cypress boards to form a basement. Parts of the floor down here were bricked, including where the furnace sat.

The furnace heated a chamber, which sent warmed air coursing through a series of ducts connecting to the rooms above. The system was as old as the house, and had been a luxury when it was installed. And to think, Boudreaux had considered a wood stove in every room of his mother's boardinghouse first-class. Shoot, a man could get used to hot air heating, gaslights, opulent furniture, and carpeting in every room.

A tall colored youth descended the narrow steps into the dingy space and looked to either side of him. Boudreaux figured Billy for about seventeen. For the past two hours, they'd shoveled coal from a pile dumped on the north side of the house, down a chute and into a large bin inside the dank lower level.

"Working good?"

"Seems to be," Boudreaux answered.

First firing of the season. Before this morning, there hadn't even been any fuel brought inside the house. Coal had been sitting in the yard since October, Billy told him, but the household had been preoccupied with sickness, death, and funeral arrangements. There'd been a couple of cold spells before Thanksgiving, but the family had made do with the fireplaces.

"That's all you got, Mister Clay."

Boudreaux reached into his pocket and found six bits, which he held out to the young man.

"No, suh, I get paid ever' week." He waved the coins away, but Boudreaux shook his head.

"Take it, Billy. You've done a full day's work, and it's only eight."

A flash of teeth lit up the young man's face. "Yes, suh, I will." He graced Boudreaux with a quick salute. "Thank'e and welcome home." He started up the steps. "Be out at the barn if you need me."

Boudreaux's stomach growled. Unless Billy could cook, he wouldn't need him. Worse yet, Miss May, Billy's grandmother, was the cook, and Billy informed him earlier that Olivia had given her the week off. Now he began to wonder where the other three servants were. He wasn't positive, but he thought they should be here by now.

He tilted his head and listened to the unfamiliar sound of water draining from Olivia's bath. She'd drawn it almost an hour ago. A whole damn hour. And here he was down in the cellar shoveling coal so she'd be warm. Hell, he hadn't even had breakfast yet.

Behind him the cellar door squeaked, and he turned at the same moment a breathless, restless, where-have-you-been voice said loud and clear, "Troy!"

At the threshold above him, he found its source, her eyes wide and her lips frozen into a smile. He cocked his head to one side. "Hello, Katie."

"I wonder where Millie and Simon are?" Olivia stopped at the kitchen entrance almost as fast as Katie dropped Boudreaux's hand.

"I don't know about Millie and Simon, but I have had the pleasure of meeting Miss Harder," he said.

"I see that."

Katie stepped back to untie the scarf beneath her chin and

pulled the broad-rimmed hat from her mop of unruly golden curls. She reached for the top button on her coat. "I'm sorry I'm late, Olivia. We did get that frost last night, and I had to gather a little more firewood for Mama." She licked her lips, then gave Boudreaux a nervous smile. "It feels good in here."

"I had to get the house warm, so my lovely bride could bathe in leisurely comfort."

Olivia narrowed her eyes. "Perhaps my morning toilet was not long enough to suit you, darling."

He laughed at her. Laughed! If he thought, on top of everything else, he was going to live under her roof and make a fool out of her by diddling the —

"Your sudden burst through the kitchen door just now did surprise me. I heard you pull the plug in that tub not two minutes ago."

She always left the scented water in the tub until her toilet was complete. It made the entire upstairs smell good.

"And I do believe," he said, "you scared the color right out of Miss Katie's rosy cheeks."

Yes, well that remark and his sweet smile certainly managed to put the color back into Katie's plump cheeks. This Boudreaux person was managing to throw Katie completely off kilter. Not surprising, considering he was a handsome man, and handsome men tended to challenge Katie's less-than-circumspect judgment.

"I wondered when the household servants would arrive," he continued, his attention now fully on Olivia. "I understand you've let the cook off."

"All week. When Aunt May left yesterday, we thought there would only be myself in the house. She was fond of your father."

Olivia shifted her gaze to Katie. "I was wondering if Millie said anything to you yesterday about being late this morning?"

"Oh." Katie took another step away from Boudreaux. "They'll be along any minute, I imagine." The young woman coughed, then brushed past her and out of the kitchen.

Olivia frowned, found Boudreaux watching her, then set out after Katie.

43

❧❦

$\mathcal{B}$oudreaux had no sooner followed Olivia across the kitchen threshold than the front door slammed.

"Well," a haughty voice said as he came around the grand staircase, "I see you've already made your way here." Boudreaux caught Katie's quick nod to an older woman, dressed in a dark coat. The woman's gloved hands, clasped in front of her, held a bag. A hat sat atop her head. Perhaps it was the cold that left her face pinched, but not the cold entirely.

Behind the woman, stood a tall, lanky man, hatless, his bald head gleaming from sunlight streaming through the foyer's second level windows. Simon and Millie Dumont, man and wife, personal bookkeeper and housekeeper, and Simon had sometimes doubled as Lionel Augustus's gentleman servant. Neither made any move to enter farther into the house, nor did they remove their winter outerwear.

Katie mumbled something to Millie, then moved aside when Olivia reached them.

"Millie, whatever is wrong? You are almost an hour late, and why have you come through the front door?"

Millie's eye caught Boudreaux's, and she raised her chin. "So this is supposed to be your husband, Olivia?"

"He is."

"That's not the way I hear it."

"I beg your pardon?"

"He's a stand-in, I'm told. Someone you've found to pretend he's your husband so you can argue the marriage has been consummated and you won't have to share —"

"Now you wait one minute, Millie —"

"No, you wait, young lady," the older woman said, shaking a gloved finger at Olivia. "I don't care who of you gets Mister Augustus's money, but I do care about morals and the proper behavior of a young woman. Living in sin with this...man" — she nodded to him, standing behind Olivia — "would cause your stepfather to disown you, and your mother to roll in her grave, proper aristocracy that she was. You should be ashamed of yourself."

44

He figured one of two things would happen to Olivia if he touched her right now. She'd either remain hard as stone or she'd explode into a thousand pieces and take Millie Dumont with her. How he wished he could see her face.

"Simon and I have no intention of working for you until you rid yourself"—Millie looked him up and down—"of this person, and start living like a decent human being." She raised her head. "When he's gone, we'll come back. In the meantime, we want our pay for this past week."

Olivia straightened, ominous despite her stature. "How dare you presume to tell me how to live and what my mother and uncle would or would not approve as far as I am concerned. You never knew my mother and a scenario such as the one you described is one my granduncle may well have written. You have overstepped your bounds as a servant in this house."

Millie paled, and for a moment, Boudreaux thought Simon would suffer an apoplectic fit.

"Millie," Olivia continued, the hint of a tremor in her voice, "you worked for my uncle almost nine years. You know the family well enough not to have taken such a ludicrous tale at face value, yet you immediately turn on me. I have much bigger concerns than the approval of the hired help."

Olivia whirled, and the satin in her black skirt hummed with the spin. He stepped out of her way, and she stalked past him.

"I'll give you your pay," she spat over her shoulder, "but you will not be coming back. Ever. You are both fired."

"Millicent?" Simon whispered.

"Hush," Millie said, "it was to be expected." But from the look on her face, she hadn't really "expected" to be dealt with in quite this manner.

Olivia turned and glared at them. "Come with me."

Millie started after her, Simon followed.

Boudreaux pursed his lips, then turned and found a wide-eyed Katie. Don't worry, he mouthed, and reassured her with a smile before following the others to Lionel's elaborate office. He heard Katie behind him.

45

"You'll give us references, of course?" Simon asked. In front of him, Millie watched Olivia writing a draft at the desk. Except for shushing Simon, the woman hadn't said a word since Olivia started talking.

"Yes, I will give you references, but rest assured, I will note the perfidious reason I let you go."

Millie sucked in air. "Now, I've worked for—"

"Finding work really shouldn't be a problem for you, Missus Dumont. Approach Agatha Augustus for employment." Olivia's nostril's flared. "She is, without a doubt, the reason you have so recklessly lost this position. I'm sure she'll be willing to intercede with Aunt Connie, who will put you to work scrubbing floors. Why, she was complaining just the other night that Sally was ineffective. In time you should be able to work your way back up to a supervisory position if you grovel to Mabel." Olivia glanced at Boudreaux, looked at the draft, then motioned him to the desk. "Your signature is at the bank. You'll have to sign this. The first test of your signature, darling. For Millie and Simon's sake, I do so hope Mister Demarche has no doubts as to your true identity."

Yeah, Clay Boudreaux's signature was at the bank all right, but so was hers. He took her place behind the desk and perused the draft. The pay seemed more than it should have been, and he considered Olivia had provided them a little extra.

"I'm sure there will be no questions," he said, and with an air of confidence meant for Olivia, he signed the draft, then leaned back, waving the paper in the air to dry the ink. When he caught Olivia's eye, he passed her a sassy grin. Her lips tightened, and she reached to take the draft, but he handed it to Simon instead.

The now quiet Millie drew in a breath, looked at the amount on the draft, then at her husband, and with a final thrust of her chin, she looked at Olivia. "I—"

"Use the back door, please."

Millie hesitated a moment, then followed Simon out. Katie stepped out of their way, then glanced at Boudreaux.

"That's all the excitement, Katie," he said, "you can get to work. Looks like you've got free rein."

She slipped out the door and down the hall. From the kitchen, he heard the back door slam behind Millie and Simon.

"That was rather brutal, don't you think?"

Olivia made a half-pivot and looked down on him. "Brutal, Mister Boudreaux? This in defense of a woman who told me I needed to start living like a decent human being? Perhaps I should have increased the amount of their allowance for the kind words she said about you."

"She may have honestly been concerned with your best interests."

"My best interests, your ass..."

"Why, Olivia—"

"This moment has been waiting to happen since I graduated school last spring. I never trusted her. She's been convinced from the moment Uncle Lionel hired her she'd be needed only until I was old enough to assume responsibility for running the house."

"It sounds like her fears may have had some basis."

"She's undermined my efforts to assert myself for the past year." Boudreaux watched her wring her fingers into knots and out again. "I didn't want to give her the boot anymore than Uncle Lionel did. Besides, he liked Simon."

"Well, what did you intend to do?"

"I had intended, until this morning, to keep her and let her run the house. Goodness knows I've got enough to do now trying to run..." Olivia clamped her mouth shut and stared at him.

"Continue, Olivia. Run what?" He looked at the shining surface of the desk before him, then at her. "The Augustus empire?"

"Well, as of this time yesterday, you were quite dead."

"Quite. But now I'm quite alive."

"And you're already sitting behind my stepfather's desk."

"My father's desk." He sat forward, his gaze locked on hers. "As per his wishes. And Millie's gone, per yours, so you've got the house."

"Haven't things worked out divinely?" She turned to go.

"What did your uncle say about Millie's not respecting your position?"

"I never troubled him with such bickering. He was sick, and there was no reason for me to make it an issue. I had plenty to do taking care of him. I can forgive Millie not wanting to relinquish her position in this house. What I can't forgive is her conniving with Aunt Aggie."

"How do you know it was Agatha who talked to them?"

"Ask your newfound friend Katie why they were late this morning. There is no doubt in my mind they were waylaid at Uncle Duncan's on their way to work. This entire, embarrassing episode was concocted by Agatha Augustus."

More embarrassing, he wondered, than the consummated marriage scheme? "So here we are, you and me, alone with my newfound friend Katie."

She stared at him.

"Do you ever consider you're being manipulated, Olivia?"

She blew out a breath. "Provoked would be a better word."

Her mettle sounded strong, but the look in her eye when he'd pointed out her possible misstep whispered doubt.

"And do you know more of this incident than what you're telling?" she asked.

"I'm simply putting my brain to use, sweetheart. Given what you told me just now, Millie must have anticipated termination."

"And Katie," she said, "do you think she planned on being fired?"

"I don't know. I really had nothing to do with any of this. But, on the subject of Katie, what does she do here?"

"She's worked for Aunt Aggie for years. We hired her a couple of years ago to do ironing three days a week, but ever since Uncle Lionel got so bad, she's taken over much of the washing from Auntie May, too."

"Do you know of any other services she performs?"

Olivia walked to the study door, looked up and down the hall, then pushed the door shut before bringing herself to attention in front of the desk. "What other legitimate purpose would she serve in this house that I would not be aware of?"

"I note you qualified your response with legitimate."

"I did, indeed."

"She seems rather..."

Olivia drew a breath. "Spit it out."

He grinned. "I'm surprised you didn't fire her."

"For what, being indiscreet?"

"How do you know she was indiscreet?"

"I know Katie."

"Was Lionel screwing her?"

Her cheeks reddened. "If I knew the answer to that tasteless question, I would not share it with you."

"There's a lot you're not sharing with me that you should."

"Perhaps you should reword your question."

"All right, Olivia, was Lionel intimate with Katie?"

"To the best of my knowledge, Uncle Lionel had no relationship with Katie other than as her employer."

"Who did?"

"I wouldn't know."

"Oh, yes you do."

"Very well, but I'm not ready to trust you with information that you so obviously want." She pivoted in the direction of the door.

"Olivia?"

"Yes?"

"As the new housekeeper, are you going to rustle us up something to eat?"

"I'm sure that, for a bonus, Katie would whip you up a hearty meal. I know how to feed myself."

Chapter Seven

B ack here, at least at low tide and no rain, as was the case this morning, the sloping bank rose a good two feet above the brackish waters of Epico Bayou. Live oak and cypress flanked the stream. Months ago, a large pine had lost its footing on the bank, and still lay half-submerged in the water. When they'd been younger, she and Lydia and the Augustus boys would play on such nature-made structures, over the bayou or not. The boys would have even jumped from the trunk into the water. None, however, with the possible exception of Julian, would have done so in early December.

A few yards from where she stood, the woods went wild, a wall of vegetation interspersed with palmetto, teeming with poison ivy and jagger bush, wisteria and spring-blooming magnolia trees, the trunks of some as great in girth as the ancient live oaks. A formidable barrier for a stranger to the bayou, but man had breached that wall millennia ago and Europeans had begun settling this area at the close of the seventeenth century.

Olivia had been told that when she was a toddler, her mama feared taking her outside, terrified of alligators and cottonmouths. Rebecca Fontaine Lee Augustus had never voiced concern for diamondbacks or coral snakes, only cottonmouths. But Rebecca Lee hadn't come from the Coast, or even the Piney Woods, where she'd met Olivia's father. Her people were from Madison County, north of Jackson.

Her mama died, and Olivia never developed a fear of alligators. They fed at night, Tom Buscher told her, but watch for snakes in the fall and always leave them be. Still, he taught her to recognize the poisonous from those not, the pit vipers from the

50

coral, the cottonmouth from the harmless water snakes, and for a while, during her prepubescent years, she'd explored the woods behind her home. That had been well before Lionel Augustus, her granduncle and stepfather rolled into one, granted her wish for finishing school in Madison county. She'd completed her last term this past spring. She'd not ventured into the wild since she'd returned.

The screen door slammed, and she heard footfalls on the back porch steps.

"Olivia."

She narrowed her eyes on the bayou waters, then pivoted and glared at Julian Augustus striding her way. Oh, to surrender to the promise of those wild woods.

"Katie and I searched the house for you. What are you doing out here?"

How unfortunate Boudreaux had not stopped him inside. Did the man serve no purpose at all?

"What do you want, Julian?"

Almost upon her, he stopped. Prudent of him.

"I've come to take you home."

She started around him. "I am home."

He reached for her, but she stepped wide to the side of him.

"Don't you dare touch me."

"You can't stay here with that person," he said, but he did drop his hand.

"With what person?" She kept moving away from him, back toward the house. He caught her arm.

"The man who claims to be your husband."

She jerked free. "Claims to be my husband? And if he's not my husband, pray tell, who is he?"

"He's Troy Boudreaux, Clay's brother."

Her heartbeat quickened in anticipation of information to add to what she'd already gathered. "Why do you say that?"

"Because Clay died in a fire."

She waited, but knew after a moment he wasn't going to tell her anything new. Julian had always been foolish. Uncle Lionel used to say that was because he assumed people were as stupid as he was.

She sighed. "Well, he claims that he most certainly did not, and I believe he's living proof that is the case."

"That man is Troy."

She batted her eyelashes and smiled. "Yes, but why assume I'm not part of the deception, Julian? After all, Aunt Aggie implied I was." She started away, throwing up her arms as she went. "Lord knows what I'm going to do with the man after the will is read. Kill him, too, I imagine."

"Olivia," Julian said when he caught up with her, "this is not a joking matter." He touched her arm, and again she spun on him.

"If you dare lay another finger on me, I swear, I will slap you."

"What the devil is wrong with you? Aunt Aggie is an idiot. I had nothing to do with that."

"What about the letter, Julian? Tell me. What about the letter?"

"What letter?"

"The letter I wrote Troy Boudreaux offering him who only knows what to kill his brother."

"You did that?"

Sweet Jesus. "Julian, I just realized how right Uncle Lionel was about you." She started to turn again, and he jumped in front of her.

"Quit walking away from me."

"I want you to leave my house."

"I'm not in your house, and I'm not going home without you."

"I'm not leaving," she said, and sidestepping him, she started up the steep steps to the back porch. "This is my home, and I'm sure not leaving it to my husband, and you aren't staying here, because you are even less welcome than he is."

She heard him climbing up behind her. "So you don't think he's Clay either?"

From the porch, she looked down on him five steps below. "I don't wish to discuss him with you at all. I don't trust you. I don't trust your brothers and sister or your mother, and most especially Aunt Aggie. Why I've had moments over the past twenty-four hours that I've even considered doubting Uncle Duncan."

"You know Troy is being sought in connection with murder?"

She continued to glare at him.

He took one more step up. "And you're living under the same roof with him."

"What are you talking about?"

"Something to do with Margo Flores's death."

"Oh, please, stop this. Howard's evidence regarding that poor woman is selected to suit your family's interest."

"Have you slept with him?"

The acid which surged into her throat prevented an immediate response. Given what she might have said, the moment's respite was probably for the best, and she coughed.

"That is absolutely none of your concern, but in case Aunt Aggie asks, the answer is yes."

He charged up the remaining steps. Olivia raised her arms to push him at the same moment the back screen flew open, and Boudreaux stepped out. His appearance slowed Julian's attack and stifled her push, but she did shove hard enough to force Julian back a step, off balance. In the space of a blink, Boudreaux had his arm around her waist and her snug against him. She wanted to push him down the steps on top of Julian, but didn't try. He hadn't hit her yet, but Julian would have. He had hit her when they were little, and but for Boudreaux, he'd have hit her now. She knew it.

"Cousin Julian, I presume?"

Julian relaxed against the handrail. "Troy and I aren't kin."

"I'm Clay."

"I don't believe you're Clay."

"Believe it and go home. Now."

"Only if Olivia comes with me."

"Olivia doesn't want to go with you," Boudreaux said and squeezed tighter with the arm he'd hooked round her waist. She looked up to find him looking down at her.

53

"Or do you?" he asked.

She held his gaze and wondered if—

"Olivia, look at me."

She did. Julian no longer leaned against the railing, but stood straight, his hand extended to her.

"Come back home with me," he said. "We'll get to the bottom of this."

"For whose benefit?"

"All of ours."

"There's no benefit for you. Clay and I are the heirs"—she tilted her head so she could see Boudreaux—"unless I receive information from authorities in Galveston County, Texas, that Clay is dead."

Boudreaux's lips covered hers, and she'd have been shocked speechless if she hadn't already quit talking, if she had even been able to talk. He smelled of soap and sandalwood, and his pristine white shirt, open at the neck, was damp. Not wanting to encourage Julian, she squelched the urge to push the man away, and instead, raised her hand and pressed against his chest. He pulled back.

"Please, darling," she said with a tight smile, "not in front of company."

Julian glared at them, then started up the steps. Boudreaux released her and blocked his way, at which point, Julian finally reversed course and crossed the yard to the barn.

"How dare you!"

He put his finger to his lips, and motioned to the kitchen door. She leaned close. "You persuaded Katie to cook for you?"

"I don't think it would have taken much persuasion, but no, Betty Joy is here."

"Betty Joy?" Olivia pulled the screen open and stepped through the open door. He followed. The young Negress, whose acquaintance he'd been making when he heard Julian and Olivia on the back porch, stepped back through the larder door, a bright smile on her face.

"Mawnin', Miss Livy. Grandma done sent me. She be so worried 'bout you. 'Fraid you'd starve yo'self to death grievin'."

"Thank you, Betty Joy." Olivia glanced at him. "Having you here does help my appetite immensely."

The girl, Boudreaux figured her for fifteen or sixteen, looked at him. "Now you can spend some time with yo' new husband 'stead of cookin' fo' 'im," she said. "Grandma's gonna be so pleased to know he be alive." Betty Joy went back inside the larder from where she called, "She say you jest went and fell into little bitty pieces when yo' uncle Duncan told you he was dead."

Olivia glanced at him, then averted her eyes. She couldn't hide the color rising in her cheeks though.

"He says he's hungry." The girl stuck her head out of the closet and looked first at him, then Olivia. "It's gittin' late. You want me to feed 'im breakfast or dinner?"

He said breakfast the same time Olivia said dinner.

"Dinner its gonna be then," Betty Joy said as if he hadn't spoken, and she disappeared back inside the larder.

Olivia stuck her tongue out at him, then departed through the kitchen door. Boudreaux decided on the larder, where he found Betty Joy gathering potatoes. "So, what is for dinner?" he asked.

"I so sorry, Mister Clay, but ain't nothin' here for breakfast, but taters. Eggs ain't been gathered in two days, but I can go out to the chicken coop right now and wring the neck of one of Mister Lionel's fine pullets—oh that po' man loved my granny's fried chicken—and fix you up the best dinner in no time."

"Fried chicken?"

"Yes, suh."

His mouth watered. "How long's it gonna take?"

"Be ready by noon. Gonna make you a nice tater salad, too."

"What—"

"Black-eyed peas. Left over from last night." She nodded at a jar of cornmeal on the pantry shelf. "Cornbread, too. Don't you worry." She shook her head. "Don't got dessert, though. Might have to talk Miss Livy into doin' that fo' you. She makes the best fried peach pies of anyone on the bayou. Mister Lionel said her

55

pies tasted like them her grandma Lee used to make up in Marion County."

Odd, considering her grandma Lee died years before she was born. "And who taught her to make 'em?"

Betty Joy shrugged. "Got the recipe I guess."

His mama had made a mighty fine peach pie, too, and he couldn't help but wonder if those two recipes weren't one and the same. Didn't matter, though. He figured his chances of getting a fried peach pie out of Olivia today were downright slim.

Someday maybe, Boudreaux thought, standing in the door of Lionel Augustus's office and watching Olivia working at the desk. She looked up; he stepped in and closed the door.

"More letters?"

"Plotting your demise."

He took a seat in that wing chair in front of the desk. "Yes, well, I do wonder about that."

"How so?"

"I've always understood there is a possibility you didn't write that letter."

"Even if I didn't, that doesn't mean I'm not writing one now." She folded a piece of familiar-looking stationery and pulled an envelope from the stack on her left.

"Has anyone ever told you that you have a wry sense of humor, Olivia?"

"No."

"I wonder why?"

"Because anyone who knows me, Mister Boudreaux, knows I do not joke."

"Ain't so, sweetheart, right now you're responding to condolences."

She returned to the envelope. "So, you've rifled through this desk, I see."

"I've rifled through a number of things in this house." His grin was more for her than him, but she didn't see it. "Not near about everything, though."

She pretended to ignore him, and he was sure she was pretending.

"Why did you let me kiss you?" he asked.

Her head jerked up like someone had yanked a bridle on her. "Why did you do that?"

"To convince that ass you were happy here with me."

"He already knew that wasn't so."

"He left."

"Because he knew I wasn't going to go with him."

"Because you let me kiss you."

"And what do you think would have happened if I'd slugged you?"

"You'd already told him you slept with me."

"I qualified that statement by telling him —"

"It was for Aunt Aggie's sake, I heard you, but that wasn't going to keep him from beating you."

She looked back to the desk, but she was no longer writing. "I'd have pushed him down the steps if you hadn't intervened."

"He'd have given you a black eye, then I'd have had to kill him."

"How gallant of you."

She returned to her work, and he rubbed his jaw. "You are my wife, Olivia. If anyone is going to beat you, it's gonna be me. Why was he so angry?"

"Clay would know the answer to that."

"Because he intended to marry you himself."

She continued writing, regarding his questions with supposed indifference.

"But he should have gathered, by now, that you had agreed to marry Clay."

She looked up then.

"Unless, of course, he believed," — Boudreaux waved a hand in front of him — "for whatever reason, Clay would never arrive at Epico Hollow to claim you."

"I am assuming you imply I am rejecting Julian due to his failure to eliminate Clay?"

"Did he know you were dealing with Troy?"

"And do you really expect me to answer that question?"

"I'm hoping you've become so tangled up in this twisted plot you'll slip up."

"I can assure you that I am not tangled up in anything. Julian wants Clay to be dead. He thinks I'll marry him—"

"Why would he?"

"Why indeed?"

A leading question filled with possibilities. "Have you double-crossed him, sweetheart?"

She stuffed the letter inside the envelope.

"Was he going to blackmail you into marrying him?"

She rose. "He has nothing he can use to blackmail me with."

"There's the letter."

"It's my understanding Troy has the letter."

He sat forward. "Yes, but if you all believed you were working with Troy, Julian would have known about the letter."

"If Julian were working with Troy alone, he would have still known about the letter."

"That's true, but—"

"And that would leave Troy"—she widened her eyes —"with the damning piece of evidence, which he could then use to compel me to do his bidding."

"Which I have not done."

"You've insinuated yourself into my home and my life. From my point of view, it is as likely that you are the person who has double-crossed Julian and the rest of the Augustus clan."

"We're not getting very far here, are we, sweetheart?"

She started around the desk. "No, we're not, but I have no intention of standing still, either."

"You're up to something?"

"You may rest assured I am."

"Tell me about the poison."

"Actually, I don't know that there was any poison."

"What did the autopsy show?"

"Do you think that by displaying knowledge of the events

surrounding Uncle Lionel's death you will convince me you are Clay?"

"I am Clay."

"Clay could have told his brother everything told to him."

"He could have, but he didn't."

"So you say."

"It's irrelevant at this point."

"Irrelevant to whom?" She started to the door.

"Olivia, let's presume for a moment that I am really Clay and you are his devoted wife and we are both trying to uncover what happened."

"Troy could be filling in missing pieces."

"He could, but whether you betrayed your partners or Troy betrayed his, or we both did, we might prove to be each other's only friend at this point."

"Friend is an overstatement."

"Then we'll leave it at partners in crime."

"Fine. What do you want to know about the autopsy?"

"Did you realize they were trying to frame you before or after you decided to double-cross Clay?"

"Mr. Boudreaux, I suddenly recall why I do not wish to be your partner in anything. Now, if you'll excuse me, I have important things to take care—"

"I'm spoofing with you. Tell me about the poison."

She blew out a breath. "This last month before Uncle Lionel died, Aunt Connie or Aunt Aggie were always bringing or sending dishes for him. Truth is, Mabel prepared most all the meals, but everyone in that house had access to them.

"The first time, I almost gave him Aunt Aggie's chicken broth. His stomach had been so queasy, and I thought it truly a considerate gesture on her part. But when I told Uncle Lionel where it came from, he refused to eat it. He was desperate that I not eat any either. Referred to it, as a matter of fact, as her 'infamous' chicken broth. He told me to throw it out and not eat anything else that came out of that house.

"I knew that Doctor Tasker took hair and nail samples, but

then I found out he also removed the liver for testing. Poor Uncle Lionel lay at the livery for four days, waiting. I was afraid someone might be able to get to his body and taint something."

"You didn't tell them you weren't feeding him the foods they sent over, did you?"

"I thanked them profusely for every heartfelt gift."

"Duncan asked for the autopsy?"

"Yes, and I don't understand why."

"To frame you for—"

"I don't believe that. I can't help but believe Aunt Aggie was the one behind the request."

He frowned, and she waved her hands in front of her, palms up. "He caters to her," she said. "It makes his life easier."

"Olivia, do you really believe your Uncle Duncan knuckled under to her insistence for an autopsy without questioning the reason for it?"

She didn't say anything, and after a moment he said, "They were trying to frame you. But for me, the question remains, were they trying to frame an innocent or eliminate a partner in crime?"

"They were trying to eliminate the heir, you fool."

Boudreaux received a great deal of satisfaction in both the way her eyes widened when he rushed her and the grimace she made when she hit her hip on the corner of the desk while backing away from him. His fingers sank into her upper arm, and he yanked her around the side of the desk, then shoved her toward the chair. She locked her knees. He couldn't force her to sit, but she did stumble a bit, and he left it at that. "I won't be called a fool by the same very stupid woman who tried her best to make one out of me. You haven't succeeded yet, so you might want to exercise some discretion, Missus Boudreaux."

"Let me go, you bastard."

He tightened his grip when she tried to wrench free. "Darn it, Olivia, you'd better—"

"Better what?" She sucked in a breath, but fought him still, and he knew he was hurting her, but dammit she was such a stubborn little witch. "What will you do, Mister Boudreaux?"

He yanked her hard, and she eased her struggle. "Beat you."

"Oh, thank the Lord, I was afraid you were going to kiss me again."

His mouth dropped open, then curled into a little grin. "Stop fighting me."

"Let me go."

He did, and she staggered back a step and started rubbing her arm. "Then stop accusing me of murder," she said. "If you're Clay, you aren't a fool. You're an ass." She braced and bit her bottom lip. "And if you're Troy, you are a fool for coming here."

He stepped away. "Perhaps I am, but I'd appreciate your keeping your name calling and your opinion to yourself."

"Are you done with me?" she asked.

"Almost. What was the family's reaction when the coroner's report showed nothing wrong?"

"I wasn't with them when they received word. No one has given anything away in front of me." Again, she looked him in the eye. "Nor would I expect them to."

"That tactic would have eliminated only half the problem, anyway."

"Not if whoever it is succeeded in killing Clay," she said, holding his gaze. "And that person or persons certainly didn't require my complicity to attempt that."

True, but that didn't mean they didn't have it. She was staring at him, daring him to voice that thought out loud. He wasn't going to. They'd baited each other enough in the past twelve hours. He was tired, so was she. The fatigue showed in her eyes and in her voice. "There is simply no end to the possibilities, is there, sweetheart?"

"Including those implicating Troy, or even Clay, Boudreaux."

Olivia watched him walk to the door, the impressions of his cowboy boots making a path behind him across the wool carpet. She liked the look of those boots.

The cat ran in when Boudreaux opened the door, and he watched the beast a moment, then looked at her. "Chester pees in

61

the corner behind that plant over there, you know?" He nodded to a Boston fern, then winked at her. "Tell me Clay discussed that with his brother."

Not a particularly interesting topic for discussion between brothers to be sure, but there was nothing to guarantee Clay hadn't said something to Troy. Certainly someone had mentioned Chester's bad habit with one of the two men from Galveston. Uncle Lionel, no doubt, who had probably also mentioned his long-standing threat to kill the animal.

Boudreaux left the room, headed toward the kitchen, and Olivia sighed in relief. With one more glance to the door, she addressed her last envelope and hid it inside the stack of completed thank-you letters.

"Hey."

She startled, then cursed him under her breath. At the door, Boudreaux graced her with a questioning grimace that caused her heart to slam against her ribs. The moment stretched on and on. Finally, he stepped into the room, reached down, grabbed Chester by the scruff of his neck, and lifted him from where he'd settled in the wing chair in front of the desk.

"Betty Joy says we've got a good hour and a half before dinnertime. You get those letters ready; I'll take them to the post office." He wrapped the cat in one arm and patted him on the head.

"I've more to do."

"There's some rule of etiquette that requires they all go out on the same day?"

She shook her head.

"Then I'll take what you've got."

Chapter Eight

"The boat is still out front." Sunshine filtered through a cloud of dust at the point where Epico Hollow's drive disappeared into a canopy of trees. Olivia moved away from the kitchen window and looked at Betty Joy, dusting cornmeal into a cast-iron skillet on the stove. "He took the wagon?"

"Yes'm."

Olivia slipped the letter she'd drafted into the pocket of the old work coat hanging by the back door as she removed the coat from its hook. "I wonder why? I thought he was going to the post office."

"Y'all is out of food. He says he's gonna stock up this mawnin' while he's waitin' on my cookin'."

For certain, the cupboard was all but depleted. Keeping the house functioning hadn't been a major concern over the past two weeks, and with only Olivia to feed, and her not eating much, Millie had allowed supplies to dwindle. Then, too, a variety of dishes, all brought by friends and neighbors for Uncle Lionel's wake, still covered the dining-room buffet.

"Did you give him some idea of what to buy, because I'm not comfortable with a man—"

"Oh, Miss Katie done gone with him."

"She did?"

"Yes'm, so it'll be all right. Miss Katie'll know what to do."

Olivia just bet she would. The laundress was not the person to restock the pantry. Boudreaux should have asked Olivia herself or waited until after the noon meal and taken Betty Joy to the grocery.

She grasped the knob to the back door. Things were anything

63

but right around here, and matters seemed to grow murkier with each passing minute.

"Miss Livy, if you see Billy out there, could you tell 'im to bring me some wood? We almost out, and the chicken's gonna need some tendin'."

"He's at the barn?"

"Choppin' wood."

The door closed with a click, and a chilly gust of wind tugged Olivia's hair. She pulled the coat around her and started down the steps. Five minutes ago the thought of chicken frying in the skillet had her mouth watering. Katie and Boudreaux alone in a wagon on lonely bayou back ways had pretty much dried up that anticipation. She put her free hand in the deep coat pocket and clutched the letter. In the distance she could see Billy in the sunshine, chopping wood. He'd stripped off his jacket, and sweat dampened the chest and underarms of his cotton shirt.

"Daddy's sayin' we got a cold winter comin'," Billy said when she drew close. "Says he knows by the fur on the caterpillars. We gonna have some freezin' nights this year."

Freezing nights they might have eventually, but if not for the wind, she wouldn't need the coat atop her dress.

"Thought I'd chop some extra wood," he said. "Y'all havin' coal in the big house now, might be I could take some home?"

"Take all you need, but right now, Betty Joy says she needs some in the kitchen."

"An' she done tol' you to tell me to bring it, didn't she?"

"She did. She's cooking."

"Oh, she ain't got nothin' on that stove she can't leave. She ain't got wood so nothin's gonna burn."

"She—"

"Jes' plain lazy. She don't like climbin' them stairs to the kitchen is all."

"Neither does your grandmother."

Billy bent and picked up a small block of wood. "Daddy says there'd be a gas stove in that house if Grandma woulda let ol' Mr. Augustus done what he wanted a year ago."

Olivia smiled. "From what I heard, she told him if he wanted to continue to eat her fried chicken he'd best leave her wood stove alone."

Billy wiped his brow. "Sho' nuff now. Smart folks, they don't go and make the cook mad."

"Good, we are agreed. Take Betty Joy her wood and when you're done with that"—she handed him the letter and a nickel—"would you take this to the post office for me?"

He nodded.

"I do not want Mister Boudreaux to know about that letter."

He looked at her, then at the letter, and said, "Yes'm. Won't say a word to him if'n that's how you want it."

Billy could read; he would know where the letter was going and did, no doubt, wonder why. But after all the years his family had worked for hers, Olivia trusted him not to betray her. "Don't say anything to Betty Joy, either."

"No, ma'am, I won't."

Olivia turned in the direction of the house.

"Real pretty horse that Mister Clay done put in the barn."

She looked back at Billy.

"Brought a fine golden stallion here from Texas. Ol' Mister Augustus would have sho' took to him. Have you seen 'im?"

No, she hadn't. She'd given no thought as to how Boudreaux got here. Conjuring himself up in a puff of smoke would seem more like him than his riding in on a fine horse.

"How did you get in here without anyone seeing you?" Olivia pushed the office door closed. Speaking of demons and smoke, this man, by all accounts, really should be a ghost, if for no other reason than someone died in that boarding-house fire.

"Walked right in the front door," he said from his seat behind Uncle Lionel's desk. "I saw your guest and Katie Harder leave together."

"Do you know who he is?"

"Do you?"

She stared at him. "He says that he is Clay."

"And do you believe him?"

"I believe one of you is lying."

"Or maybe we both are."

Unsure of her ground, she dropped her eyes and approached the desk. "Why did you leave yesterday?" she asked. "You said you'd wait until everyone was gone. Instead, I found him."

He leaned back in her stepfather's fine leather chair. "I saw him sneak in the house. I didn't want him to see me."

"If you know he's not—"

"I don't care about that right now. I don't want him to know I'm here. What have you told him?"

She sank into the upholstered chair in front of the desk and looked him in the eye. "About you? Nothing."

"Why not?"

"I don't trust him."

"Good girl. What did he tell you?"

Demurely, she looked down at her lap and plucked lint from her black dress. "Nothing I intend to share with you under the circumstances."

He flexed his jaw. "You don't trust me either?"

"I do not. I want you to confront him."

"No."

"And the reason you won't?"

"I thought he died in that fire. Now, finding him here, alive, I know something more is going on."

Heart thumping, she said, "Then you know the fire wasn't an accident?"

He stared at her long and hard. Finally he said, "That's right, sweetheart, someone tried to kill me, and up until yesterday afternoon, I thought they'd killed him."

"And you're assuming the attempt on your life is on account of Uncle Lionel's estate?"

"Yes, Olivia, I am."

She raised her chin. "Why, when everyone else thought Clay was the one who died in the fire, did you think Troy had?"

"Well, it was obvious to me that Clay didn't die in the fire."

66

"But why did you think Troy had?"

He puffed up his cheeks, then blew out a breath. "There were five boarders in that house. They'd been awakened by gunshots right before the fire started. They all made it out. I slept in the same back room Troy and I had shared as kids—there were two feather beds in it. Whenever Troy came to town and stayed overnight, he slept in the other bed.

"When they got the fire out, they found two bodies. Nate Phillips naturally believed one of them was mine." He hesitated a moment, then averted his eyes. "When I showed back up shortly after, I assumed"—he nodded, then again looked at her —"Troy had spent the night and he was one of the two men who'd died. Did he tell you anything about the fire?"

"Only that two men died in it. He thinks he was meant to be one of them."

"He being Clay, you mean?"

"Yes, I think he believes..." She bit her tongue, then said, "Do you think he believes you actually died in the fire?"

This particular Boudreaux seemed to give that question some thought, but perhaps he was only mulling his answer to her. Finally, he sat forward. "He very well might. Did he mention one of the dead men having a bullet in his chest?"

"No." But he really hadn't confided much in the way of fact she could separate from sarcasm and subterfuge. "Do you know the name of the man who was shot?"

"Nope."

"So no one knows who actually died in the fire?" she asked.

"Is that good, Olivia? Dead men don't talk, you know." He swiveled in Uncle Lionel's chair and looked out the bank of windows at Bayou Bernard. "I thought my brother had. Now I know he didn't, but Clay Boudreaux was supposed to."

Her stomach had tightened with his weakly veiled accusation. "And do you know that because you thought you'd killed him and only realized yesterday that you hadn't?"

He spun in the chair and stared at her, and she steeled herself. "Is that why you don't want to confront him?" she said.

"And why would I want to kill my brother?"

"Your brother claims to have a letter."

"And?"

"According to him, I wrote it, and in it, I recruited Troy to kill Clay. Do you know anything about it?"

He opened his mouth, she thought, to speak, but a short laugh escaped instead. "That does create a problem for you, doesn't it?"

"Do you know anything about that letter?"

"Did you write the thing, sweetheart?"

"Quit calling me that," she snapped, "and do you think I'd admit it to Clay if I had?"

"Would you admit it to Troy?"

"I didn't write it."

He grinned. "He calls you that, doesn't he?"

"What?"

"Sweetheart."

She placed the heel of her hand against one aching temple and closed her eyes.

"My name is Olivia, and at the moment, I am not the least bit interested in being anyone's sweetheart. I want you to reveal yourself to him."

"And if I'm Clay?"

"And if you are?"

"Then I'd be a fool to trust you, Olivia. Even if I'm Troy I'd be a fool to trust you."

So she'd been told.

He turned back to the bank of windows stretching along the north wall of the room. "How did your relatives take Clay's" — he tossed back his head and pointed with his chin to the road, down which the other Boudreaux had left with Katie — "turning up very much alive?"

"They think he's an impostor."

He smiled at that. "It would be interesting to learn why they say that."

"The letter one of them wrote perhaps?"

"The letter implicating you in murder." He grabbed the edge

68

of the desk and brought the chair back around to face her. "Before we go and fess up that I'm here, I think we should recover it, don't you? What if it falls into the wrong hands?"

"It already has, and I'm—"

"Not if he was the intended recipient."

She clamped her mouth shut, and he narrowed his eyes on her. "Listen to me, Olivia, and listen good. I don't want him knowing I'm here. Your bloodthirsty relatives think Clay's dead and that they're dealing with an impostor. Only you know Clay is still alive, and I want to leave it like that for now."

"But I don't know which one of you is Clay."

"And you don't know where that letter is either, so I'd advise you to play along."

Her gut cramped. Was that a threat? The two men could be working together and didn't want her to know it. Or they could be at odds, and she still didn't know which one she was married to, which one she should be allied with, if either. She thought back on the other man's exchange with Aunt Aggie the evening before, on Lydia's subtle suggestion that those two actually understood each other quite well. "Why weren't you at the house the night of the fire?" she asked.

"I was out of town."

"Were you with a woman?"

"It's not really any of your business, but no."

"Were you the father of Margo Flores's baby?"

"No, I was not. Who told you I was?"

"Howard was in Galveston. He sent word to the family that Clay..." She waved her hand. "Oh, it doesn't matter."

"That Clay, the man you were to wed, was already obligated to another woman. Is that what cousin Howard implied?"

"Yes."

"Margo was pregnant. Troy offered to marry"—he curled his lips—"you're thinking big brother was doing little brother a favor, aren't you?"

"It wouldn't be the first time brothers have done that for each other."

69

"A pretty big sacrifice on Troy's part, don't you think?"

"Clay could've made it worth his while, but the woman might not have agreed."

His countenance darkened. "Her death was an accident. She fell off a horse and broke her neck."

And if the Boudreaux boys were working together in pursuit of Lionel Augustus's fortune, she could be the next woman to fall off a horse and break her neck. She rose and started for the door.

"Olivia."

She stopped, and he rose from his chair and rounded the desk. This Boudreaux, like the other one, was astute and attractive, though a little taller. He, too, wore cowboy boots. The two men looked like brothers, and they were close enough in age that she could not tell which was older.

"I don't want him to know I'm here, do you understand?" He loomed close, and she twisted from him when he reached to touch her face.

"Then you need to leave," she said, "before he gets back."

Chapter Nine

At its most convenient, the trip from Epico Hollow to Handsboro was a short flatboat ride hugging the south shore of Bernard Bayou to the Lorraine Road ferry landing. The large grocery was less than a block south of that point on the west side of the shell-paved Cowan Road. Boudreaux and Katie, however, entered Cowan Road at Pine Street, farther south still, after traversing two miles of bayou back roads, the longer trek necessitated by bringing a wagon to market.

The trip proved pleasant enough, though, and not all that time-consuming, under an hour. Katie was an amicable companion, though somewhat reticent when he guided their conversation to exactly what had caused Millie and Simon's poorly considered challenge to Olivia this morning. She had warmed to him again by the time they reached the grocery. Before entering the store, where he left her to fill the order, she'd pointed across the shimmering Bayou Bernard. There, on the north shore, about a mile east, he reckoned, of Lorraine Road, stood a massive wooden complex, and she asked him if he'd been over there yet. He told her he had not, and she asked him if he knew what the structure was. Not sure if this were some sort of test, he hesitated before answering, then opted for the truth, and that was he did not know. The Lee-Augustus Lumber Mill, she told him. His mill.

Ah, yes. He knew there was a mill. Forty years ago it was the Lee Mill, fifth largest sawmill in the nation. It had made a comeback after the War, backed by Augustus money, but the ensuing decades had depleted the forest along the streams and bayous that brought timber to Bayou Bernard, and though the industry still did well for itself in Handsboro, the largest mills had slipped

71

eastward to the Pascagoula River and its tributaries. No matter, Lionel Augustus had adjusted with the times, acquiring virgin timber and building larger inland mills. He bought a brickyard in Handsboro and even had an investment in a shrimp cannery at Point Cadet in Biloxi. And there were log towns and turpentine stills north and south of Hattiesburg, and spur lines all over the Piney Woods. Good Lord, he thought, urging Toby down Cowan Road and across Main Street Handsboro, tippin' his hat to the ladies, for whom he stopped so they could cross in front of him, and wavin' to shop owners and gentlemen and old Confederates playin' checkers and no doubt tellin' war stories on the covered porches of buildings lining either side of the busy intersection, what in heaven's name had he gotten himself into?

At some point south of Main Street, Handsboro merged with the eastern fringe of Mississippi City. He didn't know exactly where, but he figured it was around the point where the business establishments petered out to be replaced by clapboard cottages enclosed by white picket fences set back from the quiet, tree-lined route. Less than a mile farther, he came to the junction of Cowan and Beach Boulevard, paralleling the Gulf of Mexico. He turned west. He was roughly a mile from Texas Street and the Gulf View Hotel. A popular watering hole, with a different name years before the War, it had been renovated since and remained a popular tourist resort.

He pulled the wagon off just shy of the courthouse, one block early and one block north, to confirm for himself that the Stars and Bars of the Confederacy did still fly over that hallowed hall of Harrison County justice. Satisfied, and with no small degree of pride, he walked past the jail onto the lawn of the Gulf View, weaving his way through live oaks and magnolias before ascending broad wooden steps to the hotel's veranda. He gazed a moment on the gulf, its waves sparkling like lightning bugs between the tree trunks and low-reaching limbs. A cool breeze brushed his cheek. Not a bad place to hole up.

Boudreaux rapped his knuckles on door 213.

"Who is it?"

"Me," he said and waited for the door to open.

"Ah"—Sandifer Hudgins winked at him—"Clay Boudreaux and right on time. Actually, I only beat you to the hotel by about three hours. You didn't have trouble with the quarantine?"

"Just showed 'em Deputy Boudreaux's credentials, and they waved me on through."

"Yes, well, I guess Texas sheriff deputies, like the darkies of old, are immune to yellow fever." The man motioned him into the room. "Do you have Clay's credentials?"

Hat in hand, Boudreaux stepped into the luxurious room, dim and cool after the warm sun outside, despite the slow fire burning in the fireplace. Hudgins closed the door behind him.

"Actually, I ended up disembarking in New Orleans. Rode in on horseback yesterday afternoon. Fewer restrictions that way."

"I figured you'd be here later in the day, given last night was your first with your new bride."

Boudreaux snorted. "She's even less enamored with me than I am with her."

Hudgins guided him to an upholstered, balloon-back chair, then sat in its mate. A delicate pedestal table stood between them. "You told her you were Clay?"

"I did."

Hudgins frowned. "And she didn't, at least, pretend to be pleased?"

Boudreaux looked the older man in the eye, and Hudgins cursed. "You confronted her with the letter, didn't you?"

"I couldn't help myself."

"Did you even give her a chance to react to your being Clay?"

He sat forward, elbows on his knees and rubbed his eyes. "Not really."

"Dammit, our plan was to convince her you were Clay. What did she say about the letter?"

"She denied writing it."

"Yes, she denied writing it. Did she ask how you came by it?"

"Nope."

Hudgins cursed under his breath and stood. "I wish you'd stuck to our plan."

"I'm sticking to the plan, letter or not."

"Except now she knows you don't trust her."

"She'd already been told Clay was dead, so she doesn't trust me either."

Hudgins threw up his hands. "Well that's just dandy. What the hell compelled you to bring up the letter?"

Gut tight, Boudreaux rose. He stood a good two inches taller than Hudgins. "Somebody tried to shoot me in New Orleans, that's what. I don't like being double-crossed."

Hudgins stared at him, then blew out a breath. "You think Olivia was trying to kill you?"

"I do. With Clay dead, she no longer needed me."

"I never considered her trying to eliminate Clay's killer. Do you know who the shooter was?"

"No."

Hudgins ran a hand through his hair. "She's obviously working with somebody else." He rounded his chair and retook his seat. "I understand, now. You were angry. Sit back down, and let's think this out. Things are more complicated than I thought. Has the family heard anything official from Galveston?"

"No, and I don't expect it will anytime soon. Nate's not gonna pronounce Clay dead until he's sure Clay's dead."

"Clay is gone. He's going to have to make his suspicions known sometime, and soon. Perhaps we should go ahead and tell Olivia the truth."

"Absolutely not. The plan is to divvy up after the reading of the will, and I say we stick to it. We're wading in quicksand here Sandy. Telling her the truth will give her an advange over us."

"Yes, you're right." Hudgins flexed his jaw. "I'd try and expedite the reading of the will, but Duncan is the executor and that would be a sure-fire way to alert him."

"You think he'd be suspicious of you?"

"Possibly...and Katie? Do you agree you can't trust her?"

"I do. She's in thick with more than one of the Augustuses,

but I'll tell you straight, she has no qualms when it comes to dealing with a Boudreaux either."

"Money?"

Boudreaux smiled. "Not exactly."

Hudgin's grunted. "Let me tell you something, son. Katie's fast, but she's not easy. She's on a mission for somebody, and that somebody *ain't* a friend of yours, I guarantee it. Any fringe benefits she's providing you aren't worth the risk. You need to get her out of your house."

"I've already considered that, but she knows too much. I don't want to send her back to the Augustuses angry. "

"She'll be going back to the Augustuses, angry or not, and on that note, have you met Aggie?"

"I have. She says she needs to talk to you."

"How long do I have?" Olivia asked.

"They ain't back," Betty Joy said, "and the chicken ain't done fryin'. Fat, young pullet. Gonna make a fine meal fo' yo' new husband."

She stepped around Betty Joy. The kitchen was warm and heavy with the scent of frying food, a pleasant smell to Olivia. Earlier, she'd found Betty Joy setting the dining room table. Had the girl asked, Olivia would have told her the kitchen table was fine for the noon meal, but Betty Joy was trying to make the occasion special for the newlyweds, so Olivia let things be.

She grabbed a checkered dishtowel, red and white, from the drain surface. "Billy brought you plenty of wood?"

"Sho' did. Don't have no trouble with him when you're the one doin' the tellin'."

Stretching for the cupboard above her head, Olivia pulled down a box of sugar cubes. "Your grandmother has no trouble with him."

"She sho' don't, and she'd beat his butt if she did. But I ain't nothin' mo' than a little sister."

"You're fortunate," Olivia said, filling the towel with sugar, "I've often wished for a big brother."

"Oh, but you don't need one such now, not with that fine man to take care of you."

To smile pained her, but Olivia managed. "You like him, don't you?"

Dismay swept Betty Joy's dark eyes. "Don't you?"

"I don't really know him yet."

"Don't have to know 'im. Just sit back and look at 'im."

"It's not that simple." She folded the treats in the towel, then held it up for Betty Joy. "I'll see how well I like his horse. You know what people say, know the horse, know the man."

"Folks say that?"

Olivia laughed and pulled the back door open. "Not that I've ever heard, but they should, don't you think?"

*B*oth sets of barn doors, one front and one back, were open wide. Usually the front doors were closed, the rear kept open to allow their animals easy access to the corral behind the structure. Inside, dank air, laden with the stench of alfalfa and manure, assaulted Olivia's senses. She closed her eyes to adjust to the dimmer light; her nostrils adjusted, too.

Billy was gone, but she found the stallion in a shadowed stall. The horse whinnied with her approach and moved his formidable body toward the gate.

"Hello," she said and climbed upon the lowest rail.

He laid his ears back.

"Don't be bad; I've brought you something." Slowly, so as not to upset him, she unwrapped the dishtowel in her left hand. He flung his head to the side and snorted.

Olivia picked out several cubes, then stretched her hand between the rails to put the sugar beneath his nose, and he nuzzled her palm while he ate. She repeated the gesture until the sugar was gone, then climbed higher to reach the space between his ears, but when she scratched, he shook his head.

"It's all gone."

As if he understood her, he snapped, and Olivia half-jumped, half-fell from the stall.

"You'd do better trying to make friends with me than him," Boudreaux said, and Olivia turned to him, standing at the door of the barn. He'd gotten back none too soon, given Pompeii's temperment, and eyeing first the horse, then the girl, he came on inside.

"You could, you know?"

"Could what?" she asked.

"Make friends with me."

"I don't believe you want to be my friend."

"That's because you assume the horse is dumber." He stopped in front of her and bent his face close. "I'll show you. Scratch me...well, not between my ears." He looked toward the loft and touched his upper lip with the tip of his tongue. "Let's see, between my what would be good?"

"Go away."

"My shoulder blades, I think. Ha, you thought I was going to say something off-color, didn't you?"

"Regardless of what you said, what you implied was vulgar, and you know it. But no matter what part of your anatomy you want scratched, I prefer scratching the horse."

"The horse doesn't like you."

"And suddenly you do?"

"You'd be useful for scratching things."

"Get Katie to do it," she said and turned away.

Ah, he suspected he was going to run into conflict about that. "I needed someone to purchase grocer—"

"You might have asked me."

He allowed his mouth to fall open, then he laughed. "I'll be darn. You'd have wanted to ride into Handsboro with me?"

"No, but I would have."

"You were busy. I asked Katie."

"Really?"

"You want to come help her put the groceries away?"

"I do not."

He shrugged and stepped around her.

"What did you two talk about?" she asked.

He tilted his head slightly her way, then glanced at Pompeii. "I don't know which one of you I should keep my eye on."

"What's going on between you and Katie?"

"Nothing is going on between me and Katie."

"Bull. I noticed something earlier. You know her."

"I do now."

"Why did you want to get away with her?"

"We needed groceries."

"Katie does not do the purchasing in—"

"Millie did, but you fired her this morning."

"I am not stupid"—she grabbed his arm and tried to force him around, and he allowed her to, just a bit—"I know something is going on."

"Perhaps we could trade information."

"I've told you everything I know," she said, her voice higher. "At least you know for sure who I am."

"And you know who I am, because I've told you."

"Oh"—she stepped in front of him, placing herself between him and the stall—"I can't tell you how reassuring I find words from your lips."

Pompeii moved, and Boudreaux tensed. "I'm glad to hear it."

Olivia curled her hands as if to strangle him, but she stepped back not forward, and he reacted immediately, grabbing and yanking her his way at the same moment the horse lunged against the rail and nipped air where her ear had been. Boudreaux raised his fist. Olivia cried out, and Pompeii lumbered back, out of reach. Boudreaux stopped his attack and pivoted to Olivia, who was rushing forward, he assumed, in defense of the damn horse. She stumbled—sweet Jesus, she was a clumsy woman—and he reached out to steady her. She collided with him, and he staggered back.

Heat seared his shoulder, and drowning Olivia's muffled cry with a curse, he twisted away from Pompeii's head. Numbness followed the burning ache down his arm and up his neck. He raised his other hand and touched the torn shirt, finding blood where the horse's bite had penetrated flesh.

78

Olivia jerked him around, eyed the wound, then threw herself upon the rail and hit Pompeii between the eyes.

"Bad horse," she cried and jumped back before the animal could retaliate.

Immediately, she turned on Boudreaux. "And you," she spat, "look what you've done. I wanted to make friends with him. Now I probably never will."

"I didn't do anything."

"You came out here. You interfered. You distracted me and the poor dumb beast with your perverse analogy."

"That poor dumb beast doesn't understand perverse analogies, Olivia, and I came to get you. Betty Joy is putting dinner on the table as we speak, and I had to put Toby up." He waved at the old workhorse standing outside the barn door. "I don't want you trying to make friends with Pompeii anyway." He dropped the apologetic tone from his voice. "He's meaner than an ol' red wasp and a lot bigger."

"He takes after his owner," Olivia said, and she stepped to one side of him and snagged Toby's leads.

"Leave him, Olivia. Billy'll do that."

Thank the Lord heartbeats were quiet. Despite Boudreaux's instruction, Olivia led Toby through the barn and set him loose in the fenced pasture out back, praying all the time her partner in crime didn't make an issue of Billy's absence.

When she came back in the barn, she found the insufferable man in front of his horse's stall talking to the beast and offering it a carrot...a darn carrot! The horse shook his head, then took the treat. Boudreaux rewarded the hateful thing further by scratching its neck.

Whether he sensed or heard her, Olivia didn't know, but he said, "Teach you to try and steal my horse."

She studied the two of them. Alike they were, both of them handsome, treacherous, vicious, deceiving, and dangerous.

Chapter Ten

Boudreaux did put on a clean shirt before joining Olivia in the dining room, but wouldn't let her do anything about the horse bite. "It can wait until after we eat," he told her, then inhaled the meal, rained praise on Betty Joy, and hinted to Olivia about some fondness he had for fried peach pies. Despite the implication he'd starved himself for this meal, he ate with decorum. He didn't lick his fingers, though he eyed her a couple of times, and she suspected he wanted to.

"Betty Joy," Olivia called when he finally wiped his mouth and placed his napkin beside his plate, "the meal was perfect; for certain you've inherited your grandmother's flair."

"You're a good cook, too," Boudreaux said and winked at the girl when she smiled at him.

"Could you put the kettle on?"

"I've already got coffee made if that's what you all's wantin', Miss Livy."

"No, I need to clean Mister Boudreaux's wound."

The girl eyed his shoulder where a small spot of blood had stained his white shirt. "What you gone and done, Mister Clay?"

"Miss Livy, as you call her, upset my poor—"

"His horse bit him, Betty Joy."

"But it was her fault."

"Any horse does that"—Betty Joy picked up his plate—"lookey at that blood on yo' nice shirt. You need to shoot that thing."

From his seat at the head of the table, Boudreaux nodded at Olivia. "Should I shoot her, too, you think?"

The girl wore a smile all the way to the opposite end of the table and Olivia. "Oh, Lordy, no, we don't wanna shoot our Miss Livy."

Olivia folded her napkin and laid it beside the plate. "Make sure that water is boiling, would you, please?" she told Betty Joy when the girl removed her plate.

Betty Joy laughed. "We got enough chicken left for y'all's supper tonight."

"You take it on home for you and your family," Boudreaux said. "It won't be eaten here."

"You want one of them fine hams then?"

"No supper for us tonight, Betty Joy, but do you make white bread?"

"Sho' do. I'll get to it soon as I get dinner cleaned up."

The girl left the room, and Olivia locked her eyes on him. "Why don't you want her to cook for tonight? I thought you were in a constant state of hunger."

"Unlike those of you who are starving themselves to death, my appetite is fine. What's wrong with you anyway?"

She rose and motioned him up. "I've had things on my mind. Food hasn't been one of them."

"Murderous intrigue?"

He followed her out the dining room door and into the hall. "Justice," she said, "and you didn't answer my question." Her hands itched for Uncle Lionel's special medicinal bottle. She was going to pour the antiseptic on the bite. It would burn like the devil, and she wasn't going to blow on it, and given the position of the wound, he certainly wouldn't be able to...

"We've been summoned to dinner."

She stopped, and he moved around her to continue up the graceful stairs. "Where?" she asked and started climbing again.

"Uncle Duncan and Aunt Connie's."

"Oh, did you and Katie go visiting during your jaunt in to town?"

"Billy gave me the invitation when I got back."

"Billy's back?"

Boudreaux shot her a curious glance. "He left?"

81

She hoped she didn't blanch. "He told me he needed to go to town."

"Well," he said, continuing up the stairs, "he told me he got the invitation from Julian. I'd assumed Julian delivered it to him outside and didn't risk coming to the door, considering his treatment this morning."

Olivia rubbed her own aching shoulder, suffering now from yesterday's crash through the balcony. If Billy had crossed the Bayou in the flatboat, he would not have passed Uncle Duncan's house. Maybe Julian had—

"What's wrong, Olivia?"

"Nothing. I'm simply concerned about Billy talking to the rest of the family, you know?"

"Haven't they always talked?"

"Of course, they have. But this is"—she waved her hand in the air—"oh, never mind. I'm probably being silly, but I'd hate to think we couldn't trust Billy."

Chapter Eleven

"Oh, no you don't," Boudreaux said. "You're not pouring that stuff on me."

Olivia held the bottle away when he reached for it. "The skin is broken," she said, "the bite needs to be cleaned."

He snagged the bottle by its neck and wrested it from her. "The skin will burn away after you put that on it." He sat down on a three-legged stool she'd drawn up near the pedestal sink and held the bottle of clear liquid up between them. "I pulled this stuff out from under there this mornin' and smelled it. Brought back a painful memory. Do you know what it is?"

"Uncle Lionel's special disinfectant."

"Lucy Lee's"—he nodded curtly—"your paternal grandmother's, 'Pearl River Spirits.' Clean, clear spring water, from when the Pearl really did run clear, liquid lye, and one tablespoon of muriatic acid per gallon. Years ago, before your granddaddy made lumbering pay for itself, she made this in pickle barrels and offered it for sale at two bits a pint. Fools actually bought it. Don't know how often they used it after the first time, but they did buy it."

"It works."

"Did you ever use it?"

"Uncle Lionel put it on a cut once."

"Cured you of cuttin' yourself, didn't it?"

"Cured me of letting him know when I did."

He set the bottle on the floor. "I thought you knew."

"I didn't know my grandmother concocted it. How do you know so much about it?"

"Like I said, I had it used on me once, too." He hooked his

83

thumb in the direction of the cabinet. "There's iodine in there and peroxide."

Obviously, he'd snooped through this room like he had her stepfather's office and bedroom, not to mention the kitchen pantry. She reached for the tincture of iodine."

"That'll stain. Use the peroxide."

"The iodine stings, that's what kills germs, and you're a sissy."

"The peroxide kills germs, and it will clean up the dried blood, and you, sweetheart, are a sadist like your father."

She stopped unscrewing the cap on the peroxide bottle. "What is that supposed to mean?"

He picked up the terry cloth she'd placed on the edge of the sink and held it out to her. "He's who used the Pearl River Spirits on me that one and only time."

"You knew him?"

He waved the rag in front of her. "Take this, and yes, I knew him. Darcy Clayton Lee. Mama named me after him. I was still pretty young when he was killed, but he used to visit Mama and Daddy often. He'd always waste a lot of his time on Troy and me when he was there.

"I was six when he poured that fire-juice on my scraped knee. Me, him, Daddy, and Troy were visiting a forest of yellow pine he wanted to see during his visit. I slipped crossing a shallow creek. Cut my knee on a rock. He went to his saddlebag and pulled out that stuff, told me it was gonna make it all better. I can still remember Daddy's, oh, no, then his tellin' me, after the deed was done, it was okay if I washed it off in the stream."

"And did you?"

"I did not. I was a tough little tyke and my good buddy Darcy Lee told me it was good for me. My poor knee burned for a damn hour, I swear."

"I washed mine off."

"Ha, so don't be calling me a sissy."

She finished unscrewing the bottle cap, then soaked the rag in peroxide. "Fine, but I'm not a sissy either; I'm smart. Can you move your shoulder?"

"Yep."

He didn't roll his shoulder or move his arm to prove he spoke the truth, and Olivia pressed her fingers into the smooth skin above his right breast. "The bite is near your collarbone. There's a nasty bruise around it."

"A year ago he got my ear. He was eyeing yours."

She tilted her head so she could see his face. "I'm sorry I misjudged the beast," she said and returned to her work.

He maneuvered so that her knees were between his thighs. "You make a habit of that, don't you?"

"Of what?"

"Misjudging."

She scooted from between his legs and dropped the washrag in the sink. "If you're referring to my misjudging beasts you are probably correct. When it comes to misjudging people, however, Mister Boudreaux, you must be declared a master."

He rose and reached for the clean shirt draped over the side of the claw-foot tub. "You're done, I take it."

"I quit." She averted her eyes when he caught her watching him dress.

"Thanks for cleaning it."

With one hand, she squeezed the peroxide from the rag. "You'll be sorer tomorrow."

He raised his chin to fasten the top button of his shirt, then reached for the buckle at his waist. She returned her focus to the rag in the sink.

"There's a red dress in your wardrobe," he said. "I want you to wear it tonight."

She looked up, no longer compelled to avert her eyes when he started unbuttoning his britches. "You've been in my wardrobe?"

"And every drawer in your room." He tucked his shirt. He didn't even have the courtesy to look at her, concentrating instead on his darn belly and the button he maneuvered back into the buttonhole of his pants. "Even under your bed."

She crushed the rag, slammed it into the sink, then fisted her wet hand. "Who do you think you are?"

He looked at her then. "I had to make sure you didn't have any weapons in there."

"Weapons my hind foot. You wanted to plunder my things."

"I didn't plunder anything. You didn't even know I'd been in there."

"Bull. There are guns throughout this house. And what of the butcher knives in the kitchen? Do you intend to confiscate every one of them so I don't cut your damn throat?"

"Language, Olivia, language."

"Don't you dare presume to monitor my choice of words, you fiend."

"Fiend?"

"Yes," she hissed, "and I'm being kind."

He blew out a breath. "Someone tried to kill me. The evidence indicates that person might be working with you. I will do whatever's necessary to find out every thing I can about you."

"No such evidence exists that I've seen, and from the information provided me, the person you claim to be is dead, so you keep out of my room." She stepped around him and yanked his bloodied shirt from the floor. "Sweet Jesus"—she straightened and glared at him—"is there nothing in this house you do not feel free to violate, Mister Boudreaux?"

Her heart was yammering against her chest and when a slow grin curled his lips she got so mad at herself she considered hitting him, because she knew what he was...

"I've yet to violate you, Missus Boudreaux."

"And you had better not attempt to."

"If the way you've been studying my manly chest for the past fifteen minutes is an indicator, my exploration of you will hardly be a violation."

"You are disgusting."

"I'm not the one ogling you."

She shook her head and reached for the rag in the sink. "Well, I'm not half naked, am I?"

"You told me to take my shirt off."

Dirty wash gathered, she started to the door, but he blocked her way. "If I asked you to take that damn piece of monastic attire off, would you?"

"Get out of my way."

He stepped aside. "Then I could ogle you, and we'd be even."

She turned when she reached the safety of the door. "I am pleased to learn that the manner of my dress discourages your ogling, Mister Boudreaux."

He had turned to watch her retreat, but didn't follow. "Which brings me back to that red dress."

"I beg your pardon?"

"I really do want you to wear that dress tonight."

Beneath her black-clad breast, her heartbeat picked up speed. "I am in mourning."

"There's no requirement for a young woman to endure a period of mourning for her great-uncle."

"He was my stepfather. A very-much-loved stepfather." She wet her upper lip with the tip of her tongue. She'd watched Lydia do that, in the company of men, a thousand times. This one narrowed his eyes. "Why do you wish for me to wear that dress?" she asked.

"I want the family to think we're getting along famously."

"Famously?"

He smiled and took a step toward her. "That we're getting along well if you prefer."

"That we like each other, you mean?"

"That we've known each another," he said and stopped in front of her, "and still like each other."

"Like each other better than ever, perhaps?"

He nodded. "Yes."

She stepped through the door and turned toward the staircase. "I'll think about it."

"*I* went to find Betty Joy," Boudreaux said. "You can smell that bread all over the house."

Olivia shifted her gaze from her reflection in the mirror to him, crossing the foyer behind her.

87

He was toying with his shirt cuffs, not really looking at her, and she reined in her quickening heart with a soft snort and the neutralizing thought that he'd probably pilfered a pair of Uncle Lionel's cufflinks.

She returned to her reflection, pretended to adjust her bodice, then shifted her gaze to find him staring at her in the looking glass. He was dressed in black trousers, black jacket, and white ruffled shirt with a western tie. She drew in a breath, touched the locket Lionel Augustus had given her on her sixteenth birthday, then turned to face the whole of him. His polished boots caught the light from the gaslight overhead, and a shudder ravished her body. Good Lord, he was a handsome man. "And did you?"

His eyes swept her body. "Did I what?"

"Find Betty Joy?"

"No. Katie neither."

"I told them a few minutes ago they could leave. They're not ones to dawdle. What did you need them for?"

Boudreaux's gaze moved from where it had lingered on her bodice and found her eyes. "What do you mean?"

"You were looking for a servant, for heaven's sake. What is wrong with you?"

He smelled of soap and of his woodsy, masculine cologne, seductive and more subtle than his brother's (and Olivia had no doubt they were brothers) bay rum. This Boudreaux's jaw was smooth and firm. He had shaved—his skin would be cool—and Olivia resisted the urge to touch his face.

"Nothing's wrong with me," he said. "It's my turn to ogle you, is all. Thank you for wearing the dress. You're beautiful."

A sweet and unexpected compliment. She watched him a moment, then ducked around him half expecting him to touch her, but he didn't try. "Whatever I need to do to stir the plot, darling, and thank you."

"It's cold out," he said and followed her to the door. She reached for her coat hanging on the coat tree, and he chuckled. "I'm looking forward to seeing Julian's face when you walk in wearing that dress."

88

She looked at him over her shoulder, and her hand fell on air. He reached over her and grabbed the coat.

"So I'm wearing this dress for...Julian?"

"I told you my reason for wanting you to wear that dress, but I'll be interested in his reaction. Here."

Her heart had created that rhythmic thud, thud, thud in her ears. "So, you're trying to make him jealous." She slipped an arm into one sleeve.

"I think he's already jealous."

She pushed her other arm into the empty sleeve, pulled the coat closed, and faced him. "You're trying to instigate trouble?"

"I wouldn't mind provoking him."

"And are you intentionally using Katie to provoke me?"

He wrinkled his brow. "You're doing that on your own."

Maybe he just plain didn't care if she were provoked. Maybe he considered her that unimportant, but she was finding his using her as a sexual provocateur particularly worrisome in the wake of her encounter with the other Boudreaux earlier in the day. She couldn't help but imagine the two brothers working in tandem to undo the spoiled heiress, who they believed had never liked Clay Boudreaux to begin with.

"Oh. Well, perhaps I can help you provoke him," she said.

"I beg your pardon?"

"You play with Katie to provoke me, and I'll play with Julian to provoke him."

"Olivia," he said slowly, "that is not the same thing."

"Oh," she said, and placed the tip of her index finger beneath her chin, "how characteristically stupid of me. That should provoke you, shouldn't it?" She trilled a laugh. "But since we are working together to uncover information about this tangled plot, and since you wish to provoke Julian by using my person, I'm sure you'd sanction my seduction of the foolish lad."

"That was not my intent."

"Oh, then please forgive my confusion."

"I think we need to have a little talk."

She started buttoning the coat's tiny buttons. A hundred of

the stupid things. No, a thousand. She hated this coat, and tonight she hated it more than ever. "A little talk about what?"

"About what I expect from you tonight."

Her fingers tangled in a buttonhole. She jerked them free and whirled on him. "Expect from me? You slip around with Katie and carry on whatever amorous betrayals you've started and expect me to sit back and not return the favor?"

He raised an index finger.

She covered it with her hand and smiled. "Oh, no, no, no, darling, I insist on doing my part in unraveling this convoluted plot." Good God, what if both the Boudreaux boys and Julian were collaborating against her? She removed her hand from his and, calmer, pushed another damn button through the proper hole.

"Olivia?"

She found the next buttonhole, too, and hadn't even looked.

Boudreaux watched her nimble fingers finish cloaking the provocative red dress in black. Her eyes, defiant and beautiful, she kept fixed on him.

"Believe me," she said, "I will tangle with whatever you plan on tossing my way."

A challenge he had no choice but to accept. "But will you win?"

"That is my intention, yes."

"What is your plan?"

"You tell me. You're the one who wanted me to wear this dress. Now I find out you want me to wear it for Julian."

He blew out a breath. "What's your relationship with him?"

"What's your relationship with Katie?"

"There isn't one."

"And I don't have one with Julian. Do you want me to establish one?"

He ground his teeth. "I don't want you to do anything. I simply want to confirm there's not already something going on between you two."

"I think you want to confirm there is."

His palms were starting to sweat. "And is that your plan for tonight?"

She turned and reached for her hat on the petticoat table near the door. "You've given me no reason to confirm or deny anything to you, sir." She placed the hat on her head and, watching what she was doing in the mirror, started pushing pins into the headgear and the smart coiffeur beneath it. "Truly, I have no idea which tactic would be in my best interest."

"I'm what's in your best interest."

She yanked on a glove. "Did Billy bring the surrey around? We're going to be late."

"I could care less if we keep them waiting."

"They have a fine cook."

"Probably healthier for us both if we miss dinner."

"What do you mean?"

He stepped closer. "Poison."

She squeaked and splayed her gloved fingers over her breast. "Oh my," she said in a blatantly faux high-pitched voice, "whatever do you suggest we do, sir?"

He smiled at her antics and loomed over her, forcing her to strain back against the table edge. "Eat only what they eat."

Pretense gone, she moved her hand from her breast to his and shoved at him. "You aren't serious?"

He stepped back. "Certainly as serious as you are, and no, I don't think they'll try to poison us tonight. The poison of choice is arsenic, and if done subtly, the process takes too long. Right now, they're holding out hope that Clay Boudreaux is dead and I'm an impostor."

He peered out the floor-to-ceiling windows that graced the front foyer. "The surrey is out there. Let's go."

Chapter Twelve

oudreaux sat to Olivia's left, next to Duncan Augustus, who
was at the head of the table. Lydia sat across from him, and
Julian was next to his sister and across from Olivia, stunning
in the red dress. Shoot, he couldn't have planned better if he'd
been asked to assign seats. Julian all but drooled, glancing re-
peatedly at Olivia's provocative décolletage, then glaring at him.
Julian's jealousy was eating him alive. What that jealousy was
based on, Boudreaux didn't know, but he hoped to learn something tonight about Olivia's relationship with the man most likely
to have seduced her. He glanced at her next to him. Funny, he
was having more and more difficulty imagining her seduced by
anyone.

Glittering crystal glasses, half-filled with white wine, already
sat on the immaculate table when the party entered the dining
room. No sooner was Olivia seated than she reached over and
switched her glass with Lydia's. The voluptuous redhead smiled
at the gesture. Then, almost as an afterthought, Olivia switched
Boudreaux's glass with Uncle Duncan's and winked at the man.

"What was the point of that, Olivia?" Aunt Agatha said from
her seat on the other side of Julian.

Head high, Olivia turned to the old woman.

"Olivia was merely making a most conspicuous point, tied, no
doubt, to the autopsy request," Duncan told Aggie before catching Olivia's eye. "You should have switched your glass with your
Aunt Aggie's, my dear."

The harridan looked at him, then said sweetly, "Why I do
nothing without your tacit concurrence, little brother."

"Complacency, Aggie, is the better term." Uncle Duncan took

a sip of wine from the glass Olivia had placed in front of him. "But it is of no consequence tonight."

"Yes, well, there's much to be said for complacency"—Aggie turned to the woman sitting at the opposite end of the table from Duncan—"as opposed to recklessness, is there not, Connie?"

Connie took a sip of her own wine. "I wouldn't know. I'm faulted more for stupidity."

Duncan's gaze rested on his wife, who smirked at him, then he said to Olivia, "You do intend to eat, do you not?"

"Only what you eat, Uncle Dunky."

Uncle Dunky?

"Well, Ollie, my sweet girl, I intend to eat plenty, but I don't know that following my lead is your best course." He glanced at his wife. "Anyone here wishing to poison you would be as likely to poison me."

Aunt Connie cleared her throat, then set down her glass. "If that hasn't happened after nearly forty miserable years, dear, I doubt you have a thing to worry about now." Her gaze focused on Agatha. "At least from me."

"Mabel is the cook," Agatha replied. "She'd taint his food if you asked her to."

Connie graced her sister-in-law with a most unpleasant smile. "I'd never ask. In your case, however, I wouldn't have to. I do believe Mabel would act on her own."

A door in the dining room's far corner swung open and an aging Negress, loaded down with a platter of steaming rice and what appeared to be a bowl of a rich, ingredient-laden sauce, stepped through. "I'm hearing you in here, Missy, and you'd best hush now. I'm too old to risk my eternal soul for the likes of a witch already condemned to Satan's fires, no matter how much my sweet Lord Jesus might approve hastening her there."

Lydia perked right up. "All this talk of damnation is making me hungry. Oh, Mabel, it smells divine."

Mabel set first the bowl, then the platter, in the middle of the table.

"Ah, crawfish étouffée," Duncan said.

Mabel looked at Aggie and said, "Yes, suh, good ol' craw-fishes." She cackled, took Agatha's plate, and heaped rice onto it, which she smothered with étouffée. She pushed the plate in front of Aggie. "For an ol' crawfish. You be the taster."

Agatha placed a portion of the food on her fork and the fork in her mouth. Boudreaux wondered if she'd carry the charade so far as to grab her throat and fall facedown into her plate. She swallowed, put down her fork, and said, "It's too salty."

"You speakin' to me, old woman?"

"You're the cook, aren't you?"

"Just wanted to make sure it was me you had in yo' sight. Most us folks never sure who you lookin' at."

"Yes, but I am always clear as to whom I am addressing."

"Hmmph," Mabel forced out and started for the door. "You mean from the stupid words come out yo' mouth?"

From time to time growing up, there'd been some real trials and tribulations brought to his parents' table, but Boudreaux had never witnessed a mealtime like this. With Mabel's departing words, Duncan Augustus made a show of standing and reaching for the rice. "If Aggie finds it too salty"— he passed the platter to Olivia—"that means it's perfect, which is good, because my appetite is in grand agreement with me this evening."

Boudreaux glanced at the man, then found Olivia studying both of them. She was as paranoid about him, no doubt, as he was about her. But in defense of himself, he wasn't on a pet-name basis with these people.

Duncan Augustus had to be well into his sixties, but was still handsome, bearing a striking resemblance to his older sibling, Lionel. Green eyes, a strong, straight nose and wide mouth, and a head full of hair, now highlighted with silver. The calculated ruthlessness was there, too; Boudreaux saw it in the way the man placed food on his fork, transferred it to his mouth, and chewed. Duncan looked up, met, then held Boudreaux's gaze in silent challenge. Slowly, a mocking smile molded his lips and...

"You hardly look in mourning, Olivia," Agatha said, diverting Boudreaux's attention.

94

"I am no longer a widow, Aunt Aggie." Fork in one hand, Olivia wriggled her shoulders and breathed in deeply. "I rather enjoy dressing for my man."

Julian's face clouded, but Boudreaux knew Olivia's perform-ance was meant for him, and her defiance grated. More than that, given their discussion before leaving Epico Hollow, who was she referring to when she used the words "my man"?

"Are you sure you're no longer a widow, Ollie?" Duncan's gaze slid from Olivia to him. The man smiled pleasantly, his ex-pression disconcerting at best.

"Of course, I am," Olivia answered, and Duncan dropped his gaze. She hadn't exactly exuded confidence when she spoke, but she hadn't sold him out, either.

Aunt Connie coughed. "And on that subject, did your trip to Hattiesburg prove fruitful, Aggie?"

Agatha Augustus's good eye settled on Boudreaux. "Sandifer was out of town. But I know where to find him."

"You wish to speak to Mr. Hudgins?" Olivia asked her, then followed the old woman's skewed gaze to him.

"I do indeed," Aunt Aggie said.

"And where do you think he is?" Olivia asked.

"You're not aware of your lawyer's whereabouts?"

"Not as a rule."

"And you, sir?"

"I am," Boudreaux answered.

The old witch raised a brow.

"He's working my case if I'm not mistaken."

Agatha's gaze shifted to Olivia. "You may rest assured, girl, that is the truth. His case."

Oh, good lord, Olivia was going to say something indiscreet, he knew it, and beneath the table, he reached for her hand in a subtle effort to head her off.

"I've been sitting here looking at you, Deputy Boudreaux," Constance Augustus said. In relief, he looked to his hostess's end of the table. "You favor your mother's father, except for...ah, I just realized"—she looked at Duncan, then laughed, not a hearty laugh, but a short little thing, more akin to a bark—"he has his father's eyes. Do you see it, dear?"

Duncan didn't look at him, but furrowed his brow at Connie. Aggie placed her fork on her plate and dabbed at her mouth with a napkin. "I don't see Edwin or Lionel either one in him. I agree he favors Hugh Henry, but Hugh was Troy's grandfather, also."

Constance turned to the older woman. "I am aware of that, Agatha."

"Then what was your point?"

"I was making conversation." Connie raised her glass in mock salute. "Remembering old times and old friends. You and Elaine, for instance."

"Elaine and I weren't friends."

"Of course you were, Aggie," Duncan said. "Elaine was—"

"Beautiful, and you liked to keep company with her," Connie said with a syrupy smile, "in hopes that she would attract you a handsome beau."

Agatha turned an equally faux smile on Boudreaux. "Your mother and I were friendly acquaintances, but I removed myself from her company when she decided to use my brother as a fine bull stud."

His gut quaked, and at the same time, the hand beneath his tightened into a fist. "That is bullshit," Olivia said.

Connie sucked in an audible breath, and Duncan said, "Ollie, you are absolutely right. Lionel was never once used unless he wished to be, and"—he turned to his older sister—"Agatha, you could not have been more rude if you'd planned it."

"But I did plan it, Duncan."

"Subterfuge for me, perhaps?" he said. Again, he turned his hard visage on Boudreaux a moment, then refocused on Aggie. "I will thank you to remember Olivia and her husband are guests at my table."

Beneath that table, Olivia freed her hand, and for a moment, Boudreaux didn't think she was going to let this rest. Duncan, however, turned to her with soupspoon raised. "See here, Olivia, I'm trying the gumbo; why don't you taste it."

⌖

$\mathcal{O}$livia hadn't fibbed about Mabel's cooking, and the étouffée was perfectly seasoned. Aggie's remark had been what Boudreaux suspected at the time, a failed attempt to provoke the Negress. He was on his last bite when a foot caressed his shin between the kneecap and the top of his boot. He glanced across the table to Lydia, who wet her top lip with her tongue—much the way Olivia had done earlier in the afternoon. He held the auburn-haired beauty's gaze. She was a wily widow, and that pretty, painted face of hers lent wicked vibrancy to her innuendo.

Her foot climbed higher to caress the inside of his thigh. He smiled at her and lifted his wine glass to—

Olivia slapped his hip, and he leaned her way. "What?"

"What is wrong with you?" she whispered.

"Why do you ask?"

"You had the silliest smirk on your face."

A laugh rolled out of his chest; he couldn't stop it.

Lydia dropped her foot, but it was the straightening in her chair that drew Olivia's attention, to which Lydia responded with a shrug and a smile. Olivia smiled back at her, then looked at him askance.

Uncle Duncan touched his arm. "A joke you'd care to share?"

Boudreaux wiped his mouth with his napkin. "I fear I would embarrass Olivia if I did. My beautiful bride has...well, suffice it to say she requests we make an early evening of it."

Across the table, Aunt Aggie made a sound of disgust, and to spite the woman, Boudreaux kissed Olivia's temple. He caught Julian's glare when he did.

Duncan rose. "You can have your man—such a well-chosen word, Olivia—to yourself in a bit. Right now, I need to talk with him."

Boudreaux, his stomach tighter than the smile he pasted on his face, rose after Duncan. The man had an ace up his sleeve; he'd been enjoying his dinner too much not to, and Boudreaux couldn't help but wonder if this trump he held might be related to the subtle clash he'd had with Aunt Aggie earlier.

97

"Francis and Julian, join us in the study."

Olivia rose with Francis, who sat on her right, but Duncan stopped her with a glance. "Just Mister Boudreaux, my dear. You and I will talk later."

Boudreaux looked at her half-standing beside him. "Sit down. I'll be back."

Olivia damned them all. That man's talking behind closed doors with her Uncle Duncan and the boys was insufferable. She didn't know if they were at loggerheads or united, but her biggest fear right now was that the four were smoking cigars, sipping brandy, and plotting how best to manage her fortune. She trusted Uncle Duncan would never hurt her physically. She equally trusted him to manage her money if he could get his hands on it.

"Thank you," Olivia said to Sally when the young colored woman removed her plate. A chill convulsed Olivia's body. Not only was she worried, she was cold. Despite being relatively new, this house lacked the efficient heating system Olivia enjoyed at Epico Hollow. The dress she wore, the one he'd wanted her to wear, with its low neckline and sleeveless bodice had been a bad choice for this cold December night. Olivia hadn't even brought a shawl and now considered asking Sally to fetch her coat.

"Coffee?" Lydia held a graceful porcelain pot above the china cup to the right of where Olivia's dinner plate had been.

"Please." She pulled the cup closer before reaching for first the sugar, then the cream. Across from her, Lydia retook her seat. Olivia spooned sugar into her coffee, and it occured to her that the only sound she heard was the clink of her spoon against the rim of her cup. She turned to her right and saw that Aunt Connie watched her. As curious as her aunt's interest in her spooning sugar in her coffee, it wasn't nearly as disconcerting as Great-aunt Agatha's glower.

Olivia reached for the creamer, and when she glanced around again, she found they were all still watching her. She slowed her stirring. Uncle Duncan was gone, and she was the only one having coffee. The only one using sugar and cream, and that droll challenge she'd tossed out to her uncle earlier no longer amused her. She stopped and set her spoon aside. Lydia caught her eye, and she curled her lips into a smile before pouring her own cup of coffee.

"I usually drink mine black," she said, reaching for the sugar and cream, "but for you, tonight, little cousin, I will indulge."

"You've made a grievous display tonight, Olivia."

Aunt Agatha was a master of overstatement. Olivia sipped her coffee. "I am sorry you feel that way, Aunt Aggie. I was so pleased with my performance."

"You've not heard..."

The pocket door to the dining room slid open, and Olivia turned and watched Julian slip into the room.

"Can I talk to you alone?" he said to her.

"Julian," his mother began, "your father..."

Julian already had his hands on the back of the chair, wiggling it to bid her rise. "Please," he said, but she was as eager as he. Across the table, Olivia saw one of Lydia's eyebrows arch, but the redhead said nothing. There were no more protests, and Olivia went with him.

"We know Clay is dead," Duncan said to Boudreaux, "we received notification three days ago. Nothing has changed."

Boudreaux sipped the smooth brandy, which warmed its path down his throat and into his stomach. "Except that Clay has shown up very much alive."

"Except a man who claims to be Clay Boudreaux has shown up."

"I am Clay Boudreaux."

On Boudreaux's right, Francis placed his hands behind his back and rocked on his heels. "We don't think so."

"Who then do you think I am?"

"Troy Boudreaux."

"Why would you think I'm Troy?"

Duncan raised his hand, silencing Francis. "I have my reasons."

"Such as?"

"Such as Troy Boudreaux having been commissioned to eliminate his brother for a suitable sum."

Despite the line of cannon booming in his chest, Boudreaux
smiled at Duncan Augustus. "I'm shocked you would admit being
privy to such information, Uncle Duncan."

The older man's lips tightened, and he straightened in his
chair. "My lovely niece told my son. Now, we're getting nowhere
playing this game of Machiavellian chess. How much will it take
to make you simply disappear?"

"I believe you've already tried that."

Duncan frowned at him.

"My attempted assassination in New Orleans?"

"When was that?"

"Two nights ago."

"What happened?"

This really was getting tiresome. "Your man missed."

Duncan Augustus studied him a long moment, then shot
Francis a furtive glance. Julian wasn't there to make eye contact
with. He'd slipped out no sooner than the brandy was poured,
and Boudreaux knew the bastard was with Olivia. What was
worse, Duncan hadn't sent Francis after him, and Boudreaux
couldn't help but wonder if separating her from him hadn't been
planned from the start.

"And did you miss, sir?"

"I did not."

"You identified the culprit?"

"No, he fell into the river."

Again the man looked at Francis before giving Boudreaux a
nod. "I know nothing about your problems in New Orleans, and
I will admit that Clay's untimely death came as an unexpected
boon, undeserved as it might have been. Now you, a man who I
believe is trying to take advantage of a young widow, have shown
up wreaking havoc with my sudden good fortune. Needless to
say, I am perturbed. So, I ask you once again, how much will it
cost to get you to leave Mississippi and never return?"

100

Boudreaux took another sip of the brandy and sucked in a cooling breath. "To come up with enough money to buy me off, Uncle, you'd need Lionel Augustus's fortune, and you don't have it. I do. So the real question is, why do I need you?"

Francis moved closer to his father. "You conspired to murder Clay. We will see to it you hang."

"The mastermind behind that particular plot, I believe"—he refocused on Duncan—"is Clay's widow, and I have the evidence."

"Thank you for confirming that," Francis said. "That assures us you are indeed Troy."

Boudreaux's attention jumped to Francis, then fell back to Duncan, who sat quietly studying him. "If you find comfort believing that, please continue to do so."

"We have other evidence which casts doubt on your claimed identity."

"And that is?"

"Tell me, Mister Boudreaux"—Duncan brought his index fingers together to form a steeple beneath his chin—"what does Olivia say about your being Clay?"

"She's pleased I'm alive."

"Then you must not believe she wrote the letter you accused her of writing."

Francis lined himself up behind his father's left shoulder.

"Of course he doesn't, Dad. Clay Boudreaux wouldn't live with a woman trying to kill him."

"Clearly another indicator you are not who you claim to be," Duncan said. "That further leads me to suspect you are giving Olivia little choice but to support your claim."

"Ask her."

Duncan graced him with a politic smile. "I don't have to." And he reached into his desk drawer and pulled out a letter. "Seems our sweet Olivia has attempted to contact the U.S. marshal in New Orleans." He removed the correspondence from the envelope and unfolded it. "She says here that she has additional information regarding the death of Clay Boudreaux and one other in Galveston, Texas, in which she believes premeditated murder to be a factor." Duncan refolded the letter and put it back in the envelope.

"I want to see the letter."

"Why?"

"To confirm you're not making it up."

"I think you know it's true. As you should have learned by now, you cannot underestimate Olivia."

Boudreaux shook his head. "I really must insist on reading it for myself."

Francis shifted his weight, and now Boudreaux looked him in the eye. Only one door led into the room, and it was within his range of vision. It remained closed.

He held out his hand.

Duncan sighed and laid the missive in it. "You—"

Boudreaux stuffed the letter inside his jacket pocket. Duncan clenched his jaw, then reached inside his desk drawer.

"Don't."

Duncan, his hand wrapped around the butt of a pistol looked up, then down the barrel of a Colt .44. Boudreaux's gaze jumped to Francis, who froze, his hand inside the lapel of his jacket. He'd been too quick for Duncan's eldest son, but the man had his hand on his gun, Boudreaux knew it. Reaching over, he confiscated Duncan's pistol. He didn't take time to look at it, but guessed it to be a .38 from its weight and feel. He put it in his pocket and rose, not taking his eyes off Francis.

"Unless you want to lose your father," he said, "I would advise you to place that pistol on the desk. Right now."

Inside his coat, Francis's hand moved.

"Careful."

"This isn't the time, son," Duncan said. "Do what he says."

Francis laid the gun on the desk, and Boudreaux seized it, too.

"Who are you working with?" Duncan asked. "Is it Agatha?"

Well, hell, that question told a tale now didn't it? "I thought you were her partner of choice, Uncle."

102

"Depends on the scheme. Does she know who you are or does she think she's been double-crossed?"

Boudreaux returned his Colt to its shoulder harness. "Seems I'm having trouble convincing everyone who I am."

"I'm not going to let you get away with this, you know."

"With what, Uncle Dunky, taking the letter?"

"Clay Boudreaux has as much to gain from Olivia's demise as she does from his."

"That may be true, but then he wouldn't have Olivia, would he?"

"Does he want Olivia?"

"He hasn't decided for sure. Speaking of which, I need to have a little chat with my bride."

"*I* cannot believe you've taken that bastard's side in this."

"Really, Julian, what did you expect me to do? Run to the loving arms of my family?"

"Better with me than him."

Air caught in Olivia's throat, and she coughed. "I know how self-serving you are."

"If you're referring to that letter you told me about this morning, I don't know anything about it. Why would I do that? I want to marry you."

"But if you recall, I do not want to marry you. You intended to coerce me into marrying you with a murdered man and that damning letter."

"To the best of my knowledge, the fire was an accident."

"And who would believe that, under the circumstances?"

"What circumstances? The so-called letter implicating you?"

"Really Julian, you must get your father to keep you better informed. At least one of those men was murdered. Fire or not, he had a bullet in his chest."

"Are you sure?"

"Of course I'm sure. So an accidental cause for the fire has been ruled out."

He seized her shoulders. "I swear I had"—she twisted away,

103

and he threw up his hands. "I had nothing to do with it. I would not send the woman I love to prison. I couldn't marry you there, could I?"

She folded her arms beneath her breasts. "I really don't know. Certainly, if I were incarcerated or hanged, you'd have free reign with the money, wouldn't you?"

He shook his head. "If anyone in the family betrayed you, I know nothing of it, and I certainly know nothing of a murder."

No, neither Julian nor Uncle Duncan would have framed her for murder. They wanted her to marry Julian and them get everything. There were others, however, who would not necessarily consider that agenda in their best interests.

None of them trusted the other, and she wasn't about to trust any of them with her best interests. Her hope rested with the U.S. marshal in New Orleans, who might very well take that letter Boudreaux claimed to have and throw her in jail.

Julian reached to touch her, but she pulled away. "I saw you two tonight," he said. "Hardly the affection I expected between newlyweds."

"We've only just met."

"If you were mine, we wouldn't even be here tonight. You'd be wearing that dress for me alone."

Not if you were a panderer, I wouldn't—and it disappointed her that Julian's thought and not Boudreaux's most closely paralleled her own regarding her wearing this dress. And, in an act of self-righteous magnanimity, wasted because Boudreaux wasn't there to witness it, she thrust her chin and said, "What goes on in public, Julian, is not what goes on behind closed doors."

Julian ruffled up like a rooster in a cockfight, and she pushed at the door, which rolled open a crack before he spun her around to face him. His fingers bit into her arm, and he shook her. "What kind of a fool are you?"

She tore free. "Not nearly as big a fool as you and the rest of the family need right now."

"What is that supposed to mean?"

"It means leave me alone. I don't want anything from you.

Nothing. And something else. My relationship with my husband is my business, and none of yours."

"And is what he does your business?"

"I beg your pardon?"

"He left Epico Hollow with Katie Harder this morning. Did you know that?"

Olivia's heart skipped an anticipatory beat. "They went to buy groceries. You saw them when they passed your house?"

Well, of course, he did. He was standing there, looking at her, listening to her. He had to hear the excitement in her voice. Well, who cared what he thought, he wasn't capable of indepth thinking, anyway. What did the foolish boy know?

"Did you follow them?" she asked.

He opened his mouth, she swore to say yes, but then he closed it. "Suffice it to say," he said, "he was seen a little later at the Gulf View Hotel."

"So," she forced through clenched teeth, "was Katie Harder seen at the Gulf View with him?"

"Surely you can guess the answer to that."

Yes, she could, and she also knew how Julian expected her to guess. Either he was purposefully hedging in fear of being caught in a lie if he knew Katie hadn't been at the Gulf View, or he had not seen her at the hotel, which didn't mean the woman hadn't been there, somewhere.

Julian, teeming with confidence, squared his shoulders. "He went into a room upstairs."

"Which one?"

He sniggered. "The one he'd put Katie in, I'm sure."

"The number, Julian."

"What does that matter?"

She narrowed her eyes on him. "You lost him, didn't you?"

"I don't need to tell you everything I know, Olivia, and I won't. You know darn well that man is not your husband, and you've made it obvious to me you suspect he's carrying on with Katie."

Given the snottily superior look on Julian's face, she couldn't

105

even be sure Boudreaux had gone into a room. Julian might have seen nothing more than the man go inside the hotel entrance. Katie's being with him would actually simplify matters for her, but she couldn't tell Julian that. The real point was, if not carrying on with Katie, what was Boudreaux doing at the Gulf View? In fact, it was possible the person Boudreaux met there was Julian himself.

"Well?" he yelped.

She startled, more irritated than frightened by his tone. She cocked her head and looked at him. Possible, but not probable. The complexities of this charade mitigated against Boudreaux's partnering with Julian. "I'll have to ask him."

He stuck his face so close to hers their noses almost touched. "Your husband is dead. This man you're living with is an impostor and you..." Julian's eyes widened, then he straightened and gave her a giddy laugh. "He's blackmailing you, isn't he?"

Given his denseness, Olivia had wondered over the years if Julian was an Augustus at all.

"Of course. That explains your odd behavior," he said and raised his hand to her face. She stepped back. "Come on, honey, I understand why you're acting this way now. It's not as if you're betraying Uncle Lionel. Clay is dead."

She raised her arms to fend him off. "Leave me alone."

"We'll get the letter back."

"The only thing that I can think of worse than him having that letter would be its falling into your hands."

His hand circled her neck, and he pulled her toward him. "I'll give it to you, I promise. I can get you out of this, my love." His breath, ripe with the smell of tobacco and brandy, fanned her lips. Nausea swelled her stomach, and she strained back. Her sore shoulder ached from trying to keep him at bay, and she forced out between clenched teeth, "I'm not interested, Julian. I've..."

The pocket door rolled open.

"...already got a partner in crime," Boudreaux finished.

Chapter Thirteen

Boudreaux had listened to them only a short time through the partially opened pocket door. Julian made his offer to help her find the letter; Olivia declined, citing lack of trust as the reason. Why she didn't trust him is what Boudreaux really wanted to know, and he wished he'd heard their conversation from its start.

She stood at the wide portal now, staring at him, and for a moment, he held her gaze; then he turned to Julian, who bristled.

"You're blackmailing her."

"No, I'm not."

"I'm married, Julian," she said.

"This man is not—"

"There is no doubt in my mind Clay Boudreaux is very much alive," she said and stepped through the door into the wide, central hall, which extended the length of the house.

Julian fixed his eyes on Boudreaux. "She's being coerced."

Boudreaux opened his mouth to speak, but Olivia, moving away from them, called back, "Not really, given a choice between you and him."

Boudreaux watched her back as she moved away. All she'd really said was that given a choice between the frying pan and the fire, she'd temporarily chosen the fire. She was biding her time, counting on the U.S. marshal.

"You don't know who this person is," Julian cried after her.

She stopped in the hall and faced them. Julian was at the door. Boudreaux stood between them. "But I know who you are," she said.

⋙⋘

$\mathcal{B}$oudreaux watched Olivia push the last pin into her hat, then take her coat from Sally. "Thank you for another delicious dinner," she said to Aunt Connie who, along with Lydia, had joined the five of them in the dimly lit hall after their closeted meetings.

"I'm sorry you two are leaving so soon. I'd hoped to get to know my nephew better."

"There will be other times for that," Duncan said, his eyes steady on Boudreaux. Boudreaux nodded at the man.

"Of course there will," Olivia said, turning her head briefly to offer Julian a sweet smile, "and I want to make an early evening of it, if you recall. Do tell Mabel the étouffée was the best it's ever been." She peeked around Aunt Connie into the dining room and called, "Good night, Aunt Aggie, darling."

Lydia rolled her eyes, then took both Olivia's hands in hers and kissed her cheek. "Pretend she said goodnight and pray she doesn't get up." Lydia turned to him and offered her hand. "I do so hope we will be seeing more of each other, cousin." She rubbed her thumb across his knuckles before stepping away.

Boudreaux reached to take Olivia's arm and found her look inscrutable. He closed his hand over her bicep and...

Bang! Bang! Bang!

He jumped despite himself, and Duncan, apparently rattled as much as he, cursed under his breath and started to the front door. Boudreaux dropped the hand that had reached for his Colt. The racket was nothing more than the exuberant use of the knocker by someone outside. He watched Duncan pull the door wide.

Dosh Brogan, Olivia whispered to him when he asked, recently appointed county sheriff upon the untimely death of the duly elected official last month. Uneasy now, Boudreaux hung back and listened as best he could to Duncan and the sheriff talk in hushed tones of New Orleans, the river, and Howard Augustus. With each low word that passed between the two men, his heart pounded harder. His escape was blocked. He tightened his hold on Olivia, and in his stomach, Mabel's fine dinner turned to bile. Francis and Julian joined their father as the conversation continued, and finally Connie edged forward.

Suddenly Connie covered her mouth with both hands and shrieked. Olivia took a step toward the group gathered at the front entrance, but he tightened his grip on her arm. She looked up at him, and he shook his head.

"No!" Connie screamed again. Duncan moved to take his wife in his arms, but hysteria ruled her now, and she backed away. He persisted, managing to wrap his arms around her, and she fell against him, sobbing. Lydia hovered at the fringes of the group in the doorway. Agatha finally joined them in the hall, and Duncan motioned for her, but Connie shoved Duncan away and slapped at Agatha. "Don't you dare touch me." Lydia touched her though, without protest, and Julian said something to his father, then joined his mother and sister. Francis stayed where he stood and talked to the sheriff.

Boudreaux's hold on Olivia must have hurt her, because she tugged her arm, and he glanced down to find her dark eyes wide.

Aunt Agatha moved into the shadows on Connie's right, until Connie screamed at her to get out of her sight, and Aggie started up the stairs. Again Olivia tried to pull free. Boudreaux wasn't about to let her approach Connie now, but their silent tug-of-war had done its damage. Lydia, her arm around her sobbing mother's shoulders, turned to look at them and Connie's eyes locked on Olivia a heartbeat before her face contorted into a twisted, hate-filled mask. "Are you working with her or against her? Two greedy, selfish bitches determined to keep everything for your-selves no matter the price."

Olivia stiffened beneath his hold.

"God in heaven, you are your mother's daughter," Connie spat out, nearly choking on her words. Olivia extended her free arm. "Aunt Con—" she managed before Connie tore herself from Lydia's hold and, hand raised, rushed at Olivia.

"You get out of my house, too!"

Boudreaux let go of Olivia's arm and caught Connie's fist in his right hand. She snarled, twisted, then stared at him, as if only now realizing he was there. Unbelievably, she laughed, and the sound took him aback, as it must have, given the sudden quiet, every person present. Then she renewed her struggle against his hold. Francis moved up behind his mother and took her by the shoulders.

"Let her go," he demanded.

Boudreaux put himself between Connie and Olivia and did as Francis said. The son pulled the mother away, and she whirled on Duncan, ashen-faced, still by the door. "Do you think Darcy's pleased tonight, husband? Poetic justice, wouldn't you say?"

For a moment, Duncan stared at her, then at him, still shielding Olivia at his back. Duncan turned to Lydia. "Sugar, take your mama upstairs."

"What has happened?" Olivia asked Francis, who turned instead to Boudreaux.

"Howard's dead. New Orleans police fished him out of the river this afternoon."

Julian strode up to them. "He was murdered." The vehemence in his voice was almost as poisonous as his mother's. His hatred, however, he directed at Boudreaux.

"No, he wasn't." Again Boudreaux took Olivia's arm. She resisted his hold.

"I need to help Lydia."

"It's all right, Olivia," Lydia said from the foot of the stairs. "Mama wouldn't welcome your help, I don't believe. Thank you, anyway."

Lydia escorted Aunt Connie up the stairs. Counting Aggie, that made three down. The other three stood between him and Olivia and the door, and there was always the off-chance that mad woman, Constance Augustus, would return with a double-barreled shotgun before they made their escape.

"Let's go, Olivia."

She offered no more resistance, and Boudreaux guided her around Julian, all the while keeping him and Francis in his line of sight. At the door, he came face to face with Duncan, still talking to the sheriff. Duncan turned and settled his eyes on him.

In front of Duncan, Olivia hesitated. "I am so sorry—"

"Shut up," Boudreaux said.

Duncan never looked at her, but he did reach out and touch her hand. She squeezed his fingers, and he squeezed hers in return. "We'll talk later, Mister Boudreaux," Duncan said.

Boudreaux pushed Olivia onto the broad porch and pulled her down the steps to the surrey. She raised her skirt to step up, but he seized her around the waist and bodily swung her into the carriage. For the second time, he looked back at the house. Julian and Francis had emerged onto the porch. Duncan stood in the doorway, the sheriff behind him. Boudreaux felt the Colt pressing against the inside of his arm.

"Why—"

"Hush." He had rounded the carriage and climbed into the seat. "Do not distract me."

She looked over her shoulder to the porch. "The lanterns?"

"The horse can see." The waxing moon was already high and near full, and he was thankful for the tree-shrouded drive home. He glanced at Olivia and flicked the reins. "We don't want them to be able to see us."

He drove quickly for the first quarter mile up the deserted Epico Way. Occasionally, he looked behind him. The narrow peninsula that ended at Epico Hollow was host to only two home-sites, Duncan Augustus's and Epico Hollow itself. The bulk of the land between them belonged to the Epico Hollow estate.

The thick, mixed bayou forest of pine, cypress, and oak formed cave-like walls on either side and over them. At his side, the dark form of Olivia sat still and quiet. The news of Howard's death and her aunt's reaction to it had stunned her. He slowed Toby to a walk.

"I must offer my—"

"No, you must not," he said. "You are not offering anything to those people. Not sympathy, not help, not one damn thing."

"I've known Howard all my life, and I love Uncle Duncan."

"Howard deserved to die. I'm not sure about Duncan yet."

He heard her soft intake of breath, and irritation, frustration, and raw anger seethed through the pores of his skin.

"What world do you live in, Olivia?" He shook the reins to

111

speed Toby up. "Do you remember how your Aunt Constance acted toward you when she heard the news?"

"She doesn't like me."

"She hates you. You and your Aunt Agatha and your mother. I don't know what she's got against Aggie, but she'd hate you for no other reason than you were born to Rebecca Lee."

Olivia shook her head. "It's more like she blames me, me and Aunt Aggie, for Howard's death."

"Should she?"

She jerked her head around and stared at him. He eased back on the reins. "Think about this, Olivia."

On his left, the forest thinned as the peninsula narrowed and he could see the shimmering waters of the bayou. He could see Olivia's face now, too, pale in the soft glow of the moon hanging well above the distant tree line. He didn't know how well she could see him, since he faced away from the light, but she seemed to study him.

"You killed Howard," she said after a moment.

"Yes." He turned to the surface of the water expanding in front of them, but he could feel her gaze.

"It was Howard who tried to kill you in New Orleans?"

"Apparently."

"You didn't know it was him?"

"No, Olivia, I didn't know." He regretted his clipped response, but he was scared. He hazarded another glance behind them, then looked into the black forest on their right. A hundred yards or so beyond, where he couldn't see, ran the smaller Epico Bayou, and dead ahead, clearly seen from Epico Hollow's broad front porch, Epico Bayou emptied into the much larger Bayou Bernard. "We're lucky we got out of that place tonight. Things are going to get worse from here on out."

"Are you going to be arrested for Howard's murder?"

"No."

"But the family knows."

"There was no murder, Olivia. It was self-defense."

"But can you prove that?"

"Is that desperation I hear in your voice?"

"I don't want to be alone out here now that you've managed to anger everyone."

"It wasn't me Aunt Connie was calling ugly names tonight."

"That's my point."

"In addition to the police report I filed in New Orleans, there were three other witnesses who gave statements. As far as the law is concerned, I'm cleared of wrongdoing."

"Oh."

In the distance stood the house that Matthew Lee built, the one Lionel Augustus later acquired thru Darcy Lee, Lionel's beloved stepnephew and Olivia's father. Inside, dimly-lit gaslights flickered in welcome, and Boudreaux's nausea subsided.

"Well, other than that, Missus Boudreaux, how did you enjoy your evening?"

Chapter Fourteen

"How do you think I filled the pantry if she wasn't shopping for me?" Boudreaux closed the kitchen door behind them. "Where's the key to this door? Given the course this evening has taken, we need to lock up tight tonight."

"Mister Yates filled the order. He does it for me routinely." Olivia looked at the door. "On a nail inside the pantry. The only time that door's locked is when we go up to bed and usually not even then."

"Best for now, I think, we keep it locked. At least at night."

She nodded, but he didn't see. "It's warmer in the carriage house than it is in here," she said.

"Might be safer, too." He hung his hat on the back of a kitchen chair. "And so you know that I know, Millie did the shopping, not you."

She turned up the wick on the lantern glowing in the middle of the kitchen table, then moved to the pantry. "And how would you know that?"

"My father told me how this household functioned."

"Your girlfriend told you this morning on the way to your tryst. She also told you Mister Yates would fill the order." Olivia handed him the key, and he locked the door, then opened the one leading to the lower level of the house.

"Hand me that lamp. We needed groceries," he said, when she did, "and you were busy."

"There was no reason for you to take Katie shopping. None. If shopping was what you were interested in, you could have asked me to stop what I was doing, or you could have waited until after dinner and taken Betty Joy."

114

"Or I could have simply told you to do it."

She stared at him.

"I needed to talk to her alone, which I did. I left her at the grocery, and I came back to pick her up." He stepped onto the landing, then took two steps down.

"Then what were you doing at the hotel?"

He turned on the narrow stairwell and looked up. Olivia had stuck her head through the door, her shadow on the wall as black as the coat she wore and that elaborate hat still perched atop her head. Despite her petite size and unmatched beauty, she looked ominous in the golden glow of the lamplight.

"Meeting someone," he answered.

"Julian?"

Now that was an interesting question. "Why would you think that?"

She eased through the door and stepped down to the landing. "Because he was there."

"Do you think he would have made you aware of that if he were meeting me?"

"He didn't tell me about your meeting, and yes, I believe he would try and misrepresent his reason for being there if he could work it to his benefit. You can't trust him, you know. I will always be his first priority." She moved toward that first step.

"Don't you come down here." He looked down the stairs. The space below was dark, and for the span of a heartbeat he thought of Butler's dead Yankees. Then he looked back at her. "I don't trust him. I didn't meet him. And if you really believed you were his first priority you wouldn't be expressing concern right now over the possibility of me working with him."

She stopped at the edge of the landing. "Very well," she said, "then what was Aunt Aggie hinting at about you and Mr. Hudgins?"

"Mr. Hudgins is my lawyer."

"He is my and Clay's lawyer."

"Exactly."

"Aunt Agatha implied that you and he are up to something."

115

"If your doubts are getting the best of you, you had better remember he was Lionel Augustus's lawyer, too. Surely you believe your uncle trusted him?"

"Actually, Uncle Lionel trusted Benford Hudgins, Sandifer Hudgins's father. The elder Mr. Hudgins and Uncle Lionel were close friends, but Sandifer was a junior partner. As such, he was privy to all Uncle Lionel's legal affairs. He took over everything when his father died two months ago."

"Hudgins and Hudgins represented Darcy, too, didn't they?"

"And Mama after Daddy died."

"Your mother and Lionel had the same lawyer?" Now, that was something he had never given much thought to—not that he would have—and dammit, given the way Olivia was looking at him at the moment, he wished he hadn't spoken that thought out loud.

"Why," she asked slowly, "wouldn't she have had the same lawyer? She was Darcy Lee's widow, then Uncle Lionel's wife."

He started down the stairs. "You're right. I wasn't thinking."

A floorboard moaned, and he turned around.

"You know something. Tell me."

"I don't know anything, Olivia. I guess I figured she had some old stuffy family solicitor up in Madison."

"Why do you think she would have needed her own lawyer?"

Four steps below her, he faced her fully. "I don't," he said, but he knew from the plea in Olivia's dark eyes that she suspected her mother might have, indeed, needed legal representation other than that provided through her husband.

"Then why did you say that?" she asked.

"I didn't mean anything by it." But he knew that she knew he did.

"Perhaps I should find my own lawyer," she said.

Now there was a thought. "I'll let you have Sandifer if you really want him."

"I don't know that I do."

She'd let her questions about her mother go; he didn't know for how long, but he'd take the momentary reprieve. "Olivia," he

116

said. "Aunt Aggie has convinced herself I'm Troy. Therefore, she assumes that any dealings I have with Hudgins are for no good. Now, you go back up and let me feed the furnace."

Olivia wasn't in the front room. Boudreaux called for her, his initial irritation expanding into anger, then concern. He took the steps two at a time, but didn't find her in her room or his. His heart was walloping his ribs by the time he bounded back down the stairs. She couldn't have been foolish enough to leave alone, not with the relatives probably wanting them both dead—unless, of course, she'd gone to meet someone. He peeked in the open office door. The room was dark, its air heavy with an unpleasant smell, hauntingly familiar, and he hesitated, wondering if there were a parallel between the scent of fear, which he swore a man could smell, and cat urine. He spoke Olivia's name in the darkness. She didn't answer, but he couldn't fathom her cowering in this inexplicably ominous place in fear of him, and he returned to the front room to find it still empty. His stomach, queasy since their departure from Duncan's house, cramped, and he spun around into the foyer...and spied her hat on the petticoat table near the front door, which was ajar. He yanked the door wide.

The meandering, low-lying limbs of two gigantic oaks framed her silhouette against the silvery sky. She was alone, looking out over Bayou Bernard, and he braved the encroaching shadows and went to her.

She glanced over her shoulder at his approach, then turned back to the water. The moonlight caught her platinum tresses, and he stopped, the last of his fear-fed anger seeping from his body and disappearing into the chilled air, replaced with a sweet warmth generated by her beauty.

He stopped at her side, and his arm brushed her shoulder. She shifted away without looking at him.

The night was clear and cold, the sky a tapestry of blue velvet glowing in the mist of the moon. Silver piping fringed a stratum of clouds to the south, and on the surface of the quiet bayou, shimmering moonlight reflected back until it disappeared into the

117

distant tree line. Serene beauty lay before him...and beside him. A perfect night for a man to be awash with emotion next to the woman he loved. He resisted the temptation to dip his head and kiss the back of Olivia's neck, but he did lay his arm over her shoulders and draw her close.

"What are you doing out here?" he asked.

"Meditating."

"About me?"

"Some." She continued looking out at the moon-swept water. Less than three miles as the crow flies, more if one counts every twisted foot of the stream, the languid, brackish waters of Bayou Bernard emptied into Big Lake, which emptied into Biloxi's Back Bay and finally into the Gulf of Mexico.

"I'm sorry for what Aunt Aggie said about your mother," she said softly. "It was a terrible, nasty thing to say about her and Uncle Lionel. Even Aunt Connie was appalled."

"She was trying to get a reaction out of me."

"But you didn't react."

"No, you did. Thank you."

"I defended my stepfather."

"Nevertheless, your rather frank response gave me pause to think before I spoke."

She fidgeted and moved her head. He couldn't see her face, but he bet she smiled. "I gave a lot of thought to my choice of words, I'll have you know."

"Word, if I recall and that was bullshit. I must say, Olivia, you have a quick, sharp mind."

"Thank you."

"Did they teach you any more good words at that fancy finishing school?"

"I learned that word at Epico Hollow many years ago."

"Did you use it in the presence of your stepfather?"

"On rare occasions." She turned her head and looked at him. "Are you going to tell me what you talked about with Katie?"

"I wanted to find out if she had any dealings with your Uncle Duncan and his family."

"She ironed for Aunt Connie two days a—"

"I mean passing them information about what went on"—he nodded in the direction of the house—"inside those walls."

"Did she?"

"Oh yes, she was a spy within."

"Why would she?"

"Love and money."

Olivia turned to face him, and he dropped his arm. "Uncle Lionel was generous with her," she said. "She was well-paid."

"I would guess she was better paid for the information she passed than for her ironing."

"And Howard was who she was involved with. I always thought there was something going on between them."

"And Francis."

Her mouth fell open.

"I think that was probably while you were in school."

She closed her mouth. "Are you going to tell me who you met at the hotel?"

"No."

"Was it a woman?"

Given that he was irritated to the point of cutting out Julian Augustus's tongue for having told Olivia he was at the Gulf View Hotel, Olivia's misconstruing his visit was a relief. "I am in need of a good woman."

"Trying to sidestep the issue with sophistry, sir?"

"With what?"

"You're purposefully trying to mislead me by deflecting the conversation to an irrelevant point, which you assume, for some reason, I would be interested in knowing."

She started to the house. "Well," he said, following behind her. "I wouldn't consider your need for a good man irrelevant, if you told me you needed one."

She rushed up the steps to the porch, then looked down on him. "And what would you do"—her voice sounded suddenly weary—"if I told you I were in need of a man?"

Not waiting for an answer, she pushed the front door open

and stepped into the foyer. He followed her inside and locked that door. "I'd provide you one."

She gave him a haughty smile and slipped her coat off. He caught it and turned his back long enough to find the coat tree.

"Well, I don't need whoever you have in mind."

"Whoever, Olivia? What is that supposed to mean?"

He didn't touch her, but two steps up the spiral staircase she turned on him as if he had.

"It means I don't require whatever it is you presume I need."

He relaxed his grip on the newel post. "My statement to you was a supposition. I didn't presume you needed anything."

"Oh." She turned away.

"Wait a minute. I'm not done thinking about your answer."

She ascended no farther. "I'm tired. Do you really need me in order to think about it?"

"I do." He leaned against the post. "Did you mention the letter to Julian?"

"The one implicating me in Clay's murder?"

"Attempted murder, and yes."

"I did. He says he knows nothing of it."

"Well, that explains how Duncan knew about it, if he didn't orchestrate the ploy himself. Do you believe Julian?"

"I believe Julian knows very little about anything, but in defense of him, in this particular case, I have yet to see a letter myself."

"That reminds me," he said and reached inside his jacket pocket. "Do you recall seeing this one?" He held it up, still in its envelope. "Someone signed your name to it, too."

Her cheeks, which had been rosy from the cold, paled to the color of her hair, and he feared she was going to topple off the steps. Her gaze moved from the letter to his eyes.

"I want Billy removed from my employ first thing in the morning." Hand on the rail, she started up the stairs.

"Is that all you have to say?"

She stopped. Her back was to him, and she took a moment before turning. "Did he give it to you?"

120

"Worse, I got it from Uncle Duncan."

She raised her chin, and he saw the subtle movement of her throat when she swallowed. For the first time since he'd confronted her yesterday in Lionel's bedroom she appeared totally vulnerable. "So, you are working with them?"

"No, Olivia, I took it from him at gunpoint after he showed it to me as proof you don't believe I'm Clay."

She closed her glistening eyes. "I cannot believe Billy betrayed me."

"I don't know that it would have mattered anyway. A U.S. marshal isn't going to rush over here from New Orleans based on something like this"—he waved the letter. "If we were lucky, he'd have gotten in touch with Nate Phillips in Galveston for more information. If we were unlucky, he'd have come to Brogan, who would have probably gone straight to Duncan Augustus. What were you going to tell Marshal Hamm, anyway?"

"Is that the U.S. marshal?"

Boudreaux nodded. "Yep. Wilford Hamm. You know he's in his sixties and been through three wives. He has few kind words to say about women anymore, so I doubt your feminine wiles would have worked on him."

"You seem to think they work well on everyone else, why not him?"

Ah, there was his feisty Olivia.

"Was it Lydia?"

"Lydia?"

"Who you met at the Gulf View?"

He smirked. "I couldn't find a woman, Olivia. Seems I'm still in need."

Those shimmering eyes still shimmered, but her body stance softened. The red dress suited her coloring, like its velvet folds suited her body.

Thus encouraged, he said, "You know, Olivia, we're probably in a lot of danger way out here by ourselves in this big house. We'd be safer if we shared a room."

Slowly, she started down the stairs. His gaze dropped to the hem of her dress, then moved up, over her thighs to the gentle curve of her slender hips and flat belly, to linger on the swell of her breasts above the décolletage. She was almost to him now, her lips parted, her eyelids half-closed.

"Do you mean a room or a bed?" she murmured.

"Bed."

"Does this mean I have worked my wiles on you, Mister Boudreaux?"

He breathed deeply. "In a manner of speaking."

"Is it a good woman you want or a bad woman and a good whore?"

He knew what she was up to, but wasn't sure she would play the game out. "I wouldn't necessarily classify a good whore and a bad woman as one and the same."

"Of course." She tossed back her head and breathed in. "One would certainly consider a virgin murderess a bad woman."

"And without a doubt, a lousy whore." His gaze slipped to her lips. She stepped closer—his gut constricted—and her fingers touched his shoulders. The scent of gardenia engulfed him. She rose on tiptoe and, pulling him down, brought her cheek to his. Her breasts pressed against his chest, and he hardened. He swore her lips touched his ear, but perhaps it was no more than her sweet breath.

"One does not have to be a whore to act like one, Mister Boudreaux."

He sensed her intention to push away and quick as a king snake spying a wild bunny he wrapped her in his arms. "But that doesn't rule it out."

She squealed when his lips covered hers, and he tangled his fingers in her hair when she found his wounded shoulder. He braced against the pain she inflicted and pulled her head back, forcing her mouth open. Still against her will, he grasped her tighter and thrust his tongue inside. She never surrendered, making it a hard-won kiss, conquest being his only pleasure, and a dubious one at best. As he lessened his hold, she pushed him back, but kept her grip on his shoulders. With tear-filled eyes and

122

trembling lips, she ground out, "I might be a whore, sir, but who-ever's whore I am, I am not yours."

"Not yet."

Olivia shoved him, he was sure, with all the might she could muster, then hurried up the stairs, but not so quickly that he missed her sob.

"I could work with you on improving your feminine wiles, if you want," he called after her.

Above, on the landing, she leaned over the damaged rail. "No, thank you. I now know why you were unable to find a woman to take care of your needs this morning."

That was a good rejoinder, and he grimaced with the slam-ming of her bedroom door.

Chapter Fifteen

Without opening her eyes, Olivia searched beneath her pillow for Clay's one letter to her, then remembered she'd put it on the bureau beside her bed when she crawled beneath the covers hours ago. Recalling the reason, she left it where it was.

Outside, the north wind sighed softly through the limbs of the ancient live oaks. Her shoulder ached, and she pulled her hand from beneath the pillow and rolled to her other side, away from the bureau and her link to Clay Boudreaux. The mattress was soft, the bed warm, at least where she lay, and she snuggled underneath the blankets and closed her eyes. She would have slept, but for the plaintive cry penetrating the wind. Again the faint yowl, and she sat up.

Light from the foyer chandelier shone beneath her bedroom door, and she reproached herself for the crumpled shadow on the floor in front of the wardrobe. Her red dress. She was normally careful with her things.

Again Chester cried beneath her bedroom window. Between the time he'd come to live with them as a kitten twelve years ago, up to the present, he must have wakened her a thousand times. During the day he slept on her bed, but he preferred his nights outside—except when the temperature was disagreeable. As she had grown into a young woman, he'd grown into a persnickety old tom. Tonight was bitter, but if she got up, she risked waking Boudreaux.

Again Chester meowed, and Olivia threw back the covers. In the hall, she discovered the master bedroom open wide, brightly lit, and abandoned. Downstairs, the backdoor clapped shut. Tentatively, she touched the newel post at the top of the stairs.

124

"Dammit, I'm going to wring your neck," she heard him say, and for the span of a heartbeat, Lionel Augustus was alive again, walking the halls of Epico Hollow and threatening the life of her red tabby. At that point, realizing Chester was safe and warm inside, she considered going back to bed. But she'd used the word safe too hastily. If her stepfather had indeed been the person uttering those words, she would have returned to her room, but the man chasing her cat tonight was not her stepfather.

With Boudreaux's next curse, she started down. The house was quiet, and she kept quiet, too, descending the dimly-lit stairs. In the foyer, a light emanating from the back hall guided her way. Cautious, she peeked into the recess behind the stairs, where the Augustus boys used to hide and jump out at her and Lydia when the girls had been very small. The light from the open office door twelve feet down the hall proved the hiding space empty, except for the pile of spindles Katie had stacked against the wall the day before and—she wrinkled her brow—Chester.

He meowed when he saw her, and she snatched him up to silence him, then stiffened when she heard movement in Uncle Lionel's office. Quiet prevailed. So quiet, in fact, she didn't want to move in fear that he'd hear her. After a moment, Olivia patted the cat on the head, and turned back the way she came. If she were careful, maybe she wouldn't have to face Boudreaux again tonight after all.

"God dammit, Katie."

Boudreaux's words were low and wet and spoken as if he were strangling on them. What passion that implied she wasn't sure, but she dropped the cat and turned around. Lips tight, Olivia padded soundlessly to the open office door.

Boudreaux, his back to her, stood to one side of the swivel chair where Katie, she guessed, sat facing the windows. He straightened, then whipped around to face her. She jumped at his sudden movement, catching her own reflection in the glass and realized that was how he knew she was there.

"What are you two doing in here?" she asked, and recomposing herself, she started toward them. "It's three in the morning."

125

"Olivia," he said, "stop."

She glanced at him, then to Katie, who hadn't moved. Olivia could see more of Katie reflected in the window than she could of her hidden in the chair directly in front of her. Behind them the clock ticked monotonously on the mantle, and Olivia's heart pounded harder. She swallowed and came on.

"Don't come any closer."

She turned on him. "Why not? What do you think you can keep hidden from me?"

"I don't want you to see this," he cried and moved to stop her when she reached for the chair.

"Too late—you're caught."

The chair spun, and a dark, ugly Katie with bulging eyes and tangled hair revolved into Olivia's line of sight. Olivia fell back with a cry and splayed a hand over her racing heart. Hackles raised, a shudder racked her body, and she stepped away from him. "Oh God, what have you done?"

"I didn't do this."

Her gaze darted to Katie, then back to him, and he held up a hand. "Hold on."

She stepped back, toward the door, and screamed when he reached for her.

"Olivia, I didn't..."

She spun in the direction of the door, but he'd stepped on the hem of her nightgown and had her stopped. She dropped to the floor when he reached for her a second time, and she twisted and pulled on the nightdress with both hands, hollering at him the whole time to let her go. He raised his bare foot, releasing her, and she scrambled to her feet, whirled, and crashed into the wing chair that sat in front of the desk. It fell backwards, her in it, and she sucked in a breath when pain numbed her shin.

"Olivia, listen to me."

She climbed from the fallen chair, screamed at him to keep away, and fell again when he tried to help. She rose on her own in front of the fireplace, then held to the mantle, while she rubbed her aching shin. Boudreaux blocked the path to the door.

He held out his hands, palms up. "I did not kill her."

"Then let me go."

His brow furrowed. "What are you going to do?"

"We need to get the sheriff."

"I know that."

"Then go. Go now!"

"I can't leave you here alone."

"Then I'll go."

"Now, listen to me, Olivia."

Dear God, her leg hurt so, and her knees weren't going to hold her up much longer. He couldn't let her go; he'd have to kill her, too. She sucked back a sob and looked around, then lunged for the fireplace poker at the same moment he grabbed her right arm. She cried out once and turned, hitting him with her left hand, while he wrenched the poker from her right. She shoved him, and he grunted. With that moment's reprieve, she eyed the door and started to make a run for it. But her foot tangled in the hem of her nightgown, her ankle bent sideways, and her body finally buckled. Fire scorched her ankle, and her knees gave way.

Chapter Sixteen

Boudreaux jerked awake. Olivia moaned, and he rose from the rocker next to her bed. She had moved her head, but otherwise remained as he'd laid her—he glanced at the round face of the clock by her bed—two hours ago. Despite the steady rise and fall of her breasts, he hadn't been able to wake her, and under those circumstances he sure had no business falling asleep. But he had.

Chester lay on her other side, watching him. The cat's jumping up on the bed earlier had seemed so natural that Boudreaux decided the act must be routine. Cats belonged outside at night. At best, they should be relegated to the kitchen, but he'd let the animal in to shush its cries, and now he let it be.

Olivia reached for her head, then struggled to sit up. He shot to his feet, more concerned by her sudden movements than relieved by the fact she'd opened her eyes. By the time he reached her side, she was searching beneath her pillow. He bent down to stop her at the same time she jerked the pillow up. She stared at the mattress a moment, then started to cry.

"Is this what you're looking for?"

Glassy-eyed, she looked at him, before shifting her gaze to Clay Boudreaux's letter he was brushing against her hand. With a sharp intake of breath, she crushed the missive in her fingers, pushed it beneath her pillow, lay down, and closed her eyes.

Pain in her ankle woke Olivia, but it was her aching head that suggested she not move. Suggest it might, but she couldn't continue to lie as she was. Carefully, she rolled to her back.

Oh God, now the room was spinning. She placed her palms

on either side of her head and pressed, and in some strange, night-marish way, pressing her temples caused her stomach to swell. She curled into a fetal position and sank back into her original place. Too late. She pushed up, off the pillow.

Behind her, the mattress gave at the same moment an arm cir-cled her shoulders from behind and held her up. "Go ahead," Boudreaux said.

With each retch, pain sliced her back and limbs, but mostly it pounded her head. Water splattered her face, and for a moment, Olivia prayed she would return to oblivion. She gagged again and would have fallen face first into the blue-speckled bowl and its foul contents, but he held her tight against him and balanced the bowl on the mattress with one hand.

"It's okay," he whispered against her hair. She shook, or tried to shake, her head.

"Looking at that"—her voice rasped, and she tried to point—"is making me sick."

"If you're done, I'll move it."

She managed a nod, and he rolled her onto her back, then touched a water droplet on her face. "You look like a ghoul."

Katie's bulging eyes and swollen tongue eclipsed the hand-some visage hovering over her, then that vision, too, blurred, and she closed her eyes and started to cry. "Katie's a ghoul."

She felt a wet rag on her mouth, her cheeks, and her nose, and she opened her eyes, then drew in a stuttered breath. He wiped away her tears. The cool rag was comforting. He was comforting. "I didn't kill Katie," he said.

"You were standing over her."

"I had just found her. I went into that room after the stupid cat, which I had kindly come downstairs and let in the house."

She stared at him, and he held her gaze.

"Why would I kill her, Olivia? Tell me."

"She knew what you were up to."

"All she knew is that I wasn't Troy."

"Maybe she knew that you were."

"I'm not."

Olivia laid a forearm over her eyes. "It feels like my heart is pounding inside my skull."

"In a manner of speaking it is."

She uncovered her eyes. "Did you do this to me?"

"You don't remember what happened?"

"I remember seeing you. You were angry I caught you with Katie." Her breath hitched. "And I remember thinking you would have to kill me next."

"Yeah, I figured that's what was going through your head. You tried to get away from me, and when you did, you fell and hit your noggin on the corner of the hearth. Damn thing was sharp, too. Your blood adds a nice contrast to your hair."

Her eyes widened and she touched the side of her head.

"Probably needed stitches, but the bleeding's stopped."

Tears filled her eyes. "I can't remember. I don't know if you're telling me the truth."

"Olivia, think. If it had been my plan to kill you last night, you'd be staring at the devil right now."

"You are the devil."

Her terror of three hours ago was gone, but she still feared him. He could see it in her eyes, even if he didn't hear it in her words. He didn't want her to be afraid of him, at least not because she thought he was a woman killer.

"What are you going to do now?" she asked.

"It's daybreak. As soon as Billy gets here, I'll send him for the sheriff."

"I mean about me."

"I'll get him to fetch the doctor, too. Somebody needs to take a look at your head."

"You're going to let me talk to the sheriff?"

"Short of cold-cocking you again, Olivia, I don't see that I have much choice. I can't imagine he won't want to talk to you, and I didn't kill Katie."

"Why was she in the house?" Softly spoken, but an accusation none the less.

130

"I don't know."

Olivia narrowed her eyes on him. "She wasn't here when we left last night, was she?"

"Not unless she was already dead, and we didn't know it."

Chapter Seventeen

"Sheriff done got here, Miss Livy,"—Betty Joy rushed to where Olivia was trying to rise—"wish you'd stay put like the doctor done told you to."

Pain jabbed Olivia's ankle, and she gave herself a moment's respite before looking up. Betty Joy was studying her with an empathetic grimace etched on her beautiful dark face. The girl had a sick, widowed father whom Olivia loved dearly and a grandmother she loved even more...and a gentle, hardworking brother—Olivia's eyes blurred—whom she was going to fire this morning as soon as she laid eyes on him.

"I have to get down there, Betty Joy. I must see the sheriff."

"Well, Dosh, you know that's what I get paid for"—Doctor Maurice Tasker let go of Katie's hand—"and I'm damn good at what I do." The smallish man stood straight in his wrinkled suit and glared at Sheriff Brogan, half a head taller. The Harrison County sheriff was a large, powerfully built man with heavy jowls and thinning hair. Beneath an open coat, he wore the same flannel shirt and overalls he'd been wearing at the Augustuses' house the night before. One thing was certain, Boudreaux thought, the doc was smarter and both men knew it.

"Now I put the temperature in this house at about sixty-five right now." The doc removed his spectacles and rubbed his left eye with an index finger, then waved the glasses in Boudreaux's direction. "Clay here says the house was colder most of the night. Given the condition of the body, I say she's been dead around twelve hours, give or take a couple of hours either side."

"So she was killed when?"

Doc Tasker sighed.

"Nine o'clock last night," Boudreaux told the sheriff.

"Give or take an...sweet Jesus, Olivia, what are you doing out of bed?" The doc shot across the room like he'd been fired from a cannon, and Boudreaux's gut twisted up like a hangman's noose. "Girl," the doc said, "I told you I'd be back up as soon as I was done down here."

"I've got her, Betty Joy," Boudreaux said, taking Olivia's elbow. Gently, he squeezed her arm. "Afraid you'd miss something, sweetheart?"

The doc was steering them toward the settee at the back of the room. "Not much exciting going on now. I told you your ankle's sprained. Not bad, but it's gonna swell if you don't listen to me and keep off it."

She looked up at Boudreaux. "I thought my presence might be beneficial."

Not to him it wouldn't be. He and the doc maneuvered her onto the couch.

"Are you dizzy?" the doc asked.

"A little. Doctor Tasker, you think she could have been dead as early as seven?"

"It's possible, and even as late as eleven."

Olivia found Boudreaux's eyes, and he thought he might choke on his heart, now lodged in his throat.

Brogan, still standing by the desk, asked, "What time did you two leave here last evening?"

"About seven," Boudreaux said, never taking his eyes off Olivia's.

"Was Miss Harder still here when you left?"

"She'd gone for the day," he answered.

Brogan stepped toward them. "You're sure?"

Olivia hadn't even blinked, and her implication couldn't help but be obvious to the other three people in the room.

Brogan stepped closer to the settee and said sharply, "Miss Olivia?"

Now, she looked at the sheriff. "I'm sorry?"

"Was Miss Harder here when y'all left for dinner at your aunt and uncle's?"

Boudreaux balled his sweating hands.

"I..." A wide-eyed Olivia turned, as did the sheriff, toward the hall door in response to a din emanating from the back porch. The back door opened, and a man's voice cried Olivia's name. Betty Joy, who stood closest to the exit, stepped into the hall at the same moment another voice admonished the first and yet another, decidedly feminine, shushed both the men.

The back door slammed shut, and footfalls started out of the kitchen toward them. Already in the hallway, Betty Joy called, "She be in here, Mister Augustus."

Julian stepped around the girl, saw Olivia, and rushed forward. Uncle Duncan, a scowl on his face, peered around Betty Joy, then moved her gently out of the way. "She's in here, Agatha."

Duncan was halfway to the settee when Agatha Augustus froze in the doorway, one eye fixed on Olivia. Her cock-eyed gaze flitted to the doctor, who was, Boudreaux noted, visibly annoyed by the intrusion.

"Floyd said she was dead," the biddy snapped.

"You appear disappointed, Agatha," Doc Tasker said.

"Hmmph. Thank the Lord the news is false, but I see no reason to upset the family for nothing. We've been through enough."

"Well, blame poor old Floyd, but don't get testy with me. It was a long night for me, too."

"It would seem it was a long night for a number of us," Duncan said and squatted in front of Olivia. "Entertaining morning guests in your dressing sacque is not a habit of either a Lee or an Augustus woman. His eyes shifted to the blood in her hair. What happened to you, Ollie?"

"Supposedly she fell and hit her head," the sheriff said.

Julian shot Boudreaux an ugly look before taking a seat beside Olivia. "Or someone tried to beat her into submission."

Olivia successfully resisted Julian's effort to take her hand, but she did let her Uncle Duncan hold her other.

"We came down to let Chester in—"

"Oh my God!"

Olivia looked up at the same instant Uncle Duncan's fingers squeezed hers, and he looked around to where Agatha stood in front of the desk, staring at Katie's body.

"Darn it, Agatha. Are you trying to wake the dead?" the doctor said.

"You could have warned us that thing was in here," she snapped back.

Duncan rose. "Katie's dead?"

"So, Floyd was right," Julian said and stood, also. "There was a murder here."

"Clay found her around three this morning," Olivia said.

"I'd just stripped down to my long handles after getting back from your place, when Billy come for me," Brogan told Duncan.

Julian approached the recomposed Agatha. "She looks awful."

Aunt Aggie slapped his arm with a black glove. "She's dead, you half-wit, of course she looks awful."

"Strangled?" Duncan asked.

"Yes," the doctor answered.

Duncan turned and faced Boudreaux. "Why?"

"I was getting to that," Brogan said, "when y'all busted in here."

"Well, man?"

Boudreaux wasn't sure if the question was meant for him or for the sheriff, but if Duncan's unwavering eye meant anything, the question was for him.

"You can answer that as easily as I can, Uncle."

"Me?"

"Yes."

"I had no reason to do this to Katie."

Agatha grabbed Duncan's arm and, shoving him aside, took his place in front of Boudreaux. "You did this," she said, then turned to Brogan. "You are aware, Sheriff, that we don't think this man is who he says he is. We also think he and Katie knew each other before he made his presence known two days ago. She knew his true identity and was a threat to his flimflam."

Boudreaux frowned at the woman, then looked at Duncan, who was also studying her pretty damn hard.

"She knew I wasn't Troy Boudreaux, if that's what you mean, Aunt Aggie."

The old harridan started for the door. "I'm going to be ill."

"Betty Joy," Olivia said, "would you help Aunt Aggie?"

"I don't need help," the woman said and disappeared into the hall. Betty Joy turned to Olivia, whose nod clearly told her to go anyway.

"Why was she in your house last night?" Brogan asked, drawing attention from Aggie's abrupt departure.

Julian took a step Boudreaux's direction. "Because he was diddling her. She threatened to tell Olivia, so he killed her."

"You're an idiot," Boudreaux said.

"Gentlemen," the doctor said, "I'd barely gotten back to sleep when Billy knocked on my door, so could we all please refrain from wild accusations, name calling, and poor use of the Queen's English?"

"Where were you all night, doc?" Boudreaux asked.

Tasker made a sibilant sound and returned to Katie's corpse. "There was excitement all over this little part of the bayou last night, but I joined the fray around four."

"Oh?" Boudreaux looked at Duncan, who ignored him. Julian volunteered nothing either. Boudreaux flexed his jaw and rested his gaze on Brogan.

"There was a shootin' at Mister Augustus's 'bout two this mornin'."

"What happened?" Olivia asked. She hadn't moved one part of her body where she sat on the settee, but despite her pale skin and veiled eyes, she was alert.

"A fella walked in on Aunt Aggie in the kitchen," Julian said. "We were all awake, what with happened to Howard. She started screaming and wouldn't stop. Claimed he was a rapist. Dad came running with a gun and shot him."

"You killed him?" Boudreaux asked.

Duncan looked at him, then turned away.

"Fella's name was Cecil Moon." Tasker squinted at Duncan, who didn't look at the doc. "One bullet through the heart."

"Any sign of a break-in?" Boudreaux asked the sheriff.

Julian jerked. "I told you, he walked in the back door."

"They don't lock their doors either," Olivia said.

"People get shot walking through other folks' doors in the middle of the night, and that's how it should be." Brogan stuck his thumbs in his waistband and watched Boudreaux. "Honest ones don't make a habit of doin' it."

Doc Tasker cleared his throat. "Dosh, come over here. I want to show you something." The sheriff approached the corpse followed by Duncan, Julian, and Boudreaux.

"See these bruises?" the doctor said, pointing to Katie's neck. "I've still got to check her entire body. She's got a couple of broken nails. No skin under any of 'em."

"Probably clawing at a heavy jacket," Boudreaux said.

The doc looked up at him. "Except for that there's no indication she put up any sort of a fight."

Boudreaux nodded. "She was surprised and overpowered."

Julian snorted. "Because she knew her killer."

"I can't rule that out, cousin, and she knew every man in this room."

"Then how do you know she was surprised?" Duncan asked.

"An educated guess. I am an officer of the law."

"Maybe, maybe not," Duncan said. "Personally, I think she trusted you. Your acquaintance with the woman has been suspiciously covert, you are very possibly a fraud, and you have been implicated in the shooting death of your brother in Galveston."

"I beg your pardon?"

"You heard me," Duncan said and turned to Olivia.

"He wormed his way into her confidence, Ollie. Seduced her with the promise of Lionel's estate, but you and I both know how greedy Katie could be. She made demands on him he wasn't willing to give. He no longer needed her, so he shut her up for good."

137

Boudreaux inserted himself between Duncan and Olivia. "I'm Clay, I didn't even know her before yesterday morning, I didn't kill her, and"—he cocked his head at Duncan—"I thought I was supposed to have died in a fire."

At that, Duncan narrowed his eyes, but Brogan, unaware of the confusion passing between Boudreaux and Duncan, swaggered forward and stopped in front of Olivia. He hooked a thumb in Boudreaux's direction. "Is he threatening you, Miss Olivia?"

Boudreaux couldn't decipher the look she gave the good sheriff, and his gut knotted tighter. She could offer up his ass right now, not only by concocting a compelling story that he'd beaten her, but for Katie's death as well. Olivia looked him over, head to foot, glanced at her Uncle Duncan, who watched her with great interest, then turned back to Brogan.

Boudreaux's heart pummeled his chest, and he resisted the urge to wipe off the sweat forming on his forehead.

"For Christ's sake, Olivia," Julian cried, "you can be done with him right now. Just tell us the truth, and Sheriff Brogan will lock him up."

Brogan nodded at Olivia, then reached for Boudreaux's arm. "I think we might jest have us enough here to make an arrest, Mister—"

"It was my understanding," Olivia said, "that Katie was killed between seven and nine."

The sheriff stilled, and Doc Tasker, who had been standing by Katie's body listening to this railroad job, said, "That is correct, and..." He cursed under his breath, when Olivia started to stand, but it was Boudreaux, being closer, who reached for her, and she grasped his arm.

"Then he could not possibly have done the deed."

Julian pushed around in front of Brogan. "You were with him every minute between seven and nine?"

"We've already established Katie left before we joined you all for dinner. Either she was killed while we were gone, and we did not find the body, or he would have had to kill her after we got back."

138

Boudreaux watched Aunt Aggie slip back into the room.

Brogan looked at the doc. "I thought you said it could have been as late as eleven?"

Duncan pursed his lips with the doc's affirmative nod, then said, "What time did you retire, Ollie?"

"We went to bed around ten."

"So he could have sneaked back down here," Julian said, "let her in, and killed her."

"He didn't."

"How do you know that?" Julian asked.

"Because I was with him."

"She's lying," Aggie said and took Olivia's place on the settee.

"I'm sorry?"

"Really, Olivia, you never could fib. I've just come from upstairs, and nosey old woman that I am, I took the liberty of looking in both your and Lionel's bedrooms. Since I know that as of the day of the funeral, Lionel's room was impeccable, I can only assume the mess in it now, to include a disheveled bed, was made by your houseguest. Your bed has also been slept in."

"We used both beds," Olivia said calmly.

"Ha," Agatha barked out. "Do you really expect us to believe that?"

"I do." Olivia turned to her Uncle Duncan, then glanced to Brogan who listened with rapt attention. Actually, Boudreaux was feeling rather rapt himself. "We started out in Uncle Lionel's bed," she continued, flashing her grandaunt a smile along the way. "Then we played a game of chase."

"Chase?"

"Yes, chase. Do you really need me to explain chase to you, Aunt Aggie? It's the same basic game you played as a child. Someone takes off running, another follows in pursuit."

"I won," Boudreaux said. He didn't think he could muss up her story by speaking then.

"I let him." She sighed. "That's when we ended up in my bedroom."

For a moment, her audience stared at her in silence. Then

Duncan placed his hands behind his back and said, "Well, my dear, I hope you know what you're doing."

Olivia moved her hand down Boudreaux's arm and tangled her fingers with his. Duncan watched. "Indecisiveness is the sure course to defeat," she said to her uncle.

Duncan blinked. "Not so sure as making the wrong decision."

Tears filled her eyes, and a dimple appeared on her chin. A real smile, deeply felt, and Duncan Augustus smiled in return. Boudreaux bent close to her ear.

"A Lionelism, I take it?"

She nodded quickly and swiped a tear from her cheek.

Julian cursed and turned his back on them.

"I'll help you sit back down, now," Boudreaux said. "Do you mind sitting by sweet Aunt Aggie?"

"That will be fine."

"Well, on that note"—Doc Tasker nodded to poor Katie—"we can get the body out of here. I'll get you my report, Dosh. It will say death by strangulation."

"And what about Olivia?" Julian asked of no one in particular.

"A post mortem on her can wait, I think." The doc winked at her on his way back to the desk. "But I do need to do a medical exam."

Brogan let out a heavy breath. "I'll go get Billy started hitching up the wagon."

Olivia watched Boudreaux block Uncle Duncan's exit.

"I don't know why Katie was in my house last night," he said to the man, "but you and your family knew we'd be gone."

"Did Katie know you'd be gone?"

Had she? Olivia had had no occasion to discuss their plans with Katie, but Boudreaux had spent the morning with the woman and, she could assume, Katie had been with him when Billy placed the dinner invitation in his hand.

"She would have still needed a reason for coming back here," Boudreaux said.

"Which could have been as innocent as having forgotten something."

Boudreaux's nostrils flared. "Was she working for you when she came back?"

"Is that why you killed her?"

"I need to know if you sent her here and why."

"If I did, I wouldn't tell you." Uncle Duncan stepped around him, and Boudreaux turned, his eyes on the older man's back.

"Did you not want to pay Moon; is that why you killed him?"

Duncan pivoted. "What the hell are you implying?"

"Seems strange is all, this fella ending up dead at your house the same night Katie is murdered in mine."

"There's nothing to tie him to Katie's death."

"Maybe somebody sent him here to kill Katie," Julian said.

Uncle Duncan's gaze shifted to his son.

"Maybe somebody sent him here to kill a fair-haired woman," Boudreaux countered.

With one quick step, Uncle Duncan brought himself toe to toe with Boudreaux, and Olivia held her breath. They were close to the same height and their noses nearly brushed.

"Let me tell you something, mister. I don't give a damn if you are Lionel's blood or not. You don't mean a bit more to me either way. He didn't dig you out from under your rock until he realized there wasn't going to be legitimate offspring to carry on his name. My most sinister plan for Olivia was, and still is, to make her an even greater part of the family. That's not a secret; she's aware of that desire on my part, as was my patriarchal brother, whose last demeaning gesture towards me was to sabotage my efforts to run his empire by dragging his heretofore unwanted son into the family. Clay's role was to cheat me out of something I wanted. If I'd hired an assassin, it would have been to kill you, not Olivia."

Boudreaux had stood stock still and borne every hateful word. What he was thinking, Olivia had no idea. Perhaps his resolve was indicative of an impostor, perhaps of a man who'd steeled himself to a lifetime of rejection by his father. For her part, she put herself in Clay Boudreaux's shoes.

141

"Please, Uncle Duncan," Olivia said, "that's enough. That's not true," she said to Boudreaux.

Boudreaux flexed his jaw, but he didn't avert his gaze from Uncle Duncan. "I really don't care, one way or the other, Olivia."

Olivia turned to Aunt Aggie, sitting beside her. "I'm tired. I wish you'd gather Uncle Duncan and Julian and go."

"Duncan," Agatha said, rising, "let's go. Julian"—she started to the door—"unfortunately, there's naught for us to do here this morning."

A strange look passed over Uncle Duncan's face, and he turned and stared at the woman, glanced at Boudreaux, then settled his gaze on Olivia. "His being Clay would not rule out his being a threat to you," he said gently. "You could actually be in even greater danger. You do realize that, don't you, Ollie?"

She touched her tongue against her upper lip. There was really nothing she could say.

With one last look at Boudreaux, Duncan turned on his heel. "Let's get out of here, Julian."

Olivia watched Boudreaux stare after Uncle Duncan, then her gaze met Doctor Tasker's. The man shook his head before turning to Katie's body. Brogan moved, too, which appeared to bring Boudreaux out of his stupor.

"I'm going to check out back," he said.

She started to get up.

"Sit back down."

One hand grasping the arm of the settee, Olivia sat back. "I was going up to bed."

Boudreaux nodded. "Sorry. I'll help you."

Chapter Eighteen

Brogan hovered behind and to one side of him. "That could be anybody's print," the sheriff said.

"When did it rain here last?" Boudreaux asked.

"Saturday, and it rained good."

Three days ago. He looked around the yard. He'd made it halfway to the barn before coming to a bare spot scarred with fresh prints.

"Here's somethin', Mister Clay."

Boudreaux looked over from where he squatted to Billy ten feet away.

"See here. This print's made by a boot, not a shoe like what I wear and the sheriff here." Billy nodded at Brogan who followed Boudreaux over. "And this here's a low spot; still has water from the rain. I betcha' this print was made last night."

Boudreaux looked back at the house, where Doc Tasker was coming down the back porch steps headed their way. This spot was in line with the route a man on foot would have taken from the porch to the road.

"You did good, Billy. Thanks." Boudreaux focused on Brogan. "I'd like to compare this print with one of Cecil Moon's boots, if I could?"

"You're thinkin' Moon killed that girl in there?"

"I'm thinkin' he could have."

"Then marched hisself on up the road to Duncan Augustus's place?"

"Eventually."

"This weren't a rape here, Deputy Sheriff Clay Boudreaux of Galveston County, Texas."

Boudreaux's gaze passed from the man to Billy. "I think the doc might be ready for that wagon."

The young Negro trotted off, and Boudreaux again squatted by the print. "It wasn't an intended rape there either, Brogan."

"Then what was it?"

"A payment."

"What the devil you sayin', mister?"

Brogan had shown little interest in the crime scene, inside or out. Shoot, Doctor Tasker knew more about evidence than this lout. Boudreaux stood and faced the man. He was smaller in girth, but he could look the sheriff in the eye. "Let's suppose someone hired Cecil Moon to commit the murder. Once the deed was done, he would have been in a hurry to get out of town, and he would've wanted his pay before he left. Duncan paid him all right, with a bullet through the heart. Assured him the skunk would never talk and saved him some money to boot. Meanwhile, I'm sitting over here with a dead body in the house and all of a sudden I'm the prime suspect for having done the killing. Presto, one obstacle between the extended family and Lionel Augustus's fortune removed. And if Olivia were the target, we're both out of the way."

"I don't believe for a minute Duncan Augustus would be part of no woman killin'."

"I'm not interested in your personal feelings on this matter, Sheriff. Just do your job. I'll bet you my next paycheck that if you take one of Cecil Moon's boots and bring them to this yard you'll find"—he pointed to the boot print in the soft earth near his feet—"it matches."

Brogan stepped forward and smeared the print to a slick surface. "Doesn't mean a damn thing, 'cept that after he killed Miss Harder the bastard went back up the road to kill hisself another woman, Deputy Boudreaux or whoever the hell you are."

Doc Tasker stayed Boudreaux's punching the man by grabbing Brogan's arm. "I saw that, Brogan." He was bookish, the doc, but from what Boudreaux had seen of him, he wasn't to be trifled with.

"Maurice, I don't need no phony Texas deputy comin' in here and besmirchin' the name of our good citizens."

"I'm tired," the doc said, "tired from want of sleep, and I'm tired of your ineptness, and I'm tired of listening to you bully the citizens of this county. I know my job, and I was elected by said citizens because they know that—that's more than you can say. If you want to keep your appointment until the election, you'd best start doing yours. What you did here is called tampering with evidence. If Duncan Augustus is innocent, he has nothing to hide."

Brogan whipped the slouch hat off his head and wiped his forehead with the sleeve of his jacket. "Can I put Miss Harder's body in the wagon, now?"

"That would be much appreciated."

Brogan smashed the hat back on his head and stomped toward the porch, bellowing all the way at Billy to get the goddamned wagon pulled up.

"Moon's body is at my office," Tasker told Boudreaux. "I'll send the boots back with Billy." He looked at the damp ground. "I hope you can find another print."

"And my wife?"

"Olivia's got a headache and some strained muscles"—he winked—"of course, some of those may be from playing chase rather than the fall, you think?" The doc had Boudreaux's full attention now, and the little man smiled. "But her eyesight and coordination are normal. I don't expect any ill effects from the concussion. God gave her a hard head."

"In more ways than one."

Tasker handed him a folded piece of paper and nodded. "Her dosage for the laudanum. She says Lionel had some left over in the kitchen. She needs to be resting, and that stuff will leave her little choice."

The doc turned in the direction of the house, then pivoted. "I don't think Duncan Augustus would hurt Olivia, not physically and not purposefully. You're barking up the wrong tree there." He nodded agreeably. "But like I said, if he's innocent, he can handle the investigation. And another thing..."

145

Boudreaux waited.

"Lionel wanted you here. He has for years. I don't know a lot about business, but there's always rumors bandied about. Duncan is a poor businessman. He's botched everything Lionel ever backed for him. It wasn't spite that prompted your father to draw you into the picture."

"Well, it wasn't good business, Doc. I'm a lawman."

The good doctor smiled. "Well, what's left, son?"

Chapter Nineteen

"Laudanum's in it, Miss Livy. Yo' husband put it in there himself." The delicate teacup tinkled when Betty Joy set it on the bedside table. "Doc Tasker told him to give it to you. I saw what he put in. Not nearly as much as I saw grandma give Mister Lionel one time, so I reckon it's all right for you to drink it. Says it will ease the pain and help you sleep."

Betty Joy's concern for her worries was sweet...and comforting, but Olivia couldn't help but wonder about the girl's sudden hedging as regards the likeable Mister Clay.

"Where is my husband?" she asked.

A knock sounded on the bedroom door. "He's here."

And sure enough he was, tall and handsome, one of those big Texas Stetsons in his hand and a denim jacket over his arm. "I've got somebody here wants to talk to you."

He stepped aside, and Billy appeared in the doorway, twisting his gray tam in his hand. Olivia stared at him, and he hesitated. "Could I, Miss Olivia, talk to you?"

She held her chin high, then briefly wallowed in the hurt his betrayal had caused her. Betty Joy bowed her head and slipped from the room. "Come in," Olivia told him.

Billy hurried in, then slowed when he reached the foot of her bed. She thought he might wring that poor hat to shreds.

"I swear, Miss Olivia, I didn't do what I done to go against you. Mister Julian told me when he come by yesterday mawnin' that you was in danger here with"—he turned and looked at Boudreaux lingering in the doorway—"Mister Clay, and you was scared, and that I was to watch out for you. So when you give me that letter to send to the marshal over in New Orleans, and said

147

I wasn't supposed to say nothin' to Mister Clay about it, well I figured fo' sho' Mister Julian and his daddy needed to know about it for yo' own good. So, I went up the road and told 'em, but they wanted the letter and yo' Uncle Duncan said he'd mail it hisself."

"Oh, Billy, I would have gone to Uncle Duncan myself if I'd wanted him aware of that letter."

"Yes'm, yes'm, I know that now, and I didn't really want to give 'em the letter, but they said it was best I did, and I done let 'em know I had it, so I couldn't lie. Wish now, I'd told 'em I'd already mailed it."

"And I wish you'd given me credit to know what I was doing and never gone to them at all."

"I'm sorry, Miss Olivia, I won't ever let you down again, I swear to sweet Jesus I won't."

"Did you take money from them?"

His eyes widened. "No ma'am, I surely did not."

She frowned. "They didn't offer, did they?"

"No ma'am, they didn't." Then he gave her a little grin. "Offered me cut wood, though."

She started to speak.

"Didn't take any of that neither." He grinned broadly. "Didn't have a way to get it. Told 'em I might stop by today if I have the wagon."

"Make sure the wagon is empty and take every piece they've got." She smirked. "They don't have a furnace."

Billy laughed. "Yes'm, I will, I sho' will." He sobered suddenly. "And I'll bring the wagon back in the mawnin'," he said. He'd started twisting that poor cap again. "And I'll stay the day." He stepped forward. "I'll go to New Orleans myself, Miss Olivia, and bring that sheriff back if you want."

Weary, she relaxed into the pillows. "That's all right, Billy, it doesn't matter now."

Billy turned and looked at Boudreaux. "What am I—"

"I don't think you're fired, Billy."

"No, go on back to work now. Everything's all right." Olivia

148

met Boudreaux's eyes, then glanced at Billy, who was watching them. "And I'll hold you to that promise."

He gave her a tight-lipped grin, took two steps back, put the mistreated hat back on his head, and disappeared.

Boudreaux watched him go, then came full into the room. "I'm glad you made your peace with him. He was pretty upset when he found out you were mad at him."

"I could have killed him last night."

"I don't think he'll second guess you again." He raised his chin and used it to point at the teacup beside her bed. "I put laudanum in it. Doc told me to. It'll help you sleep. How are you feeling?"

"My head hurts."

He nodded. "I've got errands to run."

Her heart started to race. "You'll be gone all day?"

"I hope not."

"Where are you going?" But the look in his eyes told her he wasn't going to tell.

"You drink your tea. We'll talk when I get back."

"If that were your intention, we'd talk now."

He put his back to her. "How much I discuss with you will depend on what I find out today."

"You could have killed her before we left."

He stopped short and turned back.

"You entered the foyer from the direction of the kitchen. Made a point of saying you were looking for her or Betty Joy."

"She was gone. And you and I both know I could have killed her after you went to bed. Now I've got to get some things done."

"You're leaving me here alone, drugged, after implying that you believe I was the person the killer was after last night?"

"I'm going to tell Billy and Betty Joy to stay close until I get back."

She sat up. "I was hoping perhaps you were only trying to rile Uncle Duncan. You do believe, then, that I was the intended victim?"

He drew in a long breath, then sat at the foot of her bed. "It's

149

a suspicion I have, but Duncan and his sons were all together last night. It doesn't seem reasonable they tried to frame me by supplying me with an alibi. And I know, and I think you realize too, I didn't kill Katie. If someone did hire Moon to kill you, Katie's being a victim of mistaken identity is a reasonable conclusion."

"Could there be someone else who wanted Katie dead?"

"Probably, but I don't know who all she was working with. She'd managed to get herself in the middle of a mess. Now I've got to go."

And go he did. She glanced to the little bureau beside her bed where the tea sat growing cold, touched her throbbing head, and grimaced when she flexed her bad ankle. Again she looked at the tea with its promise of sweet nothingness. She sighed, tossed back the covers, and got up.

Chapter Twenty

"See here, Miss Olivia, here's that second set I told you we found. Don't match the boots Doc Tasker told me to bring back fo' yo husband."

Olivia looked back a short distance to the worn, wet spot in the yard where Billy had pointed out a set of tracks that did match Cecil Moon's boots. Boudreaux had found them earlier, before he had doctored her tea and before he'd brought Billy up to face her almost an hour ago.

"Don't match Mister Clay's neither. He be the only one other than me hangin' 'round this barn that I know of, but I'll be on the watch now. Ol' Floyd say he saw somebody yesterday in the woods close to Mr. Duncan's place. Said it looked like whoever it was he was headed our way.

"See this point at the toe here? Yo' husband says it's made by cowboy boots, and there ain't many around here wears 'em."

Olivia's heart labored in her chest. "Did he indicate to you that he had some idea who made these tracks?"

"No ma'am, he didn't, but it did look like to me that he gave some thought to the matter."

Billy gave her a hand. She took it, and he pulled her to her feet.

"You didn't let anyone else see his telegram before you gave it to him?"

"I didn't, I swear. Doc Tasker told me when I left his place not to let nobody have them boots 'cept Mister Clay. Said it dealt with the law, and I could go to jail. That was befo' Mister Clay said anythin' to me 'bout how mad y'all was 'bout that letter you asked me to mail. But I still got the feelin' from the doc I'd best do what I was supposed to from here on out, 'cause you white folks was all at one another's throats."

Given the way Katie had died, Olivia wondered if Billy had intended the pun. He turned to help her into the surrey. "I ain't sure you oughta be doin' this. You don't look good."

"I don't feel well, either, but I am sure I should be doing this."

"I go and get myself back in your good graces," Billy muttered as he walked around the carriage, "now I'm gonna fall outa his."

"All the more reason not to do anything now to put yourself back out of mine. Other than what he asked you, did he give any indication what was in that telegram?"

"He got real still and quiet," Billy said, climbing into the carriage. He picked up the reins. "Just stared at it a minute, but he didn't say nothin' to me.

"Now, I told him to take the bridge down past the mill to Handsboro, then Commerce to Tegarden on into Mississippi City, then go west on Beach when he gets to the water. Figure we'll meander along behind 'im on back roads I know. That way we won't catch up with 'im or pass 'im comin' back. He'll probably be there and back before we get there."

And him returning home to find her gone would prove a problem of its own, but she'd face that when she had to.

"I know that boardin' house he was askin' 'bout. It's not a bad place. People there mostly workers buildin' Gulfport. Sailors, too, and lumbermen. Got a bar joined to it, but the owner don't tolerate drunkenness. His womenfolk work there, and don't much happen in the daytime anyways."

"Can you get in?"

"Oh yeah, they serve all folks, but I think you'll be better off by yo'self. You and me together liable to draw more looks than you alone. Either way, I think they'll mind their own business. You got money?"

She looked at him. "We're going shopping?"

He laughed. "Shoppin' fo' info'mation I thought. Tongues, they get real loose when you offer folks money."

Chapter Twenty-one

"I'm looking for Leigh Mosure," Boudreaux said.

The barkeep looked him over, then turned back to the well-worn surface of the bar and kept wiping. "I'm Mosure."

"I'm Deputy Clay Boudreaux of Galveston County, Texas, and I'm trying to confirm the whereabouts of your cousin Ralph Labat."

Mosure studied Boudreaux, as if he knew what was coming. "He was in Galveston last I heard."

"We need to talk. Private."

Hands now braced on the bar, the man turned to a young woman spilling coffee into two mugs. He said something to her in coon-ass French. She looked his way and responded in kind, positively it appeared. Beyond her, another dark-haired woman slapped a cloth on the bar and yelled something to an unseen person beyond a partition.

"Over here," the man said, and led the way to the end of the bar.

The place was dark, chilly, and quiet, at least during the afternoon. Not so outside where could be heard muffled shouts and hammers and saws and, God only knew what other industry, added to the cacophony created by the construction of a city.

Beyond the small bar, the room expanded into a restaurant of sorts, where a few diners, most appearing to be hard-working construction laborers and merchant sailors, sat digesting their noon meal. In the other direction, an exit led directly to a flight of stairs, and the rooms, Boudreaux reckoned, which made up the boardinghouse. This place lacked the feminine hominess of his mother's former establishment back in Texas, but was, from all

153

accounts, a decent refuge for transient builders and dreamers of Mississippi's proposed port city, Gulfport.

"What's with Ralph?"

"He's dead," Boudreaux said, his voice low. "Found with a bullet in his chest in what was left of a burned-out boardinghouse in Galveston five days ago. Sheriff there was finally able to piece together enough information found on his remains to identify him. He located the hotel where your cousin was registered, and that led us to you."

Leigh Mosure turned to catch the best of the afternoon light shining through the front windows of his restaurant, then blew out a breath.

"I'm sorry," Boudreaux said.

"Let's go in the back; I don't want the girl to hear. Not yet."

"Relative?"

"Ralph's baby sister."

Mosure opened the door to a small room, lighted by a dingy window overlooking a cleared wasteland dotted here and there with desolate, small frame buildings. The man nodded to a chair in the corner, and Boudreaux pulled it closer to a roll-top desk pushed against the wall next to the window. Mosure eased into the swivel chair in front of the desk. "What happened?"

"All we know is that before the fire started, residents in the house heard two shots. None of 'em were quick to stir, but two minutes later they realized the building was on fire, and they got out. Your cousin's was one of two bodies recovered. The coroner found the bullet in his heart, so we know the bullet killed him. We figure the fire was to cover up the murder. Do you know what he was doing in Galveston?"

"Working." Mosure waved his hand. "Him and me threw up this place a year ago when they decided for sure they was gonna dredge the channel from here to Ship Island."

"Dredging hasn't started yet."

Mosure looked him in the eye. "Powers that be been makin' promises about this city for the past fifteen years, but it'll happen this time. That fella Jones is gonna dig that channel himself.

Ralph thought so." The man sighed and looked down at his feet.
"Before we come over this away, he was a Hancock County
deputy. He liked that kinda work, but there was more money to
be made workin' private for folks, you know."

The look in the eye, the prudent words told Boudreaux all he
needed to know. Here on the Coast, Ralph Labat had kept busy
working for dangerous people. He had probably been dangerous
in his own right—that was how he'd stayed alive.

"Do you have any idea what he was working on in Galveston?"

The man scraped a hand over his face. "Haven't heard a word
from him since he left. Usually his work don't take him away, but
he said this job was worth the journey. Didn't give much concern
to not hearing from 'im."

"When did he leave?"

Mosure thought a minute, then turned to a calendar hanging
by a nail on the wall. He flipped back through the pages. "Three
weeks...no, more. Left the twenty-eighth of October."

"Do you know who hired him?"

"Woman in Handsboro."

Boudreaux's heart skipped a beat. "Do you know her name?"

"Lee. I remember 'cause of Robert E."

"Did you see her?"

"Young, pretty."

"Blond?"

"Light-haired, yes.

"Do you have any idea what she hired him to do?"

Mosure shook his head.

"Your cousin registered in one of Galveston's nicer hotels
under his real name."

"Can't think of why he wouldn't have."

"We suspect the reason he was killed had everything to do
with why he was in Galveston."

"Need to find the woman, then."

Boudreaux sighed. "Yeah. That's the next step."

Mosure rubbed a shaking hand over his face, and the poor man
still had to tell his female relation her brother was dead.

"I have a difficult question to ask you, Mister Mosure, but your answer might help me catch his killer."

The man nodded.

"Is there any chance Ralph Labat was hired as an assassin?"

"Them that hire killers, usually hire 'em to kill those like them, but lack the courage to do the job themselves."

"Or don't want to be caught."

If Mosure took offense, he didn't let it show.

"Did he keep records of any sort?"

"No."

No, he wouldn't, and that's one of the reasons he came at a high price. Boudreaux was surprised this man even knew Olivia's last name. That was as indiscreet as her damn letter.

"I may need to talk to you again."

The man said nothing, and Boudreaux rose.

"I'm sorry for your loss."

Mosure rose, too, then stuck out his hand. "I hope you catch who done it."

Yeah, Mosure wanted the killer caught, but Boudreaux figured he was done helping. Too many skeletons in Labat's closet.

The dark-haired woman Mosure had identified as Labat's sister stopped her cousin at the end of the bar and whispered hurried words. Boudreaux kept moving. He was almost out the door of the establishment when Mosure caught up with him and without a word, nodded to the end of a long, trestle table. Boudreaux narrowed his eyes. A woman dressed in dark clothing and wearing a gargantuan hat piled with feathers, flowers, and netting on her head, sat with her back to him.

"Josie said she come in a few minutes ago, asking after a tall man in jeans, a big Texas hat, and cowboy boots." Mosure looked him over. "Josie reckoned she was talking about you."

Boudreaux frowned. "Is she waiting for me?"

"Think she came in to see if you'd been here. When Josie hesitated, she offered her five double eagles to tell her."

Five double eagles! "I reckon she told her she'd seen me."

"For a hundred dollars, you bet your Texas ass." Mosure

156

smiled. "And for twenty dollars more, Josie told her you was in the back room with me. I'm guessin' she's hopin' you'll leave without seein' her."

Boudreaux studied the petite form shrouded in shadow.

"Do you know her?" Mosure asked.

Boudreaux pursed his lips. "The real question," he said, starting her way, "is, do you?"

Olivia closed her eyes with the sound of what she knew to be Boudreaux's heavy footfalls, and she cursed her stupid self. His fingers bit into her wrist, and he yanked her out of the chair, causing it to topple. The rest of the room quieted.

"Hello, sweetheart," he said, "fancy meeting you here."

Her heart was in her throat constricting her breathing, and the pressure on her wrist hurt. On top of that, he twisted her injured ankle when he yanked her around and started her toward the man he'd been sequestered with in the back of the building.

"Is this the woman who met with Ralph Labat?"

"Nah," the man said. "This woman's hair's white. The one I saw was the color of honey." He pointed to his front teeth. "She had a gap here, and she was fatter. This one is skinny."

Olivia yanked her wrist from Boudreaux's grasp, and he blew out a breath. Mosure smiled. "Might be she's not too skinny."

Boudreaux looked her over, his gaze stopped at her hat, then he looked back to her eyes. "I don't know if I could stand any more of her."

"What do you mean, following me?" Boudreaux said, when they stepped out on the porch.

Olivia closed her eyes to the blinding sun, small comfort for the splitting headache it aggravated.

"Well?"

She blinked her eyes open and raised a palm to her forehead. "Surely that stupid question does not require an answer."

He looked around. "You have the surrey, I take it, or did you walk here?"

"It's a block up, behind that little building."

"A block up?" he repeated, and Olivia watched him shade his eyes and, with great to-do, comb the Spartan-like expanse of newly cleared land. "Shoot, sweetheart, you must see with the same vision as that fella Jones."

"Most of what I see is, or was, through Uncle Lionel's eyes. I know he has friends, men born and raised here, who are disappointed the railroad didn't terminate in Mississippi City. It was supposed to, once, you know, a long time ago." She looked at Boudreaux and found he was, at least, listening to her. "Jackson has diddle-dawdled on the railroad and the port issue for three-quarters of a century. Now, private money is funding both. Uncle Lionel said that was for the best."

"Entails less compromising of the vision, I reckon. Your head still hurting?"

She nodded.

"Probably the weight you've got on it. Sweet Jesus, that hat alone would attract attention. Did you pay money for it?"

Carefully, she started down the steps. "It was my mother's. It's twenty years out of date."

"You were trying to hide beneath it?"

"I needed a disguise," she said and kept walking, despite the growing pain in her ankle. Half a dusty, visionary block up the road, Boudreaux motioned to a little colored boy across the street. He stood in a shaded alley between two new buildings, and he held Pompeii's bridle in his hands. If she'd noticed them on her way in, she'd have never entered the Longleaf Inn. The boy came running, a smile on his face. The horse lumbered behind.

"What would possess you to leave that animal with a child?" she asked.

"Pompeii likes kids. He likes Negroes, Mexicans, and Indians, too." Boudreaux smirked at her. "It's the dark skin, I reckon." He handed the boy a coin, two bits she thought, which earned him another smile, Pompeii's reins, and a salute. He patted the boy on the head. "He loves this little tyke. What he especially does not like are white women, particularly light-haired ones."

"That is absurd."

The boy laughed, then took off running. "Hey," Boudreaux called after him. The boy turned, and Boudreaux flipped him a silver dollar (she was sure this time), which the youngster adeptly caught.

"Oooowee!"

"We're big spenders, my woman and me," he hollered after the child. The boy waved once more, and Boudreaux turned to her and started them in the direction she'd indicated. "I do like the dark blue on you though."

She frowned at him.

"If I give you a silver dollar, will you smile at me? Oh, that's right"—he snapped his fingers—"anyone who can bribe a bargirl with six double eagles probably wouldn't be impressed with a silver dollar."

She stopped. "You think it was too much?"

He stopped, too, and Pompeii nudged him in the shoulder, which caused him to stumble. "Way too much. She'd have talked for a half eagle. What were you thinking?"

Olivia drew in a ragged breath, then shook the dust from the hem of her dress. "Billy told me people will talk if I bribe them. I really had no idea what to offer."

"Billy?" Boudreaux shook his head and started moving again. "Good ol' Billy. Did you bribe him to tell you where I was going?"

She raised her chin and, ignoring the pain in her ankle, caught up to him. "I didn't have to. He's unwaveringly loyal to me, now."

"Shame I'll have to fire him."

She grabbed his arm, with little effect. "Oh no, you won't." Her leaden legs ached in her effort to keep up with him, not to mention her pounding head and piercing ankle. The day was pleasantly cool, but she was hot in the dark velvet. "He never made you any promises."

"His letting you out of the house with you hurtin' the way you are is grounds enough to let him go as far as I'm concerned."

"He couldn't make me stay there, you know that."

159

"He didn't have to tell you where I'd gone."

Boudreaux was walking fast, not looking at her, while she struggled alongside the horse. Of course, he cared about how she ached and sweated.

"He only told me what you'd asked him. He didn't know I'd come after you, didn't want me to, but, at least, he didn't let me come alone."

"Well, there's that to say for him," he tossed over his shoulder. "What else did he tell you?"

"Nothing." Yes, Billy had mentioned the telegram he'd picked up for Boudreaux at the Western Union office this morning, but she wasn't ready to fight that battle. "Will you please slow down?"

He turned around. Stopped now, Olivia raised a shaky hand and moped sweat off her forehead with her glove.

"God, you're a stubborn little witch. Look at you." He walked back and surprised her by wrapping his arm around her waist. Pulling her close, he supported her body with his. "Come on, we're almost there, or I'd put you up on Pompeii."

Careful not to make a sound, Lydia turned the knob to Olivia's bedroom, pushed the door wide, then frowned at the pristine room with its neatly-made bed. The carriage house doors had been open when she'd driven up. She'd expected the handsome spoiler to be gone, but from her father and Julian's description of Olivia this morning, she had been certain her cousin was in bed recovering and probably sound asleep.

She stepped back into the hall and pulled the door closed. The entire house was quiet. Billy was gone from out back and Betty Joy didn't appear to be inside. She hadn't called for the girl for fear of waking a sleeping Olivia.

Lydia looked at the closed door to Lionel Augustus's bedroom. Perhaps Julian had been mistaken in his assessment of the tale of chase Olivia had told earlier. Determined not to wake her, if she were indeed sleeping in the master's bed, Lydia tried the door. Though not nearly as neat as the room her Uncle Lionel had inhabited, its empty bed was made.

160

In the mirror on her left, she caught movement, then saw a man, his back to her, and she smiled.

"What have you done with your bride?"

He whirled, and Lydia's smile melted away. "I am so sorry. I assumed you were Clay."

He looked as shocked as she felt, but he didn't miss a moment to start heading her way. "Cousin Lydia," he said, half statement, half question.

"Yes, and who are you?

Gently, he took her arm and pulled her all the way into the room. "I am Clay Boudreaux." He pushed the door, and it closed with a resounding click. "And I can't tell you how sorry I am that you've caught me in here."

Chapter Twenty-two

Hot cup of tea in hand, Boudreaux stopped. Despite the dark room, he could see Olivia's small form swallowed beneath the covers on her four-poster bed. She moved, and he hoped she might have heard him and would turn her head to the door, but she only cuddled further into the pillow.

He set the cup on the bedside bureau. "You asleep?"

"Go away."

"Are you hurting?"

Carefully, she rolled onto her back. "Only my head down to my shoulders and my ankle up to my knee."

"I've got you another cup of drugged tea. You really should reconsider and drink it." He sat on the edge of the bed and reached for the matches and the chimney of the coal oil lamp. "Why don't you have a gaslight?"

"There's a sconce on the wall over there, but the chandelier was such a big, ugly thing, and it interfered with the canopy."

The soft glow of the lamp lent color to her cheeks and muted the pain straining her lips and eyes. "How's your stomach?" he asked.

"Better now that I'm not lying on the backseat of that carriage."

"I'm not taking the blame for that. Stopping for you every five minutes, we'd have never made it home. You didn't throw up again after you stretched out."

"That seat was hard and the road was harder. It's no wonder I'm aching now."

"Sit up." He reached for the spare pillow. "You're aching because you stumbled and fell, then you didn't listen to your doctor.

162

And the roads here are good. You should drive along some of ours in Texas. Okay, you can lie back now."

He looked at Chester, beside her on the bed, then reached for the tea. "Here," he said to Olivia. She looked at the cup, but she didn't take it.

"What are you doing up?" she asked.

"Can't sleep. I'm trying to read, but I don't get far."

"You doze?"

"I lose my concentration."

She turned her head slightly on the pillow, and finally took the tea from him, followed by a sip. "What are you trying to read?"

"I picked up that copy of *The Three Musketeers* you were reading to Lionel."

"I never get bored with anything Dumas writes. I—"

"Bored is your word, mine was concentration." His gaze dropped to her lips, then to the lace at the neck of her prim nightgown.

"And where is your concentration now, Mister Boudreaux? Or have you ceased to think at all?"

He laughed. "I assure you I'm deep in thought. If anything, I have too much on my mind beginning with our mystery"—his gaze held hers—"and your role in it."

"Oh, silly me. For a moment there, I thought you were talking about the forces working against you and me, together. Well, I assure you, sir, I'm as innocent as you are."

"What you mean is as innocent as you think I am, which might very well mean you believe me not very."

"All right, I'm more innocent than you are."

"Drink the tea," he said. He hunched over with his elbows on his thighs and rubbed his eyes.

"The woman was Katie," she said.

He turned to her.

"The woman you were looking for in Gulfport."

"I know."

"You thought it was me?"

"Apparently she identified herself as a Miss Lee."

Olivia's heart skipped the proverbial beat. "Do you know why she was there?"

"Do you?"

Carefully, and that only as to not spill the tea, she sat forward off the pillows. He straightened, too. "Of course I do," she said, "I had a nefarious issue, which needed attending. I sent Katie so no one would recognize me, then I told her to use my name."

He edged closer. "Lie back and finish the tea. I don't think you sent Katie over there."

"Then why did you ask?"

"Because I knew it would fluff you all up."

"And you find pleasure in agitating me, Mister Boudreaux?"

"That, too. You're quite pretty when you're agitated, as you put it."

"Bull. No one is pretty when they're angry, and you are wandering further and further from my question, which, I suspect, is your true purpose."

He peeked into the cup. "One more swallow should do it, then maybe I can get some sleep, too."

"Do you know why—"

"Finish the tea," he said, "and I'll give you an answer."

A useless one, no doubt, but she did drink the last of the tea.

"I went there to find out what I could about a man named Ralph Labat."

"And what does he have to do with Katie?" she asked.

"I don't know." He inched closer, and she sank farther into the pillows.

"You suspect something."

He sank a fist into the pillow and loomed over her. "Maybe. How's your head?"

"Better."

"The laudanum's working."

"Tell me what you think."

"I think someone is trying to frame you for some nefarious deed."

"I told you that the first night we met."

"Yes, you did, but then as now, I'm still not certain if I am up against someone trying to frame an innocent Olivia or double-cross a double-dealing one."

"Get away from me."

He drew closer. "Who's trying to frame you, Olivia?"

"I—"

She should have known he didn't expect an answer. He dipped his head, covered her lips with his, and pressed her into the pillows. It was a gentle kiss, one she could have fought off, if she'd wanted, and she suspected he thought she would. When she responded by twisting her head in invitation, he pulled back and looked at her. Then he placed his thumb on her chin and tugged down. His mouth claimed hers at the same time she ceased to breathe. Heart thumping, she threw her arms around his neck and raised off the pillows. He filled her mouth with his tongue, and after a brief hesitation, she touched hers against his. He groaned, then his arms relaxed, and she felt his hands on her wrists, gently extricating himself from her embrace. He pushed her into the pillows. "Well, Missus Boudreaux, who is seducing whom here?"

She caught the tease in his voice. "I'm the one doing the seducing," she said. Her tongue had thickened. She needed to say something else...she hadn't answered his question. She looked at him. Worse, he hadn't answered hers, and now she couldn't even remember what it was. "You're purposefully distracting me."

"Here," he said and helped her sit up, before removing one of the pillows behind her head. "Time for nighty-nite." He stood, and when she rolled away from him, he pulled the covers over her shoulder. "You can be pretty distracting yourself."

She forced her heavy eyelids open and stared at her dressing table against the wall. "Those were terrible things Uncle Duncan said to you this morning."

"If I'm not really Clay, what does it matter?"

She tightened her lips. "Uncle Lionel cared for your mother — she was your mother no matter which one you are."

165

She tried to see him over her shoulder. She couldn't, but felt him tuck in her blanket, so she knew he was still there.

"He didn't talk about his relationship with Elaine Boudreaux, not with me, but at the end he wanted me to understand what happened and why you wouldn't leave Texas and come here and live with him." Again she tried to see him. She'd invited a response; he didn't accept, and she feared he was going to leave her. She rolled over. He was there, watching her with a sweet softness in his eyes, and he retook his seat beside her on the bed. "It was your mother's decision to leave Mississippi."

"I know that, Olivia."

"Uncle Lionel's first wife had come back."

"So had Edwin Boudreaux. He wanted to take Mama to Texas to be near Mama's daddy. They both wanted to try and make a life together. Granddaddy was a strong, neutralizing force."

"Hugh Henry Gibson," Olivia said. "I've heard stories about him."

"Did you hear the one about his leading thirteen troop up a little hill in Pontotoc County and capturing five Yankee cannon?"

"Nathan Bedford Forrest watched him do it and gave him a field commission of lieutenant colonel. Yes," she said, "I heard it a thousand times."

"Yeah, the number of cannon grew over the years, so did that rank. Granddaddy told me he didn't even know cannon was up there. He and those men with him had been cut off from the main force. I don't think they knew exactly where they were in relationship to anything but that hill. Somebody had started a rumor at some point during the day that there was a sutler's wagon on top of it. Union. He said he'd have much rather had the sutler's wagon. Couldn't eat cannon, and they were hungry. Besides that, he found out later, too much responsibility came with his new rank, whatever it was, and he never saw any damn pay. Those were his words, not mine."

"I heard he handled the responsibility admirably."

Boudreaux gave her a thoughtful look. "Admirably, Olivia? Granddaddy did his duty, and he'd have done that no matter his rank. And as for that particular story, don't place too much store in it. I figure it's more bunk than truth."

Her heartbeat quickened. "By that, I assume you mean he knew there were cannon?"

His sobriety fell away. "Spoken like a true daughter of the Old South. That says a lot, you having been raised by a Yankee."

She raised her chin, certain his words were meant to belittle her unwavering faith. "My—"

"Your nineteen-year-old father was with Hugh Henry Gibson that day"—he grinned—"looking for that chuck wagon. I know."

She sucked in a breath and started to sit up, but he placed a heavy hand on her shoulder. She knocked it away and sat up anyway. "The cannon was pounding the Confederate line, and your grandfather himself told Forrest—"

"God only knows what my grandfather would have said to General Forrest if he ever really had occasion to talk to him. And how do you know so much about what happened? For sure Lionel Augustus didn't tell you. He was minding a Union sutler's wagon somewhere no doubt, but not that one."

"Tom Buscher told me the story, time and time again. And there was no sutler's wagon, there were cannon and—"

"Stop," he said, then patted her quilt-covered thigh. "You said Tom Buscher, and that explains everything."

"And what is that supposed to mean?"

"I knew Tom, Olivia. He visited us in Texas with your daddy more than once. The man could embellish a story, sweetheart, and he was not without prejudice. I can assure you that not once did Nathan Bedford Forrest ask my grandfather's opinion on anything."

"I never said he did, but even then that doesn't mean your grandfather didn't give it."

Boudreaux snorted, then asked, "Where did y'all put Tom?"

"We took him home to Marion County. He wanted to be buried near his mama and daddy in the old slave cemetery behind the family plot, where my daddy and granddaddy and grandma Lee are. Take me back to my people, he said, and we did."

167

"Good man, Tom, and if it makes you feel better, my mama said the same thing about them knowing what they were doing that day. I reckon she was right. The cannon was pounding the Confederate line. I concede there was no way they couldn't have known it was there. Now, go to sleep."

She closed her eyes. Conceded, her left hind foot. "I know what you're doing," she slurred.

"What?" he said against her ear.

"You give me a meaningless victory in a battle you don't want to win to take my mind..."

Chapter Twenty-three

"Good morning." Lydia breezed into the house, then looked over her shoulder and gazed at Boudreaux through half-closed lids. "Mister Boudreaux."

"Call me Clay." He pushed the door shut with one hand, and Lydia smiled.

"But is that your name?"

He shot her a smile of his own. "It is."

She stuffed her gloves in her pocket, then started unbuttoning her coat. Obviously, she planned on staying awhile, and he perked up, wondering what he could make out of her game. A tantalizing body in a form-fitting green velvet skirt and jacket emerged from beneath the coat she handed him. He tossed it on the chair next to the petticoat table and followed her into the front room, watching with appreciation while she smoothed her hands over her derriere. He was no fool. Every move she made was for his pleasure, and when she stopped to rest her eyes on him, he leaned his shoulder against the parlor entry.

"Have any arrangements been made for Howard?" he asked.

"Daddy and Julian returned early this morning with the body. They were in New Orleans all yesterday afternoon and most of last night. The bureaucracy over there can be so difficult sometimes." She started pulling the hatpins from her hat. "Poor Mama has been in such a state. Daddy is really the only one who can control her, and he doesn't seem interested in putting forth the effort. Aunt Aggie's of no help. I swear she is going out of her way to provoke her. The two loathe each other, they always have. Mama is being so difficult, even interfering with Sally and Mabel, which she absolutely never does. Mama hasn't really had anyone

169

to grieve for in my lifetime, and I'm told it's much worse when it's your child." Lydia lifted the little hat from her head. "I do hope Mama goes first. Nothing against Mama, of course, but Daddy is so much easier for me to cope with."

Boudreaux might have been able to muster a bit more sympathy for Constance Augustus if he hadn't seen the threat she posed to Olivia two nights ago.

"You smell like soap. You just got out of the bath." Approval oozed between the syllables, her words designed to put the subject back to where she'd begun when she sailed through the door.

"I've found a full-sized tub in my own house quite a luxury."

She stepped forward. "I can't imagine life without one, and I do so approve of clean, nice-smelling men."

Watching her movements, the provocative tilt of her head and the glow in her eyes, he straightened.

"What brings you here, Lydia?"

"I came to check on our little Olivia. I stopped by yesterday, a little past dinnertime. Neither of you were here."

"Betty Joy didn't mention that."

"Betty Joy, I'm told, was fishing in the bayou and didn't see me." Lydia wet her lips. "Given what I heard of Olivia's condition yesterday morning, I'm surprised she got out."

"We had a pleasant day touring Gulfport."

"Mm. Not many places to go there."

Boudreaux wondered if she knew of their trip to Mosure's boardinghouse, but decided to place no significance on the visit, whether or not Lydia was aware of it. He moved closer and watched her stiffen in anticipation. "The trip wore her out, I'm afraid. She's still sleeping this morning."

"Soundly?"

"Drugged."

A slow grin moved over her pretty mouth. "For how long?"

"Hours. I take it you have something you want to discuss with me." He cocked his head and waited for her to come to him. He was sure she would.

And come she did, her now smoldering green eyes locked on

his. Lydia knew seduction, and he'd be willing to bet she knew raw sex, too. Another step...and another.

"I do," she said, and tore open his flannel shirt. Her thumb grazed his left nipple, and he hardened. He didn't think he could have helped that if he'd tried, which he didn't. She melded her body to his, and he bent his head and kissed her. She groaned and pressed her breasts against his chest. Her velvet fingertips feathered his belly. His physical response was as he expected, but he forced his emotional one blank, then braced, readying himself for her touch. One hand reached for his belt, the other stroked his jeans-clad penis. "Oh, God, Troy," she murmured into his neck, "I suspected you were in need of a woman."

"Clay," he corrected and caught her hand. He had no doubt her direct address had been purposeful. "But I have a woman, Lydia."

She pulled back to look into his eyes. "Have two." She freed her hand from his and started unbuttoning the jacket to her ensemble. "At least in my case you're not screwing your brother's wife." She wriggled out of her jacket exposing a high collar, lace-fronted blouse. From the looks of her, she was trussed up tight in a corset. Extra work he wagered would prove worth it.

"I suspect," she continued, "Olivia is very much aware of that, and if she is, despite her entertaining chase tale I heard about, you have yet to consummate your marriage"—she giggled—"or your brother's marriage." She shrugged one shoulder, smiled, then said, "If that's not the case, then I'm willing to share you with her. I'm not in the least hesitant to put a handsome man to good use." She caught his hand and pulled it toward her breast. "If you do not touch me," she said, "I shall surely die."

He twisted his hand and caught her fingers, then pulled them to his lips. "Olivia believes I'm Clay." He kissed her knuckles.

She brought her lips to his—she was almost as tall as he. "I think she has her doubts, but at the moment, I do not care."

"Why are you really here, Lydia?"

"Daddy is giving you one more chance to come to terms."

"And he seals the bargain with his daughter?"

171

She laughed, a melodious, feminine sound. "My ploy. Daddy has no idea I'm rubbing thighs"—and she did just that—"with you at the moment."

He hoped his smile conveyed disbelief; he meant for it to.

"Well," she recanted, with a wink, "maybe some idea, but he certainly doesn't sanction my misbehavior."

Boudreaux dropped her hands and went to the parlor commode containing the liquor supply. "Tell me again why your father believes I'm not Clay." He held up an empty glass for her.

"Yes, please, to repress my inhibitions."

He couldn't help but smile at that.

She took a seat on the settee. The same spot, he noted, where she'd sat three days ago when she'd come visiting with Aunt Aggie. "We have additional information," she said, "which supports our belief. And it explains why Howard attempted to kill you in New Orleans."

"Because I'm the true heir?"

She smiled sweetly. "To protect Olivia from an impostor."

"It sounds like the kind of cock-and-bull story people might believe, except that I'm not Troy."

"Oh, we believe Howard's attempt to kill you in New Orleans confirms that, indeed, you are."

"You are going to explain how?"

"Of course I will, to convince you to give up this charade and get out of town while you still can."

He handed her a snifter of brandy. "Go ahead, convince me."

"It's quite simple. Troy decided to murder his brother and assume Clay's identity for Lionel Augustus's fortune."

"So you're convinced Troy agreed to Olivia's proposition?"

She rolled her eyes and took a long swig of the brandy. "To someone's proposition, yes. We know that fire was no accident. Daddy suspected that to be the case from the beginning. The fact that the man inside the burned-up building had a bullet in his chest confirmed that."

Boudreaux twisted his head and studied her, and that seemed to please her.

"Howard, of course," she continued, "would have recognized both you and Clay; he'd been dogging your heels off and on for weeks. Believing, as did everyone else, that Clay had died in the fire, he immediately realized your plan was to assume Clay's identity; he tried to kill you before you reached Olivia."

"If he happened to realize such a plot, why didn't he just go to the sheriff?"

"Oh, really, Troy."

"Well, shoot, I want to make sure I know as much as you do about what I did."

"Again, quite simple. Olivia was set to inherit. Despite Aunt Aggie's ploy to break the will based on consummation of the marriage, there was only one way for Daddy to get his hands on Uncle Lionel's money—short of killing Olivia, that is."

"And Aunt Aggie."

"A good point, though I actually think he'd kill Aggie before he'd kill Olivia."

"Whom he plans on marrying off to one of his sons."

"Julian, to be specific, which he couldn't do if some impostor moved in claiming to be Clay."

"Expose him as a fraud."

She frowned, and he smiled.

"Your scenario works, Lydia, but only if Howard knew he was shooting at the real Clay Boudreaux. And on that point, you do realize that the only way Howard could have known about the bullet in the man's chest before his own untimely demise was if he were in the boardinghouse that night."

"I'm sorry?"

"Was he the killer?"

"Troy Boudreaux is the killer, and we intend to prove that."

"And I suspect it's equally likely that Howard is the killer, given he knew about the bullet."

"Why do you think Howard knew about the bullet?"

Boudreaux stared at her. "Your father mentioned Clay's shooting death yesterday morning. Hell, he knew about it before the Galveston County Coroner passed that information to me. If

Howard didn't pass that information to your father, then how did he know?"

Lydia's mind was working, and he reckoned at this point she was as confused as he was. What he feared most was that she wouldn't answer him.

"Julian told Daddy," Lydia said at last. "Julian got his information from Olivia."

Chapter Twenty-four

"Her ankle's swollen, but she seems to be doing fine otherwise."

Boudreaux reached for a biscuit and tried to focus on what the doctor was telling him. What he really wanted was for the man to have his say and go. He wanted to talk to Olivia himself, and the doc's surprise visit had forestalled that.

"She says she's sore," Doc Tasker continued, "and I'm sure she is."

Not as sore as she deserved to be. The doctor looked him in the eye, and Boudreaux's heart took off in a ragged trot with the thought he'd spoken out loud. He hadn't.

"She says she's been up and around," the doc said.

Boudreaux passed the wiry, little man the cloth-covered basket filled with Betty Joy's hot biscuits. "She insisted on accompanying me to Gulfport yesterday."

"She didn't tell me that."

"No, I didn't reckon she did. It was a stupid thing to do." Boudreaux handed the doctor the butter, then a bowl filled with peach preserves that Auntie May had made and sent with Betty Joy. "But my point is, she has been up and around."

"Well, she needs to take it easier than that. I'm not going to tell you to sneak the stuff into her, but offer her laudanum when she complains. Send for me if the nausea returns or she starts complaining about dizziness. I think if there were going to be any serious repercussions from that head injury they would have declared themselves by now, but we sure don't want to take any chances." The doctor buttered a biscuit, while Boudreaux stuck what remained of his in his mouth. Then the doc looked at him pointedly. "She was probably afraid to stay here alone given what happened to Katie."

Boudreaux nodded and picked up another biscuit. "That's what she said, but I had to go. Took her with me. I regretted it later, but"—he shrugged—"it was too late by then."

"Do you..."

Boudreaux looked up.

"Have you come up with any more information as to why Katie was killed?"

"Doc, I've got so many ideas I can't untangle one good one that stays solid from beginning to end."

Chapter Twenty-five

The faint rumbling behind the walls grated on Boudreaux and the late breakfast he'd shared with the doc was sitting pretty heavy on his stomach right now.

The doc had left, but Boudreaux's answer to the man had taken on a driving force of its own. How had Olivia known about the bullet? And could he trust Lydia's words? He'd seen enough of these people to know they were not only ruthless but also, at least some of them, smart. Any wedge, real or invented, they could force between him and the woman in the bathroom upstairs, they would hammer in.

He took the winding stairs two at a time, then almost collided with Betty Joy coming out the bathroom door. "Is she in there?"

"She's bathin'." Betty Joy pulled the door shut.

"Is she in the tub?"

"Yes suh."

"Naked?"

Betty Joy nodded, covering a smile with her hand.

Trapped. He was glad for the short interlude with the girl; it had calmed him somewhat. He watched Betty Joy disappear down the stairs. Inside the bathroom, the water still ran, and he rapped hard on the door. "Olivia, I'm coming in."

"Don't you dare!"

On the other side of the steam-filled room, he saw her jerk forward from where she'd been relaxing against the back of the tub. She floundered, then raised sleek, wet arms and yanked the towel from her head. Her long hair fell over her shoulders and, he suspected, into the water. Below the rim of the tub, where he couldn't see, she struggled with the towel.

"Would you please leave."

He closed the door behind him, his heart thumping from his race up the stairs and more so by the provocative beauty muted by the mist. "I need to ask you something."

"Your question can't wait?"

"Are you decent?"

"Decent?"

"Are you covered up?"

"With a towel, now go away."

Ah, how he relished the indignation in those dark eyes, which grew wider with each step he took. The towel did cover her, but outlined every mound and curve above the water line, and floated freely under it. Her hair, almost the same color as the towel, was indeed in the water and floated underneath and sometimes on top of it. She had splayed a hand over her chest to hold the towel in place. The room was somewhat warmer than the rest of the house, but the steam testified her water was hotter.

Boudreaux sat on the edge of the toilet.

"What do you want that couldn't wait?"

His gaze moved over her, huddled at the back end of the tub. The water was still running, and he reached over to turn it off.

"Do you know anything more about how those men in Galveston died?"

She remained expressionless, but she was no longer focused on her vulnerability. Her mind was working, backtracking, he bet, because his was too. His poor brain had strained since the enticing Lydia Pique had divulged the source of her knowledge. Olivia pursed her lips. "They were murdered."

"How?"

"In a fire."

"That's not murder, that's an accident."

"Not if it's set. You, yourself, told me the fire wasn't an accident."

"That's because I had evidence you conspired to kill Clay."

"Clay's death really was an accident?"

"Clay's not dead."

178

"Someone is," she said.

"Two men, and at least one of those men was murdered."

"He didn't die in the fire?"

His gaze dropped to the water-soaked towel hugging her breasts. "He died before the fire."

"How do you know?" she asked, her eyes wide and her voice so soft he scarcely heard her.

"You really don't know?"

She shook her head.

She was lying, or lost, or both, but he was sure now that she did know more than what she was admitting to him. "All right," he said and rose.

"Are you going to tell me?"

"Will you stand up and drop that towel?"

She blinked at him. "I will not."

He shrugged. "Then I'm not going to tell you."

"Wait."

On impulse, he stooped and wrapped an arm around her wet body. Straightening, he pulled her to her feet and pressed her against him.

His kiss was demanding, but more rough than brutal. Her heart raced beneath her breast, but instinct warned her not to resist him. He was angry, angry at her, and she wasn't sure why. One of the two men who died in that fire had been shot before the fire was set. She knew that. God, she remembered. The first Boudreaux had told her...and she'd told Julian. And now this powerful and, at present, frightening man knew she knew—and he wanted to know how she'd found out. She'd messed up.

He pulled back and studied her face.

"I can feel your heartbeat through the towel, Olivia."

The dripping towel offered more misery than comfort, but she kept it draped against her. It dripped into the tub, and water ran in rivulets down her legs. A shiver racked her body. "Please go," she said softly. For a terrible moment, she thought he wouldn't, then he kissed her forehead, released her, and left.

179

Chapter Twenty-six

"When did she leave?" Olivia asked Betty Joy.

"Right after Doctor Tasker got here. Don't know when she got here, but she was buttonin' up her jacket when I peeked in that big front room. Ain't no tellin' what other of her clothes she had off befo' I looked in."

Olivia whimpered at Betty Joy's unexpected tug on her head, and the young Negress covered her mouth with her hand.

"I'm sorry, Miss Livy, I forgot yo' po' head. Guess I was wishin' I was combin' out Miss Lydia's hair."

"Did Doctor Tasker see her?"

"No ma'am, but her carriage was out front. Don't know if he realized it was hers. Don't think he'd 'ave thought much about her bein' here, anyways, 'less he saw her puttin' her clothes back on like I did.

"Only reason I seen her was 'cause I was plannin' on dustin' that room today. I seen Mister Clay step out of there to let the doctor in the front door. Hope that means the doc and me interrupted things befo' she got too many of her clothes off."

What would it matter? The fact that Boudreaux intended to sleep with Lydia said all that needed to be said.

"Grandma says Miss Lydia killed that old man she married, askin' of his po' ol' body what it weren't able to give. Married him and screwed him to death. Says all she ever wanted was his money, and she got it, too."

No doubt that was true. Lydia would hardly have found the old man sexually attractive. By all accounts, even when young, Pique had not been handsome. He'd lost his first wife to yellow fever during the War and hadn't delved into matrimony again

180

until two years ago, when he'd married Lydia. Lydia's reputation preceded her; but the notoriety didn't concern her then, and it didn't disturb her now. It must not have concerned Louis Pique either. He expired on top of his young wife's naked body (at least, that's how Uncle Lionel pictured the death scene) three months into the marriage, a victim of heart failure. Ollie, her granduncle had told her upon hearing the news, the pervert got exactly what he deserved. I'm just sorry the horny old goat died happy.

Lionel Augustus had rarely been graphic when addressing her, but that particular occasion had conjured up his baser self, that and the fact he'd had more than his usual dosage of Kentucky bourbon that evening. Uncle Lionel hadn't liked Pique. Indeed, he'd considered his seventy-nine-year-old competitor an imbecile with dubious judgment.

Betty Joy looked at Olivia in the mirror, then returned to combing the tangles from the mass of curls. "She's gonna sleep with yo' husband, if she gets a chance."

"And how was my husband when you saw him?"

"Oh, he was all right. Took Doc Tasker right up to see you. Miss Lydia snuck out while they was upstairs, and when he come back down, first thing he asked me about was gittin' him and the doc some breakfast. Never did ask 'bout her. Guess he wanted food more than he wanted Mistress Pique."

Maybe he was being discreet. Olivia's stomach knotted up. Maybe he was done with her, maybe he needed sustenance to renew his vigor after... So many maybes, but she did wish she knew what all the two had discussed while she slept. Certainly that bullet in the dead man.

Betty Joy laid the comb down and picked up the whalebone brush. "You got beautiful hair, soft, like silk. Grandma says she never seen any other white woman with hair the color of you and yo' mama. Too light to be gold, she says, too young to be gray."

"Thank you. And you have your grandmother's complexion. Aunt May has the loveliest skin I've ever seen. You and she will be young forever." Olivia turned on the stool and smiled at the girl. "Now, if we're done complimenting each other, will you find

181

my husband and let me know what he's doing at the moment?"

"He was headin' out to the barn last I saw. Betcha he's goin' off somewheres again. Said I was to bring you breakfast and give you another dose of laud'num 'cause yo' head was hurtin' again after that talk y'all had while you was tryin' to take a bath."

Oh, he did? Well... "My head is hurting a bit. Would you put the medicine in the tea?"

"Sho' will."

Olivia ate hot buttered biscuits and peach preserves in bed. The tea she poured down the bathroom drain.

Chapter Twenty-seven

The door to Uncle Lionel's bedroom hung open. Boudreaux had drawn back the curtains, brightening the room and its heavy furniture; and the clean, pleasant scent of Boudreaux's cologne seasoned the air, so different from the stench of the sick room the past two months. Bright and fresh the room might be. Neat it wasn't.

Stomach aquiver, Olivia limped across the threshold into her contender's domain, its bed unmade and its floor decorated with dirty clothes. Boudreaux's saddlebags lay on the floor next to her uncle's armoire. She doubted this room had ever looked so lived-in before. Of course, Millie and Katie had been around to keep things neat, and Olivia frowned at the off-hand chance that she was failing, at least in this regard, as housekeeper. She shrugged. A good reason, then, for being in here.

She pulled open the door to the huge armoire. Her uncle's clothes hung in front of her, his shoes neatly spaced at the bottom of the chest. To the left, a series of cubbies and drawers held his smaller personal items. Her vision blurred. Everything was as Lionel Augustus left it the day he died.

She blinked the tears away and stilled her trembling lips. The solution, of course, was to close the door to the armoire, which she did, and she sat on the floor next to Boudreaux's saddlebags.

He'd unpacked little. In addition to the telegram that had sent him to Gulfport yesterday, that notorious, implicating letter could be here. Her fingers touched the worn surface of the saddlebag, and the intimacy of this violation eclipsed her anxiety. Not since she'd handed the letter intended for the U.S. marshal to Billy had she felt any kind of power over Boudreaux.

The scent of leather filled her nostrils. Downstairs, he called to Betty Joy and when the back door slammed, her heart skipped a beat. Moments later, she heard the rythmic thump, thump, thump as he hurried up the stairs, and ignoring the nausea swelling her stomach, she unfastened the tie to the first bag, turned it up, and dumped it.

Hardtack, camping gear, a knife. A floorboard on the landing creaked, and with an echoing curse, she opened the second bag and dumped it, too. A slicker and cold weather clothing. An extra pair of socks. She felt deep inside the bag...

"What are you doing?"

Olivia drew in a breath, twisted, and found him watching her from the hall, just outside the room. "Another stupid question you needn't ask. I'm cleaning your room, of course."

"To tag along with one of those jokes you never make?" He entered, and she began stuffing the clothing back into the second bag. He bent on a knee and pulled the one saddlebag from her and started putting his belongings back himself.

So much for that initiative. She stood up with some difficulty; her ankle ached more today than yesterday. He noticed, because he grasped her hand to steady her. "Sit down on the bed," he said and went back to repacking.

"I probably should go," she said, eyeing the book on the table beside the bed.

"You could have cleaned up one mess before you dragged out another."

"I wanted to get into both bags before you caught me. I thought you'd left." She went to the table.

"The letter is not in this house, Olivia."

She sat on the bed and picked up *The Three Musketeers.* "The letter wasn't what I was looking for."

"What then?"

A paper marked his page, and she opened the book to that spot and a Western Union envelope. She laid the open book on the table and removed the missive. "The thing that sent you to Gulfport yesterday," she murmured.

She heard him curse, then move. She had the telegram out of the envelope by the time his hand grabbed her wrist, and she screamed at the same moment she crushed the message in her fingers.

"Give it to me."

"No." She raised her free hand to fend him off. He placed his thumb on her wrist, and when he started prying open her fingers, she elbowed him in the ribs. "Stop it," she cried.

"You're going to tear it."

"You're the one who's going to tear it. I want to read it."

Keeping his hold on her wrist, he flung her back on the unmade bed. She yelped, then kicked out at him, hitting him in the thigh. "Dammit." He rolled on top of her and pressed her into the mattress. His legs now disabled hers, but she held onto that telegram, now a wadded ball of paper in her palm.

"You're hurting me, get up!"

He shifted his weight, and she'd have probably been better off if she'd stayed still, but she was determined to wriggle free and read the telegram. This time, he jerked one fisted hand above her head, then the other, and caught both wrists in one hand. Being crushed and squashed and jerked about wasn't going to be worth it if she lost the darn thing, and she growled when he finally managed to pry the telegram from her clutches. He raised his body off her high enough to stuff the abused piece of paper into his shirt pocket.

"Well, madam," he said, looking at her, captive beneath him, "seems you've gotten yourself into a fine fix."

Heart racing and body aching, she arched against him. "Let me up."

"In the master's boudoir, pillaging his things, violating his secret correspondence, when you already know more than you should."

He appeared scarcely winded, but the struggle had worn her out. Again she forced her body off the mattress in a fruitless effort to push him off her. "Let me up, I said."

Despite what she considered a valiant resistance, he forced

185

her hand-shackled wrists back to the mattress, and the rest of her followed.

"We're supposed to be partners," she said. "Only you're withholding information."

"I'm withholding information, sweetheart?" He rolled off her and released her wrists. He didn't move any farther, though, but lay next to her, on his side, his head propped up on one arm. "Who told you the man who died in Galveston had a bullet in his chest?"

She didn't think her head could hurt any worse, but suddenly it did. "What makes you think I know anything about some bullet in that dead man?"

"Seems it's common knowledge with the Augustus clan, and I'm told you are the source. The worrisome part is, the word got out here before I knew it.

"Did Billy tell you about the footprints?" he continued as if he didn't really expect her to say anything more.

"He said Moon's matched—"

"Did he tell you about the ones for which we have no candidate?" His gaze dropped to her lips, then returned to her eyes. "Cowboy boots, Olivia." He winked when she started to speak. "One size larger than mine. I've already checked."

She sat up and scooted a little farther away from him, and he grinned when he saw her eye the pocket in which he'd stuffed the telegram. "Don't try it. You've risked all the getting physical with me you dare, for the moment."

She studied the challenge in his eyes and hoped hers matched his. "Is that a threat, Mister Boudreaux?"

"Could be."

"Of what? A beating, or rape?"

"Why don't you try one more time to get your lovely little hands on this telegram and find out?"

She moved to the edge of the bed and stood up. Her head was hurting so badly now she was having difficulty seeing straight. "Betty Joy said she caught you with Lydia this morning."

He frowned. "Caught me?"

186

"Oh, I do apologize. I forgot of whom I spoke. Perhaps she rescued you from Lydia or was she too late?"

"Who's trying to draw us off the subject this time?"

"The subject is Lydia. She's the person who put the idea in your head that I knew the dead man in Texas had a bullet in him, is she not?"

"You do know he was shot, Olivia, and you are a damn poor liar."

She thrust out her chin. "You are absolutely correct; that's why I don't, as a rule, lie. I did know the man was shot, and if you are really Deputy Sheriff Clay Boudreaux, why the devil didn't you know before me?"

"You knew before the coroner did."

She rolled her lips together.

"Olivia, you do realize, don't you, that the only way the person who passed you that information could have known before the coroner is if he or she did the shooting, or has been in contact with the shooter?"

Or, and her heart sank, he was the real Deputy Boudreaux and authorities in Galveston actually knew from the moment the body was found. She breathed in. "I've only your say on that."

He compressed his lips. "Who told you?"

"I'm not going to tell you."

"I beg your pardon?"

She folded her arms beneath her breasts. "I'm not going to tell you." She averted her eyes with that, but looked back when he rose. "I am not going to tell you. Not yet."

"Olivia," he said. She backed against the table when he took a tentative step toward her, and he stopped. Her nostrils flared.

"I want to see the telegram," she said.

"Are you going to tell me —"

"No."

"Then I see no —"

"Well, I do. I'm the one who has the most to lose."

He braced with the choked emotion in her voice.

187

"I'm the vulnerable one, here," she continued. "I'm the one who has been abused and knocked in the head"—his mouth fell open—"in my own home. I am the one who doesn't even know who you are."

"I've told you I'm—"

"I have no proof of that. You know who I am, mister." She snatched at the satin sash holding her robe closed, then pushed away from the table, and she laid it between them on the carpet.

"If you cross that line, you can forget about me ever cooperating with you on anything again. I want to know who Ralph Labat was, and I want to know why he led you to Gulfport where you discovered Katie pretending to be me." She looked him in the eye, then nodded to his shirt pocket. "I want to see that telegram."

Chapter Twenty-eight

Deceased Labat, Ralph. STOP. *Registered Lone View 1 Nov.* STOP. *HOR Gulfport, County Harrison, Miss.* STOP. *Long Leaf Inn.* STOP. *Shot 44 Heart* STOP. *Not C.P.* STOP. *You do honors.* STOP. *Where's your brother?* STOP.

"You do honors?"

"Nate Phillips wanted me to notify next of kin here."

Olivia looked up at him. "And you did that?"

"Yesterday." Boudreaux sat down next to her on the bed and pointed to the first line in the message. "Ralph Labat was one of the men whose remains Nate pulled out of my mother's boarding-house. He was shot with a Colt .44. The other man we've always known was a friend of mine"—he pointed to the C. P.—"Charlie Phelps. He wasn't shot."

"How do you know it was a Colt?"

"If it had been anything else, Nate would have said so. This fella Labat had registered at the Lone View Hotel in Galveston back on the first of November. That's how they were able to track him back to Gulfport."

"Who was he?"

"We have his name, Olivia. Turns out he was a partner with his cousin in that boardinghouse we were at yesterday, but he made his primary living as a private investigator."

"And Katie hired him?"

"Pretending to be you."

"To do what?"

He shrugged. "Maybe to get some information to dissuade you from marrying me. I don't know." Oh, good God, he didn't like the way she was frowning.

"You never know. I'm tired of your half truths. Maybe you don't know, not for sure, but you suspect. You don't think Katie hired this man on her own, surely. Tell me what you think he was doing in Galveston."

His gaze held hers. I don't even know who you are, she'd told him. Well, he didn't know who she was either, not in the figurative sense, but if she wasn't a murderess, the answer to this mess had to lie elsewhere.

"I think the man could have been bought as an assassin, and it's only a gut feel, but I think Katie hired him to kill Clay."

"Who do you think Katie was working for when she hired him?"

"I could make a lot of guesses there, to include Aunt Aggie or your Uncle Duncan."

The twitch of her head said no to Duncan.

"Francis," he said.

"Francis and Uncle Duncan work together, as does Julian. I don't believe they'd ever hire an assassin."

She might not believe it, but he still had his doubts. "Can you believe Howard?"

She bit her lip. "Possibly."

Given the suspicions he knew she harbored, he thought she might suggest it had been Troy. She didn't, and he weighed the advantages and disadvantages of Olivia's not learning about that liaison. He couldn't come up with anything definitive.

"Katie knew Troy, Olivia."

Her mouth dropped open. "Katie knew you."

"Not before two mornings ago. She mistook me for Troy, that's how I knew she knew him."

"Why would she, you're not twins."

"And we're not doubles either," he countered. "I had my back to her. Only when I turned around did she realize she was talking to the wrong man."

"Then why didn't you tell me about Katie and Troy the night you told me of her indiscretions with Francis and Howard?"

"Because I didn't trust you."

"And do you now?"

"I'm taking things slow."

He'd purposefully softened his voice, and he watched for her reaction to it. She did respond, with a tender look, then averted her eyes and rose. "Well, I don't trust you either, and it's a pity Katie is..."

"She's what, Olivia? Not around to confirm my story?" He bent, picked up the discarded satin belt to her robe, and stood, holding an opposite end of the smooth fabric in each of his hands. Its middle drooped to his knees. "Her absence is convenient for a number of people, I suspect, but all she could have confirmed in my case is that I am, indeed, not Troy Boudreaux."

She eyed the belt, and he grinned at her.

She watched the satin tie loop over her head, then felt it at her waist. Before her racing heart could pound another beat he'd tugged her against his chest. He sat on the edge of the bed and pulled her into his lap. She didn't resist his tentative hold, but drew a shaky breath. "What game now, Mister Boudreaux?"

"Seduction." He snuggled his face underneath her hair, then kissed her neck, and when his tongue ravished the inside of her ear, she closed her eyes and sucked in a breath. Warmth and wetness teased the space between her legs. "Stop," he said, when she wiggled. "Let me do this, it won't hurt you."

"It will," she breathed out, "if I fall prey to it."

"I won't let you." He kissed her chin, then ran the tip of his tongue down her neck to the base of her throat, and damn her treacherous soul, she tilted her head back to give him easy access. Immediately, she placed her hands on his shoulders and pushed gently, but when she started to speak, his lips found hers and he pushed his tongue inside her mouth. He released her lips, but not her body, and he kissed her jaw line, his mouth again moving relentlessly toward her ear.

191

"Why did he say it like that?" she managed, tilting her head to accommodate his caress.

"Why did who say what like that?" he mumbled against her ear.

Olivia lifted the hand holding the wrinkled telegram, but he was nibbling on her ear, and she was certain he didn't see or care. Part of her didn't care either. Gently she nudged his head with hers. "Your Nate Phillips said 'Where is your brother?' How come he didn't say, 'Where's Troy?'"

"Well, Olivia, I know my brother's name is Troy."

"I don't."

"Yes you do—"

"I do not. For all I know, your brother's name is Clay."

"The telegram wasn't for you. The telegram was for me, and I know Nate is referring to Troy."

"Well, he might have considered I would read it."

"Listen to yourself. You do understand, don't you, that Nate doesn't realize you don't believe I'm Clay?" Inside her robe, his hand found a flannel-covered breast. She startled and returned to herself enough to take his wayward hand and use it to steady herself as she wriggled off his lap.

He leaned after her, but didn't rise, instead holding on to her hand and helping her. Thank sweet Jesus, he didn't try to pull her back, because she'd have let him. "Your wiles are working well this morning," he said.

"And so is your seduction."

Now he tugged on her hand, but she freed herself. "Do you know where your brother is?" she asked.

That sobered him, and he rose, much more steady on his feet, than she was. "No, do you?"

192

Chapter Twenty-nine

"Special delivery for a Deputy Clayton L. Boudreaux."

"I'll take it," Boudreaux said.

The young man clasped the envelope to his chest. "Sorry sir, I need to see some identification."

Olivia had risen when he did at the knock on the front door and limped after him into the foyer. "I'll vouch for him, David."

A smile spread across the face of the tow-headed teenager, and he snatched the cap from his head. "Afternoon, Miss Lee."

Olivia brought herself up to where he stood searching the billfold he'd retrieved from the pocket of his coat, but any effort spent looking for identification would be wasted. This kid was so enamored with Olivia, he could probably pluck the package out of David's hands at this point, and the young man wouldn't even miss it.

"This is Clay Boudreaux, my husband."

David's stupid smile persisted, but he did shift his gaze to Boudreaux and held out a hand as large and gangly as he was. "Howdy, and welcome. We all sure thought you was a lucky man till we heard you was dead." At that point, Boudreaux might as well have disappeared. David turned back to Olivia and handed her the package. "Straight from the New Orleans Police Department," he told her. She took it, but with an "oops," he snatched it back and shoved it into Boudreaux's hands. "Sorry," he said, and placing the cap back on his head, he handed Boudreaux a pencil. "Need you to sign for it, Mister Boudreaux."

This person was dressed in a uniform of sorts, blue pants and a wrinkled white shirt. Boudreaux figured there was a matching jacket somewhere, too, but the warm, fall day precluded the need.

193

"Here you go."

The kid reached for the receipt, then tipped the brim of his cap at Olivia, whom he had scarcely taken his eyes off of, and turned from the door.

"Hey?" Boudreaux was getting so doggone irritated he considered withholding the tip in which David apparently had no interest.

The young man pivoted, focused, blinked, then took the two bits with a bright "thank'ee much."

Back straight, feet grounded, Boudreaux pushed the door, and it shut with a clap. "Good Lord." He turned to Olivia, who was looking at the package he held. "What an idiot."

Olivia batted her lashes. "He likes me."

"Obviously. You'd think he'd be a little more discreet in front of your husband."

"You're dead, remember?"

He shook his head and turned on his heel.

"What's in the package?" she asked.

He looked over his shoulder. "I don't know."

"But you're going to open it?"

"Preferably without an audience." He had his back to her, but her voice told him she was keeping his pace.

"It's about Howard?"

"Probably."

"I—"

He stopped and turned. "Tell you what. I'll look at what's in the envelope, then I'll decide if I'm going to let you see it."

She jutted that pretty chin of hers. "You can't be my partner, then an alleged officer of the law whenever it's convenient."

"First let's see if this is worth the battle we're waging."

"All right," she said, then wailed, "where are you going?" when he again turned his back on her and started across the foyer to Lionel Augustus's office.

"I'll call you."

"Not on your life."

Yeah, it would have been too good to be that simple, but he

did manage to make her sit on the distant settee while he forced aside the memory of Katie Harder and sat in Lionel Augustus's chair, then tore open the envelope.

The New Orleans Police Department had sent two missives, one on standard-size paper, the second much smaller. Boudreaux read the larger document first, then picked up the second, glancing up only once, when she rose from the settee and started his way. He passed her the larger message without looking at her again.

Found this H. Augustus's belongings. Thought it might be of use.

(Harry

Harland Thibodeaux,
Captain of Police
New Orleans Police Department

The letter was typed, but whoever sent the thing signed "Harry" above Harland Thibodeaux's name.

"What did he send?" she asked.

Boudreaux acknowledged her question by leaning back in the chair and waving the "this" found in H. Augustus's belongings. "A telegram."

"And what does it say?"

"Come sit in my lap, and we'll read it together."

She chose to ignore his ridculous condition for reading the telegram and turned instead to the closing on the letter she held. "Do you know this man?"

"Met him the night Howard tried to kill me. We became fast friends. Professional courtesies, you know." He pushed back from the knee hole. "At the time, of course, we didn't know I'd shot Howard. Apparently, the New Orleans police were able to match him up with unclaimed baggage after they recovered Howard's body and identified him." He patted his thigh. "Come on."

There was either nothing of importance in that telegram, or

195

he was creating a ruse to dissuade her looking at it. "This is silly, Mister Boudreaux. Let me see the telegram."

"I've stated my terms."

Olivia heaved in a breath and watched him swivel the chair slightly, keeping his face to hers as she limped around the desk, but when he reached for her, she snatched the missive from his fingertips and backed away with a victory laugh. He smirked, but didn't pursue her. Sure now she was not only safe but also that he intended to let her see the telegram, she focused on the hand-written words filling out the pre-printed form.

Survivor not desired (Handsboro. STOP.

"This is the reason Howard tried to kill you?" she asked.

"I reckon so."

She found his eyes. "I didn't send it."

"I never said you did."

"You're thinking it."

"Actually, I'm not."

"Who do you think sent it, then?"

"I suspect Duncan Augustus."

He was studying her face, his gaze moving between her lips and her eyes. She shook her head.

"You don't think so?"

"No."

He stood suddenly, and she moved back around to the front of the desk.

"What are you going to do?" she asked.

"Are you asking in regards to yourself or to the telegram?"

"The telegram, of course."

"Try to find out who sent the thing."

"Where'd he go?"

Olivia tightened her hold on the locket around her neck and

silently cursed this Boudreaux for his uncanny ability to sneak up on her, and the other one for leaving her vulnerable. "Where do you hide," she asked softly, "to always know when he leaves?"

The other Boudreaux boy stepped into the front room. "Comforting, isn't it, to know I'm always close?"

Olivia swallowed. As comforting as the spectre of Katie Harder's body in Lionel Augusutus's chair. "And why do you risk Betty Joy or Billy seeing you?"

"I know what Betty Joy and Billy are doing right now."

So did she. Betty Joy was gathering eggs, and the tell-tale sound of Billy's ax, chopping wood, had stopped minutes ago. He would be securing the barn for the night while he waited for his sister to finish her work so they could go home. The only way this particular Boudreaux could know what everyone at Epico Hollow was doing at any given time was if he were lurking in the woods along the bayou, watching. Either that or—and Olivia shuddered at the thought—he had a hiding place inside the house.

"Answer me, darlin', where did he go?"

"He received a special-delivery letter from New Orleans this morning. Something in it apparently sent him on this latest journey."

"Do you know what the letter said?"

She studied him a moment, marked her spot, then put her ancient copy of *The Horrors of Oakendale Abbey* on the table next to the settee. "No, he wouldn't let me see it."

"Probably had something to do with Howard's death if it came from New Orleans."

"You know he killed Howard?"

"I do."

"How?" And her mouth dried up as he approached where she sat.

"Newspapers. Talk on the street." He leaned close. "Whispers in the bayou." She pulled back, then rose from where she sat. He straightened, too and shrugged. "You pick."

"Another partner I'm not aware of."

"Maybe."

197

"Seems Howard could as easily have targeted you," she said.

"I was a boat ahead."

"And how could you know that?"

He took a step toward her. She hadn't moved far from the couch. Despite her weakening knees, this time she stayed her ground.

"Very well, Olivia, I was ahead of Troy, that I'm sure of. I beat him here, remember?"

"You thought Troy was dead."

"We've been over this."

"I wondered if your story had changed."

"It hasn't." He gave her a good, long look and nodded to the settee. "Would you like to sit back down. You look pale." Then, eyes locked on hers, he said, "Is there any information on who killed Katie?"

Her heart was pounding in her poor head again, and the darn room was brighter than it should be. It was as if he were reading her mind, then playing on her fears, and she'd give anything for Billy or Betty Joy to come into the house right now. "Your brother thinks someone hired Cecil Moon and he killed her."

"That's the fella killed at your uncle's place two nights ago?"

"Yes."

"And my brother thinks Duncan hired him to kill Katie?"

"To kill me. He thinks it was a case of mistaken identity."

"But you don't think so?"

Her ankle was aching. "I don't think Uncle Duncan hired him."

"But someone did?"

She didn't know the answer and wondered if this man did. Or was he fishing, believing she knew more than she was telling?

"Maybe someone really did want Katie dead." He grabbed her arm with those words, and she squelched a cry. "Sit down," he said. "You're white as a sheet."

Heart in her throat, she did. Afraid to throw off his offending hand, she held fast to the arm of the settee until she no longer felt his touch. He sat beside her, and she sucked in a calming breath before she found the courage to look at him. "Your brother told me Troy knew Katie."

He searched her eyes. "Did he? That must explain your sudden frailty. First you're suspicious about Margo, and now you're thinking I killed Katie, too." He rose, then looked up, appearing to study the intricate carvings on the ceiling. "He could be Troy, you know." He looked at her when she said nothing. "You asked me if I knew her. Aren't you going to ask me if I killed her?"

She pressed her knees together to stop their knocking. "I really don't want to know at the moment."

"Smart answer. Do you trust him any more than you trust me?"

With her life, with her physical well-being, right now? Yes, she did, and she again damned her Boudreaux for not being here.

The other one flexed his jaw when she didn't answer. "Does he trust you, yet?" he asked.

"If he did, I'd be with him now, wouldn't I?"

"That makes you angry, doesn't it? He's gone and you're here alone, entertaining a man you believe is a killer."

"I'm not alone here, and he thinks the killer's dead."

"Defending him. Sweet. Have you slept with him yet?"

Her breath caught. "I don't know that he's my husband."

"And that makes a difference to you?"

Now she felt the long lost color surge back into her cheeks, and she stood and faced him. "How dare you claim to be Clay and say such a thing to me."

He snagged her wrist and yanked her to him. "I don't underestimate the power of sex, honey, nor do I doubt a beautiful woman's willingness to use it to obtain her ends. Then again, maybe I just wanted to know." He dipped his head to kiss her, but she twisted her body, offering him a cheek instead.

"Not even a kiss for your husband?"

"I don't know that you're my husband any more than he is."

"Then am I to believe you haven't kissed him yet either?"

She yanked her wrist free and glared at him.

"Does he know I'm around?"

"He's beginning to suspect something."

"He's supposed to think I'm dead, unless you told him otherwise."

He'd brought his face closer to hers than she liked, but there was no way she was going to back down, not this time. This man did not like her. Worse, he had no respect for her; he'd made that clear when he'd dared to ask if she'd slept with his brother, as if that act were nothing. If this man were Clay, how could she possibly ever be a wife to him?

But it didn't mean he wasn't Clay, didn't mean Troy wasn't a threat to him. Shoot, maybe he deserved to have Troy as a threat. Her heart beat faster, but despite her wishful thinking, how did she know that other man wasn't a threat to her, too? God, how did she know he wasn't outside this house right now, waiting, knowing this man was in here, toying with her.

"Well?"

She lifted her chin and looked him in the eye. "I've told him nothing. If he suspects you're alive, blame the Galveston County sheriff." She heard the back door open, then slam. "That should be Betty Joy. It's time for you to go."

He didn't rush, but studied her, his look unreadable. "I've angered you?"

"Angered me? As a man, as a husband, you disgust me."

He twisted a corner of his mouth. "My asking about sleeping with my brother is what's got you riled, isn't it?"

"Get out."

His smirk blossomed into a grin. "With all that's happened, I didn't peg you for a virgin."

"Virginity has nothing to do with it. Virtue does. What I am, is a married woman."

"You know, Olivia, you might turn out to be all right after all."

"I doubt that you will, though. Use the front door."

Chapter Thirty

"Still hurting?"

Olivia opened her eyes. She'd heard him come in the back. She'd been resting, nursing her aching head, and listening for him, praying all the while the other one didn't come back. Seeing him now, dressed in his cowboy boots and jeans, his stetson in his hands, he was the most handsome man she'd ever seen in her life, and she pushed aside her anger and her doubts at his having left her behind.

A smile spread across his face, and she wondered what look she must have on hers.

"Pleased with the present specimen, ma'am?"

With a not unpleasant shiver, fueled by the fever heating her cheeks, she snapped her book shut.

"It's a pity, Mister Boudreaux, you are not as pleasant to talk to as you are to look at."

"Obviously your headache hasn't stunted your venom."

She laid the book in her lap aside. "You should know that headaches increase venom."

"I'll try to stay clear then." He turned from the doorway and started across the foyer. She grasped the arm of the chair and, not thinking, flung herself toward the door, then limped after him to the kitchen, the price of forgetting her ankle.

"Where are you going?"

"Back out to rub down Pompeii. I sent Billy and Betty Joy home. Looks like rain. I came in to make sure you were all right."

"I appreciate your concern."

If he noted her sarcasm, he didn't let on. She did hope Billy and Betty Joy beat the rain home. She felt bad about that, but she

201

hadn't wanted to be alone here at Epico Hollow, not with that other Boudreaux person materializing at will.

"Wait," she cried when he reached the back door, "I need to get some sugar."

He went on out anyway, while she pulled the work jacket from its peg, then watched him cross the yard in the direction of the barn. She didn't follow until she'd filled the jacket pockets with sugar cubes, and she caught up with him at the yawning entrance to the ancient frame structure.

"What did you find out?"

He didn't look at her, but pushed the second panel of the barn door wide. "About what?"

She threw her shoulder into the door, stopping it. He looked at her then. "About who sent the telegram."

"I need light in here, would you move?" He added a please when she didn't, so she did.

"You know, Olivia, a man should be able to find sanctuary in his barn...by himself."

"I wasn't aware you were in need of sanctuary." She gave her head a little shake. "I was sure you found my company as pleasant as I found yours."

He glanced at her. "I do—like looking at you, I mean." He hooked the barn door to keep it from swinging shut. "And you shouldn't be on that ankle."

"I've been off it most of the day."

"You should still be off it."

"But I'm suffering to be with you."

He snorted and stepped around her. "A little colored boy, about eight, sent the telegram. Gave the operator a gold eagle and was savvy enough to tell the clerk how much change he expected back, which was most of it. I assume, from the telegraph operator's account of the story, the boy was told he could keep the change."

"Did the clerk know the boy?"

Boudreaux unknotted Pompeii's cinch and, with a grunt, removed the horse's saddle. Olivia stepped back, out of the way.

"He'd seen him around, but doesn't know his name or where exactly he lives."

"So someone hired this boy to go in and send the telegram."

Boudreaux settled the saddle on the top rail of an empty stall. "I assume so, Olivia, unless a little eight-year-old colored boy masterminded murder out in Texas. Hand me that brush back there, would you?"

She stepped in muck, then stretched to snag the horse brush hanging from a rusty nail in an ancient two-by-four.

"Are we going to try and find the boy?"

"We, Olivia?"

"Yes," she hissed, "we. I have no idea if you're telling me the truth. For all I know, you went and had tea with the person who sent that telegram."

"We'd be tossing shots"—he laughed suddenly and looked at her. "What's that called?"

She frowned at him.

"That play on words I just made?"

She thought back on what he'd said. "A pun, you mean?"

"Yeah." He grinned and turned back to the horse. "A pun."

Olivia drew herself up close to him and punched him in the arm. "You've gotten off the subject...again."

He stopped the brushing, straightened, and turned to her. "Was there more to be said? No, I'm not going to try and find the boy. I doubt he could tell us who sent the telegram anyway."

"Then what's next?"

"We need to get Pompeii into his stall and feed him. Where's Toby?"

"That's not what I meant, and you know it. Toby's in the corral."

He nodded to the gate of Pompeii's stall, and she limped over and pulled it open.

Boudreaux straightened from where he filled a tin can with oats, then tensed watching Pompeii nuzzle Olivia's hand. She was feeding him sugar again, but the horse was mean and stupid and would not hesitate to bite the hand that fed him. He should geld the big stud, but the beast was a magnificent piece of horse-flesh, and he wanted to breed the animal to a fine brood mare. He looked at Olivia. Or a filly. One with good temperament.

Olivia reached into the pocket of the ragged jacket and pulled out more sugar. "Ah, you are a sweet boy, Pompeii. Here." From where she was standing on the bottom rail of the stall, she could see over the top one. Her hair was down, pulled back with a rib-bon loosely knotted at the nape of her neck. Curly tendrils had pulled out, framing her face, and the effect made her look even younger, vulnerable...more feminine. He figured she wore it that way today because of the cut on her head and the headache she couldn't get rid of.

She reached, playfully arranging the mane between Pompeii's ears, which suddenly flattened. Boudreaux dropped the oat-filled can and sprang for Olivia. The horse nipped the underside of her arm above the elbow. She jumped from the stall and stumbled.

Boudreaux charged past her and onto the rail, from where he smacked Pompeii in the nose with the heel of his hand, and the horse shied back and bared his teeth.

"I need to take you out behind the woodshed," Boudreaux said and turned on Olivia. "I need to take you out there, too," he said, thankful it was her underarm and not her face. "You know the horse is mean. He's not your stupid cat."

"I don't feed sugar to my cat," she spat, rubbing at her arm beneath the jacket sleeve. "But I do feed it to Toby, who is also not a pet." She blinked back the tears and looked away.

His fear and anger subsided. The bite had hurt, and he fought her for, and won, the injured arm, which he caressed in the same area she'd been rubbing. The jacket had done a lot to protect her. There was probably no blood, but for sure there'd be a nasty bruise.

"It's okay," she said and managed to extricate her arm. "I've been bitten before."

"By Toby?"

"Chester."

She turned away with his smile, and it occurred to him that her feelings were hurt more than anything. "Ah, it seems you have a weakness for mean, dumb beasts, Olivia."

"And what would you expect," she snapped. "I'm surrounded by them, but that particular one will get no more sugar from me."

"I won't act that way if you're ready to risk giving me some sugar."

She raised her eyes to his and reached into her coat pocket. Then extending her hand to him, she said, "Here."

He took the sugar cubes, but before she could pull her hand away, he grasped her wrist and pulled her into his arms. "I had something sweeter in mind."

She didn't try to pull away, and he saw her eyes glance to his lips, then back to meet his gaze. With that offer, he bent his head and kissed her lips. Heat warmed his blood, which filled his manhood, and he resisted the urge to grind his erection against her pelvis.

Carefully, he pulled her closer, but when he maneuvered his right hand over the left cheek of her derriere, she pushed at him, and he let her go. She bowed her head, and he thought she was going to ask him something. The moment passed, and he moved around her. A gust of wind tore through the open doors of the barn, creating a wind tunnel that cooled his skin and billowed her skirts.

"Rain's comin'. We need to get Toby in."

"It's going to get cold again?"

"'Fraid so."

Outside, the cloud-shrouded sun was already sinking behind the bayou forest to the west. Thirty yards in front of him flowed the choppy waters of Epico Bayou. Here, on this side of the stream, the bank was cleared to the water's edge, but on the south side, tangled woods, thick with giant cypress, encroached on the normally lazy stream.

"Your father was a strict man, Mister Boudreaux?"

He turned, almost bumping her.

"Edwin Boudreaux, you mean?" She nodded, and he said,

"Nah, Mama was the real disciplinarian. Daddy moved out to his ranch when I was ten, Troy was eleven."

"What happened to Elaine and Edwin's love to bring them to that? Do you know?"

"You mean in addition to her giving birth to another man's child?"

"Yes, well, I thought they'd dealt with that."

"And they had. Their relationship wasn't so bad really. Their need for space between them built up over a lot of years. The catalyst, of course, was the War. Elaine McHugh Gibson and Darcy Clayton Lee grew up on farms in Marion County. Their families were neighbors and the two were life-long friends. I think there was even a hint of young romance, but the Boudreauxs moved into their little enclave in the early fifties, and by all accounts I've heard, Mama was smitten immediately. She considered Edwin Boudreaux a handsome, black-eyed devil. Granddaddy said they were a family of pirates, but they all got along real well. Edwin and Darcy became best friends. The sons and the fathers and uncles and cousins all went to war together. Darcy stood up for Edwin at his and Mama's wedding in December of '62. A little over a year later Edwin suffered a minié ball to the groin. Almost killed him, and it did threaten his virility."

Olivia knew Edwin Boudreaux had been seriously wounded in the War, but hadn't known the details of his injury.

"Then, two weeks after Troy was born," Boudreaux continued, "he nearly died of mumps. Left him impotent.

"Daddy's folks and eventually Mama's lost the land after the War. Your father, of course, managed to hold on to his, but he had help in the form of his stepuncle, who, as it turned out, loved him dearly and decided to make Mississippi home. That's how my mama and Lionel met, through Darcy. Lionel was married, but he wasn't happy."

"Oh, I know," Olivia said. "Sonja was her name, and from what Aunt Connie and Aunt Aggie have intimated over the years, she was quite a shrew."

"Suffice it to say shrew is a kind word compared to those my granddaddy used to describe her."

"Oh?"

"I'm not repeating 'em. Anyway, Mama was in a marriage with a man who was no longer capable of having relations with her. Edwin Boudreaux left a suicide note and disappeared for three months. Everyone thought he was dead. But despite all that, and what happened between Lionel and her, Mama and Edwin had a pretty good relationship. Troy was his, but he was just as good to me. It was his infirmity that caused him bitterness.

"As the years passed, Mama tired of dealing with his melancholy, and when he finally moved out to his ranch, they were content living apart. Us kids moved back and forth between them at will except during school months. Then, we were mostly with her in Galveston."

"Both of you?"

"Troy didn't move out to the ranch permanent till after he got out of school. Mama and Daddy both wanted us to finish high school. Mama was the second generation of her people to be born in the Piney Woods. They came to Spanish Louisiana from South Carolina in 1794. Edwin Boudreaux's people had been in the Piney Woods probably fifty years or more before that. Mama came from educated stock, so did Darcy Lee. Your granddaddy Lee might not have come to Mississippi until the 1830s, but your grandma Lucy's people had been here at least as long as Edwin Boudreaux's. When the Boudreauxs settled among the Lees and Gibsons on the Pearl River, Edwin and Darcy learned their letters alongside my mama in Hugh Gibson's cookhouse."

"I knew they'd all grown up together. I didn't know they'd learned to read and write together."

"Well, they did. They were all very close."

She and Boudreaux had stopped during their talk, and now Toby came to them, ignoring Boudreaux's scratching once he smelled the sugar in his jacket pocket. The horse almost knocked him over before he managed to get the cubes in his hand.

"Here, I've got some more," she said and pushed Boudreaux

out of the way. "It's hard to believe you and Troy were at odds, raised the way you were."

"We weren't at odds."

"What about the boardinghouse and the girl, Margo?"

"We weren't in competition for either one. Lionel finished paying off that boardinghouse after my granddaddy died. That insured Mama and I had a home. It was always understood I would get it. Edwin Boudreaux had the ranch. He wanted Troy to have it. My job kept me in Galveston, and Troy made a good rancher."

"I was led to believe you didn't like each other."

"Did you consider who was leading you?"

Certainly Julian Augustus had, but any skepticism she harbored about the love lost between the Boudreaux boys had been swept away by this man's brother, whichever one he was.

"If you two got along as well as you imply, why didn't Troy bring 'my' letter to you immediately?"

He glanced down at her. "I have the letter, don't I?"

"Because Troy gave it to you or because you were the intended recipient?"

"I'm Clay."

"All right, did Troy give you the letter?"

Her stomach clenched with the realization he was weighing his answer, and she desperately needed to know why he felt he had to.

"I found it in Troy's things," he said finally.

For the first time this afternoon, her heart throbbed harder than her hateful head. "So he didn't bring it to you?"

He looked away, disquiet in his eyes. "I thought he died in the fire. I don't know where he is right now, so I can't very well ask him, can I?"

"Did he need money?"

"Need money or want money?"

She blinked at him.

His smile was decidedly unpleasant, and he shook his head. "I'm not Troy trying to kill Clay."

"Then could he be trying—"

"Because of your offer?" he snapped.

She compressed her lips.

"Not even if you did make such an offer." He reached over her shoulder and grabbed Toby's harness. "And we need to change the subject."

The trees shivered in the breath of wind that coursed across the narrow pasture and slapped Boudreaux's chilled cheeks. Sweet Jesus, where the hell did Olivia think she was going with this conversation?

She overlapped the front of her old jacket and held it closed. The temperature was dropping. He looked back around, over her head, to the looming darkness of the woods across the bayou, then pulled on Toby's harness. The big horse plodded along behind him. "Sky's looking bad."

Olivia fell into an awkward gait at his side. An occasional ray of sunlight managed to fight its way through the gathering clouds and highlight her silvery tresses. She looked tired, and her limp underscored her frailty.

"Uncle Lionel had a wonderful old gelding named Josiah," she said.

The cold air added color to her cheeks, and with her sudden, unspoken acquiescence to change their conversation, a softness entered her voice.

"He died four months ago. Uncle Lionel was beginning to feel so poorly by that time he didn't replace him."

"You don't ride?"

"I prefer a carriage. I broke my arm from a fall"—he smirked and her eyes narrowed—"when I was nine. Uncle Lionel considered horses treacherous and riding side-saddle increased the hazard, but he seemed determined that I should be ladylike, and may I ask what you find funny about my broken arm?"

"And broken bannister rails and broken heads and sprained ankles. Your granduncle realized a long time ago that you were accident prone. He wouldn't let you ride, would he?"

"I wasn't accident prone between the age of nine and your

showing up here, and he would have, if I'd persisted. He spoiled me terribly. But riding was not an important matter to me. He sent me to that finishing school in Madison County, near where Mama was raised. That's what I really wanted."

She rubbed her temples. Her head was hurting again. Gently reared or not, she was tough...and smart. Not just book smart, but smart about life around her.

"Did they teach you business there?"

He grinned when she looked at him, because he knew damn well they hadn't.

"They taught me to be a lady. What I needed to know about our business I learned from Uncle Lionel."

"Well, unfortunately, he didn't teach me much about our business."

"You, or Clay, should have come back sooner."

Or not come at all. He flexed his jaw. But no matter what, he had a history here. "My granddaddy Gibson called his farm in Marion County The Shadows. It was a small place, based on wild cattle and lots of pine trees."

"I've been there." She looked at him. "Have you?"

"No."

"Uncle Lionel took me to Daddy's and your people's places lots of times. You and I still own my daddy's place." She waved at the magnificent house a short distance to their right. "Epico Hollow was Matthew Lee's summer home before the War. His first lumber mill is part of the estate. The business office is in Handsboro just —"

"East of the ferry landing on the bayou. Katie pointed it out to me. I went there yesterday. That's probably why you overtook me in Gulfport."

"Indeed." She studied him a moment, then said, "My mama's family home was called Tupelo Gum. It was plundered and burned in the summer of '63. Uncle Lionel never took me there. I found it on my own."

"It was a large cotton plantation, Olivia. Lionel's business was timber."

"There was more to it than that. It was as if he didn't want to associate with anything that was part of her."

Boudreaux didn't say anything, and he heard her draw in a deep breath, all the while maintaining a stoic visage.

"The columns and two of the exterior walls still stand," she said. "On a full moon when you stand in the pecan orchard and look toward the corner where the walls are standing, it looks like it's never been touched, the way it must have looked when my great-grandfather built it."

"And how in the world would you know that?"

She gave him a sheepish smile, and he felt better for her. "I went out there when I was in school."

"At night?"

"I loved it best at night. I had a friend who would sneak out with me."

He started to ask if the friend were male, but thought better of it. It was a girl's school, after all.

"The site was disconcerting, I admit, but calming, too. An owl was there one night, hooting, and I believe to this day my grieving granddaddy knew I was there and was calling out to me."

The hair rose on the back of Boudreaux's neck. Again he looked over the top of her head to the darkening bayou. "He died at?"

This time, she followed his gaze. "Raymond."

"You should have called to him that night."

"I considered that," she said, moving forward again when he did, "but I'd have had to been out there alone."

"Don't think your friend would have liked your conjuring up ghosts?"

"It needed to be a private thing is all. Like when one talks to a grave."

He understood that. "Who owns it now?"

"I don't know. It doesn't matter anymore."

It must matter. Why else would a teenage girl risk expulsion, and no telling what sort of danger, by sneaking off to a deserted plantation ruin in the middle of the night? She knew more of past

211

events than she would admit, and he wondered once again how much of her mother resided in Darcy Lee's daughter.

"Some things are worth holding to, Olivia, and some are best left go. Then there are the others—the ones that we don't really want to change no matter how much we should. Those always look best in the moonlight."

"A philosopher, Mister Boudreaux?"

"A poet," he said softly. Then added, "She was more than Darcy Lee's wife, Olivia. She was his wife, too."

Olivia averted her eyes. "I can never remember even trying to imagine them in the moonlight."

"It's not too late."

"It is." And she laughed. "The columns of Tupelo Gum are there. Once upon a time the place was real. Even today, there truly is something to see in the moonlight. With Mama and Uncle Lionel the night is moonless. It's even worse with Mama and my real daddy. I know everything about him and my granddaddy Matthew. Where they came from, how they got here. Their land, their loves, and their dreams. Most of what I know about Mama comes from a few surviving letters and my grandmother's Bible. But about Mama and Daddy, as man and wife, there's nothing."

"There's you."

Olivia dismissed his words with a shrug, but he sensed she felt the old slight. One, he suspected, she didn't fully understand.

"Timber and timber stores," she said. "Darcy Lee had the know-how, and Uncle Lionel had the capital."

"And the business knowledge, not to mention the political connections."

"You know something, don't you?"

She was fishing, and his gut burned. "I know lots of things."

"About him and her?"

Inwardly, he cursed. She'd been leading up to this question all along.

"Your father—"

"Not about her and Daddy. About her and Uncle Lionel. He didn't like her. Do you know why?"

212

Olivia was right about that. Lionel had not liked Rebecca Lee, that much he did know. "I don't know what was between them."

"Tell me what you do know."

His stomach was knotting up. Sweet Jesus, he didn't know enough to tell her doo-diddly-squat, and anything he did say, honestly, would cause her more harm than good. "I think it had more to do with her relationship with your father than with him."

She caught his hand. "Did Mama and Daddy not get along? Is that what it was? And Daddy died an unhappy man, and Uncle Lionel never forgave her?"

Lord, she was grasping, and he had no desire to provide answers, even if he could. "You should have asked your Uncle Lionel those questions."

She held his gaze. "I did. He said I was worried over nothing."

"Then you're probably worried over nothing." He broke eye contact and turned toward the water.

"What do you keep looking at?" she asked.

"My sixth sense is telling me..." Somewhere in the heavens the thickening clouds parted, and sunlight sparkled off the dark, rippling surface of the bayou.

"Telling you what?" she said and looked at the woods.

Light flashed. Boudreaux lunged for Olivia and heard her grunt at the same time she, and his shoulder, plowed into the ground. Toby's scream and the simultaneous crack that ripped the air apart absorbed the pain piercing his shoulder.

Toby lurched into the fence, then stumbled. "Get up," Boudreaux hollered at Olivia. A second shot churned up the dirt eight feet the other side of where she lay, then he had his arm around her waist and was half-dragging her into the barn. He shoved her toward the stalls. Pompeii shied and backed into the barn wall. Boudreaux grabbed the rifle he had propped against the door frame, yelled at a wide-eyed Olivia to get out of sight of the damn barn door, then turned toward the abandoned horse still outside, head bowed, but standing, supported by the corral

213

fence. Toby held his right hoof off the ground and pawed the air. He'd taken that first bullet.

At the side of the barn door, Boudreaux raised the rifle, then braced and exposed himself, pumping .44s from his Winchester in the direction of that instant of light. Pompeii whirled aimlessly in his stall; Toby didn't even flinch.

The air stilled. Clouds had closed the heavens. There was no movement across the bayou, and he figured the shooter was gone, high-tailed it when the shots missed. He looked at the wounded horse, then back at Olivia, watching him and waiting, her arms wrapped round her torso.

Boudreaux leaned back against the wall of the barn, pulled cartridges from the pocket of his jacket, and reloaded the rifle.

"Toby's hurt," she said.

"Shot."

She made a funny sound, then stepped toward the door.

"Dammit, Olivia, keep away."

She turned back, still hugging herself. "You're going to shoot him?"

God, she sounded like she was going to cry. "Not if I don't have to."

He stood and faced her. She was white as a sheet, and he wondered how he looked to her. Suddenly her eyes filled with tears, and she bowed her head. With equal quickness, he pulled her into his arms and held her, telling her everything was all right, the shooter was gone. She cried harder, so he squeezed tighter, and finally she wrapped her arms around his waist, and her shaking stopped.

"It's not necessarily something I want you to do, sweetheart, but do you think, for Toby's sake, you could let me go?"

She felt foolish, but when she pushed herself away from him, he held on to her long enough to give her a gentle kiss. She drew in a stuttered breath, and he handed her a bright red kerchief. "Let me see about Toby. If I can get him into the barn, we'll close the doors, and we won't need to worry about the shooter."

And what of tomorrow and the next day? For a moment, Olivia stared at the soft, dark dirt inside the barn and breathed in the mixed scent of manure, hay, and pungent alfalfa. Queasy, she sat hard on the moist ground, then leaned forward, head bowed and, supporting herself with her arms, fought back the nausea.

In the waning light beyond the barn, Boudreaux coaxed the struggling horse forward, and she went to them and grasped the halter on Toby's good side. The going was slow, but they got the big horse inside the barn. He went down before they could get him in a stall, but Boudreaux said it didn't matter. He closed the doors, lit a lantern, then removed the bullet in the horse's shoulder, Olivia doing her best all the while to hold the beast and keep his head immobile. Her own aching head took a couple wallops for her effort, and sometime between the time they started and the time they finished, thunder and lightning rolled in on the wind. Rain followed and now roared over them like a freight train.

"The bullet didn't break any bones. He'll probably be all right if he'll get back up."

"Do you think we can coax him?" She moved out from under the big head and forced her stiff body up. Boudreaux, who'd worked awkwardly on one knee, rose with her.

"Nah," he said, "we'll leave him for the night. He'll get up on his own if he's going to. He won't like being down too long." A raindrop hit his head, and when he looked to the rafters, she saw a second hit his cheek. "This couldn't have waited until we got inside, could it?"

"Oh God," she said, "do we want to risk going inside the house?"

Chapter Thirty-one

"You kept looking back, across the bayou; I saw you."

Boudreaux moved into the front room after Olivia. "I told you I had a feeling. Maybe my brain saw something my eyes didn't. I don't know."

"A feeling? Your brain saw something your eyes didn't?"

"I can't explain a sixth sense to you, Olivia. Sit down," he said, nodding to the settee, "and take this." He held out a brandy cordial to her, and with a shiver, as much from fear as from being cold and wet, she yanked a knit throw off the back of the brocade couch and laid it over the seat. Her skirt wasn't as wet as she feared it was dirty from the floor of the barn.

"If I were trying to have you killed," he said, "why did I push you out of the way?"

"Me? What makes you think he wasn't trying to shoot you?"

He stared down on her. "Who's he?"

She felt the color drain from her cheeks. "The shooter."

"And who do you think that was?"

"Somebody who wants you dead."

"You sure seem a lot more rational at the moment than you were a minute ago."

She shot to her feet. "I'm upset about the horse."

"Bullshit, I swear to God, if you're working with somebody you don't trust, you better tell me now."

Fear, anger, doubt, then resolve. The emotions moved across her face like clouds crossing the sky on a windy day. She set the empty little glass on the commode. "It could have been any number of people and either one of us could have been the target."

216

He stepped away from her and picked up the whiskey bottle. "Yeah, and maybe somebody had it in for poor old Toby."

"Do you think it was a bad shot?"

Her voice was calm, and he lowered the bottle, after taking a swig, and looked at her.

"Do you really think someone was shooting at the horse? No," he added, "whether one of us was the target, or if the person was just trying to frighten us, it was definitely a bad shot."

"Maybe someone is trying to put us at odds."

"The only way that would work, Olivia, is if that someone knows we doubt each other. The only person I voice my distrust to is you. Of course, there's your letter to the U.S. marshal. Have you said anything to anybody since Katie's death?"

She shook her head.

"Julian?"

She looked at him. "Lydia?" she countered.

"No."

"Are you sure there's no one else, outside my family I mean, who might find it useful to foment discord between us?"

He furrowed his brow, alert to the possibility she might be aware of his visits to Sandifer Hudgins at the Gulf View Hotel. "No," he said, realizing he'd again thrown her trust away if she were aware of the man's presence.

He couldn't read her face, but she nodded, then started for the door. "I'm going to get a bath and go to bed."

Inwardly he cursed. "There's collards and peas left over from dinner," he hollered after her.

"I'm not hungry," she called from the foyer.

Boudreaux took another swig of whiskey, sucked in a breath, and crammed the cork into the mouth of the amber bottle. He wasn't hungry either. They'd checked the cellar and every nook and cranny downstairs. He still needed to check upstairs, where she'd run off to. He turned the interior bolt on the front door, then started across the foyer. Tomorrow he was going to get Billy to help him find a good watch dog.

"Did you check under your bed?" he asked when he peeked

217

in her open bedroom door. She closed the third drawer to her highboy and turned his way. In her arms, she held clean clothes.

"Trying to frighten me?"

"You're already plenty scared. So am I."

She placed her clean clothes on the bed, then knelt down and raised the bed skirt. "I doubt I could find anything under here I should be more afraid of than you."

"And should be says it all, doesn't it, sweetheart? Should be, but aren't."

"Nothing here," she said and rose. "And so you'll know, I still think there's something you're not telling me."

"I could say the same."

"Fine." She tried to push past him, but he blocked her exit.

"I haven't checked the bathroom," he said.

"There's nowhere to hide in the bathroom."

"I'm not trying to kill you, Olivia, and I'm not trying to make you think someone is trying to kill either you or me, but someone really is trying to do exactly that. I know the names of the likely candidates. Do you know of someone I might should add to my list?"

"Why does it have to be me withholding information? You know things I don't. You ride off in the middle of the day without telling me where you're going."

"Those trips are all leads sent to me in those telegrams from Galveston."

"Which I don't see."

"You've seen the important one."

Arms folded over the clean clothes she pressed to her breast, she pushed at him. He stood firm. "Now what about you?" he said. "Do you know something I don't?"

"About what? Your accomplice"—she squinted—"my accomplice. *Our* accomplice."

"Who is?"

"You tell me."

"I can't."

"Of course you can!" Without warning, she threw her clean

218

clothes at his feet and limped back to the small bureau beside her bed, from the top drawer of which she yanked out the ragged letter from Clay Boudreaux. "He's the man who wrote this letter."

His mouth went dry. "I wrote that letter."

She screwed up her pretty face, crushed the letter in fingers-turned-talons, and moving toward him with rushed, ragged steps, threw the paper ball into his chest. "No, you didn't," she snarled. "You couldn't have." She bent and started snatching up her clothes. Done, she rose on tiptoe and pressed her body against his, her face as close to his as her petite body could manage. "Because the man who wrote that letter does not exist."

He stiffened, shocked still. "What is that supposed to mean?"

"It means that if I knew for sure you were the man who wrote that letter, I wouldn't have any more decisions to make."

She stepped into the hall and stalked away, and he rolled his eyes to the ceiling. "Well, thanks a lot, Mistress Boudreaux, for clarifying your mumbo-jumbo bullshit for me."

The bathroom door slammed, echoing through the house.

Chapter Thirty-two

"Depends on how good a shot you are," Boudreaux said.

"If I had intended any shot for you," Duncan Augustus responded, "you'd be dead, and I wouldn't be enduring this meeting out here in the hellish cold with a man I hate. The same holds true for Olivia, but I've already told you, I'd never hurt her, and despite your attempts to poison her against me, she knows that."

"I'm glad you brought up the subject of poison, Uncle, because it's my understanding you requested the autopsy of Lionel Augustus's body."

The man's green eyes held steady.

"Why?" Boudreaux asked.

Duncan turned on his heel.

"Someone was trying to poison Lionel and frame Olivia for murder," Boudreaux called after him.

The man kept walking. "You're not nearly as smart as you think you are," he said.

Boudreaux started after him. "What was Katie doing in my house the other night?"

Duncan caught his horse's reins.

"And now the shot last night."

Boudreaux stopped pursuit when Duncan suddenly turned on him. "I sent Katie to Epico Hollow that night to retrieve the letter Olivia allegedly wrote recruiting Troy to kill Clay. I figured if I could get my hands on it, I'd free her from your extortion."

Boudreaux's heart was pounding so hard he almost choked. "You were behind—"

"The only reason I knew about the damn letter was because

Olivia accused Julian of being party to its drafting. Knowing the situation as I do, I immediately confronted Katie. You may have gathered in the short time you knew her that she lacked reputable character. She confessed she wrote it."

"Did she tell you why she wrote it?"

"She did not."

"Did you ask?"

"I didn't have to."

"Would you tell me the answer?"

"I would not."

Boudreaux drew in a breath. "Who else knew she was at my house that night?"

"Only Francis."

Boudreaux studied the man, who studied him right back. Finally Duncan said, "He is not the answer."

"Olivia was the target then. Someone hired Moon to kill her, and he thought he had."

Duncan reached for the pommel of his saddle. Giddy at the thought he'd actually learned something, and frightened that the man would leave without him learning more, Boudreaux took two more strides his way. "He came to your house for his pay."

"Not to me he didn't." Duncan swung into the saddle. "From where I was standing, looking down the barrel of a gun, it was a break-in."

"You requested the autopsy..." Boudreaux cocked his head, and when he did, revelation, deep and dark, crossed Duncan Augustus's face, then fled, but with its passing, realization washed over Boudreaux. "Hell, you weren't trying to frame Olivia. Lionel was already a dead man. He wasn't the intended recipient of the tainted food, Olivia was." Boudreaux let loose a little laugh, then stepped out of the way of Duncan's prancing black gelding. "You were making sure she hadn't been ingesting poison. Who is doing this, Uncle?"

Duncan reined the animal full around to face him once again.

"I found the arsenic in the kitchen pantry two days before Lionel died. Its use in my house is not unprecedented, but the

221

stuff is usually stored in the barn. I was suspicious, is all. It's a moot point. The autopsy showed no poison in Lionel's body, and Olivia doesn't seem to be suffering any ill effects."

"Because she threw the food out."

"And I'll wager that's because Lionel told her to."

"It doesn't mean the attempt wasn't made."

"No, it doesn't, but nothing can be proved at this point."

"You suspect someone."

Duncan leaned low in the saddle. "No one I intend to discuss with you. For all I know, Mabel was trying to poison Aggie. My sister has wreaked havoc with Connie since I felt compelled to move her in, and Mabel has spent her life protecting Connie. And as for those shots fired yesterday, it's as likely you were the target as Olivia."

"Which brings me back to you, Francis, and Julian."

"Only if you're Clay Boudreaux. Anyone else—"

"Agatha?"

Duncan sighed. "...would have to kill Olivia and Clay both. Since Lionel's siblings are next in order to inherit, you've limited your suspects to me and mine. But, tell me, as of yesterday afternoon, who here knew for sure you were Clay?"

"Aunt Connie knows who I am."

"Yes she does." Duncan straightened in the saddle and looked down on him. "But let's assume the bullet was meant for Olivia."

"All right."

"From where I'm lookin', the person who has the most to gain from Olivia's death is Clay himself."

"I was with her."

"You were; however, there are such people as accomplices."

"I seen 'im over there. Took the skiff. What's he lookin' fo'?" Auntie May asked.

Olivia laid an arm around the shoulder of the stout Negress, then strained to look out the kitchen window. "Someone shot at us late yesterday afternoon. He's probably looking for something that will tell him who it was."

Auntie May turned from the window, where she was drying the breakfast dishes, and Olivia dropped her arm. "Shot at you?"

"It might have been at him."

A frown on her face and a towel in her hand, Auntie May stared at Olivia. "Is that how Toby got shot?"

"I'm afraid so."

"Lawdy be. Got all kinda worthless folk using rifles, whips, and ropes these days." The woman picked up another dish and started wiping. "Used to be people learned how to shoot, and who to kill. Shoot at a person and hit a poor dumb animal. Shouldn't be usin' no gun if they don't know how to shoot."

Olivia wished she'd never brought the shooting up. Everything about it seemed odd, but perhaps that was due more to her own doubts about the motive. Two people, who any number of people might want shot, but the horse was the one hit.

"You think yo' Uncle Duncan could have been shootin' at him to free you up to wed Julian?"

"That wouldn't wed me to Julian, and no, I don't think Uncle Duncan would do such a thing." Of course, there was also the matter of Howard's death.

"Girl, he ain't never been convinced you won't wed Julian."

"I've told him."

"Don't mean a thing."

Olivia was so very glad to have this woman back in the house. Early, no less. Auntie May hadn't said so, but Olivia suspected curiosity about Clay Boudreaux had gotten the best of the woman. "I really don't know who fired those shots," Olivia said, "or who they were aiming for."

"Yo' Aunt Agatha?"

"I can't imagine her walking around in those woods over there, but you know, Uncle Lionel said that when they were kids, Aunt Aggie used to sit on their front porch in Maryland and shoot turkeys two hundred yards away."

"Ain't believin' that. Uh-uh. Them eyes on that woman look two different directions. How she know which way to shoot?"

"I think she can see all right."

223

"Can see what you got, you mean, and she's after it." May picked up two plates and a platter. "That stingy old woman is gonna take everything, if her turn comes up, and not share with nobody. But let's suppose it was her doin' that shootin' last night. If'n what Mister Lionel said about her bein' a good shot is true, don't you reckon I'd be dressin' the two of you out right now?"

"You have a good point."

"Y'all tell the sheriff 'bout this?"

"I think my husband plans to," Olivia said, "but he doesn't trust Brogan."

"Don't blame 'im. I don't trust no white sheriff anywheres."

"My husband is a sheriff's deputy."

"I know it, and yo' stepdaddy vouched fo' him, so maybe we'll let him get by." Auntie May reached for a cast-iron skillet at the same moment Betty Joy, bundled up like she was one of those prospectors headed for the new gold fields in Alaska, stumbled through the kitchen door, her arms full of dirty laundry.

"You picked the coldest day of the year to want to get the laundry done, Grandma."

"Well, you shoulda done it earlier in the week."

"You never did say nothin' about no laundry. You said to keep 'em fed."

"Yeah, and I'm told you kept 'em fed good."

Olivia winked at the girl. Boudreaux had rained praise for Betty Joy upon her grandmother this morning.

"Now if you want to work here from now on, you best learn to keep them clothes clean so they don't pile up no mo'."

Olivia held the back door open.

"Still don't see why we can't wait till it warms up a bit."

"You git that wash pot goin' good. You be warm. Probably be fussin' about bein' too warm."

"Here," Olivia said, "let me help you with that so you don't fall down the stairs."

"No, you won't." Auntie May crossed the room with a quickness impressive for so large a woman. She grabbed Olivia's arm, but gently. "You go on alone," she called to Betty Joy on the back porch. "Miss Livy don't have no business outside, and if'n she got no better sense than to go out there, you make sho' you keep yo' distance from her and that man of hers, too. You tell Billy what I said."

Betty Joy's confusion creased her forehead, but the old woman waved her on. "Only when they outside, honey. Only when they outside. Go on now, go on."

Chapter Thirty-three

"How did your daddy react when you told him about me?"

Lydia Augustus Pique pushed up on one arm and smiled at the man she'd found in her Uncle Lionel's house two days ago. She had him in her plush bedroom now, warm and cozy in Louis Pique's huge Louis XV tester bed. Her husband had gloried in the massive thing, reveled in its name, which matched his own, and prided himself in his voluptuous bride, who kept him in it more than he could endure. Lydia had done right by the old man, fulfilled all his perverse appetites, and was so glad, today, to have a handsome, virile, young man to fill hers.

"I think the only thing worse than one Clay Boudreaux, in his eyes, is two. Now he knows Clay is alive, whereas before he thought he only had an impostor to deal with."

"Had he planned on killing the ringer?"

"I do believe," she said with a knowing smile, "he intended to expose him."

"Do you know his plan, now that he has a real Clay to contend with?"

"First he has to figure out which one is which."

"You're not convinced I'm Clay?"

She brushed his nipple with her thumb. "Honey, I know exactly who you are."

"Do you now?"

"I do."

He grinned. "You trust me then?"

"Hardly. " She dipped her head and licked the nipple. "I'm sure because I know the man at Epico Hollow, I've *known* you, and I knew my Uncle Lionel very well."

"All right, let's assume you do know who is who. After you've told your father who I am, then what?"

She placed her index finger on his chin and pushed down. "I can think of so many better uses for that tongue than talking right now."

He moved his head quickly and seized her finger between his teeth. She smiled, and he released her. "Who else have you told Clay is still alive?"

"Only Daddy. He's told the boys, of course."

"Aunt Aggie?"

"Actually, he confronted her with the news."

He narrowed his eyes. "I thought they'd be sharing information."

"Not anymore. Daddy rues the day he ever got involved with Aunt Aggie in anything. She's notorious for coming up with high-yield investments that turn out higher in risk than return. That's why she's living with Mama and Daddy now—she lost the house Uncle Lionel bought her with her last scheme, and Daddy had to mortgage the brickyard."

"And how did she react to his accusation?"

"In my opinion, she was genuinely surprised, but Aunt Aggie can function with a great deal of discretion when she chooses to."

"Are you telling me your father thinks I'm working with Aunt Aggie?"

"Are you?"

He smirked, then watched her hand snake beneath the covers.

"Go ahead and lie to me, honey," she said. "It won't do you any good."

He sucked in a breath when her fingers closed around his cock. "Okay, I'm not working with her."

She rubbed the head of his penis with her thumb, and he groaned. "Hmm," she said, "I do believe you are ready to play some more."

He rolled on top of her. "Tell me."

"Tell you what?"

227

"Am I lying about working with Aunt Aggie?"

"I'm saving my findings for Daddy."

"Lydia, darlin', if you didn't smell so damn good I'd swear you were filled with horseshit."

"Well, honey, the only thing I want to be filled with is you."

He laughed. "I've never met a woman as—"

"Candid?"

"I was going to say honest."

She smiled. "I know you were, but that word would have implied a character trait not suited for our present circumstance."

He brushed her cheek with his knuckles, then he kissed her. "I'm finding my knowing that I don't know with you very entertaining."

Beneath him, she spread her legs—"I don't believe that's what you find entertaining at all"—then nudged him with her knee.

"Lydia, my sweet magnolia blossom"—her mouth curled into a disbelieving grin at that, and he laughed at her—"as much as I'm enjoying my time with you, I really did hope to gather some information regarding your father's plans."

"Daddy, please forgive me," she said, breathless with faux excitement, "but I am helpless in the face of such eloquence." She pecked him on the lips. "Rumor has it that Troy and Clay are at odds and have been since some sordid affair regarding one Margo Flores, the details of which you probably know better than I. I do believe Daddy hopes the Boudreaux brothers will kill each other off, or if only one of you must go, he hopes Troy kills Clay, as he was supposedly hired to do by Olivia. Now, it's your turn."

"What do you want to know?"

She rolled her eyes in her head and cried, "Good Lord, I already know everything I need to know. I want us to play some more."

Chapter Thirty-four

Olivia blew on the gumbo-filled spoon. "Billy says Toby's up."

From the opposite end of the gleaming table, Boudreaux found her eyes. "He is."

She dropped her gaze and again dipped her spoon beneath the opaque surface of the delicious soup. "He'll be all right?"

"Billy's a born wrangler, and yes, I think Toby'll be fine."

"And the dog? You're going to keep him tied in the yard?"

"Yep. Billy thinks he'll stay, but I want to give him a day or two."

"We might get a frost tonight. If you'll put him on the back porch, I'll give him a blanket."

"He's a dog, Olivia."

"I don't care, and it won't hurt."

"How 'bout I put him underneath the porch, and you can give him the blanket." He waved an index finger at her. "But I guarantee you he won't use it."

"Thank you. Betty Joy says his name is Abraham."

Boudreaux refocused on his soup bowl. "I call him Abe and give thanks he's not a Sherman."

"And what did you do all day?"

"Avoided you."

A spoonful of chicken gumbo suspended halfway between the bowl and her lips, she looked at him. "Why do you say things like that?"

"Very well, sweetheart, I kept shy to give you a chance to make your next move."

"So you spied on me?"

"From time to time."

229

"I think you went somewhere and met someone."

He slurped his soup. "Ah," he said with some degree of exaggeration, "a good woman, maybe?"

"Julian stopped by." She pursed her lips when he jerked his head up, then returned to her soup.

"What time?"

"Early. He came the back way, walked along the water. A path we used as kids. He said he saw you and Uncle Duncan talking on the road."

"What did he want?"

"He wanted to make sure I was all right."

"He wanted you to tell him about the shooting."

She narrowed her eyes.

He dropped his spoon into the bowl. "Well, did you tell him?"

"Why do you think it was Julian?"

"You're answering my questions with questions. You do that a lot."

"Answer me."

"Because he came here early, that's why. Did he seem expectant, fishing for information?"

"Not for long."

"What does that mean?"

She shrugged and returned to her gumbo. "I sort of accused him."

"Dammit, Oliv—"

"Oh, and what did you talk to Uncle Duncan about?"

He picked up his spoon.

"As I suspected," she said, relieved her imprudence had been no worse than his. "And did he confess?"

"No."

"Julian pointed out that the person who has the most to gain from my demise is Clay Boudreaux."

"So did Duncan," he said roughly, then narrowed his eyes when he found her staring at him from the other end of the table. "So, you think I hired someone to shoot at you?"

"Only if you are Clay. Otherwise..."

230

"Otherwise what?"

She swallowed. "If you're not the real Clay, and if the real Clay didn't die in the fire then—"

He slammed his napkin on the table. "You know, Olivia, your uncle implied the same thing."

"What?"

"That Clay or Clay's accomplice is out there trying to kill you off."

Her gut knotted into a ball. "They've never believed you were Clay."

"Your Aunt Connie believes I'm Clay."

"Yes," she said, "your father's eyes, but I don't see Uncle Lionel's eyes at all, which begs Edwin Boudreaux. I mean she never did say Lionel's eyes, now did she?" Olivia held her breath and prayed she'd changed the direction of the conversation. Last night's discussion had come too close to the revelation of a second Clay Boudreaux, and she was still undecided as to what she should do about him.

"An impostor is one thing, Olivia. An impostor and the real man, that's different."

She dropped her eyes. "Did you find anything over in the woods this morning?"

"You saw me over there?"

"May did."

"Somebody could have come across Bayou Bernard from the Handsboro side. I found a place south of the point where a boat might have been pulled ashore, but it rained so much last night any real evidence was washed away. I looked for a launch point on the other side, and I found a boat. It was afloat, barely, but I don't know if I'd have set out across that bayou in it. I searched those woods from the place where I found the boat all the way back to some dirt road—which I didn't even realize was there until I stumbled upon it."

"Did you search the other direction, up Epico Bayou?"

"A little ways. Again, nothing left to find."

"For your information, the bayou narrows about fifty yards

below Uncle Duncan's house. There's an old foot bridge spanning it. When we were kids, we played in those woods on the
other side of the bayou. We'd walk all the way down the peninsula to the point. The boys used to swim across to our backyard
in the summertime. If Julian was the person shooting, I imagine
that's the way he came." She dipped her spoon back into her bowl
and looked up to find him contemplating her. "Do you really
think it was Julian?" she asked. Lord, she wanted it to be Julian,
and not Troy still trying to kill Clay, or, worst of all, Clay trying
to kill her — she blinked at the handsome man, watching her from
the other end of the table — and him, an accessory.

"How good a shot is he?" Boudreaux asked.

"Who?"

"Julian, Olivia. That is who we're talking about, right?"

She nodded. "Yes, and it's my understanding he's not very
good. Some autumns the men go hunting up in the Delta. Julian
never gets a kill. It's somewhat of a joke. Now, tell me, is Troy
Boudreaux wanted for murder?"

Shock stared back at her, and shock continued to stare at her
for a spell. Finally, he said, "Troy was under investigation for
murder in San Antonio. Julian told you that?"

"He brought it up days ago."

"Olivia, they're trying to frighten you, telling you I'm Troy
and Troy's a murderer. May I remind you that less than two minutes ago you said it was Clay who stood to gain by your death,
not Troy?"

"If Troy is working with Clay —"

"If Troy is working with Clay, Clay doesn't know it. Did you
let that son of a bitch in this house?"

"Who?"

"Julian, dammit!"

Sweet Jesus, what was she thinking? and she tried to calm
her yammering heart. "I'd appreciate your watching your language, and yes, he came into the kitchen. We had coffee. Betty
Joy was there the entire time. Do you honestly still think I would
have anything to do with Julian?"

232

He rose, thrusting his chair back behind him. "Why not? You're listening to his hokum."

Heart calmer, thoughts clearer, she shot out of her chair, too, and picked up her bowl. "Do you think I'm so stupid as to take anything he says at face value? He has wanted you to be Troy from the start."

"So, he's hinted to you that Troy is a murderer; now yesterday, he takes a pot shot at us, then comes over here this morning and points out that Clay will inherit everything once he's eliminated you."

Dishes in hand, she started out the dining room door.

Olivia dropped her plate and flatware in the sink with an unpleasant clatter, then moved aside. More gently, he placed his dishes on top of hers.

"If Lionel could concoct that water-heating stove in the bath," he said, as she poured hot water from the kettle atop the dishes, "why didn't he do something similar in the kitchen?"

"Because we already had a stove in the kitchen. Excuse me, please."

He stepped aside to let her by, then he moved forward and started pumping cold water into the hot.

"How important is it to you that we confirm Julian was the shooter yesterday?"

"It would be nice to know it was him," he said, searching her eyes, "and not some other snake that I don't know about hiding in the grass."

He watched her test the dishwater. If the situation had been reversed, he would have asked, "Who else?" She didn't. Instead, she yanked her hands from the sink, snatched the towel he held, and dried her hands. Her pretty purple eyes held a strange look, as intoxicating in its own right as the scent of gardenia on her skin.

"Is finding out important enough for you to want me to seduce the information out of him?" she asked.

His heartbeat quickened. "I beg your pardon?"

233

"Do you want me to use my feminine wiles on Julian to get the information out of him?"

"Assuming he has the answers."

"You do want me to go ahead then?"

With a forced calm, he faced her fully and wrapped his arm around her waist, then with a quick yank, he crushed her breast to his. A poof of air escaped her parted lips. "Once again, you should use your wiles on me."

Her gaze didn't falter, but her eyes did glisten. "Answer me."

"Are you comfortable doing such a thing, Olivia?"

"Answer my question."

"If you did manage to get information out of him using that particularly disgusting tactic, sweetheart, it wouldn't do either one of us any good, because I'd kill you myself."

The churning in his stomach lessened with the pucker of her chin. She pushed at his chest, and he let her go, and she turned from him and rushed out of the kitchen. He stared after her, then shook his head, pulled the shade over the window, and washed their supper dishes with trembling hands.

Chapter Thirty-five

Boudreaux could not recall the last time his drawers looked this good. Not since his mama's passing, for sure. His clean underwear and socks lay folded in the top drawer of Lionel's bureau. The remaining drawers, all containing his sparse clothing, were just as neat. Aunt May's doing at Olivia's direction, May had told him earlier this afternoon. He was officially moved into the master suite.

He pulled out a red flannel undershirt. The house was growing cold, and the warming effect of his hot bath had passed before he even got out of the tub. He'd relaxed too long. The water had grown tepid, and he hadn't wanted to restart the little stove beneath the tank to heat up more. He shivered, then rubbed the spot where Pompeii had bitten him four days ago. He should probably go downstairs and feed that furnace, but he figured Olivia was already in bed, and he was plumb worn out from traipsing through the woods and more from rowing along the bayous. What he needed was a warm woman to—

"Would you like me to take a look at that bite?"

Inside the bureau's tilting mirror stood a wanton spirit, mystical, her essence so sweet and potent she stole the air he breathed and filled his cock with blood.

He turned. Her vision wasn't a wistful illusion trapped inside a magic looking glass, and Olivia really was dressed in that silk nightgown he'd found in her drawer his first night here. Her radiant, moon-spun hair was down, her eyes dark, lids heavy. A soft smile, not truly a smile, shaped her lips.

"May I?" she said.

"Come on in." His voice sounded normal to his ears, and Lord,

235

that made him proud, because he wasn't sure his feet were even touching the floor.

She came close, and the scent of gardenia numbed his brain. She'd bathed before he did, and he was already half-drunk on the scent of her before he'd ever climbed in the tub.

For the space of a heartbeat, her eyes searched his, then she focused on the wound. One hand touched his naked shoulder, the other his sternum.

He drew in a breath. "I could sit on the bed." Again, her eyes found his. "You could reach me better."

"Do."

He closed his hand around the cool fingers scorching his chest and pulled her with him to the bed. He sat, then situated her between his legs, much as he'd done in the bathroom the day Pompeii had bitten him.

Her ensemble had a lace-trimmed robe—she hadn't tied it—and it framed the silky garment clinging to her delicate body. A body, he did not doubt, equally soft and sleek.

"How is it looking?" he asked.

"Very handsome." Gently, she touched the sore spot, then leaned closer and breathed against his ear. "How does it feel?"

He closed his eyes and composed his thoughts. "Exquisite. My left nipple feels even better."

She kissed his neck beneath his ear and tentatively brushed his left nipple with the inside of her thumb, before splaying her hand over his breast. "Yes, it does."

Beneath her robe, he placed his hands on her hips and tugged her closer. She didn't resist, and he moved his hands higher. "You're going too far, sweetheart. In a minute, I'm not gonna let you go."

"I don't want to be let go."

"Is this in response to what I said downstairs?"

"Yes."

"I could have been goading you for licentious purposes."

"You're referring to your remark regarding my feminine wiles."

"Isn't that what this is all about?"

"No, Mister Boudreaux, this is surrender, because you said exactly what I wanted to hear."

He frowned, he thought, and he remembered and...

With one adept twist he had her on her back, on the bed, his lips covering hers, and her wrists pinned above her head in a gentle, one-handed hold. He opened the robe before ending their kiss, and she turned her body to his when he caressed a breast beneath her gown. She watched his face watching hers, and when he teased a nipple with his thumb, she moaned. He smiled, then dipped his head and suckled her through the cloth and without thought, she arched her back to give him more of her. Heat warmed her pelvis, and she squeezed her thighs to enhance the sensation. He raised his head and she blinked at him. "That felt good," she said. Again he found her lips.

"I'm sorry I put my jeans on," he said momentarily.

"If you hadn't, I don't think I would have ever gathered the courage to cross your threshold."

"Yes, well, I only prolonged the inevitable and not for very long, at that." And he let go of her hands and reached for the button on his britches. She sat up to remove her robe, but didn't take her eyes off him. Her poor heart was racing, and she gave a silent thanks when he told her to wait and deserted his half-open waistband to pull the robe off her shoulders. "I knew I should have fed that furnace. You're shivering."

"It's not from cold."

His gaze held hers, and he nodded, as if he understood, and she wondered if he did. Reluctantly, it seemed, he tore his eyes away and returned to his britches. She almost asked him if he expected a virgin or if he cared, but decided, given his labored breathing and the attack he was making on his clothes that the time had passed for that question. Perhaps he really didn't care, but...

"Come on," he said, and helped her from the bed, "let's try to get you warm." He yanked back the bedcovers and waved her back on. "Now, I'll show you a reason to be anxious." He pushed his britches over his narrow hips and flat stomach. Her heart thumped against the base of her throat at the sight of his erect manhood. One muscular calf stepped out of a pants leg, then the other, and he kicked the jeans away. He twisted so that his rump faced her, not because he was embarrassed—that didn't seem to be the case—and she realized the cause must have been the expression on her face.

He lay beside her and drew her to him. She could see nothing now but his handsome face.

"I promise, Olivia, that once I've introduced my cock properly to you, it will never make you nervous again."

She started to say she'd heard those first introductions didn't always go well, but he was kissing her again. He flattened his hand over her silk-covered belly, then stroked her hip, before pulling the gown up to expose her legs and thighs. "I hate to do this"—and he smiled at her as he pulled the heavy covers over them—"but you're trembling like a rabbit."

Beneath the covers, she pressed her body closer to his.

"Skin to skin is better," he said, then hissed when she touched him. "Sweet Jesus, your hands are like ice, now."

"Yours are warm."

"I'm not nervous."

His hand covered her pelvic mound; she sucked in a breath, and when he kissed her, she touched his tongue with hers so that this time he was the one who moaned. Without warning, he pulled back, covers and all, and drew her up with him, tugging on the night gown until she rose off it, and he pulled it from beneath her and raised it over her breasts and face. She lifted her arms to help him, and the gown was over her head and on the floor.

Pressed beneath his warmth, she found herself calmer, and coaxed by his voice and hardness against her pelvis, she spread her legs. His tongue and long fingers found her breasts, and, with dizzying alacrity, he licked and suckled and kneaded, each touch sending want and need and heat to the pelvis he tortured. She writhed in response, overwhelmed by the silent demands his body made on hers. He told her to bend her knee, and he caressed her genitals with his thumb. Sensation suffused her body and surged through her limbs and her breasts to pool in her belly like warm brandy on a cold night. And in the end, she surrendered to the flames he fanned, and he swallowed her single cry of pleasure with a kiss.

She blinked at him, and he laid her back. "There's no time like now for this, sweetheart." Holding her at the back of the neck, he suckled a breast, then pushed against her vaginal opening. When she gasped, he cursed with equal gentleness and continued his attempt to enter her. Finally he reached between them and guided himself manually. He winked at her, an act as startling as the placement of his hand beneath her derriere and fiery thrust. She rued the helpless whimper that escaped her, but relaxed some-what with his kisses and whispered reassurances and the simple fact that his hardness filled her, and she expected the worse was over.

"You were mistaken about my first meeting with your cock," she said.

"Give me a chance now. The meeting isn't over."

She wet her lips with her tongue.

"Does it still hurt?" he asked, and she shook her head.

"Good," he whispered against her ear. She squeezed her thighs, him between them, and he groaned, then kissed her neck and shoulder, and he started to move. She rolled her head in response to his wet and wonderful tongue and she moved with him until he stiffened and cried out. Features strained, he pushed against her one more time, then held her to him before falling at her side. For a long moment he was quiet, then he brought her hand to his lips.

"Your fingers are warm, now."

Chapter Thirty-six

They made each other happy again during the night, but Olivia grew sore, and he tired, and the bed was soft and warm and his arms were strong and safe. They'd have slept wonderfully but for Abe waking them twice. Boudreaux never did figure out if the animal was barking at anything worth barking at.

He'd risen over an hour ago after a kiss and a caress, and she'd followed after he got the furnace going good. In the bathroom mirror, her reflection played a moment with the tatted collar of her gray, wool dress, then pinned up a last, wayward curl. Betty Joy had arrived half an hour earlier. Olivia knew because she'd heard the faint banging of pots in the kitchen as the girl prepared breakfast. Auntie May, as it turned out, was her and Clay's unofficial representative at Howard's funeral this morning.

She had started for the bathroom door when the dog barked. A heartbeat later, he barked again, then he was yelping viciously, the sound retreating farther and farther from the house.

With Boudreaux's shout, Olivia flung the bathroom door open, so that it slammed against the interior wall at the same moment a gunshot split the air out back. Olivia tripped once on the stairs, due more to favoring her sprained ankle than anything else, but righted herself. Halfway down, another shot. Betty Joy was between the kitchen sink and the back door when Olivia charged into the room and demanded to know what was happening. Poor Betty Joy had stopped dead with Olivia's entry, but when she started to speak Olivia, never stopping, cried, "Where's Mister Boudreaux?"

Betty Joy fell back, out of her way. "He done run outside after that stupid dog."

Olivia pushed the partially open kitchen door wide, then shoved the screen. From the porch, she heard Boudreaux call out again, his cry followed immediately by a third shot, farther away, but to her ears as brisk and cutting as the frigid air stinging her cheeks.

The day was clear and bright. Billy, in a run, had disappeared behind the rear of the barn by the time she reached the bottom of the steep porch steps and, hiking up her dress, she ran after him, her gait rough and painful. She was breathless and hurting by the time she plunged between the rails of the fenced enclosure back of the barn. Beyond, well into the tree line, she could see Billy, his hand curled into the dog's neck, doing his best to control the agitated beast. Boudreaux kneeled on the ground, his head down, but he got up when she all but fell through the rails on the enclosure's opposite side and ran to him. He looked once toward the thick woods and told her to stop. For a moment, she obeyed. Billy let go of the dog and told him to stay. Behind her, Betty Joy climbed through the fence and came up beside her.

"Oh, lawdy, Miss Livy, who's been shot?"

Again her heart plummeted. Boudreaux had returned to his position on the ground, and Olivia ploughed forward, oblivious to the prickly vegetation hindering her way.

"Go for Doc Tasker," Boudreaux was saying to Billy when she got to them, and he turned and looked at her with anguish in his eyes as clear as the sky above them. "He's closest, right?"

"Yes," she said.

"They probably all at Mister Howard's funeral," Billy said. "But I need to help you get 'im in the house first."

"I'll go for the doctor, Miss Livy," Betty Joy said.

"No," Billy said. "I can ride Mister Clay's horse. You can't control him." The young Negro looked back at Boudreaux. "But let me help you get 'im inside. These women can't help, not like me."

Boudreaux wiped the sweat out of his eyes with a shaking forearm, and Olivia placed a hand on his shoulder and squatted beside him to better see the man on the ground.

The chilled morning air caught in her throat, and for the span

241

of a throbbing heartbeat, she thought she might choke on it. She splayed a hand over her queasy lower gut, then fell to her knees beside them, her Boudreaux and the other Boudreaux, who lay on his stomach, his jacket pulled up and away—her Boudreaux's handy-work, she guessed—and his shirt soaked with blood. She touched the wounded man, though she didn't know why, then turned to her Boudreaux and asked, in a voice that sounded deceptively calm, "You shot him?"

Her Boudreaux stared at her, then looked at Billy, "Do you have a handkerchief?"

The young man pulled one from his coat and kneeled beside Boudreaux, still struggling to get his brother's coat off him. For a moment she tried to help, then got out of their way.

"He's losing a lot of blood," Boudreaux said, and Billy pressed the folded kerchief against the wound near the right shoulder blade. Olivia lifted her skirt and tore off a petticoat ruffle.

"Here," she said, and handed it to Boudreaux. He looked at it dumbly, and she passed it to Billy. "Tie it around his torso to keep the handkerchief in place while y'all move him."

Together, Billy and Boudreaux secured the compress, and Olivia picked up the pistol Boudreaux had dropped by his side. Carefully, she brought the barrel to her nose and...

Boudreaux grabbed the gun. "Dammit, Olivia, let it go." And she did. "What are you thinking, bringing that thing to your face?" He pushed the gun inside the waistband of his pants.

She swallowed and watched Billy drape the wounded man's arm around his neck. Boudreaux took the other side. Once they'd cleared the woods and circled the barn, Boudreaux said he'd take him the rest of the way, but Olivia put a stop to that. "There's too many stairs," she cried when he'd argued his point, rather angrily, but she'd won, because she was right, and he knew it. Billy reasoned with him, too, probably better than she could, because she was as upset as Boudreaux, only, she suspected, differently.

They put their patient in Olivia's room. Her bed had sheets on it. The guest bed didn't.

"I'll go for the doc now, Mister Clay."

242

"Thank you, Billy," Olivia said, when Boudreaux said nothing.

"And get the sheriff," Boudreaux called after him. "Watch Pompeii, you know how mean he is."

"Only thing I worry 'bout is some peckerwood sayin' I stole 'im."

Olivia watched the young colored man start down the stairs, then looked back into the room and saw that Boudreaux had taken a place on the bed beside his unconscious brother. Head bowed in what might well have been silent prayer, he raked a hand over his face. "Damn you," he said at last. "What the hell are you doing here?"

Chapter Thirty-seven

Clouds gathered in the late morning, dampening the air, but warming it a bit.

Olivia closed the office door. Sheriff Brogan, dressed in a dark suit, motioned for Boudreaux to take a seat. He didn't, but remained standing, watching Uncle Duncan, who had come along with the sheriff, challenge in his eyes and unspoken questions on his lips.

Olivia hadn't had a chance to talk to her Boudreaux. For the near hour they'd waited on Doctor Tasker, she and Betty Joy had cut the wounded man's shirt off him and cleaned the wound as best they could. They changed the compresses every ten minutes, and between theirs and Boudreaux's ministrations, they did manage to slow, but not stop, the bleeding. Over the course of their vigil, their patient had become cold and clammy to the touch, his breaths short and rapid.

She'd caught Boudreaux watching her as she worked, and God knows she rarely took her eyes off him when she wasn't focused on the injured man. It was way past dinnertime now. Doc Tasker and Boudreaux had spent three straight hours in that sick room, while she and Betty Joy had rotated as nurses, shuttling boiling water and bandages back and forth from Auntie May's kitchen. The doc found and removed the bullet that had lodged in a shattered rib, effectively nullifying all their hard work trying to stop the bleeding. Then he'd plugged the hole in the man's back, to keep air out, he told Boudreaux. Done with the patch, he had drained the blood inside and around the right lung with a hypodermic syringe he inserted into his patient's chest, underneath his arm pit. That procedure wouldn't be the last of its kind, the doc warned them. A collapsed lung and infection were both very real possibilities. The morning had proved long and exhausting.

The sheriff cleared his throat and turned to her Boudreaux. "You say the man is your brother Troy?"

"I do."

"Lydia says he claims to be you," Uncle Duncan said.

Boudreaux glanced at Olivia, moving up beside him, then he looked at Duncan. "Lydia?"

"She found him in Lionel's bedroom Tuesday afternoon. They have since become fast friends."

Again Boudreaux looked at her, and her heartbeat quickened. "He's Troy," he repeated.

"Did you shoot him?" Brogan asked.

"I did not."

"What was he doing here in Mississippi?"

"Obviously, pretending to be me."

"Why would he do that?"

"I haven't had a chance to talk to him."

"You two were working together," Duncan said.

"No we weren't. When I left Galveston, I thought my brother was dead. I found out after I got here that his body wasn't one of those found in the fire."

Uncle Duncan cursed. "Do you expect us to believe that?"

Boudreaux's gaze moved past Duncan and settled on Brogan. "Duncan Augustus is sheriff now?"

"I'm sheriff, and I find it far-fetched, too. If you didn't know he was here and you weren't working together, then odds are you two was working against one another."

"We're often at odds, Brogan, on minor things, but not things that matter. Each other's lives matter."

Duncan stepped toward Boudreaux, and Boudreaux braced. "You take one more threatening step my way, Uncle, and I'll knock you into that fireplace. I don't know what he was doing here, but my guess is he was covering my back. If he were pretending to be Clay, that made him a target for someone who had something to gain by killing Clay."

"I was burying my son this morning," Duncan said. Her Uncle looked at her, and Boudreaux did to. For a moment, she held Boudreaux's gaze, then she turned away.

"What happened?" Brogan asked.

"The dog started barking," Boudreaux began, "then took off for the woods on the other side of the barn. I took off after the dog. I was halfway to the barn when I heard the first shot, and when I got around the barn, I saw the dog with something on the ground. Then I caught sight of someone in the woods running away. I hailed him. All I had was a handgun. Doubt I could have hit 'im if I'd wanted, but I was just trying to get him to stop. I'd have gone after whoever it was, but by then I was close enough to see a man had been shot. When I realized it was Troy, I stayed with him. There was one more shot, but who it was at, I don't know. Could have been a shot trying to discourage pursuit."

"Is that what you recollect, Miss Olivia?"

She swiped at a tear. "I heard the shots. Three." She glanced at Boudreaux, watching her with a poker face, then returned her gaze to Brogan. "Clay was already with Troy by the time I got there. Billy probably saw more."

"I've talked to Billy. He was in the barn looking after one of your sick animals when them shots was fired." Brogan looked at Boudreaux, then appeared to perk up at the sight of Doc Tasker walking through the office door. "Is he gonna make it?"

"Don't know," the doctor said. "He's got two holes in his lung, not counting the one I made, and a broken rib, which is why he doesn't have a hole in his chest. Even if he survives the shot and blood loss, we've got to guard against pneumonia." He walked to the desk and laid a mangled bullet atop its gleaming surface. "Thirty-eight is my guess, and whoever shot him got up pretty close."

Brogan looked at Boudreaux.

"I carry a .44."

"You took my .38 the other night," Uncle Duncan said.

"Your only one? Seems to me you killed Cecil Moon with a .38 that same night."

246

"I have a house full of 'em."

Brogan turned toward Duncan. "Please, Mister Augustus."

"He fired his .44," Olivia said to Brogan. "I checked it," she added when the sheriff stood there looking stupid, and the man acknowledged with a blink, then dusted his flop hat against his leg.

"I reckon the best thing to do is to see what the injured man says." He looked at the doc. "He awake?"

"Hell, no, and I don't know if he ever will be again."

Olivia looked at Boudreaux. "Betty Joy saw him start after the dog. I think she can attest he couldn't have fired the first shot."

"Maybe that's not the one that hit the victim," Duncan said. "What kind of gun does the wounded man carry?"

"A .44," Boudreaux said. "It hasn't been fired."

"Lately, you mean."

Olivia sank onto the settee and watched Boudreaux turn to Brogan.

"I didn't shoot my brother," he said.

For a moment, Brogan held his stare, then turned to Duncan. "I think we should go, Mister Augustus."

"Yes, my presence is required at a wake."

Stiffly, Boudreaux turned half a step and watched the two men heading to the door. "New Orleans police found a telegram in Howard's things. Did they tell you?"

Both men turned. His words might have been for either, but he'd settled his gaze on Uncle Duncan, who frowned at him. "They said they gave me all Howard's things."

"This they'd have considered evidence and culled it out for me. It stated that the survivor of that fire in Galveston was not to make it to Mississippi. Did you send it, Uncle?"

"I want to see it."

Boudreaux stepped around the good doctor and opened the top drawer to the desk. After a moment's search, he handed the message to Uncle Duncan, who read it, then appeared to read it again. He looked up and, keeping his eyes fixed on Boudreaux, handed the telegram to Brogan, who had come up behind him. "I didn't send that," Duncan said.

"He could've sent this hisself, Mister Augustus, trying to—"

"Dammit, Brogan, the point is that whoever sent that telegram is the reason Howard's dead." Duncan looked at Boudreaux, then turned to go. At the door, Auntie May blocked his path.

"Ol' Floyd's outside," she said.

Duncan studied her face. "They've found Aggie?" A simple question weighted with doubt and worry and a subtle resignation that something must be dreadfully wrong for his yard man to come up the road in search of him when he was sure to be home soon.

"He says that they did."

Auntie May stepped back, and Duncan brushed past her, followed by Brogan and Boudreaux. Olivia rose. Doctor Tasker cursed under his breath and formed the end of the line leaving the room.

Olivia watched the male powwow at the bottom of the steep porch steps out back. The north wind was cold, but the afternoon sun warmed the back of the house. Boudreaux left the dispersing group and started back up the stairs to where she waited beside Aunt May. The only thing Olivia knew, and then only because May told her, was that Agatha Augustus was dead.

On the porch landing, Boudreaux turned her back into the house. "They've asked me to go back to Duncan's. Uncle Duncan asked if you could spare May. He thinks Mabel is gonna need help. They've still got neighbors showing up for the wake, and Aunt Connie remains useless."

Olivia looked to Aunt May, who shut the door behind them. "Lordy be, chil'," the woman said as she pulled her coat from a peg next to Olivia's worn duty jacket, "soon won't be none of you fool white folks left this end of the bayou the way you keep killin' yo'selfs off."

Pulse quickening, Olivia turned to Boudreaux. "Aunt Aggie was murdered?"

"Shot." He reached for his suede jacket by the door. "You ready?" he said to Aunt May, and when the woman nodded, he said, "Let's go."

Olivia caught his arm, but before she could speak, he said, "I have got to go. Someone shot Troy this morning. Now it looks like that same person might have shot Aunt Aggie, too."

"Be careful," she said, then dropped her hand when he said he would. He didn't kiss her goodbye.

Chapter Thirty-eight

"How long has she been dead?" Boudreaux asked.

Doctor Tasker removed his spectacles and rubbed his eyes. Sheriff Brogan's gaze moved past the little man and settled on Boudreaux, standing in front of Duncan Augustus's desk. The room possessed a bright airiness in the light of day. All the same people from four nights ago were here, plus the doc and Brogan.

Boudreaux turned to Duncan, seated at the desk and watching him also. "You asked me to come, Uncle. I figured I was part of this?"

"I thought," the older man said, "we might consolidate our knowledge."

"And I'm here. The reason I asked the doc how long she's been dead is because of that third shot, the distant one, after mine. It didn't really seem to be at me or Troy." He looked back at the doc. "I'm wondering if that could have been the one that killed Aunt Aggie?"

"Agatha's been dead between five and six hours. So, yes, it could have been."

Duncan sat forward and rubbed the back of his neck. "I heard those shots early. Thought it was hunters. We were getting ready to leave for the church, couldn't find Aggie anywhere. I finally gave up and left without her. So, you're thinking whoever shot her was the same person who shot your brother."

"Unless somebody different shot Aggie after she shot Troy."

"The man from Texas is getting warmer."

Boudreaux, as did every man in the room, looked to the office doorway, where posed Constance Augustus, one hand placed high on the doorjamb. "My sister-in-law brought her lover, under duress I am certain, into my house during the wee hours of this past morning, Deputy Boudreaux. Disgusting actually. Lydia's libido in the body of a barn door with the face of a prune." Connie snickered at Duncan, who swiveled away from her to stare out the French doors overlooking Epico Bayou. Connie glanced at Brogan and stepped into the room. Her gait was steady, her eyes bright.

"And who might that lover be, Missus Augustus?" Brogan asked.

"Now if I tell you, you won't have anything to do."

"She doesn't know, Brogan," Duncan said from where he hid behind the high back of the chair.

"He'd like you to think I don't know," she told the sheriff, then leaned over the top of the desk toward Duncan. "I've always known everything, darling."

Duncan swiveled his chair and faced her.

She straightened and looked down her nose at him. "There have been times I've known more than you did."

"I doubt that."

Connie's glare hardened. "Tom told Mabel. He saw her with him."

Duncan stared at her a moment, then his eyes narrowed and his hands, which he'd placed in front of him on top of his desk, tightened into white-knuckled fists. The change that swept over him had to be obvious to everyone in the room. Boudreaux certainly noticed. So did Aunt Connie, who laughed at her husband, before she turned and found Brogan. "He saw her with Aggie's lover, I mean."

Brogan frowned at her. "Who is this person you're talkin' about, Missus Augustus?"

Connie sneered at the man, and in obvious confusion, the sheriff turned to Duncan, who acknowledged the man's silent question by closing his eyes and slowly shaking his head. Connie watched their silent communication and, apparently satisfied, rested her gaze on Boudreaux. "Sweet, sweet Tom. He always worried over Rebecca, you understand. Felt he had to protect her and Olivia for Darcy's sake." Connie's jaw tensed, and she refocused on Duncan. "But that particular time he didn't know if telling Lionel would do her more harm than good."

"So he brought his dilemma to Mabel, who brought the information to you," Duncan said. The look of contempt Duncan gave his wife could have withered a three-century-old yellow pine. Connie Augustus withstood unscathed. "And you told Aggie," Duncan finished.

"And didn't things work out divinely."

"Like the rest of your ill-thought-out meddlings. I'd have more respect for you if I thought what you did was premeditated. But I know you're too stupid to see the consequences of what you wreak until it's too late."

"For Christ's sake, Dad," Francis said.

Connie's nostrils flared, and she squared her shoulders. "Do you miss her, Duncan?"

"Get her out of here, son."

She waved a finger at her son. "Don't move, honey. I'm leaving." With one last look at Duncan, she turned on her heel and left the way she came. She didn't wobble, and she didn't miss a step. The woman might be crazy, but she wasn't under the influence of any substance.

"Gentlemen, I apologize for my wife."

"Do you know who Aunt Aggie was..." — Julian blinked when his father turned to stare at him — "...with?" The younger man turned from his father's silent censure. "Good Lord, Aunt Aggie was seventy-six."

Francis cursed under his breath, then picked up a log and tossed it in the fire.

"Do you know who she was with, Uncle Duncan?" Boudreaux asked.

The man looked his way, then quietly said, "I didn't see her with anyone."

"If she were with someone, could you guess who it was?"

"I could guess, but that would be reckless."

So much for consolidating information. Boudreaux wished he could pull Aunt Connie aside, but truth was the woman hated his guts. He was relatively certain, had it not been so important for her to embarrass her husband moments ago, she would not have spoken to him at all.

Doc Tasker moved. "I've got a live patient at Epico Hollow," he said to Duncan. "We'll leave Aggie here?"

"Yes."

"She was shot with a .38. Seems to be the weapon of choice among the Augustuses," Boudreaux told Olivia when he got back.

He'd found her in the front room, already on her feet, as if she'd heard him come in and gotten up from where she'd been sitting. "Doc came back with me. He's gone upstairs. Betty Joy's with Troy?"

"She spelled me a few minutes ago. Your brother's still sleeping."

"My brother's unconscious, Olivia."

She nodded and turned from him.

"You knew he was here, didn't you?" The room was so still and tense, he sensed his words might echo. "You've talked to him."

She raised her chin and faced him. "He got here before you did. He told me he was Clay."

"For the past couple of days, I've suspected it was him you were dealing with."

"And I've always suspected you were dealing with someone. Even now I'm not sure it wasn't him."

"Well, it wasn't."

"Who is it then?" Her nostrils flared when he didn't answer. "I can promise you Clay Boudreaux is the only person I've been dealing with, but I had the misfortune of having two of them."

"When," he asked, "were you going to tell me about him?"

"I don't know even now what I was going to do about him. I was trying to figure out what was going on." Her voice caught. "I'm still trying to figure out what's going on."

"You should have told me he was here."

"He told me he was Clay. You accused me of hiring Troy to kill Clay. Well someone did hire him —

"Tried to."

"That's what you tell me now. You fired a .38 this morning."

Ah, he thought she knew. "Your Uncle Duncan's," he said quietly, "but I do carry a .44. Duncan knows that."

"I don't care. Did you shoot Clay?"

"I am Clay."

"Then did you shoot Troy to protect yourself?"

"In the back, Olivia?" He sucked in a breath. "Did you honestly believe the man was a threat to me?"

"Or you to him."

He shook his head. "You didn't think you could trust me?"

"I couldn't risk Clay if he were Clay and you weren't."

"But you'd risk Troy?"

"It wasn't my plan to risk either one of you. I've told him since your arrival, right on his heels, that he needed to confront you. He refused. You said you had a letter." She waved a hand in the air. "You know what it says better than I do. I made my choice..."

Her voice was trembling so, that she turned from him to the bank of windows looking out over the shimmering Epico Bayou. "I made it —"

"Last night," he said softly. "I was the one you trusted."

She hesitated, then he saw her swipe a cheek. "I don't know that I'd go that far, but you were the one I wanted to believe in."

Heart heavy, he studied her back, then touched her shoulder. He held out his hand when she turned. "Come on, I'm fixing to put your faith to the ultimate test."

Chapter Thirty-nine

She and Boudreaux had scarcely spoken since leaving Epico Hollow. He had told her, when he turned south onto Courthouse Road, and then only because she'd asked, that they were going to talk to Sandifer Hudgins holed up in the Gulf View Hotel. He volunteered nothing more, and she asked no more. She was tired and mildly nauseated. He blamed her for what had happened to his brother. He blamed her now like he'd blamed her days ago when they thought one of the Boudreaux boys had died in that fire in Galveston, and she couldn't help but believe, if she had acted sooner, trusted this man more, the other Boudreaux wouldn't be lying in her bed at Epico Hollow fighting for his life.

Now, on the second floor of the Gulf View, he stopped suddenly outside a guest-room door, and placing his hands on her shoulders, turned her to face him. She wanted to step into his arms, wanted him to hold her, forgive her, but his arms, holding her away from him, were too rigid, the fingers biting into her shoulders too hard.

"When he opens the door," he said, his voice low, "just listen, don't talk. I don't know how much he knows about who died in Galveston, but I never told him Clay didn't."

Dumbly, she nodded, and he turned to the door and knocked.

Sandifer Hudgins' smile froze in place and his gaze leapt over Olivia's head to Boudreaux, then back to her. "What is this?"

Boudreaux discreetly squeezed her upper arm. "My brother was shot and killed this morning."

Hudgins scrutinized Boudreaux a long moment, blinked, looked at Olivia, then back at Boudreaux. "Your brother?"

"I'm afraid so. Seems Clay didn't die in Galveston after all."

255

"Good God"—he hesitated—"did you kill him?"

She sensed Boudreaux seethed, but if Hudgins noted it, he didn't indicate.

"No," Boudreaux said, "he was shot in the back, in the woods near the house."

"Do you know who did it?"

"Considering he was supposed to be conveniently dead, you can guess as well as I. But what matters now is that Olivia needs to understand what's happened."

The older man's eyes widened. "And you've told her?..."

What? You've told her what? That was what the man wanted to ask, but couldn't because she was standing right here, in front of them, listening to everything they were saying.

"Nothing. She won't believe anything I tell her. No more games, Sandy. Tell her the truth."

Mr. Hudgins gave Boudreaux a furtive glance. "You're certain?"

"I can't see any other way at this point. Tell her what you know about Clay, then tell her that story you told me nine days ago. Show her the letter."

"Of course," Hudgins said, his voice solemn, "I understand." At the same time, Olivia turned to ask Boudreaux if he were referring to the letter recruiting Troy to kill Clay, but before she opened her mouth, he said, "Listen to what Mister Hudgins tells you." He started away from her.

"Where are you going?"

"I'll be out here waiting when you two are through," he answered.

"Olivia," Mister Hudgins said, "come in and shut the door. If the poor bastard hasn't bolted by now, he's not going to."

She kept her eyes on Boudreaux, who stopped in the middle of the hall. "Go on," he said, "you've been clamoring for the truth for the past six days. Let's see if you believe it when you hear it."

Mister Hudgins took her elbow and guided her into the room, and when he shut the door, he nodded to one of two balloon-back chairs in front of the fireplace. He took the other.

Olivia sat and turned her hands palms up. "Please go ahead."

Sandifer Hudgins cleared his throat. "This is difficult for me, but let me start by saying that every sordid thing your family has told you about Clay Boudreaux is true."

Her clenched gut caught fire, but she fought to keep her face void of expression. "And that would be what?"

"Your Uncle Duncan, I believe, told you Clay Boudreaux was the father of Margo Flores's child?"

Her stomach quaked. "Julian did."

"And he told you the young woman died under mysterious circumstances?"

"Yes."

Mister Hudgins leaned forward and took the fingers Olivia had tangled together in her lap. "Clay was the father of her unborn child, and he did plan to marry her, until Lionel Augustus offered you, and his fortune, to him instead. Clay tried to buy Miss Flores's silence with the promise of a large sum of money after he inherited, but Margo wanted more. She wanted him to dispose of you and marry her." Hudgins shrugged. "Shortly after, Margo turned up dead."

Olivia's heart was throbbing against the base of her throat. "How do you know this?"

"Troy told me after the fact."

She pulled her hands free and turned to the door.

"Yes, him," Mr. Hudgins said.

"He's Troy?"

"He is."

"Who am I married to?"

"By the fine letter of the law, you're a widow, but the man outside the door and myself have gone to a great deal of trouble to keep Clay alive. I'm hoping you'll be content to leave matters as they are."

"You must be insane."

Hudgins ran a hand through his hair. "Listen to me, girl. I was out of time and short on options. I did what I thought Lionel would have wanted."

"Plot to murder Clay?"

"No, Olivia, I honestly believed Clay died in an accidental house fire. I substituted Troy for Clay."

"Why?

"Olivia, listen to me. I had an obligation to ensure Lionel's son inherited."

She let loose a small cry. "You can't accomplish that by giving Troy Clay's identity.

"Yes, I can."

"Not unless Troy is Uncle Lionel's flesh and blood."

The subtle curl of his lips screamed triumph. He rose from where he sat and pointed his index finger at her. "There, you have it."

She wrinkled her brow, and he turned to the mahogany chest against the adjacent wall. From its bottom drawer, he pulled a book, then brought it to her. With a confident smile, he flipped the volume to a page marked by a yellowed piece of feminine stationary.

Olivia's heart was racing before she touched the familiar, linen paper, and she sat there, skimming the words, and they sank in. After a month of heartbeats, she tore herself from the letter and looked at him. "This is the last page. Do you know where the rest of it is?"

"There are personal comments in the full letter, meant for your stepfather's eyes alone; it would be indiscreet for me to provide you the whole thing, since what Elaine writes earlier has no bearing on the part you hold in your hand. The story validates itself."

She squeezed her thighs to keep her knees from knocking. So this was what terror felt like? Not horror, like spinning a chair and finding oneself face to face with a ghoul. This was terror, from which there was no escape, no way to fight, no reason to. Calm, irrevocable doom that swept one's body head to foot and left it without the will to even breathe. Again, she glanced to the signature at the bottom of the page. Well, she'd always known her mother hadn't written the thing.

Chapter Forty

He will never know the truth, not from my lips. Trust this, my darling, Lionel Augustus is and always will be the father. I do not feel the wrong I have done Edwin as painfully as the one I have done you. Troy gives him a reason to live and that is the one blessing I want him to cherish the rest of his life.

Edwin wishes us to try again to make a life together, and is pleased that I have distanced myself from the baby's father. Sonja's return provided the motivation for following Papa to Texas. No one will question my reason for leaving.

I do want us to be a family and am comforted knowing you wish the same for Ed and me and "our" children. My dearest wish is that you will find a woman who will bear you a legitimate son to carry on your fathers' name, but always know your blood will continue, no matter what happens.

I will always love you,

Elaine

Numb, Olivia read the closure one more time, then swallowed. "You believe Uncle Lionel is the father of both boys based on this letter?"

The lawyer sat on the foot of the bed, closer to her. "There is absolutely no doubt in my mind. Olivia, honey, you sound awful. I was certain you'd be pleased. With Troy, Lionel's blood will inherit, and you'll have a man worthy of you."

"How soon after Clay's alleged death did you approach Troy with your plan?"

"Within hours. I was in Galveston the night Clay, or rather the night we thought Clay died, remember?"

She did indeed. At the time, Mr. Hudgins said he wanted to inform Clay of his father's death in person. She'd considered that a bit strange, what with rumors of poison and autopsies abounding, her stepfather's lawyer had abandoned her to go to Texas to inform an estranged son an expected death had occurred.

"By the time I got there," he continued, "the hotel was in ashes. I found Troy at his ranch. I always considered Lionel's decision to wed you off to Clay reckless. After talking to Troy, I knew the marriage would have proven not only untenable for you, but probably dangerous as well." He retook his seat and stretched out his legs. The toe of his polished shoe touched the hem of her skirt, and she pulled her legs closer to the chair. "I was, I admit, relieved to know that Clay was no longer with us."

Heart quickening in anticipation, she looked up from the letter still in her lap. "And then he turned up again."

"Most inconvenient."

She'd led, he'd followed. Hudgins had known, before they'd knocked on his door ten minutes ago, that Clay not only had not died in that fire, but that he was in town. "Particularly," she said, "when you've already inserted another in his place."

Hudgins held her gaze. "I was working to your benefit."

"I could have done very well without a husband at all, Mr. Hudgins."

The man gripped the arms of his chair, then pulled himself forward. "I fear you and I have little choice in the matter of your present husband, my dear."

"I beg your pardon?"

"I am aware that you were against Lionel's desire to force you into marriage with Clay."

260

"And why do you say that?"

"Because I've seen the letter you sent soliciting Troy to kill your husband."

"He showed it to you?"

"I found it in his cabin while waiting for him the night of the fire, and I returned it to him. I wanted him to know I was aware of the liaison between the two of you."

"I see." And she did, truly, see. "Mr. Hudgins, may I ask you a question?"

"Of course, but I don't know that I'll be able to answer it."

"Being able to and being willing to are two different things, but here it is: Was it you who did the shooting at my house this morning?"

"Why would I answer that?"

No faux indignation, just curiosity, and she smiled sweetly in response.

"Because, Sandifer, my future relationship with you is dependent on your answer now. You see, the man you handed that letter to at Troy Boudreaux's ranch was not Troy Boudreaux."

The man stared at her.

"He was Clay Boudreaux searching desperately for a brother he feared dead. And if you are this morning's shooter, you have once again failed to relieve me of an unwanted husband. And"—she leaned back and studied the greenish-hued man across from her—"I do believe you are in need of a new partner."

Chapter Forty-one

From across the hall, Boudreaux watched the door open. Silhouetted against the far window, Olivia stood watching him. At the threshold, Sandifer Hudgins made a sweeping bow, and Boudreaux trod silently over the thick carpet and into the plush room. The door clicked shut. Olivia started moving his way, and he heard Hudgins say, "Stay where you are, my dear."

Olivia stopped. Boudreaux turned, and his mouth went dry. Hudgins stood three paces behind him, a smug smile on his lips and one of those new, short-nosed .38s in his hand.

Soul raw, he looked away from Hudgins and searched the cool, violet eyes of his bride. "I told you not to talk."

"And you told me to listen, which I did. I do wish it had been my alleged letter to Troy you wanted Mr. Hudgins to show me. I found out more in the last twenty minutes than I'd have wanted to know in three lifetimes."

His heart was raging, less at the thought of dying than the thought of betrayal by this woman. He simply couldn't believe it.

"Are you going to share that insight with me?" he asked.

"Oh, surely, son, you can figure this out." Hudgins gave him a wide berth and brought himself within reach of Olivia.

"You do know," Boudreaux said to her, "if he kills me, he'll kill you, too."

"She's my new partner."

"Sweetheart, he considers his partners expendable."

Olivia appeared not to be listening to either one of them, but she took another step closer to him. Hudgins reached out to stay her. She stopped, but didn't look at the man. "It was because of your brother, wasn't it?" she asked Boudreaux.

262

"Because of my brother what?"

"You were so angry at me that first day. It wasn't as much the thought I was trying to kill you as it was the belief your brother was dead and I was to blame."

In front and to one side of him, Hudgins fidgeted—"What does it matter?"—but she waved a hand to silence him.

Boudreaux studied her beautiful face, her eyes filled with hurt and remorse not there moments ago. What in God's name had happened?

"Two men died in that fire," he said. "One was a friend, and yes, I thought the other was my brother. I think my grief did take the form of anger that night, and I took it out on you."

"Are you angry at me now?"

He glanced at the gun Hudgins held. "I am a bit concerned. Obviously you didn't like the story Hudgins told you."

"She likes it fine"—Hudgins twisted his head to the side—"Clay, I do believe?"

Boudreaux's gaze slid back to Olivia. "Ah, I finally convinced you who I am."

"You..." She choked, then blinked back tears. "You are the man I married?"

"The license says you married Clayton Lee Boudreaux, and I am Clayton Lee Boudreaux."

She strangled the reticule clutched in her hands. "The man who wrote me that letter?"

He frowned. "The one you keep under your pillow?"

"Yes."

Hudgins blinked at Boudreaux, then fixed his gaze on Olivia, who was paying the man no heed at all. Boudreaux was heeding him though, and growing more apprehensive with each indiscreet observation Olivia put forth.

"What did you really think of his story, sweetheart?"

"I think you're too smart to have believed it."

Her eyes were bright, her voice soft, and both were begging him that she be right. He opened his mouth. "I—"

"You don't trust him," she cried, "and I don't believe that you

263

ever did. You told him he'd actually killed Troy this morning."

"He killed?"

She nodded vigorously. "His confession was the price for my friendship."

Whether she had degenerated to hysteria or her words were purposefully meant to spur Hudgins to action, he didn't know, but the man's sudden movement drew Boudreaux's attention. On his right, Olivia moved, too, slinging her reticule at Hudgins's head at the same moment she lunged at him. Hudgins ducked, but only partially dodged the blow, and Olivia caught his gun hand.

Boudreaux was on them seconds after the blast and for a screaming moment of terror, he was certain Olivia, now on the floor with Hudgins, had been shot.

Struggling to push back with the heel of his shoe, Hudgins managed to fling his left arm and shove her back. He had her down and the gun to her forehead the same moment Boudreaux clicked his hammer into place, the barrel of his .44 against the heaving Hudgins's temple.

"Mine's cocked, you son of a bitch. Now get that thing away from her and get up."

Olivia growled when Hudgins moved off her, and she tore the little pistol from the man's hand. Boudreaux bit back a curse. "Unless you're planning on using that thing on me, sweetheart" — quickly he considered reasons why she might — "I wish you'd put it down."

She blinked at him, then studied the gun. A shiver sliced through him. "Olivia!"

Chapter Forty-two

The look in her eye called to him and he listened, and for one terrible instant he considered she might use that gun on herself. On guard against the desperate prisoner at his feet and the demons vexing Olivia, Clay held out his hand, and told her everything was all right. She compressed her lips, closed her glistening eyes, and shook her head, but she laid the gun in his palm.

That crisis at least momentarily averted, he looked down at Hudgins, who studied him in abject defeat. "You might have told me who you were that first night," the man said.

"Sorry, but your sudden appearance in Texas the night Clay was supposed to have died was too much of a coincidence."

Out of the corner of his eye, he watched Olivia stoop to pick up the letter his mother had written years before. She didn't look his way, but to the window and held the letter to the light. He turned back to Hudgins. "I'm surprised you didn't high-tail it out of town the minute the other Clay showed up."

"Without my share of the money," Hudgins said, "I couldn't get far enough away."

"Haunted, are you?"

"By one of the most vicious, vindictive, bloodthirsty haints you would ever want to find."

"The lovely and personable Aunt Aggie. I'd bet whatever put you in her corner is a tale unto itself."

"A horrifying one. I thought I'd found a way out with Troy."

"So this morning, believing you'd finally managed to kill Clay, you decided to rid yourself of her overbearing presence?"

The defiance that had marked Hudgins's visage since Clay started talking lessened. Still sprawled on the floor, the man said,

"Actually, that wouldn't have been a bad idea." He looked away, then back. "You're referring to that third shot, aren't you?"

"Yes."

"Aggie's dead?"

"What are you playing at, Hudgins?"

"If you're telling me Aggie was the target of that third shot, and assuming I fired it, you're wrong, and I'm not saying another word until I have a lawyer."

"You are a lawyer, and right now you've already confessed to attempted murder, and you're a primary suspect in the deaths of two men in Texas, in addition to Agatha Augustus."

"I had nothing to do with events in Texas, and there's a number of people who wouldn't have minded seeing Aggie dead."

"But how many of those people are killers?" Clay steadied the gun in his hand and glanced at Olivia, still at the window, studying the letter. Outside the room, the distant opening of a door was followed by muted footfalls hurrying down the carpeted hall; a calm shout; a short discussion, loudly conducted; and finally the heavy knocking on a guest-room door toward the end of the hall.

"Let me put it this way, Sandy. I want to get to the bottom of this, the very bottom. Now you can trust me with whatever you have to say, or you and your lawyer can risk finding justice from Dosh Brogan's investigation of Agatha Augustus's murder. Even an idiot like the sheriff can see you're the lead suspect. Now, is it only me or do you also have the impression the fella is lazy? My guess is he'll make short work of your case. What do you think?"

Hudgins's mouth formed a tight line, and after a moment he said, "Can I get up?"

Clay looked at Olivia and found her watching Hudgins.

"Sweetheart," he said, somewhat relieved when she looked his way, "would you go into the hall, where I believe you'll find hotel security searching for the source of our recent gunshot.

She started for the door, and with the barrel of his .44, Clay motioned Hudgins to his feet.

266

Chapter Forty-three

Clay flicked the reins and coaxed the horse faster. Hudgins crisis behind them, he was worried now about his brother.

He glanced at Olivia, safe, and silent, on the padded seat beside him. He was worried about her, too. She wasn't saying much. Worse, she hadn't expressed interest in what Hudgins had to say after she left the hotel room or in the man's subsequent dispatch to the county jail, escorted by the jailer himself. As of the time they started home twenty minutes ago, Brogan still hadn't returned from Duncan Augustus's place. Something happened while she and Hudgins were behind that hotel-room door, and Olivia wasn't being quick telling him what. He touched her arm, and she inclined her head his way. Not the greatest encouragement, but something.

"According to Hudgins," he said, "Agatha approached him back in early October with the plot to kill me and challenge your right to the will. Of course, she knew she could pull it off only after Lionel was dead and preferably before the reading of the will. He says he refused to go along."

Olivia twisted on the carriage seat. "But he was in Galveston the night of the fire."

"I pointed that out. I told him it was obvious to any half-wit that his reason for being in Texas that night was to kill Clay Boudreaux."

"And?"

"He denied it. And to support his case, he offered up—"

"Elaine Boudreaux's letter."

"That's right. In his mind, that letter made Troy the rightful heir to the Augustus fortune."

Olivia shook her head. "He may have thought he had the rightful male heir, but that didn't address me, nor did it change the fact that the will reads Clay Boudreaux. Seems to me things would have been quite a mess."

"Not if Clay were dead. Rightful heir, Olivia, not legal."

"So he and Aunt Aggie must have been working together."

He started shaking his head before she finished her sentence. "They weren't, not then. Aggie didn't know about Mama's letter, and I'm pretty certain he didn't want her to know. As of the fall of this year—and who knows how many years prior—Hudgins didn't want to share anything with the woman. Not information and certainly not Lionel Augustus's fortune.

"Remember, she had tried to recruit him to help her kill Clay, so he was aware of her plan. When Lionel died, Hudgins set out for Texas. He knew Howard was already in Galveston. He says Labat's being there doesn't surprise him, but swears he didn't know about him. When he arrived to find Aunt Aggie's agent, or agents, had apparently succeeded in killing me, he rode off, Mama's letter in hand, to convince Troy that he had a moral right to Clay's inheritance, but to get it, Troy had to become Clay. Hudgins knew the will couldn't be broken and the only thing standing between you and the entire fortune was your substitute husband. His original plan was to hoodwink Troy into believing he could move into Epico Hollow with you and take everything. But Hudgins knew he was operating with a short fuse. Once the will was read, he expected his cut, not an insignificant share, by the way, and then he planned on disappearing, fast. He knew it would be only a matter of time before Duncan got somebody from Galveston over here and exposed Troy as a fraud. When he got to Troy's ranch and found your alleged letter, his plan was looking better than ever. He figured at that point he wasn't work-ing with an ethical man, and whatever you had offered Troy to kill Clay, Hudgins could promise much more, not to mention take more for himself. He also figured if Troy were willing to kill his brother, he'd have no misgivings about backstabbing you."

"Did he ask you if you killed Clay?"

"He did."

"What did you tell him?"

"How I managed to keep my wits about me that night, I will never know. I hadn't seen your letter, but I had to pretend I knew what was in it. I told him I hadn't had a chance to discuss that letter with Clay's bride. Hudgins said to pretend I didn't know a thing about it—and as Clay, I shouldn't."

"But you did confront me with the letter," she said softly.

Again he hastened Auntie May's old mare. "Hudgins had his agenda; I had mine."

She didn't say anything, and he squirmed in his seat. "Truth is, Hudgins believed you wrote that letter. He figured Aggie approached you, knowing you were opposed to the marriage, and persuaded you to recruit Troy—"

"But she already had a plan to kill Clay."

"Yes, Labat was the real plan, but placing your letter in the hands of Troy made you the primary suspect in the conspiracy to have killed Clay once the deed was done."

"Oh, for Pete's sake! Of course. That letter wasn't drafted because she thought Troy would be willing to kill his brother for money. She drafted it because she suspected he'd do exactly the opposite."

"Which was make sure you went to jail or hanged. A devious ploy, and she had Howard in Galveston to keep an eye on things. Hudgins's unwelcome interference disrupted her plan, but didn't destroy it. She just had to improvise a bit."

Olivia was quiet a moment. "What was his relationship with Aunt Aggie, did he tell you?"

"He says he offered her legal advice over the years, but I've known from the start of this charade there was more to them than that. He and Aunt Aggie were together this morning. She showed him the way through the woods to our house. Once they had Troy in sight, Hudgins says she started back. He insists he never saw Aggie after that. His escape route over the footbridge below Uncle Duncan's house was preplanned."

"Which again supports their working together."

"But not from the beginning," Clay explained. "Think back to that night we first met. Aggie knew, or at least suspected, Lionel Augustus's lawyer was up to something. The man had already intimated the same thing to me about her. That first time I met her, I wasn't sure if she suspected Hudgins was up to good or bad. I, of course, knew my role in his plan, but I wasn't sure of Aggie's place in the scheme, and that's what I was trying to figure out, everyone's role. I knew that night, without a doubt, Aunt Aggie and Sandifer Hudgins had some sort of well-established relationship."

"If they hadn't already discussed the substitution of Troy for Clay at some point, why did she conclude you were Troy?"

"I wondered about that myself, but I think I've figured it out. She all but invited Troy into the fray when she sent him that forged letter offering him money to kill me. Troy reacted by coming here to the Coast almost three weeks ago now. During that brief stay, he made a point of getting to know Katie."

"He had relations with her?"

"That's what I concluded from my conversation with her that day we went grocery shopping. However, my point is that Katie undoubtedly informed Agatha of Troy's visit. Then, two weeks later I show up claiming to be Clay. Since Aggie honestly believed she'd succeeded in killing Clay in Galveston, she immediately assumed the impostor was Troy. If she were working with Sandifer to insert me as Clay, do you really think she would have challenged me in front of you and Lydia that night?"

"No. You're right. That would have made no sense."

"When Aggie stopped Millie, Simon, and Katie on their way in to work the next morning, you can bet she told Katie she suspected Troy was back in town and now ensconced at Epico Hollow. Which is why Katie assumed she was talking to Troy's back that first morning she and I met."

Olivia drew in a breath. "And Aunt Aggie left for Hattiesburg shortly thereafter, in search of Mr. Hudgins."

"Right. She was gone most of the day. She didn't see Katie again, so Katie never had a chance to set Aggie straight as to who

I was. Now, assuming Aunt Aggie and Howard were working unilaterally to ensure Aggie inherited, you, as well as Clay, had to be eliminated. You received a reprieve that same night. Believing she'd succeeded in killing Clay, Aunt Aggie hired Moon to kill you. Because she was in Hattiesburg, she didn't know Duncan had invited us to dinner, and she didn't know Katie would be at Epico Hollow. Knowing we'd be gone, Uncle Duncan sent Katie back there to retrieve that letter you allegedly sent Troy. She'd confessed to him that she'd written it. He wouldn't tell me who she wrote it for, but I think he knew the mastermind was Aggie. I, of course, accused him."

"And Hudgins?"

"Hudgins claims he knew nothing about Moon at the time. Given Katie's murder happened before Lydia found Troy in my bedroom, I'm inclined to believe him. He didn't need or want you dead at that point."

"Do you think Howard knew about Aunt Aggie's plan to kill me?"

If the man had the ability to think, he did, but Clay didn't want to say that to Olivia. "Howard was after me, not you. He may have been duped into believing he was freeing you up to wed his baby brother per their daddy's wishes."

"He was Aunt Aggie's favorite," Olivia said. "When we were little, she took his side against the other kids. As he grew older, Uncle Duncan couldn't control him. He gambled and drank and was forever fighting and getting in trouble. He was finally arrested one too many times, and when Uncle Duncan refused to get him out of jail, Aunt Aggie did."

"I would guess that didn't sit too well with Uncle Duncan?"

"Not just that once. Over the years, she undermined Uncle Duncan's influence over him constantly. But I once heard Uncle Lionel tell Uncle Duncan that Aunt Aggie had done him the same way, only in his case it had been Uncle Duncan she led astray."

Clay nodded. "So, when things finally got to the point Aunt Aggie could no longer influence Duncan, she drafted Howard."

"Who was, Uncle Lionel said, exactly like her."

"Well, he'd become pretty important to her scheme, and his loss was a serious setback, not to mention his failure to kill me. Then Lydia discovered Troy in our house, and Aunt Aggie knew Clay was alive for sure. That skewed her plans for good, and that's when, according to Hudgins, she approached him a second time. She's the one who told him about the second Clay. That left an old boll weevil running loose in his high-cotton. He had few options at that point. He couldn't confide in me. I hadn't said any-thing to indicate I knew Clay was still alive. He figured I didn't know, and if he told me, of course, he'd have to tell me how he knew. So, this time he listened to Aggie's offer.

"Her new plan, the one put in motion this morning, was for them to get rid of who they thought was the real Clay, expose me as a fraud, then bring up your letter recruiting Troy to kill Clay. That, they hoped, would eliminate you; Aggie would inherit; and Hudgins wouldn't have to run away and make a new life for him-self." He smirked. "He was gonna marry Aggie and live happily ever after."

"You don't think he wanted to marry her?"

"I'm sure he didn't, but he would have for Lionel's estate. Personally, I think she offered him marriage as an easy way to get him to do her bidding. Hudgins needed her, not the other way around. She's used the man for sex for years."

Olivia wrinkled her nose. "Why would he—"

"She had something else on him."

"What?"

"I don't know."

"Do you think he killed her?"

"I think if he were going to kill her, he'd have waited until after he married her—another reason for her not to marry him, and she was smart enough to know it."

The horse hesitated when they came to the single-lane bridge crossing Epico Bayou. Boudreaux clucked encouragement to the beast, and after a short lurch, the crunch of crushed oyster shell gave way to the hollow clip-clop of hooves against wood. A stone's throw farther up the road they turned east onto Epico

Way, which took them past Uncle Duncan's place and home to Epico Hollow, a shade-shrouded mile away. When their house emerged round the last bend, Olivia straightened.

"What did you think of the letter Hudgins had? The one written by your mother," she asked.

The vibrancy in her voice caused him to look at her. "I know it was written by my mother. I recognized the handwriting."

She twisted her fingers together in her lap, and he followed her gaze down the narrow tunnel of live oak and magnolia, their dark foliage splattered with russet cypress and a faded mix of deciduous trees. Except for the critically wounded Troy, it should have been an almost happy homecoming, at least one filled with relief. It was neither, and he didn't understand why.

"Did he tell you how he came by it?" she asked.

"He said it was among Lionel Augustus's personal documents locked in his father's safe."

The look she shot him was incredulous. "And the rest of it?"

"He told me he kept the first page for discretionary—"

"He's lying."

"All right, do you know where he got it?"

She faced him. "I don't know how he got it or why he had only part of it."

Well, he sure as hell didn't know, and he wasn't convinced he cared. "Is it Troy's being Lionel's son that has you so bothered?"

"Troy is Edwin Boudreaux's son. All that matters to me is that you're Lionel Augustus's son."

"Olivia, trust me, I am Clay."

He wasn't sure if she laughed or sobbed. He pulled the carriage to a stop outside the carriage house near the barn and covered her hand with his. Not looking at him, she reached across her lap and covered that hand with her free one, then she rose abruptly, parting them.

"Don't you want me to be Clay anymore?"

"I'd give anything at this moment to find that you weren't."

Chapter Forty-four

Clay pulled the screen wide and pushed the back door open. Olivia walked past him into a warm kitchen, laden with the scent of frying food.

She'd managed to stay ahead of him most of the way to the house, and though he'd asked once what she was talking about, he hadn't pressed her when she said she'd tell him later. She was grateful for that. She needed to double check the first page of that letter from Elaine Boudreaux before she said anything to him. She had it. She'd had it for the past seven years.

Auntie May turned from the stove, and Olivia fought back tears. "They didn't need you at Uncle Duncan's any longer?" she asked.

"Mabel's okay now that them visitors for Mister Howard is gone, and I'm makin' supper fo' tonight; Mabel got her hands full dressin' out Miss Agatha, and she's worried 'bout Miss Connie. Says she jest ain't right." May nodded to Clay. "I got y'all's supper, too, when you ready. Dividin' one of them hams of yours between y'all. Got collards and okra, too."

Fried okra. Normally one of Olivia's favorite dishes, today its heavy scent soured her stomach.

"Billy says Troy hasn't woke up," Clay said. He pulled off his jacket and hung it on one of the pegs by the door.

"No, suh, but Doctor Tasker was here earlier, and he says he ain't got no worse either. That be a good sign I'm tellin' you. And I don't need no doctor to tell me so. I know some stuff."

At the table, Betty Joy turned out a skillet of cornbread onto a plate.

"Who's with him?" Clay asked.

"Miss Lydia, she—"

"Dammit." He tossed his hat onto a chair, and Olivia scrambled out of his way. He sidestepped Betty Joy and disappeared into the hall.

Olivia turned to the old woman. "Auntie May?"

"Miss Lydia ain't gonna hurt that man. If'n she can't screw 'im to death she's harmless." She turned back to the stove and carried on her business. Olivia looked at Betty Joy, wide-eyed, at the table, then walked past the girl and down the hall.

*L*ydia sat in a rocker at their patient's side. Clay stood between them, checking his brother, it appeared, for signs of life. Lydia was chatting away about things the doctor had told her, oblivious to the fact Clay considered she might do the wounded man harm. She rose when Olivia came into the room, and Olivia managed the semblance of a smile.

"Is he all right?" she asked.

"Seems to be," Clay answered.

"Doctor Tasker says his breathing is steadier," Lydia said, "but he still sounds terribly choppy to me. The doctor drained more blood. There wasn't much, and he said the lung was still inflated; but he also said someone should be with him all the time in case he starts coughing and spits up blood. Says we..."

We?

"...need to send for him if that happens. He said he'll be back later. I do believe he plans to stay the night."

"How long have you been here?" Olivia asked.

"About two hours. I came as soon as Mabel and I had Mama settled. She won't take any more sleeping potions. Says they're keeping her from taking care of things."

"What kind of things?" Clay asked.

"I'm hoping she means making arrangements for Aunt Aggie, otherwise I'll be the one doing it, but I do believe she'll rather enjoy putting Aunt Aggie to rest." Lydia rose, and prodding Clay out of her way, she wrung the rag in the washbowl by the bed. "Troy"—she winked at Clay—"and I took an immediate liking to each other, so I asked him to come play at my house." She mopped her patient's forehead. "Oh, how this man can play."

"He told you he was Troy?" Clay asked.

She looked at him over her shoulder. "He told me he was Clay, but I've known you were Clay since the morning you refused my offer of sex." Lydia caught Olivia's eye. "Did he tell you about that, darling?"

"Your offer of sex must have slipped his mind."

Lydia laughed, and Olivia pulled off her coat, lifted the chair to her dressing table, and placed it in front of her highboy. Using the chair as a stool, she retrieved her mother's Bible from the top drawer. Back on the floor, she looked and confirmed that she had felt Clay's eyes watching her the whole while. Bible clutched to her breast, she turned on her heel and left the room.

"Is this about Margo?" Clay asked.

Olivia turned from Lionel Augustus's bedroom window and looked at him. "Margo Flores?"

He took a step her direction and held out his hands, palms up. "Listen to me. Hudgins fabricated the sins of Clay Boudreaux in case we had to tell you I was really Troy. Margo was pregnant, but Troy nor I neither one was the father of her baby. John Muriel, the youngest son of a respected businessman in San Antonio, was. His family had interests in Galveston and that's what brought him to my boardinghouse.

"Troy and I'd known Margo all her life. Her mother worked for mine, then took over running the house after Mama died. Margo, in turn, took the job when her own mother died. Goodness knows I didn't want to. She was only eighteen and had nowhere to go, even if she'd wanted to, and she'd forgotten more about managing that boardinghouse than I ever cared to know." He snorted softly. "Can't imagine why the girl wasn't satisfied doing the same drudgery she'd watched her mama do since she could toddle.

"John Muriel offered her excitement and romance. When she turned up pregnant, he high-tailed it back to San Antonio alone.

276

If Troy and I could have forced that bastard to marry her, we would have, and if we could have found a decent man to marry her, we'd have done that, too. The overall situation, of course, didn't look good for me, her being so young and living in my house. People talk, you know."

Olivia didn't respond to that, and he thought she would have. She was paying attention to him, though, studying his face while he spoke, as if trying to memorize it, and he feared she was still searching for deception.

"Margo never tried to exploit the situation, Olivia. She was always honest about who the father of her baby was. She loved the man. Finally, Troy told her he'd marry her. He'd always been fond of her growing up, and I think he was getting lonely out on the ranch. He didn't make many attempts to meet the kind of girl a man would want to marry.

"But Margo turned him down. About four weeks ago now, she rode out to his ranch to tell him she was on her way to San Antone to find Muriel. She told Troy if the man didn't marry her, she was going to shoot him, and she had a gun with her. Troy told her she wasn't going to San Antonio, alone and pregnant, on a damn horse, and shoot anybody. He wanted her to get down and them talk about it, but she insisted there was nothing more to be said, at least to Troy. When she started to turn the horse, Troy grabbed the bridle. Margo responded by whipping at him with the reins. She missed Troy, but the reins caught the horse in the eye. It reared, and Margo came out of the saddle. Broke her neck. She was dead where she fell.

"Troy's two ranch hands, Alfie Mercy and Clem Evans, were right there. Two witnesses, Olivia, an old darkie and an old Indian."

"Who is Troy supposed to have murdered?"

Finally, lucidity. "Two weeks ago," he said, "somebody shot Muriel in San Antonio. Troy had left the ranch several days before that. None of us knew where he was, but we did know that Margo's death had affected him. He blamed himself, and he hated Muriel. That's where I was the night of the fire, on the road, almost back from San Antonio, where I'd gone to confirm Troy had nothing to do with Muriel's death."

He'd hoped for relief on her face, but she simply stood there looking at him.

"Everything I'm telling you is the truth, Olivia, I swear it."

She nodded, as if she believed him, then from the pocket of her skirt, she pulled out the wrinkled letter she'd treasured for days beneath her pillow. "I fell in love with the man who wrote this letter."

"Why?" he asked, because he didn't think there was anything on that page that would make him fall in love with anybody.

"Because you wrote, if you are willing."

"Lionel told me you were."

She nodded. "I was, in part. He was terribly indulgent with me about most things, but he could be demanding, too, especially when it came to duty. He came up with our marriage proposal almost overnight, and he was so adamant we should do this. I prayed you'd refuse, but you didn't. You didn't agree either, until I'd written you back and told you I was willing, also." She blinked back tears. "Because you asked, I was willing to marry you, and as the days passed and Uncle Lionel grew weaker and weaker, it became more than me willing to be your wife. I wanted to be your wife, and I wanted you here to hold me when he died. You weren't, then Uncle Duncan told me you were dead."

He took a step her way, but she held up a hand. "I'm not finished. When you stepped out from behind that door the day we met, I initially thought you were your brother. He'd been here earlier, then disappeared. But when I stepped closer, I knew you weren't him, and then you said you were Clay, the same thing he'd said, I was elated. When I talked to Troy, I wasn't elated. It didn't feel right, and I knew I should be elated to find out the man who wrote this letter was alive."

He thought back to that horrendous first meeting. "You were elated?"

"Briefly. From the moment we met, I suspected you were the right one, and when I realized you hated me, I felt betrayed."

"I didn't hate—"

"There was always the possibility, of course, that you weren't the man who wrote the letter. But then I thought maybe it was because you'd lied in your letter. That you hadn't really been willing to marry me. That all the time you'd been hoping I'd refuse to marry you, and I had let you down when I agreed. And on top of that, after you'd been trapped in this relationship, you thought I was trying to kill you."

"I was angry because I thought Troy was dead."

"But you did feel trapped, didn't you? Before, I mean?"

His head was starting to ache. "I felt railroaded, like you did, never trapped."

"Until you found out you'd married a murderous witch. Then you felt trapped."

"No, I didn't have time to think about our marriage. I was focused on a double murder."

"And now do you feel trapped?"

"No."

"If I'd been the murderess, you'd be free and rich."

His mouth fell open, but before he could say anything she cried, "Do you want to be free?"

"Why would you ask me that?"

She covered her face with her hands. "I want to know if you are going to be as miserable and unhappy as I am right now."

"Olivia, dammit, what is wrong with you?"

She dropped her hands. God, her face was wet with tears. He reached for her, to comfort her, to reassure her, but she backed away.

"It's the other letter," she said.

"The other letter?"

"Yes, the one—"

The door to the bedroom flew open. Lydia stood there, wide-eyed, and if he hadn't held his breath to cut off its oxygen supply, his head would have exploded right then. "What's wrong?" he forced out.

Lydia smiled. "He's awake."

279

"$\mathcal{I}$ ought to kick your butt back to Galveston," Clay said to Troy, "but Nate would probably kick it right back to me. What the devil are you doing here?"

"Keeping you alive," Troy said, his voice a whisper.

"Well, I'm still alive. Can't say you deserve any credit for that, though."

Troy lay on his right side, propped up on pillows with a wall of more pillows at his back. He started to roll over, and Clay rose to stop him. "Don't. Doc says to keep your good lung high, so you stay put."

"Who shot me?"

"Lionel Augustus's lawyer, Sandifer Hudgins. Now, could you explain why you burned down Mama's house?"

His head wobbled, but the gesture was definitely a negative.

"What happened that night?"

Clay watched Troy's gaze pass over his shoulder to where Olivia stood behind him. "Little over two weeks ago now," he began, "neighbor stopped by. He'd been to town. Brought me a letter from your intended."

Clay turned. Olivia's eyes were dry now, and she was battling Troy eye to eye.

"Hey," Clay said, and touched Troy's wrist. Troy refocused on him.

"I'd already given up tryin' to talk to you. Couldn't tell you nothin'. Decided to come to Mississippi to find out what was goin' on. Wanted to get away anyways, what with Margo's death and all."

"Well it would have sure been nice to know you were here when John Muriel was murdered. Nate pulled out every marker he had to keep Bexar County from issuing a warrant for you."

Troy drew in what sounded like a difficult breath. "Katie told you?"

"Yeah, she liked you a lot."

"Night I got back, went to Ma's house to talk to you 'bout what little I'd learned here, but you were gone. Went on down to

Shaunessey's lookin' for you. Dina told me Nate was lookin' for me and why. Sure as hell didn't want to see him, so went back to Mama's to hit the hay. Stench of kerosene hit me soon as I opened the door to our room. There was this fella holding a lantern by your bed." Troy squinted. "You were in it. I saw you."

"Charlie Phelps. Been back off the wagon about a month."

"Know that now." Troy closed his eyes. "Didn't then, though. Thought it was you."

Olivia moved around Clay to the pitcher on the bureau beside her bed. "He's talking too much."

"Nah," Troy said, "I'm all right."

"He shot at you?" Clay asked.

"Scared 'im. Missed. Idiot was tryin' to balance the lantern and was gonna shoot again. Pretty spooked myself. Not thinkin', shot back. He fell. Whole damn room went up."

Troy raised his left arm and covered his eyes. "Tried to get to you, but couldn't see you or the shooter. Scorched pretty good. Knew you was a goner, so I left you to roast. Didn't find out till I saw you here the day of the funeral it wasn't you"—his gaze flitted to Olivia—"but by then I was determined to find your killer."

"Well, I didn't find out for five days that it wasn't you in the ashes," Clay said, "then I still didn't know where you were."

Olivia handed Clay a glass of water, then told Troy to face forward. She moved her arm behind his head and raised him off the pillows.

"It was the wee hours of the mornin' when I got back," Clay told him and put the glass to his lips. "They had the fire out and had found two bodies."

"Do you want more?" Olivia asked and settled Troy back on the pillow when he said no.

Clay looked around Olivia. "Nate was beside himself. He thought one of those bodies belonged to me. No sooner did we have that crisis happily resolved than Dina comes running out of nowhere. She'd just heard about the fire. Told us she'd seen you earlier, and you were going back to the house to wait on me. That's why we were so sure you were dead. Nate just stood there close to squallin', saying for sure God wanted a Boudreaux that night. Woulda been nice if you'd shown yourself, big brother."

"Would've if I'd known you'd given me up for dead. 'Fraid if you saw me Nate would want me back in Texas, and you'd end up alone in this alligator-infested swamp."

"They got Muriel's killer. He was in the wrong part of town. Tried to fight off a thief."

Troy's only response was a soft snort.

"And would you please explain that game you were playing with Olivia?"

"Olivia"—again Troy looked at her, standing over him— "tried to hire me to kill you."

"She didn't write that letter."

"Considered that"—he coughed—"but figured somebody was tryin' to draw me into this for some reason or other. Decided to accommodate 'em. Speakin' of which, where's my redhead?"

"Your redhead," Olivia told him, "went to look after her mother."

Troy hacked again, and on the third spasm, Olivia twisted around to Clay. "He needs to quit talking."

Clay nodded, then touched Troy's arm. "You hurtin'?"

Troy pointed down to his right side.

"Bullet broke a rib, and the doctor periodically sticks a big, gawd-awful needle under your arm and drains blood out of you."

"How about some beef tea?" Olivia said. "Then I'll mix some laudanum with—"

"Whiskey."

Olivia's mouth dropped open, and Clay held up a hand. "You mix the laudanum with water. I'll give him a shot of whiskey."

Immediately she started shaking her head.

"Hey," Clay said, "the doc said so."

"He's sleeping," Olivia said, and Clay, sitting at the foot of the bed they'd made love on the night before, turned to look at her over his shoulder. "I left the door open," she continued, walking into the room, "so we can hear him. I hope he wakes up. I'm really not so sure we should have combined the laudanum with whiskey."

"It'll be okay," he said and turned back to a shiny boot in his hands, one of a pair she'd never seen him wear. He dropped the boot to the floor, rose, and held out a white linen envelope, a piece of a fine stationery set she recognized as her own. "I don't know if this will help put your mind at ease," he said, "but this is your alleged letter to Troy. Why you would think, after last night, I'd want to be free, I can't figure out."

She averted her eyes and fought back tears, praying he wouldn't see, then she took the letter, for what it was worth. He cupped his palm around her elbow, and she resisted the urge to pull away, but let him lead her to the bed, their bed of sweet sin, divinely beautiful and hatefully vile.

"Read it," he said, and she pulled the missive from the envelope. The script was precise, much like her own hand.

"I compared it to that one letter you wrote me after I agreed to Lionel's terms. You've got to admit I had cause for concern."

"Katie had excellent penmanship, and she knew where to find my stationery."

"And coming by a sample of your handwriting wouldn't have been hard. I didn't read that letter until after Hudgins told me that same tale he told you this afternoon about Troy being Lionel's son. Satisfied he'd set a plan in motion, he left and I—"

"Read this letter allegedly sent by me."

"Yes. I believed Troy was dead, and I had to know if you were responsible."

"So you came to get me."

"I came for the truth."

"You came to prove me guilty, not absolve me."

"To free me from my marriage vows, is that what you think? No, Olivia. When you grabbed me around the neck and told me you were going to help me find Clay's murderers, then see me hanged, I started to hope it might work out for us after all." He reached for her hand, and for the space of a heartbeat she relished his touch. Then she stood and pulled away.

He stood, too. "What did Sandifer Hudgins say to you," he said softly, "that makes you not want me anymore?"

"He stole you from me, and me from you with the very tool he thought would satisfy me as to who you are."

"What are you talking about?" Clay asked, and trepidation cinched his gut when her eyes shimmered with tears. She walked to the dresser and picked up a folded piece of stationery.

"This is your mother's letter," she said, and her voice broke. "The one Sandifer Hudgins had. The one that fool thinks Elaine Boudreaux wrote to Lionel Augustus twenty-eight years ago. The one he thinks proves Troy is Uncle Lionel's son."

"What makes you think he's mistaken about that letter?"

She separated two pieces of paper and waved them in front of her. "Because I have the beginning of the thing."

The tears overflowed, and he took two quick steps toward her. She hugged herself and tried to scramble back, but he caught her to him anyway and held her so that she sobbed into his chest.

"Oh, God," she said, looking up to see his face. "I wish I'd never known your touch, knowing I never will again."

His heart was thumping like the hind leg of a hound, scratching fleas on an old wood porch. "Will you please tell me why you are saying these stupid things?"

"Elaine didn't write that letter to Uncle Lionel," Olivia said. "She wrote it to my father, Darcy Clayton Lee. And that baby she spoke of? That baby wasn't Troy. It was the child she was carrying at the time. Her second baby. Oh, Clayton Lee Boudreaux, she didn't name you after her and Edwin's best friend. She named you after your father."

Chapter Forty-five

October 4, 1869

My dearest darling, Darcy,

I am sorry for the sadness I have caused you. I am undeservedly blessed with the fruit of our union and the knowledge that you are pleased also. You are the one person, the only person, I would believe such a sacrifice of. Unfortunately, or fortunately as the case might be, none but we three will ever know what you and Lionel have given up, you for your dearest friend and Lionel for you.

Ed's melancholy has disappeared, at least for the moment. It would seem he has come to terms with his infirmity. He and Papa have spanned the chasm created when Edwin deserted me. Truly, Papa understands, and he was always so fond of Ed. Edwin confessed to me that he left intending never to return. He had planned to take his own life and allow me the chance to begin anew. He faults himself a coward, but I know it was the prospect of raising Troy that brought him home again. As regards the other, I told him what we three had agreed to tell him.

Hands shaking, Clay placed the page of the letter Olivia had taken from Hudgins's hotel room and placed it on top of the one she'd pulled from her mother's Bible.

285

He will never know the truth, not from my lips. Trust this, my darling, Lionel Augustus is and always will be the father. I do not feel the wrong I have done Edwin as painfully as the one I have done you. Troy gives him a reason to live and that is the one blessing I want him to cherish the rest of his life.

Edwin wishes us to try again to make a life together, and is pleased that I have distanced myself from the baby's father. Sonja's return provided the motivation for following Papa to Texas. No one will question my reason for leaving.

I do want us to be a family and am comforted knowing you wish the same for Ed and me and "our" children. My dearest wish is that you will find a woman who will bear you a legitimate son to carry on your fathers' name, but always know your blood will continue, no matter what happens.

I will always love you,

Elaine

He read it once more before he found the strength to look up at Olivia. "You found the first page in your mother's Bible?"

"Years ago," she said, and stepped away from Lionel Augustus's dresser, where she'd waited while he read the thing. "The Bible actually belonged to her mother. Uncle Lionel gave it to me when I was twelve, along with a few other things that had belonged to Mama. I'm sure he never even looked in the Bible. I don't think he would have left that in there." She trilled an unhappy laugh. "It's as if we're performing in an old play starring more popular actors."

A marionette to be more specific, and it wasn't the first time Clay had felt this way over the last two weeks.

"I scarcely glanced at that letter when I first found it. I was a kid. I knew Mama didn't write it. I figured later, given the reference to Ed, that Elaine Boudreaux must have; she and Daddy had been dear friends. It wasn't until I saw the second sheet this morning that I understood the full thrust of what she was saying."

Clay rose from his spot at the foot of the bed. "I wonder, since you had the first sheet, how Hudgins came by the second?"

A knock sounded on the open bedroom door, and Clay turned to find Aunt Connie, already in the room. "Come now, deputy," she said, "you're smart enough to figure that out. If Sandy had it, it was because Rebecca gave it to him, and I can assure you her purpose was to use whatever is in there against Lionel."

Clay's gut, already queasy from the terrible revelation thrust upon him, knotted. He held up the letter. "You knew about this?"

"About that particular letter, no, but I knew Rebecca."

The hair on the back of his neck pricked his skin. He didn't like the feverish shine in the woman's eyes, or the contempt molding her lips. Uneasy, he glanced at the hand hidden in the pocket of her heavy coat. Her right hand. She stood, guarded, between them and the door. And he especially didn't like her getting this far into their house without them hearing her. They'd been preoccupied, yes, but she'd been stealthy.

"Did you come in the back?" he asked.

"I came in the skiff down the bayou to the bulkhead out front. May brought our supper on her way home, so I knew your darkies were gone for the day. No one saw me come in. Not that it matters at this point."

Behind him, he heard Olivia move, then she appeared at his side, and he squelched the urge to shove her behind him.

"Could I take your coat?" she said.

"No," Connie said, and the right pocket of her coat moved.

"Why are you here?" he asked.

Her dark hair, down, reminded him of a horse's mane. The wildness of it matched her eyes. The hair he attributed to her journey down the bayou, the eyes to madness.

"I came to tell you a nasty little secret, but I do believe you've already uncovered it. I gleefully assume, given the devastation on your faces, the marriage really has been consummated. It would almost be worth it to let you both live"—Clay's thighs weakened—"you knowing you defiled your baby sister"—her gaze slid to Olivia—"and you your brother. A thicket of thorns sown by deranged gardeners. I find much satisfaction knowing Rebecca Fontaine's daughter and my son's killer are the soiled fruit. Was it truly delectable, Olivia?"

He moved, more for Olivia than for him, but Aunt Connie had her back against the wall and the .38 out of her coat pocket before he could reach her. Olivia let loose a little cry and rushed to place herself between him and her aunt, but he managed to hold her to his side.

"Did I say something to anger you, Clayton Lee Boudreaux?" She blinked. "Sweet Darcy's bastard. I will find it hard to kill you, but then I must take Howard into account." She drew in a heavy breath and, apparently invigorated, turned the gun on Olivia. "There was never any hope for you. Where his features please my poor eyes, your very person pains them."

Clay sidled to put himself between Connie and Olivia.

"Do you know why?" the woman asked.

"Because I look like my mother."

"The whore who slept with my husband and cost your father his life."

Clay's tense gut balled into a solid, burning lump. Darcy Lee and two other men died in a freak logging accident. There had never, *never*, as far as Clay knew, been even a whisper of murder associated with his death.

"Your father was a darling," Connie said, then continued in a little girl's voice, "he was my nephew, and I did love him so."

"How did Mama cause Daddy's death?"

"I got even with her...and with Duncan."

"By killing my father?" Olivia said.

"Don't be stupid!"

Not taking his eyes off Connie, Clay chopped the air in front of Olivia and prayed she'd heed his warning. She did.

"Tell us what happened," he coaxed.

"He found out something he shouldn't have. He confronted Duncan and Agatha. Next I knew, he was dead."

"What did he find out?

"It concerned federal land and timber and bribes. I don't know the details, and I don't care. The point is he wasn't going to tolerate it, and they killed him."

"Aunt Aggie and Uncle Duncan?"

"Agatha and Sandifer Hudgins and whoever else they were working with. Poor Sandy had no idea what he was getting into when Agatha approached him, and you may rest assured she concocted the scheme. She was Lionel's secretary at the time, had been for years. Lionel knew how devious she was, but putting her to work appeased his guilt for selling their Maryland farm out from under her, but she never ceased wanting to thwart him.

"Aunt Connie," Olivia said in a voice that sounded almost calm, "Daddy died in a logging acci—"

"He was murdered, but it was an act of vengeance by that disgusting person who gave birth to you that caused it."

"What was your role, Aunt Connie?" Clay asked, realizing now the woman was cleansing her soul, a prelude to her final act of vengeance and her own death.

"Duncan never used discretion in his business dealings. He considered me stupid. I was protecting Darcy's interest."

"You passed him the information, didn't you?"

She averted her eyes. "And then he knew too much."

Downstairs, Duncan called Connie's name, and the woman suddenly glowed.

"I'm up here, darling," she sang out, and Clay held his breath. He'd been a fool to factor Uncle Duncan and his remaining sons out of this. He heard them on the stairs, Duncan and unknown others. His .44 was under the bed on the other side, the side he slept on. He was sure Olivia wasn't armed.

Duncan stopped short at the bedroom door. Connie had the gun pointed at him now, and Clay released that captured breath.

"I've been waiting on you, husband."

289

"Lydia's at the house, Connie. She's looking all over for you."

"And aren't you the clever one, knowing where I was all the time."

Duncan glanced at the pistol, then at Olivia, before briefly catching Clay's eye. Brogan stood behind Duncan, Francis beside Brogan. Francis stepped forward; Duncan waved him back.

"Why are you here?" Duncan asked her.

"I came to tell your niece and nephew something they needed to know."

"And that is?"

"Why that they're brother and sister, of course. Don't tell me you didn't know." She waved her left hand in the air. "Only half, really. Do you think that would make their marriage blessed in the eyes of God?"

"I think God could care less."

"Shame, Duncan. Olivia is quite upset. So, I believe, is Clay."

"Give me the gun," Duncan said.

"Oh, I have to put them out of their misery first. Then I'm going to put you out of yours."

"There's only one person in misery here," Duncan said. "You might consider using the gun on yourself."

"Dammit, Dad." Francis pushed around his father, who immediately pulled him back.

"Stop it, son. She doesn't want to kill anybody, or she'd have done it by now."

"Oh, yes, I do."

"Then why haven't you?"

"I have."

"She killed Agatha," Clay said.

Duncan didn't even blink. The man knew, Clay realized. He himself had guessed, but Duncan already knew, and probably had since she'd made that scene in his office earlier this afternoon.

"I heard Agatha and Sandy in the wee hours of the morning," Connie said to her husband. "They were plotting the demise of the person they thought was Clay Boudreaux. Floyd had seen a man in the woods days ago. Then he saw him again. You were in

New Orleans that last time, so he told Agatha about him. Told her this person had hid out two mornings straight that he knew of. So this morning, Agatha showed Sandy the way through the woods, so he could bushwhack him.

"I waited in the woods for her to get back. She was so confident and self-assured looking at me holding the gun on her. She waited there in front of me until we heard the first two shots. She told me it was done and once they'd exposed Troy as a fraud and Olivia as a murderess, you and she would have everything and Howard would be avenged. But I knew she had no intention of sharing with you. And I knew you would have never sent Howard to kill a man. I've known all along it was her. So I pressed that trigger, for Howard and for Darcy."

"For Darcy, Connie?"

"Yes," she hissed, "and I'm going to kill you for Darcy, but mostly I'm going to kill you for me." Still holding the gun steady on Duncan, she raised her chin and found Olivia. "I'm going to kill you, too, and I hope Rebecca's watching from hell."

"And Darcy? Do you hope he's watching, too, when you put his children in the grave?"

She refocused on Clay. "It is a pity I have to kill his son."

"Do you think Darcy will forgive you either one of them? Or do you care? You and I both know that hurting Darcy is what you really want, what you've always wanted."

Her gaze jerked to him. "What do you mean?"

"His children are nothing more than gravy on the meat, Connie. You wanted Darcy dead, not for vengeance against me and Rebecca, but for vengeance against him, for rejecting you."

Connie's eyes widened, and she forced an inhuman growl between bared teeth.

Duncan moved, and when he did, Clay whirled and caught Olivia in his arms. They crashed to the carpet together, their muffled fall overwhelmed by one ear-splitting gunshot followed by another. He twisted to see Connie sliding down the bedroom wall, smearing blood on the plaster surface as she went.

Duncan caught her before she hit the floor, and he stretched her out on the Aubusson carpet in Lionel's room. Francis sank beside his mother, while Sheriff Brogan blustered through an apology.

"You did the right thing, Brogan," Uncle Duncan was saying, his voice clear, but decidedly tired. "You did the right thing." Clay sat up and pulled Olivia with him. Uncle Duncan touched Connie beneath her left breast, then glanced over his shoulder at Brogan. "There's no telling who she'd have killed here, if you hadn't fired when you did." With a sigh, he rose and looked Clay in the eye. "She's dead."

Chapter Forty-six

Clay found Olivia staring out the bank of windows in Lionel Augustus's office, the chilly room in shadow and the setting sun glinting off the dark, choppy waters of Bayou Bernard.

She held a paper in her hand—what it was he couldn't guess, because he held the two pages that had, more so than the fatal and near-fatal shootings of this violent day, shattered their lives. Then he realized she held that snot-stained, wadded, and vomit-splattered missive he'd written her almost a month earlier. The one that had made her fall in love with him, she'd said, and his heart ached, for her and for him and for his mother and Darcy Lee and even for Edwin Boudreaux, all of them he'd known and loved. And he crossed the room and wrapped her in his arms and drew her spine against his breast, and he held her tight and smelled her hair despite her initial protests. Finally she started to cry, ever so softly so that he wouldn't have even known she cried, but for the trembling of her body. "You believe it's true, don't you?" she said.

He swallowed. "I believe I'm Darcy Lee's son. That clears up some things. His frequent visits. The way Mama wept and held me the day Granddaddy came with the news he'd been killed."

"I don't think I can stand living without you. I can't believe Uncle Lionel has done this to us."

"And that's the part I don't believe. Something has to be missing, Olivia. There has to be—"

"Um hum."

Reluctantly, Clay released her, and he turned to find Uncle Duncan standing behind them. He had escorted everyone out the back door minutes ago, Duncan, Doctor Tasker, Brogan, and

Francis. They'd placed Aunt Connie's body in his wagon to move her back up the road and home.

Olivia wiped away a tear and stepped around the desk. "Are you all right, Uncle Duncan?"

"What I feel at the moment," he said, "is a sense of relief. Your aunt and I haven't loved or even liked each other for a long, long time."

"But Francis and Julian—"

"Yes," he said with an air of dismissal, "the children loved her; she was their mother. Thank God they're grown. It's almost a pity, though, that Mabel's outlived her. She was thirteen when Connie was born; been with her ever since. Ol' gal's gonna take it harder than any of us.

"But things have been falling apart these past two years with my company's problems and Lionel's illness. Then this whole thing with Clay's coming back and Agatha's intervention, resurrecting old ghosts." He reached to turn up the gaslight. The room brightened, and Olivia closed her eyes. Clay didn't particularly want to face the light either.

"I need to talk to you." He spied the letter Clay held, and he extended his hand palm up. "May I?"

Clay looked at Olivia, who shrugged. Duncan's reading the thing really couldn't make matters any worse than they already were, so he handed over the letter.

"Ah," Duncan said after a brief perusal of the thing, "I thought perhaps Connie had told you outright and I could make light of the whole thing, then dismiss it as an erroneous guess on her part—and it was." He looked at Clay. "A guess, I mean, but not an erroneous one."

Clay's knees weakened.

"The first page was in Mama's Bible," Olivia said. "Sandifer Hudgins had the last one. I didn't see it till this afternoon. He thought it proved Troy was Uncle Lionel's son, too."

Duncan almost sat in the wing chair in front of Lionel's desk, then straightened and held a hand out to Olivia instead. "Could I see that locket, honey?" She unlatched it and gave it to him. He opened it, then looked at Clay. "It's been a long time since I've seen his face. That and the fact I wanted you to be Troy kept me from admitting the truth, so clear to Connie. You do have your father's eyes, but I was certain you were Clay yesterday morning after Toby was shot, and it wasn't your eyes that told me, but your entire face. It was the way you turned your head in the sunlight when you were asking me about the autopsy. At that moment, you were Darcy Lee. Funny how the tilt of a head will do that." Duncan snapped the locket shut, returned it to Olivia, and sat. "He's a tall, good-looking boy and a fine man, Lionel said of you after that last visit to Galveston. Darcy would be proud." He pointed at the impressive chair behind the desk. "Once Lionel thought Darcy would sit in that seat. I think you'll fill it fine."

Clay didn't move to take the chair, but Duncan's gaze had already refocused on Olivia. He held up the letter. "My guess is your mother found this in Darcy's things after he was killed. He should have never kept it, of course. Guess it was too precious to him to destroy." He studied the second page again, then sighed. "No doubt she gave this to Sandifer, intending one day for the two of them to attempt the deception you've recently witnessed. I wouldn't think she ever showed Sandy the entire letter, just left him believing Troy really was Lionel's son. She, of course, had the more valuable piece of information, should the need arrive. Rebecca enjoyed deception and creating turmoil, but as regards this letter, she died before she could put her plan in motion. Sandifer would have never known the truth.

"Rebecca was barely seventeen when she burst into our circle and gave the middle-aged men in unhappy marriages something to dream of at night. She discovered at an early age that she was adept at manipulating foolish men, and the older many of us get, the more foolish we become." He looked at Olivia. "She didn't intend to die when she did, honey. She wasn't even twenty-one."

He left the letter in his lap and turned to Clay. "It was always about Darcy, you know? But truth be told, it was about Darcy's daddy, Matthew, who was more a father to Lionel and me on his worst day than Peter Augustus ever cared to be. Matt was a fine

295

man, and so, too, we always heard, was his father before him. That was James Lee, the man who founded the Maryland farm Lionel eventually inherited by right of birth. A man we were in no way related to by blood.

"After James Lee died, Matt's mother wed my father, but as long as Matt's mother remained alive, Matt's position in the household and management of the farm remained secure. Mary Lee Augustus gave my father one child, Aggie, again no threat to Matt's inheritance, not in a legal sense anyway. Then Mary died, and Peter wed my and Lionel's mother, Martha.

"My father wasn't a loving man. He could sometimes be cruel and abusive, and he was always a niggardly old miser of the worst sort. Stingy with money, with his time, and with his love, if he ever had any to give. Matt was the one who took time with us younger kids and taught us to work the farm, to hunt, to fish. Daddy worked Matt hard, and he worked Lionel and me hard, too. And poor Aggie and Mama worked their hands raw keeping that big house James Lee built. James Lee had been a slave owner, so was my daddy, but Daddy said two womenfolk were enough to keep a house running smoothly. There were no Mays or Mabels at the Augustus farm in Maryland. My mama died at thirty-eight from pneumonia, plumb wore out. She kept more than the house. She did much of the farm management.

"Lionel never forgave our daddy, and Matthew told the man exactly what he thought of his hard-hearted attitude toward his women while he hoarded the money that would have paid for a good domestic. Lionel told me years later that Matt blamed our father for working his own mama to death. My father made life for Matthew untenable, and at twenty he abandoned his birthright and came to Mississippi.

"Be patient with me now," Duncan said, "this all ties together." He looked over and found Olivia. "The rest of what I need to tell is harder told to you, Ollie, but I have to do it. It concerns your mother and me and the rest of us."

Finally, Clay took his seat in the chair once meant for Darcy Lee, then he and Duncan looked at Olivia, but she stayed where she stood. After a moment, Duncan bowed his head. "To start, the hateful words you've had to endure from your Aunt Connie about your mother are true. They didn't need to be said in front of you, but they are true."

Duncan turned to Clay and said, "You knew, didn't you?"

"That she was beautiful and ruthless, yes, and that Darcy regretted marrying her."

"But there were other things your mother and grandfather and Nate Phillips and the rest of the boys from Company P never told you, because they didn't know. Things Lionel never wanted Olivia to know. Things I never wanted Olivia to know. Things brothers share with each other."

Clay thought of Troy. "And things they don't," he said.

Duncan's smile was slow in coming, but thoughtful when it did. "Yes, well, I'm coming to that, too, 'cause I'm afraid we're gonna have to drag all the cats out of the proverbial bag.

"Howard was an infant when Connie and I followed Lionel here after the War. Agatha, alone in Maryland, followed shortly after. Lionel told me he could put me to work in the timber business he and Darcy had going. Lionel spent the War years as an army quartermaster. As a result, he had good connections with the occupying forces. Some of the senior officers he despised, some he respected, and all of them he was able to use and manipulate. Same for the Republican politicians and thieves that had infested the South. Those are Lionel's words, not mine. We were from Maryland, and despite the fact we wore blue, we were Southerners in all things except dividing the Union in two.

"Connie's parents owned a small tobacco farm. They were comfortable, but not wealthy. Owned a handful of slaves, mostly domestic. Her father managed the farm with hired help, but her people had settled the eastern seaboard at the dawn of the eighteenth century and considered themselves among the elitist class. Connie was a beauty and the belle of the ball. She had her pick of men. She wed the second-born son of a man who had stolen the birthright of his stepson.

"As you often heard your Aunt Connie intimate, Olivia, I inherited her father's small operation, invested in risky schemes, and lost it. Lionel, on the other hand, inherited our father's ill-gotten gains and sold the land. Agatha never forgave him. But it was his right, and she never wanted for a roof over her head.

"Lionel invested in shipping and merchant trade and slave trading. He'd be the first to tell you the latter was the most lucrative and where he made his original fortune. He divested himself of involvement as the abolitionist movement grew and concentrated his money in textiles. Anything, he used to tell those people to weaken slavery in the South. Some of them didn't even pick up on the irony. He despised abolitionists.

"But whatever he embarked on turned to gold. My efforts turned to lead."

"He knew which risks to take," Clay said.

"And he had a good understanding of people, most of the time." Duncan's gaze shifted from Clay to Olivia. "He was not always an honest man, Ollie, you do realize that?"

"I wasn't raised to believe he was perfect."

"I think most of us have a line we won't cross. You might be dismayed to learn some of the ones Lionel did cross."

"Did he hurt carpetbaggers and federals?"

Duncan grinned. "You know he did, honey, but he hurt others as well, before the War and long after Reconstruction ended."

He turned back to Clay. "I've been pretty much dependent on Lionel for the last thirty years. When Connie and I and our then two children arrived here, Mississippi was still under martial law. Lionel had been awarded a federal lease on a timber tract in Perry County. There was a lot of wheelin' and dealin' then regarding reclaimed land and state and federal coffers, every entity involved being nothing more than a jackal tearing at a carcass, but Lionel had his contract, and he had the men to work it, those being Darcy and the survivors from that part of Marion County where we had all gathered to make a living. Six years later the Democrats all but ran Ames and his thieving cronies out of state on a rail, and Lionel and Darcy and I were sitting pretty, moving timber, planting cotton, and paying taxes and still manipulating federal contracts and the disreputable dogs who handled them."

Duncan played absently with the letter in his lap, then blew out a breath. "Federal contract manipulation fell under the purview of Lionel and his trusted lawyer, Benford Hudgins and Hudgins's son Sandifer."

Clay's stomach tightened in anticipation, and he sat forward in the swivel chair. Duncan straightened in his.

"In the interim, Connie had given birth to Julian, then Lydia. She was no longer the belle of the ball. She was tired, well into her thirties and plump, disillusioned with me and her family, disgusted with post-War Mississippi, and infatuated with the handsome, gentlemanly, and properly attentive Darcy Lee, who she saw on an almost daily basis. He had in the meantime" — Duncan held up Elaine Boudreaux's letter — "lost his one true love, a fact that only he, Lionel, and Elaine were aware of at the time. Lionel took credit for being your father, because Darcy couldn't bear the thought of Edwin learning he had slept with Elaine, but in defense of Elaine and Darcy, Ed was believed dead, and Darcy had loved her since childhood. In my opinion, Ed might well have forgiven Darcy. Neither his wife nor his best friend had intentionally betrayed him, but Darcy couldn't forgive himself.

"Darcy's marriage to the destitute Rebecca Fontaine was sudden and took everyone by surprise. She was the daughter of the Mexican War hero, Lieutenant Rupert Fontaine, who ultimately gave his life for the Confederacy, and great-granddaughter of the Revolutionary War officer and hero, Alexander Fontaine, who came here shortly after independence and helped wrest this area from the Spanish Dons."

"Rebecca was eighteen when Darcy wed her, old aristocracy, beautiful, intelligent, and vivacious, and very much aware of who she was and where she came from. She was the belle of the ball, and Lionel seemed pleased with the match. So did her mother and stepfather, an influential redeemer. Suffice it to say, Connie hated her. Not only was she jealous of the woman, she didn't like the way she treated Darcy, and she didn't approve of the way she flirted with men, meaning me."

"Publicly, Darcy and Rebecca continued their charade. The course of their married life really didn't make them so different from most of the other couples around. Sonja had made Lionel's life pure hell, and Connie and I rarely spoke.

"But Lionel and I were family, and we knew Darcy wasn't happy. He didn't like the woman, plain and simple, but by then, Rebecca had given birth to Olivia.

"Then one Sunday afternoon after the traditional family dinner, Connie approached Darcy regarding a romantic liaison." Duncan laid his head back against the chair and closed his eyes. "She was seven years his senior, she had four small children and Darcy had always considered her a favorite aunt. Needless to say, he diplomatically declined.

"Unfortunately, Agatha made a usually inattentive Rebecca aware of Connie's interest in her husband, and the much offended Rebecca decided a little tit for tat was required to satisfy the grievance."

Clay leaned over the desk, but it was Olivia who spoke. "She went after you."

"And I let her. She was beautiful and seductive...and"—he shrugged—"well, it was hardly an act of love. She only wanted to rub Connie's nose in the fact she'd slept with me, and I was too arrogant to realize it until too late. I can't tell you the disgust I felt with myself when I did. It's not that I'd been a faithful husband to Connie, I never was. That didn't bother me. It was the fact I'd slept with Darcy's wife. That night, and for the near two years Rebecca survived after, I loathed her presence.

"Connie didn't confront me, but I knew she knew. Rebecca made certain of that. Connie got even by informing Darcy of an impending contract Agatha and I had orchestrated through an anonymous partner of Aggie's for a two-hundred-fifty-thousand-acre tract of pine forest in south-central Mississippi."

"The secret partner was Sandifer Hudgins?"

"Yes, and the sweet deal was the result of a relatively small bribe to a federal bureaucrat and a Hudgins intimate, who just happened to be a federal district judge with a powerful name and a lot of tenure. Lionel wasn't aware of these goings-on, and, therefore, neither was Darcy. Lionel didn't trust the bureaucrat, and he hated the judge. Nor did he know that his lawyer's son had been drawn into the business by his resentful older sister, still chafing, or so she claimed, from the sale of the family farm.

"The agreement would have deprived roughly twenty-five small landowners of their land under the guise of a railroad right-of-way. Those were Mississippi landowners, some freedmen, but mostly white Confederates, and Darcy would have never allowed it to happen if he could stop it.

"He came to me the night after Connie told him. He said to call off the deal and that would be the end of it. Said he wouldn't even talk to Lionel, just call it off." Duncan laughed, not pleasantly. "He was protecting me. I'm pretty certain at that point he didn't know I'd betrayed him with Rebecca. Connie didn't tell him about that, just sabotaged the land deal.

"I went to Agatha and told her we needed to terminate negotiations. Back then, I didn't know Agatha's point man was Sandy Hudgins, and I don't know who he talked to or what they decided, but thirty-six hours later Darcy was dead, killed in a logging accident. I always considered his death overkill. Crooked deals and crooked judges ran rampant, but Sandy Hudgins lived in Benford Hudgins's shadow. The man dominated him. I've long suspected Sandifer insisted on carrying out murder rather than risk his father's finding out about his bribery and misuse of privileged attorney-client information, all for personal gain."

"But who was there to commit the—"

"There were always transients on those logging crews, Clay. A little bit of money in cheap pockets can buy some pretty nasty deeds."

Clay fell back in his chair, which rolled away from the knee-hole. He swiveled and looked out at the darkening bayou. "Did Lionel know?"

"Murder, yes. About Sandifer Hudgins, no. He never knew. Benford Hudgins preceded Lionel in death by only two months, and though Sandy had taken over a good portion of the case load

301

by that time, Benford Hudgins remained Lionel's attorney until the day Benford died.

"I was sick over Darcy's death." He looked down at his feet. "It still makes me sick, when I think about it. Connie appeared devastated. Despite what you heard me tell her earlier, I've often wondered if she realized what she was putting in motion when she went to him. Right after the funeral she brought the whole sordid series of events to Lionel's attention. Agatha swore she had simply passed the word to the judge. But for Connie's confession, I don't think I would have ever said a word, and I'm sure Agatha would have never said anything, unless it was to blackmail someone, which I suspect she's been doing to Sandifer for years."

"The land deal went through?"

"Nope. Lost the principals involved. Seems that federal judge liked to fish. Had a little boating accident on the Strong River on a quiet, spring morning three weeks after Darcy's funeral. So sad, Lionel told his widow at the wake."

Justice, but only in part. "Why did Lionel marry Rebecca?" Clay asked, "he couldn't possibly have liked the woman."

"Ah," Duncan said. "Now, that was about Olivia."

"To take care of Darcy Lee's daughter," she said with a heavy voice. "The child Darcy did acknowledge."

"Yes, it was very important to Lionel to care for that particular child." Duncan caught Clay's eye. "In answer to your question, I don't know exactly how Lionel proposed to her, but the gist of it was, if you want to continue to live with your daughter, you will accompany me back to Handsboro where we will marry and live till death do us part."

Clay's heart skipped a beat, and his face must have conveyed his concern because Duncan said, "I know what you're thinking, and no. Rebecca was a good mother and loved her little girl. Lionel would have never taken Olivia's mama from her.

"Officially, she died of the grippe less than a year after they wed. The same cause of death for Peter Augustus, my, Lionel's, and Agatha's father."

302

"Aunt Aggie," Olivia said softly.

"Yes," Duncan said and slowly shook his head, "Aunt Aggie. One October morning when I was sixteen, I fired at a buck and spooked my father's fine mare, within days of foaling. She charged into a split-rail fence, shattered her shoulder, and broke a hock. Lost her and the foal.

"Lionel was near twenty. Father had sent him to Baltimore to conduct some banking. Just Agatha, me, and our father at the house. Papa had a faithful hickory stick, and that morning, he beat me with it. He hit Agatha, too, across the face, when she tried to stop the beating. Aggie was never a beauty, but she certainly looked better before that blow. He hit her at an angle across the bridge of her nose and crushed her eye socket. The realization of what he'd done to his daughter sobered him, and he stopped beating me. Aggie saved my life, and she never let me forget it.

"Father died before dawn the next morning; he'd been sick all night. Lionel returned from Baltimore the next day to find his father dead, Agatha with a broken nose and one eye swelled shut, and me laid up, beaten half to death and with two broken ribs."

"Did you know what she'd done?" Clay asked.

"She fed me broth early that night. Told me she had to make Father a special soup and I was not to touch it. Since I couldn't get out of bed by myself, her warning made little sense otherwise."

"She wanted you to know," Olivia said.

"Yes. My knowing left me guilty and obligated to her. Lionel realized what had happened the moment he arrived home. Part of his silence was the price for protecting me, but truth was, we were both too scared to try and prove murder, even if we'd wanted to. Patricide in the case of a farm the size of that one would have cast suspicion on him, too."

"And my mama?" Olivia asked.

"Rebecca died early on a Monday evening. She'd been in bed for two days prior with a cold. As was customary on Sundays, the family got together after church for dinner. That particular Sunday was Lionel's turn to host, but since Rebecca was so sick, we ate at my house.

"Mabel had made a chicken broth the day before to go in the dressing. She set a bowl of it aside and sent it by Tom Buscher to Rebecca here at Epico Hollow. The doctor determined Rebecca had come down with the grippe on top of fighting that bad cold, and that's what killed her.

"Weeks later, Tom told Lionel that it had been Connie who told Mabel to save some broth for Rebecca. Connie told me the thoughtful gesture had been carried out at Agatha's suggestion."

"They were working together?" Olivia asked.

Duncan shrugged. "Maybe, but there was plenty of opportunity that afternoon for Aggie to sneak into the kitchen and poison the broth on her own. But there was no proof, and there was a valid certificate of death citing grippe as the cause.

"Again, as was the case with Peter Augustus, Rebecca's murder would have cast doubt on any number of people, including, this time, the servants."

"But why did Aunt Aggie want Mama dead?"

"Because your mother threatened something your Aunt Aggie considered hers." Duncan looked at Clay. "Do you recall Connie's scene in my office earlier this afternoon?"

He did indeed, and he nodded.

"Sandy was a handsome man, even more so in his younger days, and a womanizer. For a brief moment seventeen years ago, his wandering eye fell on Rebecca. The liaison was one Benford Hudgins would have absolutely forbidden and one Agatha, her talons already into Sandifer given what she knew of his involvement in Darcy's death, didn't feel she had to tolerate." Uncle Duncan looked down at the letter in his lap. "Rebecca, on the other hand, obviously felt she had the upper hand. My guess is, Sandifer, given a choice between the two women, was willing to take a risk with Rebecca and whatever advantage he felt this thing"—he waved the letter in front of them—"would give him over Lionel. Of course, Rebecca, knowing the whole truth, had the real advantage. Sandifer's half of the letter was no good to him as long as Lionel lived. Hence, he didn't make a move until after Lionel's death, and since his ploy was based on Rebecca's deception, the letter was really of no value to him at all."

"And Clay and I really are..."—Olivia's voice broke, and she turned from both men.

Duncan stood and crossed to her. He wrapped his arm around her shoulder and pulled her bowed head to his chest. She raised it off and pushed back.

"You knew. You've always known. How could you let Uncle Lionel do this?"

"I haven't always known. Leaving half the estate to Clay was something I'd come to accept, but I knew you'd get the other half, and I planned on Julian getting you. When Lionel dreamed up this sudden plan to marry you and Clay off to each other, he fouled up my plans completely, and I confronted him. I knew the result would be incest. That's when he told me Darcy was Clay's daddy. He had no choice really; I'd have stopped your wedding if he hadn't told me the truth."

Olivia's brow furrowed.

"Lionel was so pleased with himself. Almost giddy. Wondered why he hadn't thought of the union before. It gave him, he said, everything he wanted, his and Darcy's posterity to inherit his empire."

"That makes no sense."

"Oh, honey, it does, and it answered a question that had perplexed me for two decades." Once more he waved the letter in front of him. "And that was, why did Darcy do what he did?"

"What did he do?" Olivia asked.

"Listen up, Ollie," he said, again placing his arm around her shoulders. "You're going to like this part. What he did was marry Rebecca. I knew he loved Lionel, but marrying Rebecca seemed more of a sacrifice than any young man should be asked to make."

Clay's heart lurched into a gallop. He knew then, but Olivia hadn't caught it, and he knew that was because she was too distraught. "I think you're gonna have to spell it out for her, Uncle."

She looked at him then, and he grinned at her, because he

305

couldn't hold it back any longer. The moment they'd shared last night was pure and precious again, and they could repeat it for the rest of their lives. She gasped suddenly and jerked her eyes back to her uncle. "Mama was pregnant with Uncle Lionel's child!"

"Yes."

Olivia clamped her hand over her mouth. The act might have stayed whatever cry she was trying to restrain, but nothing stopped her tears. Duncan dropped his arm from her shoulders. "You can go to him, Ollie. You can kiss him if you like. Anything and everything. He's your husband, and you don't share one drop of common blood."

Clay met her halfway around the desk, and he held her and kissed her, and when they broke their kiss, he saw Duncan slip out the door.

Chapter Forty-seven

"Do you need help at the brickyard?" Clay asked.

Halfway through the back door, Duncan looked over his shoulder. "Fiscal, you mean?"

"Yes."

"No, I'd given up getting my hands on Lionel's money when Olivia agreed to marry you. Clay's premature death briefly revived hope, and for a couple of days there, I tried to convince myself you were a threat to Olivia. I can say I'm content that's not the case." He clenched his jaw. "Howard's been lost to me for a while now. His death was nothing more than the grand finale. The blame is mine, not yours. I'll deal with it in time.

"As for the brickyard, I've been talking to Francis and Julian about selling forty-nine percent of the business to Lydia and us becoming partners with her. She's offered to pay off the creditors. She's been wanting me to do that since her husband died. At that point, I'll probably retire and let the kids handle it. If her brothers stay out of her private life, things will work fine." He smiled—this one pleasant. "It might surprise you to know she has Lionel's head for business."

Clay was surprised actually, but he'd never had occasion to talk business with Lydia. He'd have to ask Troy what he thought about that. Not that Troy knew squat about business.

"You've always known about Olivia?"

"As unbelievable as it might seem, Lionel and I trusted each other a great deal. For the record, Katie worked for Agatha, not for me, and she had long before Agatha came to live in my house.

"And to answer your question, Lionel confided in me as soon as he knew Rebecca was pregnant. It would have been a terrible scandal. He was a respected, married man in his early fifties. Rebecca was scarcely eighteen. Lionel's wife Sonja was an invalid by that time. She died the following year."

"But he didn't tell you about Darcy and Elaine?"

"Not until the end. But he could have; he knew that. There was no reason for me to know. Later that brief liaison I had with Rebecca strained our relationship for years. I think, up until that point, he still cared for her. Darcy's death destroyed those feelings."

Clay followed him onto the porch.

"It was Julian who shot Toby, by the way," Duncan said. "I scared it out of him this morning after your brother was shot. To tell you the truth, I was afraid he might have been the one who shot Troy, thinking he was you. He says he was only trying to frighten Olivia."

One step down, Duncan turned to him again. "It'll be quieter at my house from now on. That would be sad had it not been for the hate and discontent I've lived with the past twenty some-odd years."

"Your boys are there."

"And Lydia. Do you realize there are two female corpses waiting for me at home?" He blew out a breath. "Malicious females. What nasty spectres those two will make screeching at each other up and down my halls. I believe I'll pass the house on by for the moment and meander out past the settlement at Turkey Creek. There's a beautiful mulatto out that way. She's in her early thirties now. I've been visiting her since she was twenty."

"A mistress?"

"Hardly. I've neither the wealth nor the sophistication to keep a mistress. I'm not her only client, either, and given my age, I doubt I'm her favorite. But for a few hours, every week, she makes me think I am."

Chapter Forty-eight

"Thanks, Doc, let us know if you need anything," Clay said. Doctor Tasker waved goodnight from the rocker beside Troy's bed, and Clay closed the door to Olivia's old room.

"How is he?" Olivia asked when he entered the master bedroom.

"He's not hurting as much. Doc said he ate pretty good."

She smiled, a quick little thing, but a smile nonetheless. "Yes, he did. He wants something solid. Is he asleep?"

"Yeah, thanks to the laudanum."

"And you gave him more whiskey, didn't you?"

"Doc poured it himself."

She pulled the neck of the silk nightgown up off her shoulder where it had fallen. The shimmering thing clung nicely to her body, and his groin tightened.

"Do you think Doctor Tasker will be comfortable on that cot?" she asked.

"If he drinks enough of Troy's whiskey he will."

She didn't smile at that, didn't even look up, simply pulled back the coverlet on their bed.

"What's bothering you, sweetheart?"

She looked at him. "The most important thing is what's not, and that's your being my brother."

Across from her, he helped turn back the bedspread.

"Uncle Duncan said she was a good mother, Olivia, and she loved you."

"That's not what I was thinking about. Not this time."

"What then?"

"Do you realize that for the first time in my life I'm not related

309

to any of the men who took that artillery up in Pontotoc County? I've always been so proud of that—Nathan Bedford Forrest and all."

He was around the bed and pulling her into his arms in the space of a heartbeat. Of course, that's not what really bothered her. She'd always be related to those men, not by blood, but deep within her soul; her maternal grandfather had given her that right and consecrated it with his life. No, it was the sudden change of everything that made them who they are...and the lie. "All we've done is switch daddies, Olivia. He didn't really betray you; he was always right there with you, and my good buddy Darcy Lee would have always been there for me if he'd been able."

"I know."

He rocked her in his arms. "You know, your babies will be related to a number of the men who fought on that hill up in Pontotoc County."

She pushed away and looked at him with glistening eyes, then she smiled. "I hadn't thought of that."

"And I think that's a good enough reason to crawl under the covers right now and make one of the little stinkers, what do you think?"

She answered with a kiss.

If you enjoyed *Epico Bayou* don't miss Charlsie Russell's award-winning first novel

The Devil's Bastard

Natchez on the river, 1793. The Spanish Fleet controls the Mississippi, and the Dons rule their rowdy British and American subjects with a patient hand. The location is strategic, the land fertile, and within two decades, cotton will be king. Into this web of international intrigue, the rich and powerful Elizabeth Boswell welcomes her orphaned grandniece Angelique Veilleux and introduces the impoverished beauty to a world of privilege. But power has its enemies and wealth demands a price. Rumor has it Elizabeth's success stems from dalliance with a lustful demon that still prowls her family farm of De Leau outside Natchez.

At the center of this ominous legend is Elizabeth's grandson, the handsome and dangerous Mathias Douglas who saves

Angelique from degradation and death near the end of her journey to Natchez. Mathias is the son of the doomed Julianna, Elizabeth's only daughter. Mathias's father, locals whisper, is Elizabeth's demon.

Despite the dark rumors, Angelique cannot quell her feelings for Mathias, for whom she would make any sacrifice. An outcast, Mathias is cruelly tested by Angelique's affection. Determined not to dishonor her, he callously puts her aside. But Elizabeth has other plans and offers him the family farm at De Leau to marry the girl. Soon Angelique finds herself desperately in love with the man who has conquered her body and possessed her soul.

But something in the swamps surrounding De Leau stalks her, and nightmares invade her dreams. What she perceives as Mathias's indifference to the threat leaves Angelique isolated and afraid. She begins to doubt her grandaunt's motives for sending her to De Leau, as well as Mathias' role in Elizabeth's plan. Resolving her doubts means uncovering the secret of Mathias's sire.

From Mathias and Angelique's first meeting to Elizabeth Boswell's revelation at story's end, *The Devil's Bastard* is a splendid read. First and foremost a sensual romance, it is also a well-researched historical with a haunting mystery.

Don't miss Charlsie Russell's second award-winning novel

Wolf Dawson

Ten years after the Confederate Army reported him killed in action, dirt-poor Jeff Dawson returns to Natchez, Mississippi, a wealthy man and purchases White Oak Glen, the once opulent home of the now impoverished Seatons, the aristocratic family that years ago shattered his own.

Burdened with her drunken brother Tucker and besieged by greedy relatives, Juliet Seaton struggles to hold on to what remains of her farm. Now she finds her family faced with a new menace in the form of a marauding wolf, which slaughters valuable stock and assails the mind of her alcoholic brother. Tucker Seaton warns his sister that the man occupying White Oak Glen is a ghost, who in the form of that vicious wolf seeks to destroy what is left of the Seatons.

An infant when events occurred setting her family against

the Dawsons, Juliet appears pitted against a neighbor hell-bent on avenging his sister, who died in childbirth after being violated by a Seaton male. Jeff's grandfather was part Creek Indian. Local legend states he terrorized unfriendly neighbors with tales of his ability to shape-shift into a deadly wolf. Unidentified persons lynched the colorful old man following the savage killing, apparently by a wolf, of the Seaton who raped Jeff Dawson's sister.

But Juliet finds the handsome Jeff a living, breathing man. Hot-blooded to boot. His seductive touch weakens her resolve and blinds her to the danger he poses. Jeff, however, is no longer compelled to destroy the Seatons, if he ever was; they have destroyed themselves and left the vulnerable Juliet to his mercy — mercy he's quite willing to give, though he's not ready to let the feisty beauty know that.

Into this explosive mix of fear and distrust comes a sadistic killer, and what this fiend kills is not Seaton livestock.

With the countryside ablaze with suspicion directed toward Jeff, he and Juliet overcome mutual distrust and strip away a lost generation's hatred as quickly as the clothes covering their bodies. Old lies give way to new truths, lust to love, and together, the lovers set out to uncover not only a killer, but the identity of the spectral beast haunting the countryside.

Look for Charlsie Russell's fourth novel in the near future.

River's Bend

Rafe Stone came back to Mississippi seeking justice and the house irrevocably linked to everything that makes him who he is. But the magnificent structure that began life as a one-room, French-Dominion log cabin and grew into an antebellum show-case south of Natchez has fallen into disrepair and into the hands of a savvy Mississippi City businessman by the name of Josephus Collander. The astute Collander has no use for the tax-draining piece of real estate; moreover, he needs to unburden himself of a recently acquired orphaned niece who, through no fault of her own, is wreaking havoc within his household. The house is not for sale, Collander tells the disappointed Rafe..., but he can have it for nothing, if he'll accept it as Delilah Graff's dowry.

Rafe's desperation, coupled with Delilah's beauty, makes the decision, albeit a reckless one, easy. But what secret in the siren's past would cause a seemingly kind and responsible kinsman to barter her to a stranger?

Tragedy, followed by a difficult childhood, has left Delilah jaundiced toward life, bitter toward men, and eager for the independence she is sure is coming. Instead, the financial support her beneficent Uncle Joe promised is suddenly forfeit, and he has called in his markers, compelling her to wed a man she does not know. Worse yet, her uncle doesn't appear to know much about the handsome Rafe Stone either. Adding to her discomfort, this Mr. Stone takes her to Natchez, a city where her name is synonymous with disgrace. There he moves her into a house rumored, over the course of its nearly two-hundred years, to have hosted treason, robbery, adultry, and murder. A house still reputed to harbor the specter of a vicious killer.

And who is Rafe Stone, the man to whom she has sworn her troth and under whose roof she sleeps at night? A man, who claims to be a stranger to Mississippi, yet knows more about the ominously majestic River's Bend, and its past, than he should? What is his link to the dark legends haunting River's Bend and to the ghost walking its rambling halls? Is he the personification of her nightmare or an unbidden dream come true?

Mystery, suspense, romance, and history, dear reader. Enjoy this look back to the time when the memory of the Old South blossomed into legend.

About the Author

Charlsie Russell is a retired United States Navy commander turned author. She loves history, and she loves the South. She focuses her writing on historical suspense set in her home state of Mississippi.

After seven years of rejection, she woke up one morning and decided she did not have enough years left on this planet to sit back and hope a New York publisher would one day take a risk on her novels. Thus resolved, she expanded her horizons into the publishing realm with the creation of Loblolly Writer's House.

In addition to writing and publishing, Ms. Russell is the mother and homemaker to five children and their father.

To learn more about Charlsie Russell and Loblolly Writer's House, visit www.loblollywritershouse.com.

Loblolly Writer's House

Order Blank
Tear this sheet out and

Mail order to:

Loblolly Writer's House
P.O. Box 7438
Gulfport, MS 39506-7438

Item	Price*	Qty	Total
The Devil's Bastard	$16.00	_____	_____
Wolf Dawson	$16.00	_____	_____
Epico Bayou	$16.00	_____	_____
		Shipping free:	0.00
		Total payment:	_____

Would you like a signed copy?
Tell me how:_____
_____

Send to:
_____
_____
_____

*Price includes 7% Mississippi sales tax
 For Bookseller rates visit: www.loblollywritershouse.com

Loblolly Writer's House

Order Blank

Tear this sheet out and

Mail order to:

Loblolly Writer's House
P.O. Box 7438
Gulfport, MS 39506-7438

Item	Price*	Qty	Total
The Devil's Bastard	$16.00	_____	_____
Wolf Dawson	$16.00	_____	_____
Epico Bayou	$16.00	_____	_____
		Shipping free:	0.00
		Total payment:	_____

Would you like a signed copy?
Tell me how:_____
_____

Send to:
_____
_____
_____

*Price includes 7% Mississippi sales tax

For Bookseller rates visit: www.loblollywritershouse.com